Helga Zeiner

Section 132

published by POWWOW Books Canada
author info: www.section132thebook.com

ISBN-13: 9798667652342

Prologue

Martha had thirteen mothers. Some of them, like mother Marion who was the first wife and the two young ones called Emma and Anna, hardly touched her life. But the others, mother Barbara for example who was in charge of the afternoon sewing sessions, or mother Esther who supervised the laundry duty, were mean and horrible. They beat her every chance they got. For things she did wrong in their eyes and even for things she hadn't done at all. She hated them with all the might of her twelve year old heart, each one of them. But most of all, more than any of the others, she hated her birth mother Katherine.

Mother Katherine was the teacher.

She had control over all thirty-five children who were still young enough to attend classes, seven hours a day, from six in the morning until one, every weekday. And throughout Sunday's Church services mother Katherine sat at the back of the pews erected in the community hall and watched like a hawk in case any of her pupils misbehaved.

Her mother was more mean than all the other mothers. And there was no escaping her.

"Martha, you are dreaming again! Answer me!" Woosh, the ruler sliced the air above Martha's head and landed on her back. Martha involuntarily jumped up and then slumped back again. She hadn't heard her teacher mother coming. She had no idea what had been said. She had no idea what she was supposed to say.

Woosh again. Higher up this time, on her neck. And again. Higher still, on the hands she had folded over her head to shield herself from the expected blows. Her teacher mother always did that. Hitting her shoulders and her head until she drew blood. Once Martha had lost her hearing for the rest of the day after such a punishment, and since then all voices and noises floating past her ears were bedded in a rather pleasant hum, as if the world had muffled itself with a blanket. Martha liked the subdued sounds, even if it meant that she couldn't hear her mother approaching her desk in time to protect herself.

"What am I to do with you? How will you ever learn the scripture if you don't pay attention to what I am saying?"

Mother Katherine was really upset now, Martha could tell. She knew the signs. Her teacher mother looked around the classroom. All her pupils were bent over their books, pretending to study. Martha didn't think it was fair that she was beaten more often than the others, but then, so much in her life was unfair. She couldn't understand any of it, and that sometimes made her mad like a dog with rabies. So mad, that she kicked small rocks on the roadside with her bare feet or scratched her arm with a sharp piece of metal. To hurt herself outside made her feel better inside.

"Here, recite this passage!"

Martha stared at the open book her mother had slammed on her desk in front of her.

"From here on, up to here!"

Oh dear Lord, two full paragraphs. Martha couldn't even remember one sentence, let alone a whole paragraph. Under her folded arms she looked up at her mother. She shouldn't say anything because that always annoyed her mother, but as usual she couldn't help it. "It's too long. I don't remember. I can't do it."

Woosh. "The Bishop expects all of you to become good soldiers of the Lord. We owe him so much."

The blow had not been too forceful. Martha relaxed her arms a little, hoping mother Katherine might forget about her, now that she was on to her favourite topic. The Bishop. Her second husband. Her mother never tired of telling the whole class why they all owed him so much. After all, he had taken her and her seven sister-wives and all their children to his compound in the wilderness of British

4

Columbia, rescuing them from the shameful existence of belonging to an apostate.

Her mother's voice hung in the air, gently humming in Martha's ears. She relaxed a bit more. She did not pay attention to the sermon because she had heard it all before. She lowered her eyes and tried to concentrate on the text in front of her. Terribly complicated sentences which did not make any sense to her. It made her all itchy inside, like ants crawling underneath her skin. She wanted to shout that she would never remember those words, she didn't even understand what they meant. But she could still feel the blows to her back and neck. Bending forward made her eyes all fuzzy. Dizzy. The words in the air and the words on paper got entangled and made her head ache. With her tingling skin, her fuzzy eyes and her throbbing head all she wanted to do was jump up and run away.

It had always been like that, ever since she could remember. She was forever being punished for some oversight or for her stubbornness, but she never really understood why. They always made her do things she couldn't cope with. Even after school, when all the girls from the age of four had to go to the community hall to do their sewing, she could not get anything right. Sitting still for hours, mending the clothes with needles that were too long for her delicate fingers, was just too difficult. Her body started to itch terribly when she had to sit for more than a few minutes, and she was no good at sewing anyway.

And try as she may, she could not recite the scripture from memory. It didn't stick in her brain, and when she was supposed to finish a passage one of the other girls had started, she stumbled over the difficult words and fell silent. Then her teacher mother Katherine would take out her ruler again and beat her hands or her back.

Martha knew she was not a good girl. Her mind strayed even now when she should have concentrated. Accompanied by the gentle humming in her damaged ears, it wandered back to the last time she had had to learn part of the scripture by heart. After several long and lonely hours confined to her mother's hut, the Bishop had ordered her to the hall and had told her to stand in front of his family-congregation and recite. Of course, her memory had been empty like that of a newborn.

She wouldn't have known her own name, standing up there in front of all her mothers and siblings. Afterwards, mother Katherine had given her the beating of a life-time and threatened to send her to the prison hut up in the mountains if she ever caused disgrace like that again. Oh yes, Martha was a bad girl. She had screamed and hollered and cried for hours afterwards, another terrible sin in the books of the Bishop.

If only the Lord would take her away from here and let her into his kingdom. All the misery would be at an end if she could live in his far-away land where everything was white and golden.

Her teacher mother walked up and down the corridor, still humming along like a busy bee. Martha felt safe enough to go on daydreaming. In it, her father, the real one, not the Bishop, took her by the hand and said *shhh*, be quiet, they won't notice, I'll take you away from here. I'll take you to the white and golden kingdom.

Martha had no recollection of him. She had been only three when she and her mother were taken from her birth father's farm in Alberta and sent to the Bishop's *Mountain Glory Ranch* compound. Once she had begged her mother Louise, a gentle and soft woman who had also been one of the wives given to the Bishop, to tell her about him. Very quietly, Louise had explained that it had been a terrible and sad day when her birth father told his family that he would leave the Church.

"But where did he go?" Martha had asked incredulously. "There is only the Church and nothing exists outside of it, so he couldn't have gone very far."

Louise had paled and had hushed her. "There is nowhere but the black abyss," she had said, "and we must be grateful to the Bishop that he has found it in his heart to accept us all. Never forget, he is our saviour."

Martha never stopped dreaming about her father coming to rescue her.

At one o'clock her mother dismissed the class.

This same day, Martha's hopes of one day being saved by her elusive birth father were, unknown to her at that stage, shattered forever. Walking down from the community hall to the women's quarters, she discovered blood running down between her legs. It frightened her enough to run back up again to see first mother Marion who was in charge of attending to any kind of illness. Martha thought she might die. Her stomach suddenly cramped badly, and the blood didn't stop running. Mother Marion didn't tell her what was wrong; she only explained to her that she wasn't really ill. That she should go back to mother Katherine's hut and stay there until she was clean again. The bleeding simply meant that she now was a woman and would get married soon.

About a week later, mother Katherine told her to walk with her up to the house where her husband and the first wife lived. Katherine was beaming all the way. When they got there, they had to wait in the hallway until the Bishop arrived.

The Bishop. Martha feared the man she had to call father, while she pictured the one who was her real father as a wonderful person. She didn't believe the story that he had willingly thrown himself into the dark abyss – he was much too wise for that. He had surely found a way to the Lord's white and golden throne.

Suddenly, there were sounds behind the door leading to the large dining room. Martha had never been allowed in there. There had to be a very special reason for her to accompany her mother, but she couldn't think of a single one. The first wife Marion opened the door and asked Katherine in. Martha's mother took her hand and held her close by her side. The twelve sister-wives were lined up in front of the large dining table. No one paid any attention to Martha, they only looked at her mother. Katherine didn't return their shy nods of welcome, her eyes were focused on their husband who now entered the room, greeting him with all the deference due to him. He smiled at her, opened his arms wide, beamed at all the others and announced with joy in his voice that he had decided to take a new wife. The wives bowed their heads in silent agreement. They already seemed to know who the new one would be.

Martha still wondered why she was included in this gathering, until her mother fell on her knees, thanking him for the honour of accepting her daughter as his new wife. Martha was shocked. She didn't want her father to become her husband. She didn't want to be a sister-wife to her birth mother and to all the other mothers.

"No!" she cried out.

Everybody froze. A deep frown appeared on the Bishop's forehead. His face flushed a deep shade of crimson.

"I don't want to," she continued crying, pressing her eyelids shut so she didn't have to look at him.

Her mother Katherine got up quickly and grabbed her by the elbow, trying to force her onto her knees. "Quiet," she hissed. "Remember the teachings."

Martha lost her balance and had to hold onto her mother. "No, please, no, no, no," she pleaded desperately. They couldn't do this to her! All her dreams had focused on her getting away from the Bishop's unbending regime. She feared him, loathed him; didn't want anything to do with him. She would rather die than be his wife.

A rush of rage grew inside her so quickly that she couldn't control it. All the pent up frustrations over the teachings she could not grasp and the unjust punishments she had suffered, over the rules and regulations that seemed so senseless, and the privations she had to endure exploded out of her.

"Never! Never! Never! I will not marry him. He is my father. I must get another husband. I must get away from here. I don't want him. Never! Never! Never…" she kept screaming through the shower of slaps her mother dealt out to stop her daughter's unbridled ranting.

"Never! Never! You can't make me! I won't!"

She screamed through the commotion that followed, when all the sister-wives started to whisper amongst themselves, shuffling their feet, unsure what to do.

"No, I won't. Leave me alone. Let go of me."

Her mother kept clawing and pulling at her as if dragging her down on the floor would somehow shut her up. Martha resisted her and tried to wriggle out of her mother's strong hold.

She yelled even louder. "No! I won't! I won't!"

Katherine started to sob. Some of the other wives moved a timid step forward, looking at their husband. He nodded his consent and they advanced to help Katherine subdue the hysterically screaming Martha by shoving her down and hitting her wherever they could. Finally the girl was on the floor, pinned to the wooden planks by several knees and hands. She continued to yell until, choked by the billowing skirts of the women on top of her, she had to stop.

Above her laboured breath she could hear the footsteps of the Bishop approaching.

"Let go of her," he commanded. The women retreated.

Martha got some air into her lungs again. Her whole body hurt. She slowly lifted herself to her knees and looked up at him. Tears were streaming down her face. She hated him so much. All she could think about was to defy him. She would never, never, never be his wife! She wanted to yell again, but her lungs were still fighting for more air, so she sobbed harder, feeling desperately sorry for herself. It was so unfair. Not him. Not her.

"You will fulfill the Lord's wish," he snarled at her. "Stop crying immediately. Thank the Lord for His mercy. I will elevate you to my kingdom as the Lord has commanded me. If you do not obey me, you are breaking the holy covenant." He beckoned to the other wives. "Get her out of my sight and confine her. Only when she has convinced me that she has repented her abomination will we proceed with the ceremony." He turned away to leave the room.

Martha put all her strength into one word.

"*Never!*"

The sound of her voice shook the air and hung in the silence that followed. It reverberated in her ears, travelled along her dulled hearing senses, reaching her innermost core. *Never! Never! Never!* The sound waves manifested themselves there and welled outward again like an echo. *Never! Never! Never!* screamed every part of her being.

The Bishop turned back to her, eyes frozen on her, his face twitching. Nobody dared to move. Except for Martha's heavy breathing, the room was deadly quiet. After an endless pause, he raised his arms to the ceiling and started to recite from the scripture: *"You, who have committed sins that cannot be forgiven, let your blood be shed ..."*

Katherine's hand flew to her mouth to stifle her gasp, but he had heard it. He pointed his finger at her and thundered: "You! Continue!"

She shook her head. "Please."

"Katherine, continue!"

"...and let the smoke ascend, that the incense thereof may come as an atonement for your sins..." her voice broke and became inaudible.

Nothing penetrated Martha's shield. She did not understand the meaning of what was being said. The concept that there were sins that could only be forgiven through the shedding of the sinner's blood was foreign to her simple mind. As foreign as the notion that a covenant was everlasting. *Everlasting,* she had sometimes pondered, was a very frightening word. Nothing lasted for ever; there had to be a beginning and an end to everything. She could not understand it.

What she did understand, however, was the grave danger she was in. She had to get away from the Bishop fast or she would never be able to find her real father. Her instincts told her to run. She was closer to the door than any of them; she could make it. Before she had time to think twice, she scrambled to her feet, grabbed her skirt and made a dash. Strangely, nobody moved to stop her, even when the door handle slipped through her sweaty fingers, making her lose valuable time. She tried again and the door sprang open.

Martha ran for her life. She did not hear the Bishop ordering the first wife to bring him his rifle. She did not see her mother breaking down in shame and grief. She did not feel the low-hanging branches scratching her face and arms or the roots under her feet as she ran from the house. Nothing else mattered, only to get away from there. But she did feel the bullet stinging her calf.

Martha toppled over when the pain ripped through her. She couldn't get up. The Bishop walked slowly toward her. He stopped where she was lying and looked down at her.

She was holding her calf with both hands, pressing hard to stop the bleeding. She didn't feel any pain. Her mind raced frantically. He had only shot her in the calf. Did that mean he hadn't planned to kill her?

The Bishop sank to his knees beside her and took out a hunting knife.

"May the Lord forgive you!"

Before she had a second to think, he slid the knife over her throat, from one side to the other. As her life blood spurted out of the deep gash, Martha realized what he had done and moved her hands from her calf to her throat, but she quickly lost the strength to press against the wound there. Her arms dropped next to her body and she went into shock.

The Bishop watched her final convulsions until she was limp, then he signalled to one of his sons waiting in the background.

"Let her bleed out before you dump her in the woods. Her smoke has to rise to the sky."

1

Richard Bergman was well aware that not only the tree huggers but many otherwise quite reasonable people considered land developers nothing but a bunch of greedy bastards, out to make a quick killing without any consideration for the environment. They never understood that progress in the Province of British Columbia would stagnate if no new land was made available, and that the big cities who already suffered from self-inflicted population and transportation infarct desperately needed to spread beyond the borders of their over-crowded suburbs. Richard was one of those progressive land developers and didn't give a hoot about public opinion. He loved what he was doing, and he loved the idea that he could make a bundle of money with this despised activity. So maybe he was a greedy bastard after all.

He had started in this business about ten years ago, just after he had taken up permanent residence in Canada. He had called his company Richland Ltd. because he believed in the power of positive associations and had made a profit with every single venture he had since undertaken. Sometimes more, sometimes less, but always with exceptional ease. Nothing had ever gone wrong, and he was quite convinced that nothing would ever go wrong. After all, he had a knack for finding the perfect parcels of land and turning them into desirable developments, snatched up by eager buyers.

Richard Bergman had been born in Germany. Actually, his last name originally was spelled Bergmann – the man of the mountains – but he had dropped the second *n* soon after his arrival in British Columbia.

He had been only eighteen then and had wanted to blend in with his peers. Meanwhile he had become a Canadian citizen, had matured and would have preferred the uncommon double *n*, but he couldn't really change his name back without giving the impression of being fickle. He took pride in his straightforward approach to all his business dealings. Clients and business partners alike considered him trustworthy and fun to work with.

Too much fun! Only recently, his realtor friend Tracy had spent an evening with him - not entirely business-like, but who was complaining, they were both adults - and between the sheets she had lured him into promising to look at a fabulous property up north she had listed. Two thousand acres of pristine wilderness that were, according to her, only waiting for a smart guy like him to snatch up and make a small fortune.

The following Friday, he woke up earlier than usual. Looking out the window, he saw the first morning light spreading above the eastern mountain range. A cloudless sky, promising a brilliant summer day. He decided on the spur of the moment to take his nearly new BMW for a joy ride up north to look at Tracy's listing. Business was always slow in August and he could afford to go on a wild-goose-chase. Plus he owed Tracy one. Maybe the property really was as good as she had bragged, and how would he ever know if he didn't look.

He called his assistant Daisy and informed her that he would take the day off. Half an hour later, he was on Highway One driving towards Hope. Listening to his favourite radio station he felt pleased with his decision, relaxed and slightly curious as to what the day would bring.

After Hope the radio lost reception.

He stopped in Merritt to look for a decent lunch place, settling for a quick Tim Horton's coffee and muffin because the town was preparing for some kind of Music festival and every coffee shop had a waiting line.

The longer he drove on, the more his initial enthusiasm for the long road trip deflated.

Soon after Kamloops, there was hardly any traffic on the highway and even less houses by the road side. The landscape was certainly picturesque, but it had turned into a damned hot day. The air rising from the asphalt distorted the colours of the road in front of him, twirling grey and blue with silver specks.

The idea of walking any land in this heat did not appeal to him at all.

By the time he reached his destination, about two hundred kilometres north-east of Kamloops, the afternoon heat would be at its peak, without a hope in hell for a cooling breeze. Who outside Canada would believe that it could be so dry and hot in this crazy country?

Two hours later, driving through a village called Blue River, he questioned his judgement even more. The place had achieved a certain fame because a Swiss guy had built a luxury resort there which catered to a clientele positioned between the extremely well off and the filthy rich. Apart from that large hotel complex, there was little else that held the promise of rural charm. He hardly saw any signs of civilisation. The few village houses on both sides of the highway had come and gone in the blink of an eye. Surely, the resort hotel needed workers, but it must be the only employer of any significance in the area. There was no infrastructure around that the young growing families he usually targeted, craved and needed. Where would the adults find jobs, the kids go to school, where would they all get medical care?

What on earth had he been thinking? There was no way he would invest in this God-forsaken part of the country. Best to turn around and head back. Sorry Tracy!

He could stop at the Blue River Resort, maybe have a cold beer there, call the property owner and tell him he had changed his mind. Looking for the next highway exit to turn around, he saw a sign indicating the turn-off he was supposed to take to get to his scheduled viewing. Behind him, a fully loaded logging truck closed in with crazy speed. Richard swerved into the turn like a suicidal robot and slowed down only when he hit the gravelled country lane leading from the highway into the back country. Dust billowed up behind his car. The road was quite narrow and winding, so he drove even more cautiously, careful not to kick up sharp gravel that might scratch his midnight blue beauty. Bad enough that a dust film already covered the chassis.

He was looking for a place to turn around, but the lane never straightened or widened enough. One sharp curve followed another. Suddenly, he was engulfed in a horrendous cloud of dust, produced by a car crawling along in front of him. When he fell back a bit, he could see that it was a very small, very old car. It looked like an antique, one of those tiny red pick-up trucks pictured in old country calendars, straight out of the depression area. It was a miracle that thing still did its duty. Of course it was sent to annoy him and test his patience. Penalty for my being stupid enough to come up here, he thought, while he kept his distance from the ancient vehicle trailing dust like a flag of honour.

Richard's right foot was itching to hit the accelerator and overtake the car. After another curve in the road, he saw a relatively long straight stretch ahead. Without thinking, he slammed his foot down, hurled his car into the cloud, sensing where the little truck would be, and laughed out loud when it appeared way back in his rear view mirror. His reckless overtaking must have scared its driver quite a bit. He had swerved off the road with the right set of wheels on the grass next to the lane, narrowly escaping the ditch.

Then it occurred to Richard that he might not have done himself a favour. As soon as he found the right spot to turn around, he would have to drive past that stupid thing and eat dust again.

A few kilometres further, the land to his left became steeper and the road straightened out, running parallel to the hill. In the distance, he saw a ravine breaking the hill as if a meat cleaver had chopped it in two halves. There was a lane leading into the ravine, marked by colourful balloons tied to a dried out leafless tree. This was the property marker the owner had placed for him. Unwittingly, Richard had reached the turn he was supposed to take. He could now drive on until he reached the home of the owner, or he could take this opportunity to turn around and head back.

Richard Bergman drove into the lane. His instincts told him that the little dust machine behind him would continue straight ahead. Once it had passed, he could turn around, wait for the dust to settle and head back home.

A few meters down the narrow dirt lane, he stopped. There was still no place to turn his car, but the hills on both sides were opening up, giving him a triangular view of the country in front. It was spectacular. There were meadows in various shades of green, one rolling into the other, until they touched a bright blue sky with puffy white clouds. They reminded him of his childhood. On perfect summer days, the people of Bavaria called them *Schäfchenwolken*, Little Sheep Clouds.

The landscape within the triangle was simply magnificent. He stared at it intently, wanting to take in the country's perfect flow until it reverberated in his body, calming and soothing his jangled city nerves. He wanted to soak it up, memorize it forever.

Still in awe, he started the car again and slowly followed the lane, looking back every so often to see if the little truck was following him. When a dust cloud popped up in the triangle that was now behind him, he watched it disappear again, just as he had expected. The truck hadn't turned; he was all alone in the lane. The lane wound gently through the soft hills, opening up new vistas of undisturbed perfection with every curve of the road.

If he owned this land he would make sure it stayed this beautiful. It needed big lots, connected by unobtrusive roads. It needed buyers who appreciated its natural beauty. There must be plenty of people out there who would feel what he experienced just now.

Even before he reached the home of the property owner, a weathered old cabin close to collapse at the end of the lane, his imagination was already working overtime. He would turn the large property into a cabin community for city slickers who would come up here with their families to enjoy summer and winter holidays. People who wanted to own a cabin where their kids and grand-kids could gather and have fun in the great Canadian outdoors. How many lots should he divide this into? Two thousand acres was plenty of land. How much did the owner want for it?

Suddenly, Richard felt incredibly alive and vibrant. Tracy had never mentioned the purchase price and he had never asked. All he knew was that it was negotiable and that the old guy selling the land was "highly motivated", as the realtors liked to call it. Thank heavens he had not turned back. If he ever met the driver of the dust machine, he would have to thank him and apologize to him - and wow, would he thank Tracy! This little trip up here was supposed to be no more than a welcome interruption to his daily routine; he had not expected to feel the old thrill of the hunt even before he had inspected the whole property or started negotiations. Such an amazing property, a highly motivated owner, old and probably uneducated and careless, and no other potential buyer in sight – wasn't that the ideal mix to create a bargain scenario? This could be the pot of gold at the end of his personal rainbow.

Richard drove into the yard. The area in front of the cabin was not gravelled and there were deep furrows the owner's truck must have made when the earth had been wet and soft. Now it was hard as rock, and Richard had to manoeuvre carefully so his under chassis wouldn't scrape the ground. He parked the BMW and got out. The yard with the cabin was nestled in a grove of fir trees so tall, they provided shade all day long. It made the heat Richard had expected to feel quite bearable.

A tall, skinny man stood in front of the cabin door. He wore a pair of oversized overalls which had not seen a wash for a long time. His naked upper torso stuck out of them like a crane's neck from its feathered body. His head bore a similar resemblance to the funny bird. It was narrow and bony, with big eyes staring out from a wrinkled, dark skinned face. A hat, shaped like a cowboy hat but squashed and pressed nearly flat, had several feathers sticking up, just like a crane's crown.

"Nice car," the guy said and broke into a smile that made him look even more like a scarecrow. "What is it?"

"A BMW," Richard said and extended his hand. The guy seemed pleasant enough. "I'm Richard Bergman. Tracy Wilson from the Burnaby Re/Max office sent me."

The owner shook his hand. "Bob." He pointed to the BMW. "Can't use that one if you wanna see the land."

"Are you the owner?"

"Sure am." Bob's smile widened. "Sure as you're a city boy with no business here."

Now Richard returned the smile. This guy was taunting him. "I wouldn't be too sure about that."

"You wanna buy?"

"Maybe."

"You got money?"

"Maybe. Depends what you are asking."

"Let's go look." Bob disappeared into his cabin, coming out again with a Twenty-two rifle in his hand. "Plenty of bear still around. We'll take my car."

They walked together to a brown truck as old and beaten up as its owner. Richard got into the passenger seat and wanted to buckle up. There was no safety belt. The engine started on the first try, and Bob drove out of his yard and onto an old logging road behind his cabin. The ground was bumpy, shaking both men around as if they were riding over waves of concrete. Richard grabbed the door handle with his right hand and held onto the dashboard with his left. Bob didn't seem to be bothered by Richard's discomfort. He held the steering wheel tight with both hands and kept up his speed. He knows his land, Richard thought, every inch of it, but he did not say anything. Bob was the quiet type and it was best to leave a man like that alone until he was ready to talk.

They had driven for about quarter of an hour when Bob slowed down, climbing up a fairly steep mountain. When they had reached its peak Bob stopped, got out of the truck and started to walk along a nearly hidden path. Richard followed him. Soon after, the forest opened up to a breathtaking view of the land in front of them on the downhill side of the mountain. In the distance, Richard could see a lake nestled between green hills. Its silver and light blue surface glittered in the afternoon sun like the scales of a giant snake sliding gently through the landscape. *Majestic – grandiose – awesome!* Richard realized, what spread out in front of him was pure, raw Canada. A secluded mountain lake of virginal beauty.

"Magnificent," he breathed.

Bob grinned knowingly. "Not bad, eh!"

"Not bad at all."

Bob pointed to the horizon. "That's how far it goes." Then his arm swept to distant points on his left and right. "And there, to that peak that looks like a coyote head. And there, just beyond the hill with the large Douglas fir on top, see, the one with the eagle's nest. All that's mine."

"All that land..." Richard muttered stupefied. "All that land...."

"...could be yours."

Bob had found the words that Richard's mind was still groping for. Yes, it could all be his. It would be his. In that instant, he knew that he had to have it. This land had to be his, no matter what.

"How much do you want?" he asked without thinking further.

"Three Million."

Richard sucked in his breath. Steep! Too much for his company to handle at the moment. They would have to sell most of their current projects to create the necessary cash flow. Quick sales usually meant having to lower the prices. Maybe Bob was willing to wait.

"How soon do you want to sell?"

"Three months."

It could be done. If he really tried, it could be done. He could raise the money by November.

"How about end of the year?"

"Nope." Bob cocked his head to one side and looked Richard straight in the face. "Don't have too much time left."

"What do you want to do with all that money?" Richard asked, although it was way too personal and not his style at all to enquire about a seller's motives, but his curiosity had got the better of him. What would a guy that age who lived all by himself do with three million dollars?

Bob didn't seem to mind. "Gonna go see me the world." And as an afterthought. "Before I kick the bucket."

It didn't even occur to Richard to negotiate the price. Three million was a lot for his company to handle, but it was a low price for the land. He held out his hand for a second time that afternoon to the bony old man. "Have a good trip."

Bob looked him over and contemplated before he took Richard's hand. He shook it quietly with a serious expression in his lively old eyes. "Done."

Richard knew this handshake was as good as a written and signed contract, but he felt the immediate urge to get back to his realtor, have her draft up the agreement and make it legally binding for both sides. He was not sure how he would get the money together or what exactly he would do with this land, but he was thrilled beyond any reasonable explanation. He felt like a child going to Disneyland. The future was full of promise. He didn't know where this golden opportunity would lead to, but his confidence in his own capabilities was boundless. He would make this work, big time! The thought of failure never entered his mind.

He looked around again, resting his eyes on the various landmarks Bob had pointed out to him.

"What is beyond there?" He asked of each point. Not that it mattered, he just wanted to know.

"Back there is crown land, and to the west as well," Bob explained. "Over there, to the east, you have a neighbour. But that's only one family, Americans, I think. Never met them. Bit weird apparently, but harmless. After them, crown land again."

Richard looked to the east. Beyond the eagle's nest the land disappeared from sight behind rolling hills. Whoever lived there was not important to him. Staring in the direction of his neighbour's property, he had no idea that this was the place a young girl had been brutally murdered just a few months ago.

And that, at this precise moment, a wedding was taking place.

2

The moment she had been groomed for all her life was close. Lillian was shaking with anticipation, but she tried to hide the telltale signs by sitting on her hands to squash the tremors. She mustn't worry so much; it would all be perfect and wonderful.

Dear Lord, in just a few moments she would meet her future husband! He would marry her; he would be loving and caring, and he would be the most wonderful man that ever existed on this earth. In turn, she would adore him, worship him and eventually she would love him with all her heart.

Nobody expected her to love him right away, but she would in time. Wasn't that what her mother had told her? After all, she was just a silly girl, she didn't know what was right or wrong for her and didn't understand the wisdom behind the choices made for her. Choices made by men. They always knew what was right. It was not her place to questions their motives, or those of her future husband for that matter. All she knew was that this great man had agreed to marry her, although she was a nobody, a young girl from down south who knew nothing of the world. She only knew life as it was on her father's secluded *Bright Desert Light* compound, hidden somewhere in the mountain range that separated Arizona and New Mexico.

She had never been allowed to leave this small family community, had never accompanied her father on his numerous trips to the big cities called Albuquerque and Phoenix, like some of her sisters. For some reason, she always had to stay behind. When he got his truck ready for one of his long journeys, all the girls lined up in front of the main dorm. Then their father would walk down the line, scratching his salt-and-pepper beard while his eyes wandered up and down each daughter, inspecting them with the same intensity he displayed when it was time to choose one of the pigs for slaughter. Lillian knew what he was looking for in the animals, they needed to be fat and round and healthy, but she could never figure out what he was looking for when he picked the lucky ones who were allowed to hop in his truck and go with him. She assumed he wanted them to be especially modest and demure, so she always tried hard to look submissive, hanging her head and casting her eyes to the ground when he came closer. But he had never picked her. He had always walked right by her, hardly pausing his steps when he reached her near the end of the line up. She had seventeen half- sisters, each one hoping to be the one. Sixteen of them in tears once he had chosen and she had always been one of them because he always took only one mother and two daughters.

With the boys it was different. They went with him everywhere. They went hunting in the mountains with him, coming back with bloody carcasses on the back of the truck. They spent time camping in the desert with him, bringing home sticky dripping honeycomb, fleshy cactus and agave's leaves, or other delicacies suitable for drying or making juices or medicine. They went with him to the cities to do business; an activity she had no concept of. Business was a serious and nearly holy matter, one of the mothers had once explained to her, because it usually involved meeting one of the Church Elders.

All this didn't matter now. Her father had finally taken her and her birth mother on a journey with him.

To be married to the man the Elders had selected for her.

Her future husband. The man she would worship for the rest of her life and beyond. The man who would be her saviour. Only by becoming his wife would she escape being thrown into the dark abyss of eternal suffering. Only by obeying him without question and by filling her heart and soul with gratitude and love for him would she belong to The Chosen Ones.

Lillian suppressed a sigh. Ever since she had been told to get ready for the journey to meet her husband, she had secretly prayed that he would be good looking. Oh, how she hoped that he would be handsome and young, and not old and unapproachable like her father, or fat or ugly like most of her uncles. May the Lord forgive her those prayers. Of course she would adore her husband even if he was as ugly as sin, the good Lord knew that, just as she knew deep down in her heart that it wouldn't come to that. Every time her mind drifted into a daydream about her future with this important, beautiful man who had agreed to marry her, she had to hide a smug smile. Now where were all her high-and-mighty sisters who had mocked her for having to stay home again and again! Who had told her about the strange females they had seen in the shops, showing bare arms and ankles, sometimes even bare knees, having rings in their ears and – of course she never believed that one – sometimes even in their noses. What were their stories worth now? All they ever got were shopping trips to one of the big box stores as they called it, and then they had to come home again, while she had been allowed to go on this three day journey to be delivered to HIM. Best of all, her parents would leave her with him and go back home without her. It was she who was finally free now! It was she who could change her life, satisfying her deep hunger to see and experience new things.

Ever since she had been told that she would be married to an important man all the way up north in Canada, she had pictured herself in a strange new world filled with unimaginable excitement and had felt delirious with joy and anticipation. To live in a foreign country with unknown seasons, she would discover unfamiliar landscapes, experience strange phenomena like snow and coloured lights in the sky. New sounds, new smells, new sights, new everything. She would learn many things new to her, would grow and, above all, she would be loved by somebody.

Many times, guilt tried to creep into her reverie like a big bellied lizard lashing with a darting tongue - usually when she imagined how her beautiful future husband was gazing deep into her eyes while gently stroking her neck with his cool fingers – and tried to destroy those delicious daydreams! That made her angry and she pushed the guilty feelings away. She wasn't going to let anything ruin her dreams! She had a right to them. She would be a married woman soon.

Lillian glanced at her parents. They were patiently waiting for the door to open. Waiting to finally meet the important man who had chosen their daughter to be one of his wives, for time and all eternity. Her mother's skinny frame seemed to disappear in her best dress. Had she always been so fragile? Lillian could not remember. Her father, serious and unapproachable as always, standing next to her mother, made an unusual gesture. He put his arm around his wife's waist, awkwardly, but seemingly affectionate. She thought she saw a smile flicker across his face. Her father had been so proud when he had received Bishop Jacob's letter, informing him of his desire to wed one of his daughters. For several weeks, the household had been in a state of heightened anticipation while they were all waiting for the Bishop to study the pictures and descriptions sent to him. Each daughter old enough to be married hoped to be the one. Once her father had known that the final choice had fallen on his daughter Lillian, he had immediately started to prepare for the arduous three day journey north. The Bishop had informed her father that he was in such a great hurry to seal the union, he had arranged for the Church Elders` blessing in advance. Imagine, Lillian's father had said, very soon we will be connected to a Bishop. He is one of The Chosen Ones, and with this wedding our family will become part of them.

Her father had ordered the wives to prepare a feast. The entire family had joined together to sing hymns of praise and offer prayers of thanksgiving. Lillian had been permitted to work on a new dress for herself for the wedding. Her mothers had picked a colour that matched her green eyes and complimented her fair skin. All the women and girls had helped to cut and sew and finish the dress in record time.

Lillian slowly moved her left hand out from underneath her to straighten the folds of her pretty pale green dress. It had small yellow flowers embroidered along the rim of the skirt and all along the front. She just loved this dress, it was the prettiest thing she had ever owned. Nobody noticed her gesture, which was just as well as it could have been interpreted as vanity. Her father was now talking to her mother in a low voice.

It could not be much longer now. She had to use the toilet but did not dare to ask for permission. What if her husband came to claim her while she was out peeing? Unthinkable. She tried to paint his imaginary picture in her mind again when she heard footsteps outside. He was coming!

Her parents turned towards the door, smiling, expectant, pleased. She held her breath and looked up.

"Stand up, girl," hissed her father.

She stood up and lowered her eyes, as she had been taught to do since she had been a toddler. Always lower your eyes when you hear a male voice. The door opened.

He must be in the room now. His voice took over the room, greeting her parents, thanking them for delivering their daughter into his care. Lillian was much too excited to listen to their muted polite conversation.

His voice came closer. Her eyelids fluttered. Could she risk a glance? A dark shadow fell on her, stretching out its tentacles. Two grey arms, reaching her face, one landing on her chin, the other moving around her head, settling on her neck. Slowly, one grey shadow arm moved her face up and her eyes finally fell on HIM. Part of him. A huge charcoal belly! Up, up. Buttons. Higher. A white collar, a round face. Round and burgundy like a plum. Smiling. Oh dear Lord, he was enormous! The skin of his face stretched over puffed up cheeks, watery lips.

Her shock must have been obvious, because he let go of her chin as if his fingers got burned. Lost interest in looking at her, and she was grateful for it. But maybe she was wrong and he had never planned to look at her for longer than this one split second? Cheerfully he invited everybody into his office where the marriage ceremony would be performed.

Lillian followed her parents down the hallway into another room. She was numb, did not feel anything. She had been so sure, had never imagined anything like this. Never pictured her husband blown up like a balloon ready to burst. Never seen him so enormous - so threatening. Should she beg her father to take her back home? The thought alone was so ludicrous, it stunned her that she had even considered it for one second.

Finally tears wet her eyes but she blinked them away. Be thankful, Lillian forced herself to think, he is not as old as grandfather Jonas. At the time of his last wedding he had been eighty five. This man can't be much more than forty.

Disappointment ran down her cheeks.

You will learn to love him. He is your husband and will be the father of your children. By next year, she promised herself, fighting to dry her eyes, *next year, on my fourteenth birthday, I will carry his child.*

The Bishop walked around his desk and positioned himself behind it. He directed her parents to stand on one side of the desk and motioned for Lillian to stand on the other side, opposite them. Her father prodded her back to get her moving. Once there, she did not dare to look at her future husband, so she studied as much of the room as she could safely see from under her half closed lids. There was a desk close to the wall with a window behind it. Two empty chairs in front. The office faced the backyard. From where Lillian stood, she could see the twigs of healthy fir trees gently moving in the summer breeze outside. The floor was covered with a soft carpet that showed worn patches wherever it was used most. No pictures on the walls, no flowers on the desk. The three inside walls were whitewashed. The outside wall with the window was made of logs, stained in a yellowish tint, with rough caulking sealing the chinks. The wood looked solid, perfectly capable to withstand the onslaught of heavy winter storms. Impossible to let anything in – or out.

Lillian suddenly felt trapped and gasped for air. Her heart was racing. She wanted to get out of this room. Back to the first one, where they had been waiting – before he had arrived - but she had already forgotten where this room was or what it looked like.

The door was still open and now a steady stream of women came into the room. Nobody talked. They filtered past her with the faintest rustle of their long skirts. When they had taken their place surrounding the existing group, one of them closed the door. The room was now terribly overcrowded but still quite cold. Lillian shivered and noticed that her mother was cradling her elbows with her hands. Her knuckles were white from the effort. Was she cold too, or was she remembering her own wedding? It had not been a happy time, she had once, in a rare moment of openness, told Lillian. Why had she never asked her mother the reason for her unhappiness? Lillian suddenly wanted to run over to her, unfold her arms, shake her and ask her about it. *Please, Mother, please, tell me why you have been unhappy. Tell me why you are always so sad.*

The Bishop cleared his throat, officially welcomed her parents into his family and declared that he would now conduct the wedding ceremony. Lillian finally looked up, expecting he would ask her to join him behind his desk. He didn't look back at her, so she took a small insecure step in his direction. Noticing her movement, her father shot her a warning glance and she froze where she was.

Then her father produced some papers and handed them over to the Bishop who studied them carefully. He seemed pleased with what he read. Lillian assumed those papers must be her birth certificate and other official documents. The Bishop motioned one of the women to hand him something. She gave him a bunch of keys, he chose one of them, unlocked his desk drawer, placed the papers there and locked it again. He smiled at her father. "From now on, the girl will be called Martha."

Her father frowned, obliging the Bishop to explain. "It's best for her. We have documentation for her in place which will make her a Canadian citizen. It's much easier this way, you understand."

Of course her father understood. A girl her age could not live in Canada for too long without parents or legal guardians. On the journey up here, he had wondered about that complication but had trusted the Bishop to find a solution.

But Lillian did not understand so easily. "I don't want to be a Martha," was on the tip of her tongue. She barely managed to hold the words back and swallow them before disgracing her parents.

"We shall now proceed with the wedding," the Bishop said.

The vows consisted of only one sentence.

"I take you, Martha, into the fold of my family, for now and for ever!"

Lillian was not required to reply as she had no say in it. Not now and not ever afterward. Forever! She was bonded to him forever and was no longer her father's responsibility, but the property of her husband. The words of the wedding vow signalled the moment of transition. She had finally escaped the stifling atmosphere of her father's firmly ruled empire, but for what?

Her father walked around the desk and shook hands with her new owner, sealing the deal. Then the women moved forward and formed a loose circle around her. One after the other stepped out of the circle, introduced herself and welcomed her into her new family.

"I am Marian, first wife of the Bishop – and I greet my new sister."

"I am Elisabeth, second wife, and I greet my new sister."

"I am Barbara, third wife ..."

A sickly woman, too weak to step forward on her own, was assisted by two others who propped her up and held her until she could whisper her greeting: "I am Katherine, fourth wife ..."

Martha could barely understand the words from the frail sister-wife and felt a twinge of pity for her. She seemed distraught, had been crying and looked like she was in deep pain. Then Katherine disappeared into the background again and another took her place. Martha tried to concentrate so she would remember the many names, but the women all looked the same. They all wore dresses in faded colours and had their hair combed back into a tight bun. The dresses were not as pretty as her own, they seemed to be sewn together from many different materials, like patchwork without a theme. Plain long sleeves, ruffled ankle length skirts and rounded collars, closing tight on their necks. No embroidery or other kind of trimming. Fashion was frowned upon in Lillian's family, her *past* family, too, but at least the dresses all her aunts had sewn for themselves looked a lot nicer than those her *new* family wore.

She lost track of counting how many women introduced themselves. Ten? Twelve? Thirteen? Her father had mentioned in one conversation she had overheard, that the Bishop was rumoured to have many wives. Would she be number eleven? Or number twelve? Or fourteen?

Finally, this part of integrating her into her new community was over. Her new sister-wives stepped back again. Her father turned to her, formally shook her hand and said his farewell. Then her mother embraced her stiffly and whispered *remember what I told you* into her ear.

What should she remember? To be good, to obey? Lillian's head was swimming like when she had to study long prayers, repeating the words over and over again, until they all disintegrated into some vacant space behind her consciousness where they melted into each other and lost their meaning.

Her mother nodded with a frozen face. *Remember what I told you!* Willing her to remember without letting the others catch on to their silent communication. *Remember!* Remember what?

Then her parents were escorted out by her new husband and she was alone with the other wives. Marion, the first one, took her by the hand and led her away. It was time to take her to their husband's chamber.

Lillian began shaking again. Everything had happened so fast. She and her parents had only arrived at the Bishop's compound a few hours ago after travelling for three days. It had been a long and quite exhausting drive, cramped into her father's small red pick-up, with hardly a word spoken between them. Excitement and anticipation had kept her awake most nights in the cheap motel beds, tossing around, fantasizing about her future life. To be led away now by a strange woman in a washed-out, patchy dress after a brief and cold ceremony without joy and laughter, to be led to her husband who was not young and handsome like she had imagined but old and fat, filled her with dread. All her romantic expectations were crushed by sudden fear. She felt scared, intimidated by this woman who should have made her feel embraced and wanted, but who walked silently beside her, clutching her hand with a fierce grip. The invisible shield the first wife had built around her was impenetrable. Lillian tried to wriggle her fingers to release some of the pressure, but they were held forcefully, dragging her body along.

A memory of her childhood in her father's *Bright Desert Light* compound popped up in her head. Her older brother had tied a puppy to a leash with one of those collars that tighten without release when pulled. The little dog wanted to go in a different direction but was pulled mercilessly behind her brother who did not even look back. It had been a very obstinate puppy, persisting in his choice of direction until he could not breathe any more. His legs gave way, and her brother had dragged the stupid creature on his soft belly for quite a while before realizing that he had killed it.

Lillian pictured herself falling, being dragged along the floor by the older woman, not able to release her hand until her arm was pulled out of its socket. An involuntary moan escaped her mouth and she pressed her lips together. Marion, the first wife, stopped abruptly, turned to her and looked her straight in the face. Unblinking, with a tight mouth and eyes that seemed to see through her, she said: "Martha, there is no need to fret. This is the happiest day of your life!"

Martha? Hearing her new name, Lillian froze. Martha! She hated that name already. Why Martha? Why couldn't it be a name that sounded warm and round and flowing, like … she couldn't think of one, like, well, like her own name maybe. Lillian had a pretty ring to it, she had always liked her name. But she was quick to learn, so she promised herself to keep sweet and accept her new name.

But she could not so easily accept the first wife's last comment. *This is the happiest day of your life!* Why did she say something like that? What did she mean? This could not be the happiest day of her life. Everything was wrong. Her husband was not young and handsome. And she was in a strange land, all alone, feeling cold and forlorn.

Although it was the height of summer outside, the temperature inside the house was so low it made her shiver. Lillian, no, Martha, had read somewhere that log structures were popular in northern countries because they insulated so well against the elements. But this house did not simply shield from excessive heat, it reflected a coldness way beyond seasonal comfort. It had a chill that crept right underneath her skin. Lillian, no, Martha, knew this instant that the house had a cold heart. All the people living in it had turned to ice. Why couldn't the woman be nice to her? What in the Lord's name did she mean with *the happiest day of my life?*

They reached the end of a long hallway and Marion ushered her into a small room. Again there was only one window, this one high above the headboard of a double bed, too high to be able to look outside. The last rays of evening sun threw a distorted window shaped light-patch on the opposite wall, just above a wooden dresser. It looked like a tilted cross. The bed, the dresser and a single wooden chair in the corner were the only furniture. It looked a bit like the room she had shared with her sisters back home, her *past* home. Had she really expected the bedroom she would share with her husband to be more than that? Of course she had hoped for it. She had pictured a friendly place, with warm pastel coloured walls, curtains on the window, a vase with fresh flowers, a lovingly quilted bedspread. But she had also imagined a young and handsome man who would invite her onto the soft mattress, blanketing her gently with a downy duvet, playfully unpinning her bun, letting her copper hair fall in a soft cascade. That's as far as her dreams had taken her, never further.

Marion went to the dresser, opened a drawer and took out a night gown. White, no frills. She placed it on the bed, straightened it with a slow, hesitant movement, as if she was saying goodbye to it. "This is your room now. Stay in it until told otherwise. Your husband will see you soon. Get undressed, fold your clothes and put them outside the door. They will be taken away and you will be given new ones tomorrow."

Lillian, who was now Martha, could not restrain herself any longer. "I need to go to the bathroom. And I am thirsty and hungry."

The first wife nodded. "You may use the toilet. It's opposite this room and you are allowed to go there when necessary. But you must return right away. There you'll find everything you need to freshen up. Come with me, I'll wait until you have finished."

"What about something to eat and drink?"

"No food tonight, Martha. You can drink water from the bathroom tap. I will send you some milk later, that will be enough for today."

Martha, Martha, Martha, Lillian repeated silently while following Marion to the bathroom, which was no more than a tiny cubicle with a toilet bowl and a washbasin. No mirror above the sink, but a narrow shelf with some faded cloths and towels hardened from many washes on it, as well as a bar of soap that smelled of laundry detergent and a new toothbrush still in its plastic wrapping. She relieved herself and quickly washed her face and hands with a bewildered urgency. It was all so confusing. Why was she treated like a prisoner, not like a wife on her wedding day?

When she had finished she left the bathroom. The first wife was waiting in the hallway and ushered her back into the bedroom. Her face betrayed no emotion. Lillian-Martha did not dare break the barrier with the many questions twirling in her head. Her warden did not come into the room but closed the door firmly behind her. Lillian was alone.

Lillian?

Martha!

Bewildered Lillian mumbled her new name. Martha, Martha, Martha. Then she sat down on the bed and started to cry. What else was there to do. Not long after, Marion stuck her head through the door again, ignored her tears and reminded her with an irritable voice to get undressed and place her clothes on the floor outside the door.

Lillian, no, Martha, gave up. She had no choice but to accept her name and all that came with it. The first wife would be waiting outside until she had obeyed her command. It occurred to Martha that maybe placing her dress outside the door was a tradition in this family. Maybe it was the signal for her husband to come to her! She suddenly longed for this big man to enter the bedroom. Then she could tell him how she was being treated by his first wife and ask him to help her. It was so unfair! Hastily she unbuttoned her lovely green dress with the yellow flowers, slipped into the white nightgown which was not as hard as she had feared but so bulky and large that her tiny frame got lost in it. With both hands she gathered the wide gown around her waist, lifted the hem so she would not trip over it, and cautiously opened the door to do as she was told. Marion was gone, there was nobody in sight, but

Lillian did not dare venture out into the hallway. Her husband would come soon and even if he was not young and handsome, he would love and protect her and would stop this nightmare.

Slowly she stroked the fine material of her wedding dress for a final time, then she stood up and closed the door to her room.

She did not know that she would never see this dress again.

3

The burden of his shepherd's responsibilities started to wear Brother Lucas down. He must be getting old.

All his life he had practised what he preached and had encouraged his brothers in the faith to be steadfast and unrelenting, but the raid on the *Yearning for Zion* Ranch in Texas had made the brothers paranoid. They worried about the future of their families, unfortunately with good reason. The Zion Ranch was headquarters of the Mormon off-shoot Fundamentalist Church of Jesus of Latter Day Saints, and since the authorities investigated them life had become more complicated for all Mormon sects who believed in The Principle.

Those Zion Fundamentalists were nothing but a bunch of big-headed fools. Brother Lucas had little time for them. The way they flaunted their polygamous life-style, demanding to be taken seriously by the monogamous public, was ridiculous. The Day of Reckoning was close and the immoral population of today's modern America seemed to do everything in their power to bring it even closer. Those sinners would never change and embrace the principle of plural marriage just because some arrogant Fundamentalists told them that it was the only way to save their souls.

Ever since the mainstream Mormon Church had officially renounced polygamy in 1890, many of the faithful practiced their conviction in secrecy. Of course, the Elders had always been aware of this and tolerated it as long as outward appearances were kept up. In fact, Brother Lucas knew of several Mormon Elders in Salt Lake City who presented themselves as confirmed monogamists while keeping their extended families hidden in the sparsely populated Utah countryside. Brother Lucas fully approved of such conservative behaviour, but those stupid, thoughtless members of the FLDS didn't think it necessary to protect their own.

In the old days it had been a lot easier. Nobody cared how the Mormons lived. Sadly those days were long gone. Brother Lucas was eighty now, but he could still remember well how his father with his over fifty wives and countless children had lived in one compound, undisturbed by the authorities or the public.

But over time, thanks to the aggressive approach by the Fundamentalists, the general public had taken notice of their different family structures and started to question their rights to live *The Principle*. Ignorant fools, that's what they were, the lot of them. And on top of their misguided behaviour, they had allowed a madmen to rule over them. Their Prophet, Warren Jeffs, was nothing but an egomaniac, and a criminal on top of it. The man was not suitable to be a Prophet! A Prophet had to be above suspicion. Every aspect of a Prophet's life should be dedicated to the word of the Lord, he was the mouth-piece of the Lord – a God himself.

But even before Warren Jeffs' troubled leadership, the truly faithful had been deeply disturbed by the direction the FLDS was taking. They considered the Elders too lenient and were looking for ways to preserve the old teachings. Brother Lucas was their most vocal advocate. His powerful personality was a magnet for many of those extremist fundamentalists. Many years ago he had persuaded some of them to form a secret society. It quickly grew into an important organisation outside the mainstream Mormon Church, yet within their original ideology. Its members understood their duty to protect the pure interpretation of the Faith, as Joseph Smith had decreed through his many holy revelations. They called themselves *The Gatekeepers*.

Eleven of them were at the power core of this society. Brother Lucas and the ten men he had appointed as his fellow Gatekeepers – he had decided on this odd number in defiance of the Mormon Church who was ruled by the Quorum of Twelve and the FLDS who was controlled by the Prophet and twelve Apostles - considered themselves the true keepers of the Faith.

Although their society was officially shunned by the Mormon Church, and even by most members of the Fundamentalists of the Latter Day Saints, both groups secretly applauded the Gatekeepers' spiritual strength and quietly supported them. Lucrative contracts were channelled their way because the companies the Gatekeepers had established could work their labour force cheaply and effectively. All their business efforts quickly flourished. Money had never been a problem.

At least not until now, in the aftermath of the Zion Ranch Raid, when the heathen media sat like vultures on their doorstep, waiting to rip gaping holes into the protective cover of their polygamous communities. Everybody was overly nervous. The wealthy and powerful mainstream Mormon Church had suddenly turned a cold shoulder on them, hoping enough distance from the Extremists would guarantee their own survival.

Brother Lucas knew their cowardly behaviour was wrong. When the Day of Reckoning came only the true believers, the Gatekeepers and their followers, would be allowed through the Gate that protected the highest echelon of the Lord's army. He would make sure of that, because by then, he would be at the gate, right by the Lord's side.

Brother Lucas stood up and looked around the table, studying the faces of his brother Gatekeepers. Each of them wore a similar black suit, a white shirt and a dark tie. Whenever they met, they always presented themselves inconspicuously, blending into the gentile business community to attract as little attention as possible. Throughout the year they were in constant touch with each other and often met in smaller groups, but all eleven of them only met once a year.

This year he had chosen Denver as the location of their annual meeting. Important things had to be discussed and decided on. The general business decline, heralded by the withdrawal of the Mormon contracts, would adversely affect the income of their flocks in America, Canada and Mexico for the coming year, creating a serious challenge.

The meeting went on for most of the day and finished on a dismal note. The only resolution they had reached was to dip into their large savings and disperse a portion of it to make sure their families were taken care of until the tide would turn again. The Gatekeepers hoped to ride it out, as they had so many attacks on their faith before.

It was five o'clock and all of them had a plane to catch. They shuffled their papers, thinking Brother Lucas would now close the meeting when he asked for their further attention. He had one small matter to discuss. A rather delicate matter as it involved the son of a former Gatekeeper who had passed away some years ago.

"My dear brothers, I know you are anxious to head back to your families, but I seek your advice." Brother Lucas slowly wiped his forehead with the palm of his left hand, indicating how much thought he was giving his next words. "This morning, before I left for the airport, I received a rather disturbing letter." He took an envelope out of his breast pocket and held it up. All eyes were on him now. "In it, our dear brother Peter from the *Bright Desert Light* compound south of Phoenix thanked me most gratefully that we have allocated his daughter Lillian to Brother Jacob." He paused briefly, before he elaborated. "Brother Jacob, in Canada!"

A subdued murmur went through the Gatekeepers. One of them raised his hand.

"Isn't he the son of Brother Mitchell?"

"Indeed, he is."

The murmur grew to a collective groan as the men remembered. Jacob had been the first born in a prominent Mormon family. His father had been one of the founding Gatekeepers, believing throughout his life-time that his son would succeed him in this prestigious position. Unfortunately from an early age on the boy had shown a rather over-developed sense of superiority. He could have benefited from the best education available, having the door of the Brigham Young University in Salt Lake City wide open to him, but his total disregard for the hierarchy of the University and his lack of respect resulted in him being expelled before his first term was over. Back home he continued to behave inappropriately, even toward the eleven Gatekeepers, but the

Brothers never mentioned Jacob's rudeness to his father. It was not up to them to teach the young man manners and they quietly pitied his father.

After Brother Mitchell had died, his son Jacob, who was by now over thirty years old and married, impatiently demanded to take over the family business as well as his father's seat on the council. The Gatekeepers held an emergency meeting – the only time they had ever met outside of their scheduled annual meeting – and decided to strip the obstinate young man of his powers, at least temporarily until he showed that he had learned to fit in and contribute to their society, and sent him into exile. The ruling, however, had not been unanimous. Some of the Eleven had thought a prolonged stay in the Canadian wilderness would help cool his temper, while others had thought the sentence was too harsh. It was agreed to transfer ownership of a large parcel of land the Gatekeepers owned up north to Jacob and his first wife to enable them to settle in Canada, and force him to sign a mortgage with hefty interest to keep him under control. They further agreed to review his case every year.

To this day, more than ten years later, Brother Jacob was still not allowed back. Year after year the Gatekeepers had considered his application to return into the folds of their society, but the majority had always voted against it. His compound in Canada still didn't show a profit, unbelievable after all those years, considering all the additional wives and children they had allocated to him to provide him with an extra work force. He hadn't made a single interest payment. In fact, he was draining their resources, constantly asking for additional funds to run his compound. The money seemed to disappear into a black hole.

Brother Lucas was convinced Brother Jacob would never change. He had always been troublesome; it was best to keep him out of reach of their secret society altogether. Especially in these difficult times a hothead like him spelled trouble. But if he advocated Jacob's permanent exile too openly, some of the more lenient Gatekeepers might object. Although he was their appointed leader and had absolute power, he always made a special effort to give them the feeling of being included in his decision process.

One of them now wondered aloud why Brother Jacob had been allocated Brother Peter's daughter without the consent of the Gate-keepers, as was the rule. All marriage matches within their society had to be proposed and sanctioned by them. Another asked how much they were supposed to pay for this planned transfer. Yet another complained: "Brother Jacob is a financial burden, always has been, and I don't understand why we have to pay for another wife for him. He has more than some of us have!"

"Indeed, he does!" Brother Lucas repeated again and waited patiently for the next comments, making sure his non-committal answer aggravated the other Gatekeepers even more. He did not have to wait long.

"If I remember right, several years ago we allocated the family from an apostate from Alberta to Brother Jacob to help him establish his compound!"

Everybody knew who was meant, but Brother William from Alberta had renounced the Church openly. The apostate's name could not be spoken aloud any more. His eight wives and over thirty children had been taken away from him and given to Brother Jacob. A generous gesture by the Gatekeepers, one that was supposed to finally make his compound profitable.

"Yes, he received eight wives, and since then we have sent two more from our own flocks to him."

"What is he doing with all the wives and children? Why is he still not making any money?"

Now several of the Gatekeepers voiced their indignation.

"He's draining our resourses without showing any potential for decent earnings in the near future. Does he expect us to support him forever?"

"It's not right."

"We can't afford that. Not in these troubled times. Didn't we just decide to tighten our own belts to weather the storm?"

"Yes, does he expect us to deny ourselves what is our right while he is squandering more and more of our hard earned money?"

"Exactly! We shouldn't send another wife to him. He has to learn to give before he gets."

Now they all grumbled and questioned the motives of the one who had given his consent to the new bride. They all assumed it was Brother Lucas himself. Half of Brother Lucas' face broke into the crooked little smile his last stroke still allowed him. "My dear brothers, I need to clarify something. Neither I nor, I am sure, any of you, have ever promised Brother Jacob another wife. "

Silence fell on them and they all stared at their leader.

"So, who did?"

"Brother Peter wrote to me because he was told by Brother Jacob that we approved this transfer."

It took a brief second before the Gatekeepers understood. This was an insult bordering on blasphemy! How dare an exiled brother assume the identity of the Gatekeepers for his own benefit!

They were shocked into silence.

Brother Lucas nodded gravely. "I understand your dismay. I have been rather alarmed myself. However, further to the gravity of this outrageous behaviour by one of our own, there is another small problem we have to deal with immediately. Brother Peter thanked us in his letter for the ten thousand dollars we will send him for his daughter Lillian. And, of course, before you wonder, just as I have *not* given my consent to the exchange in the first place, I have not agreed to such a payment either."

Regaining his composure, one of the Gatekeepers stood up and spoke. "How dare Brother Peter expect us to pay the bride price for his daughter? He knows very well that this is the groom's responsibility. Even if Brother Jacob convinced him that we've approved the marriage, how can he be so presumptuous to think we would take care of it? Does he really think we are so stupid to shell out money just like that?"

"It is not Brother Peter who is trying to cheat us," Brother Lucas said carefully. "There was a copy of a note attached to his letter. A promissory note written by Brother Jacob, confirming to Brother Peter that he had cleared this exchange with us and that we would compensate Brother Peter directly."

Now everybody leapt to their feet. The affront was unbearable.

"That's outrageous!"

"Inconceivable!"

"How dare he!"

"Please, my brothers of the Lord," Brother Lucas pretended to calm them down. "I understand your outrage. But we have always known the true character of Brother Jacob. He has always believed himself to be equal to us."

"Forgive me for interrupting you, Brother Lucas, but is it not more so that he believes himself to be *above* us?"

Brother Lucas lowered his eyes and let them rest on the note in his hand. "He has signed as *Bishop* Jacob."

He could have heard a pin drop. Since their brotherhood existed none of the Gatekeepers had been subjected to such insolence. The arrogance of the man! Thirty years ago, Brother Lucas and his ten appointed Gatekeepers had decided to remain humble in the face of the Lord. They were all Brothers, even he, their leader, called himself Brother. There were no Prophets, Apostles or Bishops like in the Mormon Church or the FLDS. They refused to get trapped in meaningless hierarchy, subsequently resulting in power struggles. The term Brother was good enough for them until the Day of Reckoning came, when they would be rewarded for their unpretentiousness. When they would be kings! Gods!

Suddenly they all spoke at once.

"This time he has gone too far. We ought to teach him a lesson."

"Yes, let's refuse him the bride."

"And stop sending him money! It's about time he took care of his own without our assistance."

Brother Lucas half smiled again. "Our next step has to be considered with great seriousness. There is a large family to consider. What some of you are recommending could be considered forsaking some of our own. We have never done this before. I would not want to make such a decision by myself."

"If Brother Jacob cannot support his family, we can always take them away from him. There are plenty of good men who will be pleased to take possession of the wives. Most of them are still quite young and can reproduce. And most of the children should be old enough by now to contribute to any man's wealth."

"We should give it a year without any support and then see if he has finally seen the light."

Brother Lucas was very pleased with the way this discussion went. "Shall we vote on it?"

They all nodded eagerly. Brother Lucas asked for a show of hands in support of the Gatekeepers cutting all financial ties with Brother Jacob until his compound showed a profit. This time the decision was unanimous.

"There is one small detail though," Brother Lucas concluded. "I tried to call Brother Peter on my way here, but apparently he left immediately after he posted the letter. He must be in Canada already, delivering his daughter to Brother Jacob. I can't reach him there."

The excitement had died down. The Gatekeepers felt calm now that order was restored. One of them said that if this meant they should pay one final amount of ten thousand, so be it. Brother Peter must not be cheated out of what had been promised to him. If word got out that they, the Gatekeepers, had been manipulated, it would be too big a shame to carry. Not even Brother Peter should suspect what Brother Jacob had been up to.

Another show of hands confirmed that they were in agreement. They were righteous men – nobody could accuse them of not doing what was correct, or not correcting what was wrong. Brother Peter would have their full support and Brother Jacob would be an outcast until he changed his squandering ways.

4

Martha waited for a long time. She sat on the bed, not daring to slip under the covers as she did not know if this was the right thing to do. Nobody had told her what to do while waiting for her husband to join her.

Then the door opened again. Martha looked up expectantly, but it was not her husband, it was one of the sister-wives – Martha had no idea which one – holding a glass of milk in her hand.

"Here, drink this," the woman said, extending her arm with the glass toward Martha. "Marion wants me to wait until you drink it all."

"Who are you?" Martha asked.

"I'm Michaela. But I'm not supposed to talk to you."

"Why not?"

"Please. Drink it, or I'll get into trouble."

Martha took the glass from Michaela and started to swallow the white fluid. It smelled odd and tasted even stranger, but then, she had never had a whole glass of milk before. In her father's household milk was considered too valuable to waste it on girls. The women made cheese out of it that could be sold at the farmers' markets, or sometimes the boys got to drink it. Martha wrinkled her nose. "It's not very nice."

"Please!"

Martha dutifully gulped down the rest of the milk and handed the glass back to Michaela. The sister-wife said a quick thank-you and was gone before Martha could ask another question.

The waiting started again. Martha sat down on the same spot on the mattress as before and stared at the wall opposite the bed. Soon she got bored staring. To occupy her mind she did a little mind game she had played many times to amuse her younger siblings. One of them had to think of a specific subject that was represented in nature, such as trees, or birds, or mountains, or flowers, and she had to state as many examples as she could think of while sorting them in alphabetical order. Lillian could do it – so Martha should be able to as well. Of course now she had to assume the calling part of the game too. She shrugged, concentrated and started with a subject she had done many times before - insects in general. That was easy. Then she advanced to more difficult categories - insects with two wings only. That was harder.

Soon she got tired of the game, in fact she got so tired that she carefully stretched out on top of the covers, trying not to disarrange them. Outside it had turned completely dark; only the dim shine of the farm light in the yard illuminated her room. It was cold and gloomy inside. Martha hoped for her husband to finally arrive, but the house seemed deserted, it was so quiet. She had to yawn. She was so tired. Her body felt suddenly limp and heavy. She tried to fight it, but couldn't keep her eyes open. All she wanted was to close them for a few minutes. Her feet were icy cold. Surely there was no harm in covering them. She slipped under the cover. The image of Marion's hard face briefly popped up in her mind, but she pushed it aside and thought of her mother. Sometimes, when she was hurt or sad or angry, her mother had taken her in her arms, stroked her back or her hair and said soothing things to her. Not often, because one had to be careful not to get caught showing such affection, but each time was so wonderful that she had instantly felt calm and wanted and loved. That's what she yearned for now. It was impossible to picture the man who was her husband to be gentle like that. She tried for a little while to envision his large fleshy fingers tenderly holding and stroking her, but then the image of his huge bulk forced its way into her mind and she quickly pushed the horrible vision aside.

Her cheeks were wet with tears when she finally let go of all reasoning and slipped into a mercifully deep sleep. While drifting off she remembered what her mother had said. *Make sure you fall pregnant quickly*, she had said again and again. It had sounded like a warning. *Let him do whatever he wants. Don't fight it. Make sure you fall pregnant quickly.*

Martha briefly wondered what her mother meant by that, then she was gone.

Just down the hallway, not far from the room Martha was sleeping in, a phone rang.

Marion had already opened the door to her husband's office when she heard it. She wanted to retreat quickly, but the Bishop gestured her to come in. She closed the door behind her and waited for him to finish his conversation.

"Yes, yes, of course I understand." Suppressed anger made his words sound sharp and pointed like pieces of a broken mirror. "My dear Brother, I don't know what you are talking about. Of course we'll make a profit soon. It's only a matter of time. You've got nothing to worry about."

Pause. He was listening, but not too long.

"I'm telling you, by next summer we should be well on our way to operating independently. I've got this great idea how we can make money, but until then I need some more funds."

Pause. Even shorter.

"That's ridiculous! How do they expect me to get through winter? All I've got here is a bunch of useless women and minors too young to put to work."

Pause, just long enough for him to catch his breath.

"Sure, my oldest is fifteen and I have three more ready to be integrated into the priesthood soon, but that's about it. What am I supposed to do? It's all very well for the Gatekeepers to expect a profit, they don't have to spend their days in this godforsaken wilderness surrounded by bear and moose and bickering women and spoiled children. They spend their time in spacious air-conditioned homes, being pampered by their wives."

Marion didn't dare to move. Her husband's voice had turned even more piercing. She assumed he was talking to one of his old friends in Albuquerque or Phoenix or Utah and the content of this conversation did not bode well for her. When he hung up he would need a target for his pent-up frustration. She wanted to disappear but remained frozen in position.

"No, I don't see any point in it!" the Bishop continued, shifting his tone from accusing to pleading. "You've got to help me here. Try and convince him otherwise. He'll listen to you. I can't call him. Brother Lucas won't talk to me. He fancies himself our prophet, you know that as well as I do, and once he's made up his mind he's as stubborn as a mule."

Pause.

"Yes, that's what I think! And I'll tell anybody who wants to listen. I don't care. It's about time he had his wings clipped. Trust me, when I return, I'll shake up a few souls. They'll regret what they've done to me!"

Pause.

"Sure, sure, I appreciate that. If you could put a word in for me, it will not be forgotten. My time will come and then the Lord will help me punish those who are against me." Pause. "Yes, well, thanks for warning me. I do appreciate that. It's always good to know in advance what they are up to. Bye for now."

The Bishop put the receiver back and rested his hand on it while he contemplated what had been said. Then he lifted his head, faced his first wife and growled. "Brother Lucas thinks we should be self-sufficient. He doesn't want to send us any more money."

Marion wasn't sure how to react, so she looked at him with what she hoped was the right mixture of curiosity and concern.

"I don't need to tell you what this means," he said, still looking at her with a dead-pan expression. "You will have to get those lazy women to be more productive. I can't risk being cut off by the Gate-keepers without having another source of income in place. You've all been enjoying the fruit of my connection with the Elders long enough now. It's about time you paid for your keep."

Marion only opened her mouth because her husband cocked his head and sneered at her expectantly. "My husband, forgive me, but what is it you want us to do."

"Well, just work harder! What did the women produce in the last few months? What did we sell? How much money was left over once the provisions were bought? Answer me! You should know the figures, you do the accounting!"

"They're all busy tending the fields and bringing the harvest in."

He laughed. "Ha, excuses, excuses! Give me some figures! How much?"

Marion mumbled something about having to take money from the bank to supplement the household expenses. That they hadn't really sold anything as all the vegetables and fruit were needed for their own consumption. That most of the old clothes they could salvage from the dump had been used for their own needs. The few quilts they had made out of the leftover material last winter had already been sold at the markets and nobody had had time this spring and summer to go collecting again.

Her husband lifted one eyebrow. "Well, the free ride is over. My patience is worn thin." He stood up resolutely. "Order all women to the community hall. I shall have to announce a few new rules around here!"

"When do you want to see them?"

"Now, of course."

"But, my husband, forgive me ..." Marion wasn't sure if she should even mention it. Why didn't she just leave it alone?

"What?"

"May I remind you. Your new wife. She is waiting."

The Bishop angrily shook his head. Damn this woman. She was always on his back. As if he didn't know that a juicy young virgin was waiting for him. This one was better than any of his wives, by far better than Katherine's daughter, that obnoxious clod he nearly married. The Lord certainly moved in mysterious ways. If he had not got rid of her, which had greatly upset him at the time, as he hadn't enjoyed a new young wife for quite some time, he would never have thought of writing to Brother Peter. And his daughter sure was something else! All day long he had been looking forward to see her slim, naked body splayed out on the mattress in front of him. Every time he pictured the new bride he now owned, he felt familiar warmth spread in his loins. He had purposely drawn out the moment when he would finally enjoy the rare pleasures this unspoiled child could give him. It would fade soon enough. Her skin would stretch as soon as she was pregnant, her flesh would sag after giving birth, she would be a woman way too fast. Just like all the others; those old hags the Gatekeepers had punished him with. Even like the last two younger ones he had imported from America at great expense. The delicious sweet flower of their youth disappeared too fast in the harsh northern climate.

He had wanted to savour the moment, knowing how short-lived his pleasures would be. Actually, he had just prepared himself to go and see her when Brother Mathew had called. Now his tingling anticipation had gone flat, ruined by the Gatekeepers' threat. Ah, what a shame. The girl would have to wait. Once he got his other wives straightened out, the urge would surely come back. Maybe he would enjoy it even more, having to wait until tomorrow night.

When Lillian woke up again, the sun was already brightening the room but did not manage to warm it up. She shivered. For a disturbing second she had no idea where she was, then everything came back to her. She remembered and quickly mumbled *Martha*. She was Martha now, and she was married. This was her husband's home. She was alone in a cold room with a high window, sitting on a wide bed with only a thin quilt as cover. She was all alone. Her stomach was queasy and she felt like throwing up. Just thinking about it, made her rush out of bed. She barely made it to the toilet before a small amount of milky fluid gushed out of her mouth. It tasted sour. She instantly felt better and rinsed her mouth with water before she drank some of it. Then a pang of guilt hit her. Had anybody in the house noticed her disgraceful behaviour? She opened the door and peered into the hallway. Nobody was there. She tip-toed back to her room and settled on her bed again.

After a while her ears adjusted and she heard faint noises. A door hinge squeaked; muffled sounds drifted along the hallway; a child was yelling from further away.

Full of guilt, she blamed herself for sleeping through the night. How could she? What would her husband think of her now? Surely he had come and seen her fast asleep! But he had not woken her. Realizing how considerate he had been, she relaxed a little and smiled. Nothing bad had happened.

Then she remembered Marion and her anxiety returned. Maybe he had seen her asleep and had left the room because he was angry with her? She should have stayed awake. Maybe Marion was angry too. How could she get pregnant if she slept? Her mother had never really explained to her how this all worked, how a woman actually got pregnant. She had only said, when your husband comes to you at night, you must welcome him and obey him again and again until you are with child. The 'again and again' part had been left unexplained.

Martha thought about it and cringed, torn between fear and reason. She had not waited up for her husband, so he had every reason to be angry, but maybe he understood how tired she had been and would forgive her disobedience. Her mother had said *again and again*, meaning there must be many more possibilities to get pregnant, but he might be so upset and not come again to take care of this pregnancy thing. It was all so complicated.

Her empty stomach grumbled, reminding her how hungry she was.

Quickly she pulled herself upright on the iron headboard until she stood on the mattress and could peek out the window. Outside her confinement was a beautiful sunny day. High fir trees cast their shadows away from the house and the open meadow in front of the window was still green and covered with white and purple flowers for which she had no name. Flowers like that did not grow in her home, her *old* home. Around her old compound she used to see mostly prickly pear, which had pretty flowers too, and other cactuses. And early in the year, before it got too hot, some bushes bloomed and she knew all their names too. Thank the Lord for all the books in her father's home she had been permitted to read. Nobody in the household had time to teach her the things that were written down in the books, they considered it a waste of time to study such useless information. It was much more important to learn how to cook and sew and clean. How to grow and harvest and preserve food. How to milk a cow or goat and slaughter a pig. She could do all those things too. But she really, really liked to know the names of all the flowers and all the other wonderful things the Lord had created for his universe. Maybe her husband would tell her what the pretty white and purple ones on the meadow outside were called. He was a Bishop. He would know everything.

Suddenly she heard a noise and quickly slid back down under the cover. The door to her room opened and a young woman entered. Not as young as her and not as old as Marion. And not Michaela. Maybe she was one of the sister-wives who had welcomed her yesterday evening, but Martha did not remember having seen her before.

The woman brought a bowl of food and a glass of water and placed it on the dresser. With a friendly smile she looked at Martha and was about to leave again.

Encouraged by the smile, Martha jumped out of bed. "Please don't go."

The woman halted.

"What's your name?"

"I'm Anna."

Ah, yes, Anna. There had been an Anna. She remembered now.

"I am not supposed to talk to you."

"Why not?"

Anna shot a quick glance at the closed door and whispered: "Because you are new here. You have to do your duty first."

"My duty?"

"With our husband, you know."

"No, I don't know. Please tell me. Have I done something wrong?" Martha was so excited that she could finally ask another human being all those questions burning inside her, that she forgot to keep her voice down. "Is our husband angry with me? I fell asleep, you know, and I

54

didn't even hear him. Is Marion angry with me? She said I must wait up for him." She pointed at the food. "Is this my breakfast?"

"Hush", whispered Anna. "If you're going to make so much noise, I'll leave right away."

"Sorry."

Anna handed her the bowl. "Here, sit down and eat this. You didn't have supper; you must be starving."

Martha's empty stomach contracted painfully. She grabbed the bowl. Food, yes! Hot cereal that smelled of raisins and cinnamon. She wolfed it down while Anna explained in rapid, staccato sentences.

"We know you fell asleep. Marion checked on you. She told us this morning that our husband stayed with her and not with you. She is happy, don't worry. At least for now. But don't do it again. Stay awake tonight. I must go, before they miss me."

"Wait. Don't go. I'll come with you."

Anna was already at the door, shaking her head sadly. "No, you can't go. You must stay here."

"How long?"

"Until he has seen you."

"I don't want to stay in here all by myself."

"Look, if we are careful I can spend more time with you when I bring your next meal. But not now. All the wives are getting ready to do their duties. Marion said I can stay here to look after the children and bring your meals. So just be patient."

Martha felt a surge of panic rising inside her. "What are you talking about? Meals? Do I have to stay here all day?"

Anna went to the door, opened it and looked back at Martha with a deep frown on her forehead. She placed a finger on her lips. "Sshh. Maybe later."

Martha stopped talking. Anna waved at her and slipped out of the room.

Martha waited for Anna all day long. Nobody came. There was nothing to do. Having to sit and wait was terribly boring. Her boredom started to make her nervous. She became agitated; was too nervous to make up a new mind game to distract herself.

To fill the endless empty time she started to count the seconds until they made up one minute and then the minutes to make up one hour. Then she lost track and had to start all over again. She walked from the bed to the door, five steps, and back. She opened and closed the empty dresser drawers. She stood up, looked out the window, counted the branches on the trees, the flowers on the lawn, until the light faded.

She went to the toilet once more, but it never occurred to her to venture down the hallway. What would she do if she entered another room full of women, or one with her husband present? What would they do to her if they caught her?

Then the door opened again and she jumped up, delirious with happiness that finally, finally, it happened. Whatever the *it* was, she would happily accept it. Whatever was supposed to happen to end this agonizing wait.

It was not her husband!

Another woman, not Anna, entered with a similar bowl filled with some stew, but this one did not say a word, no matter how much Martha begged. She left as quietly as she had come. When the room was sealed shut with a minute creak of the door hinges, Martha started to cry. Hot tears streamed down her cheeks and she sobbed loud and hard. She did not care who heard her; nobody came anyway. When her tears dried up and her body was weak from heaving and cramping she was so exhausted that she was not even hungry any more. Night had fallen outside. The outlines of the sparse furniture in the room developed an eerie quality, as if they were telling her that her life was reduced to the same shadowy existence. As exhausted as she was, she rebelled against the unfairness of being reduced to a contour in a lonely night. As she drifted off into an exhausted sleep, a childlike promise comforted her.

I will never eat again until I am dead. Then they will be sorry.

5

The faded quilt had 2856 octagons. Its width consisted of forty-two and the length of sixty-eight different coloured patches. 680 of them were white, or had been white a long time ago, 796 were different shades of blue, 232 were red, pink or purple, 112 were yellowish and the remaining 1036 had multi-coloured patterns.

It had taken Martha two days to figure it out and keep the numbers in her head, next to all the others she had to remember. The fir trees in front of the house had been easy to count, there were only twenty seven. Same with the grey tiles in the bathroom (48 on the floor, 12 behind the washbasin), the wide wooden planks on the bedroom floor (52) and the dresser drawers (5). More complicated were the cracks in the ceiling. Should she count them all or just stick to the major cracks and not bother with the spidery veins branching out from them?

Two full days of endless waiting.

Every time she had stared at the ceiling she got confused, then angry, and then terrified. Nobody would let her out of this room until she knew how many cracks the ceiling had. Or until she could count time, but that was nearly impossible. The only reference points she had were the moments when a meal was brought by a silent sister-wife. How many seconds lay between the breakfast bowl and the lunch bowl? Too often she lost her concentration and started to count the ceiling cracks before she reminded herself what needed to be done. The time counting was very important and she just could not get it right. Got distracted so often by useless thoughts of loathing or self-pity.

Finally, on the third day of waiting, the meal was brought by Anna again.

Martha was instantly excited. She wanted to talk to her, but could not get a single word out of her parched throat.

Anna put the breakfast bowl in Martha's hand, sat down next to her and patted the quilt where Martha's left thigh was. "It's alright, I understand. You don't have to say anything. I'm sorry I couldn't come sooner. And I don't have much time now. But you won't have to stay in here much longer. Our husband had to go to Kamloops for a few days, that's why he didn't see you. That's the delay."

"Then... why... do I... have to... wait in here?" Martha croaked, barely audible. The lack of use had made her vocal cords raspy. "Why can't I be... outside... with the other wives?"

"Because he wants it so. He wants you to be perfectly ready when he has time for you."

"Time to do... what?"

Anna's face clouded over. "Come now, I don't have to tell you. You need to be with child quickly."

Whatever that meant. At this particular moment, Martha didn't care. She didn't want to *get* with child now, she wanted to get out of this room. She was too engrossed in her own misery to notice the shadow clouding Anna's expression. Her saliva slowly started to flow again and she swallowed hard. "Why didn't you come... like you said you would? I have waited so many days... and nobody talks to me."

"I know. I tried. But Marion doesn't like me. She really doesn't. I had to go with the others to the dump, although I normally never have to go. Never. She made me go, same as Emma. I have a small child and Emma has two, we're not supposed to go. I spent two days at the dump. It was just awful." She shook herself in disgust and quickly carried on explaining. "Our husband decided that we must work harder with our sewing. We need to make more things he can sell. Marion said our husband wants four of us to go to the dump every day from now on. There is so much else to do, specially in summer, with the harvesting and all, so I don't understand why any of us should go at all. And I don't believe our husband meant for us mothers with young children to go there. I think Marion makes it up to punish some of us. Can you imagine? She made me go! I had to leave my child alone all day because the others were busy in the fields. If we don't pick the apples now, they will drop to the ground and be spoiled, and if we don't get the hay in soon, the cows and sheep will not make it through winter. I don't know what she is thinking. And I hate it so much there …," suddenly her voice quivered and faded. Tears filled her eyes and she rubbed them away with the back of her hands.

Martha could see how dirty Anna's fingernails were. She put one hand on the other woman's arm. She found no words to console her.

"Oh, it's just so horrible. Horrible. The stink of it, it's so disgusting. I can't get rid of the smell. Don't tell me you can't smell it on me?"

Now that she pointed it out, Martha got a sweetish whiff in her nose, like the aroma of rotting bananas. "Not really," she assured Anna. "It's not bad at all, really."

"It is. It hangs in my dress and my hair and we have so little time to clean ourselves. The dump always smells bad, but the stench is much worse in summer."

"But why do you have to go there?"

"We look for the clothes other people throw away."

"Why?"

Anna looked at her stupefied. As if it was the most natural thing in the world to go and collect clothes from a dump. "Well, what do you think? Because we make our dresses out of it. And things like this quilt that keeps you warm. Every evening all sister-wives and daughters meet in the community hall and we sing and pray and make things out of the old clothes. You have no idea what people throw away. We salvage some other things too, anything that can be useful. Most of the furniture in our huts is from the dump. The boys restore it for us." She suddenly stopped, hit by the absurdity of the activity she just described. "Otherwise we wouldn't have anything," she added feebly, more to herself.

Martha's eyes widened in horror. They had to work hard at her father's compound too, but *the dump*? "From the dump?" she said.

Anna nodded. "But so far I never had to go, I just helped to make things out of what the others collected, and all of a sudden Marion made me go. I spent the last two days there. Two days. All day long. The four of us were not even allowed to climb out of the trench for our meals. We had to eat our ration there. I couldn't get anything down in two days. We were only allowed home after dark, when we were picked up by our husband's eldest son. And then we had to clean ourselves and assemble in the hall to start sorting out what we brought home. You think you are hard done by, but I tell you, it's nothing compared to what I had to suffer."

"I wouldn't do it!"

Anna meant to laugh, but the sound that was meant to placate and maybe ridicule Martha's misguided comment exploded out of her throat like an accusation. Her hand flew to her mouth to stop her hysteric reaction. "Sure you would. And you will, if Marion demands it. I pray this will go away just like many of the other crazy things she makes us do, pretending they were our husband's order, because none of us can stand it much longer. Katherine is already gone over the edge, but that was to be expected anyway."

Martha was glad the conversation changed course. She didn't want to think about her future, not as long as her options were only to slowly lose her mind in this tiny room or to crawl over heaps of stinking garbage. "What about Katherine?"

"Oh you know, since her daughter has gone, she has not been herself. She used to teach the little ones, but now that she has gone mad with grief she is no use for that, and Marion has to find another one to take over from Katherine. I should thank her for losing her mind. Marion is trying out all sister-wives, one after the other, to find the best one to take over from teacher Katherine. It's my turn tomorrow and for the next few days I'll look after the school, so one of the others will have to go to the dump." Anna thought of something and giggled. "Maybe Marion will let me stay home now in case our husband doesn't like you. I'm his favourite, you know. And if he wants me and I smell so bad, he will blame her for it. She knows that. I bet that's why she wants me to stay away from the dump. I need to smell good for our husband. But don't fret, I'm sure he only wants you right now. And when he is done with you and got you with child, it will be my turn again." She leaned even closer to Martha, confiding a secret that must not be heard beyond those walls. "Don't worry. It's only you or me. Only the two of us who have to share him. He doesn't want the others. The first three who came with him from America, Marion and Elisabeth and Barbara, remind him too much of his old life. You know, back where he is from he was a very powerful man with a great future ahead of him, and he gets so sad when he's with them that he doesn't want to touch them any more. He told me that. And the others, Katherine and her seven sister-wives from Alberta, were forced on him, they have never been to his liking anyway. He would never have picked them himself. Never. They are all old! Way too old, none of them is under twenty. That leaves only me and Emma – but Emma was a mistake, he said, she is just skin and bones. That's why you are here now. But don't worry, I won't begrudge you his attention. You are so young, you will be pregnant quickly. And then it's me again. Of course, the others always nag at Marion to let them visit him, saying he must resume his duty with them, but he never will, I know that for sure." She took a deep breath and was finally quiet.

Martha was totally confused. She had learned a lot about her new family in the last five minutes, specially about the all-important hier-archy among the sister-wives, yet she still didn't know why she had to wait in here and what would happen to her after her husband had come to see her. She wished he finally would – but then again, if this only meant she would leave the room and join her sister-wives scaven-ging in the garbage dump, she might be better off in here. "When will he be back?" she asked timidly.

"Tonight. But if he is very late, you might have to wait until tomor-row for your big moment."

In the evening Anna came again, telling her that their husband was indeed delayed with some important business meetings and would come back the next day. Just one more day of waiting.

Martha felt much better knowing what to expect. At least she would be able to go to sleep without any guilt, if she was allowed to. She said so to Anna, but Anna told her not to worry about it. The staying awake and waiting rule was just another one of Marion's orders that didn't make any sense. She always demanded things that made the other wives uncomfortable or belittled them in the eyes of their husband. Marion is the first wife and likes to feel important, Anna explained, she likes to control the favours and punishments given.

That made Martha feel better. "Can I leave this room once he has been here?"

"Maybe not right away. Maybe you have to stay here until they are sure you'll be with child. I was with child very quickly. My bleeding did not come once after my wedding, so I was able to move to my own house as soon as my expected time had passed and did not have to stay here with Marion any longer."

Martha knew about the sign of the blood women shed at monthly intervals. That a husband must be found as soon as a girl became a woman and that the blood dried out once she became pregnant. That is the sign, her mother had told her. To start bleeding is the sign that you are a woman, and when it stops, it is the sign that you will have a child. She wanted to ask Anna about the house she was allowed to live in but Anna, getting nervous about spending too much time with Martha, refused to explain any more and quickly left.

Martha's heart was lighter now, but soon after Anna had left the room, it felt as heavy as a brick again. So heavy that she could barely breathe.

The next day, Anna came twice and chatted with Martha as long as she dared. That was like a miracle to Martha. Like a very special gift for which she would be thankful all her life, even though Anna wasn't overly friendly toward her. Martha could understand why her sister-wife kept her distance. They would be competing for their husband's attention, so they could never be really close; but Anna was her only connection to the outside world and her cheerful, though detached, chatter made Martha see her own situation in a slightly brighter light.

On the evening of her fourth day of confinement, the routine changed. Marion came herself and brought the dinner bowl and a glass of milk. Martha was immediately alert and in her confusion she jumped off the bed and said something very silly. "It's 2856 patches, I counted them all."

Marion lifted her eyebrows, looking like an owl with her round yellow glasses perched on her small nose. She ignored Martha's remark, put the tray on the dresser, took the bowl and sat down beside Martha. "Here, eat this."

Martha sat down and did as she was told.

Then Marion handed her the glass of milk. "Drink."

The milk smelled as if it had gone sour but it looked alright and Martha swallowed it without hesitation. She would have drunk it even if it had been off; Marion's presence petrified her. The milk left a bitter aftertaste in her mouth. It reminded her of the herbal medicine her mother had administered every time a child had been sick. That tasted horrible too, but it worked really well.

Martha handed the empty glass back to Marion without looking at her. She stared at the wooden planks, helpless to stop the counting. Five, six, seven planks, the tip of Marion's shoes peeping out underneath her bulky dress, eight, nine....then Marion got up and ruined the count. Now she would have to start all over again.

"Our husband will come and see you tonight."

A surge of excitement flooded through Martha. Yes! Finally! She jumped up again and nearly embraced the woman standing next to her. Marion stared down at her, probably thinking how impertinent her impulsive gesture was. Martha dropped her raised arms.

"Do not get excited. You must stay calm. I will now tell you what you have to do."

Martha's head bobbed up and down. Yes, of course, she needed to know what to do.

"Sit down," ordered the older woman. "Take your nightdress off."

Martha had been wearing this bulky piece of cotton twill day and night and could not be happier to get rid of the monstrous garment, but she had nothing else to wear.

"Don't worry, you will get a new dress tomorrow. Now, take it off and get under the cover."

Martha's heart was beating as fast as a woodpecker hammering into a tree trunk. She took a few short deep breaths, trying to calm herself. Quickly she slipped under the quilt with its 2856 patches – although this time no numbers popped up in her mind – pulled it up to her shoulders and started to wriggle out of her nightdress.

When she had managed to slip it over her head, Marion held out her hand and took it from her. For a split second Martha's shoulders were exposed and she grabbed the quilt with both hands and lifted it up to her chin to cover herself.

Marion made her owl face again. "Do not be ashamed. That is how the Lord wants us to be. Always think of the scripture. You can do no wrong if you do what our husband demands. Remember the teaching: *They shall be gods …*"

Martha remembered the written holy text the girls had to repeat aloud so many times in scripture class. She fell in with Marion and both recited together:

" *…because they are above all, because all things are subject unto them. They shall be gods because they have all the power and the angels are subject unto them.*"

When they had finished Marion left the room, only to return a few minutes later with a candle stick for 6 candles. This night Martha would have light. Marion placed the candle stick on the dresser and lit the candles. "After our husband has seen you, you will remain in here until I allow you to leave. It may be that he wants to see you for a few nights in a row. You must always be prepared."

Martha lay perfectly still under the quilt and watched the flickering shadows on the wall.

"When he decides that he has fulfilled his duty to the Lord, you will be allowed to join your sister-wives. There is much work to be done here. I, we, need every hand and I hope you will be a help to the weaker ones who have no strength left for the hard work the Lord places upon us."

Martha quickly nodded, indicating her willingness to the older woman.

"You will then be moved to one of the huts which shall be your new home. When the time comes, I will explain the rules of our lives in detail, but one thing you may ponder already while you wait for our husband to arrive is this: He expects total obedience and he wants you to serve him with a smile. *Keep sweet* is what he expects from all of us. You will not question his decisions, not even quietly to yourself. He is our master and we will respect his word. You will not speak to your sister-wives about any of his decisions; you will simply adhere to them. Is that understood?"

Martha nodded again. Of course she would obey him, he was her husband, wasn't he? Why did Marion feel the need to preach about this?

Marion turned away from her and left without another word. Darkness settled in front of the bedroom window. By now Martha was unaccustomed to having light in her room and kept staring at the flames. She was so excited. Tonight she would be able to stay awake until finally, finally, her husband would come and save her from this horrible prison. Surely Anna was right and it was only Marion who made up such strange rules. She would tell her husband about it and would make sure the others did not have to suffer under Marion any longer.

No matter how often she told herself to stay alert, she just couldn't. Her whole body felt heavier and heavier and she had to really fight to stay awake. It was so warm under the covers. Not wearing a night-dress made her skin feel flushed. Her whole body was warm. Her limbs were so heavy and her muscles relaxed until they were unable to move. Should she get out of bed to cool down and stay awake? She tried, but she could not. Her body refused to react to her command. She felt so sleepy, so tired and heavy, she couldn't lift an arm or a leg, couldn't move an inch, didn't want to move. What would she do outside this bed? It was cold there and she had no clothes to cover herself.

Her eyelids started to droop and her breathing became difficult. Dear Lord, what was wrong with her? She had to burp to relieve some of the pressure in her chest and smelled the same disgusting sour odour the milk had had.

If she could only close her eyes for one minute and take a deep breath, she would be able to gather enough strength to stay awake.

The candles were half burned when the door opened. Heavy with sleep and only semi-conscious, Martha registered that her husband entered the room. Part of her wanted to wake up and welcome him, and tell him about Marion and all the injustice she had suffered, and the loneliness and the boredom, but the other part wanted to drift deeper into sleep and wanted him to go away. She was unable to move. All power had gone out of her muscles and, even worse, her mind was just as paralysed. She, who normally always had millions of questions twirling like glow-worms in her brain, couldn't think of anything. She wanted to open her eyes fully and look at her husband and tell him what she had gone through, but neither her eyelids nor her tongue reacted the way they were supposed to. She could barely make out her husband's wide frame at the end of the bed. When he took the quilt in his hands and slowly pulled it off her naked body, she tried to cover herself again. She tried to beg him not to look at her – didn't he see that she was without clothes? - but only a crackling sound came out of her throat. He took no notice of her. Powerless to lift herself up and reach for the quilt that was now bunched around her ankles, she could only squirm. Her hands tried to hide her private parts.

"Don't!" he commanded her. "Do not move!" and she did not. She could not. Could only squeeze her eyes shut in shame, so she would not have to look at the big man who inspected her as if she was a broken machine he was going to fix.

"Look at me!" he commanded again, and she did lift her lashes enough to show him her obedience but she refused to see him. He remained motionless at the end of the bed and stared at her for so long that her burning body turned to ice and began to shiver. Even with her eyes nearly closed and her body frozen in fear could she feel his greedy examination. Finally, she heard him move around the bed and felt his weight settling next to her. She could not escape the draft of his heavy laboured breath gliding over her cold skin, nor his probing hands which started to work on the Martha machine. Rough hands moved between her legs and pressed her thighs so unnaturally wide apart that it hurt her hips. She wanted to scream and make him stop, but knew she must not. He was a God and she was nothing. He had every right to do whatever he wanted. He could hurt her, tear her apart, even kill her, if he did not consider her worthy enough to follow him into his celestial kingdom. She was his to do as he pleased. No crying, no fighting back. Even when he lowered his weight on her, pressing her into the mattress, and wriggled around on top of her until he had pried her open even more, the pain was numb and detached. Her mind refused to believe what he was doing to her. It was too shameful. His pushing and shoving inside her intensified to a point where it penetrated her denial and forced her to scream out against the pain that grew and grew inside her. The pain did not subside after his sweat drenched body suddenly went limp, covering her like a wet blanket. A wave of nausea rolled over her. She could not breathe. She was buried alive; couldn't move, couldn't think, couldn't retch. Slowly he rolled off her.

Her desperate gasp for air turned to gagging. She barely managed to turn her body away from him and hang her head over the edge of the mattress before a gush of vomit spewed on the floor.

With amazing speed he jumped off the bed. "Oh, for heaven's sake, how disgusting!" he said, shaking his head and pulling up his trousers.

Long after he had left, she remained lying on her side, retching and gasping and crying all at once. Eventually there was nothing left in her stomach, or in her heart, or her mind, and the pain between her legs began to dominate her. She rolled over on her other side, away from the stinky mess she had produced, and curled into a fetal position. With her arms clasped around her knees she rocked her body to soothe the pain so she could forget what had happened.

The Bishop settled at his desk. He was quite pleased with himself. It had gone really well; even the girl's disgusting lack of self control at the end didn't diminish his satisfaction. The girl was so delicate, none of his other wives were built like that. He had made the most of those exquisite moments before he had taken possession of her. There was nothing comparable to the pleasure of studying a helpless little thing like that, squirming in discomfort and shame. Nice, really nice. Pity it wouldn't be quite like that next time. It would still be good of course, many times after the first time, but not quite like that. She would get used to him looking her over, maybe even try and offer herself in an adult, shameless manner. The time he would have to devour her with his eyes would get shorter, and the time he needed to satisfy himself physically would get longer because of it. Sometimes he thought he should not touch a young girl at all. He should just look at her tiny frame, the flat chest, the slender boyish hips, the skinny arms and legs, all of her body without a hint of the womanly bulges she would develop all too soon. He should just look at her until he came all by himself - or maybe just with the help of her inexperienced little hands.

But that must never be. He was the Bishop. It was his duty to create soldiers for the Lord, he could not afford to waste his seed.

There was a knock on the door. Knowing it would be his first wife, as usual spoiling his after-glow mood, he sighed regretfully and called out for her to come in.

Marion opened the door just a crack and stuck her head through. "My husband, forgive me..."

He leaned back in his chair, folding his arms over his belly. "Marion, what is it now?"

She came into the room and closed the door. "It is just..., I need your advice."

"As usual." He smiled benevolently. What would they all do without him!

"I am not so sure what to do next. The hay has to be brought in soon and we need all hands in the fields."

"So?"

"But four of the women have to be at the dump everyday."

"So?"

She looked at the worn patches on the carpet in front of his desk. Where she had stood many times, pleading with him. Slowly she came closer. "We need everybody's help now, before the weather turns. Can I stop sending them to the dump? Please? At least until the hay is in?"

The Bishop patted his belly with one hand. "My dear Marion, how often do I have to explain to you that we need money? Do you think it grows on trees? How often do I have to explain that we have to step up our production! The women need enough material to produce their quilts. They can't make those pretty handicraft things the city people go crazy over out of thin air. Haven't I explained to you what our dear friends down in Arizona have done? Did you see any money coming into my account this month? No, you didn't! So what do you suggest we live on?"

"I know, but the hay...?"

"The hay! The hay! I've got bigger worries than that. Do I have to justify my orders to my own wife? Marion, Marion, when will you learn? Just do as you are told and all will be well. I want to see your sister-wives at the table every evening sewing and embroidering until their fingers can't hold the needles any more. Is that clear? Even with four of them at the dump you have enough of the others at your disposal for your silly haying. They just have to work a bit harder. I want to take a truck load full of stuff to the shop next time I go to Kamloops, understood? So do as you are told and stop bothering me with minor details. Hay! Please! Now, off you go and assign the women to their jobs. See how much I trust you, I leave it all to you to arrange. I only wish you would extend the same courtesy to me, your husband, and stop pestering me. Now, go!" He waved her away.

At the door Marion looked back, defeated and worn out. "My husband..."

"What now?"

"The new girl, Martha, can I put her up in Anna's hut?"

He smiled. "No. I'm not done with her yet."

6

Daisy couldn't believe that her boss hadn't even tried to negotiate a better deal. In fact, since he had returned from his trip up north a week ago, he acted so totally out of character, she hardly recognized him any more. He was so proud of his latest acquisition, he behaved like a kid in a candy store, playfully toying with an assortment of ludicrous ideas; planning his pet project from early morning until late at night. His focus was so total, so all consuming, Daisy worried that it might soon turn into a full blown obsession.

She did not share his dream. Daisy was a level-headed woman. She was 31, only one year older than her boss, had an analytical brain and liked to base her work on solid facts, backed up by thorough research. It worried her that Richard Bergman had lost his usual caution. For God's sake, he hadn't even secured the financing for the acquisition before he had committed himself to it.

"You have to see the land to understand," he tried to justify his passion to her. "We can't go wrong with this one. Believe me, I can make it work. I have developed a concept that will be so attractive to city slickers, the Vancouverites and Calgarians will snatch it up even before my fellow Germans get their land-greedy hands on it."

She didn't answer, just watched and waited, wondering when their usually productive working relationship had derailed. Until now he had always asked her opinion before he purchased any land and had respected her judgement. This time he had not consulted her, had not let her do the usual title search and other relevant background checks, had apparently over-hastily accepted the vendor's initial demand - something that bugged her most, how the hell could he not negotiate! – and had not informed her of his decision until it had been time to sign the sale and purchase agreement in the lawyers' office. Nice guy, Larry, the lawyer, nice, knowledgeable and very professional. As professional as he was, he had temporarily lost his usual unbiased attitude, and had asked Richard Bergman point blank if he didn't think he overextended himself with this purchase, and if he was absolutely sure he wanted to go through with this deal.

Richard had beamed with joy and said he was sure, more than sure, he was certain this deal was a once in a lifetime chance, something one had to grab quickly and turn into a model development. "It's my pot of gold at the end of the rainbow," he had cheered himself on, clapping his hands with a sudden inspiration. "That's it," he had said, "I've got a name for it. I will call it the Rainbow Estate!"

Daisy had sat next to him and could only shake her head, while the lawyer didn't make his disapproval quite so obvious. His tight-lipped mouth displayed enough of his reservations.

That had been three days ago, and now Richard was sitting in her office with the same silly grin on his face.

"Won't you at least listen to my concept before you make up your mind?" he pleaded. "I've got this brilliant idea what to do with the Rainbow Estate. I'm positive it'll work."

"If you can explain to me how we are going to pay for it, I'll listen to anything you have to say."

He waved his hand. "Minor detail. We need to off-load all our other assets. I talked Bob into closing end of December, so we have four months longer to get the cash together."

"*One* month," she corrected him. "The seller gave you only one month longer."

"Don't be picky! You know what I mean."

"Actually I don't." Daisy sneered. "Even assuming we will be able to sell the four flats we have in Burnaby and the duplex in Surrey at full price in the next few weeks, it won't be enough."

"I know. But we can always max our line of credit."

"Still not enough."

"The banks will lend us the rest."

"You know the banks don't finance development land in rural areas. Not the TD, the Canadian, the Royal or any other Bank."

Richard was getting annoyed with her attitude. "*Himmel-Donner-wetter,* what's the matter with you? Why do you always have to be so negative? Why can't you trust me? Haven't I always found a solution?"

"Yes, you have," she relented. "And I usually trust your instinct. But this one is such a big house number, it simply scares me. Plus, you are probably right, I haven't seen it and can't picture it."

"Exactly."

"You didn't ask me to look at it before you made up your mind."

He laughed. "Admit it, your nose is out of joint, little lady!"

"Don't get patronizing," Daisy reprimanded him with a stern face, as always refusing to be charmed by him. She put on her glasses, moved the map of the subdivision plan he had brought with him around so she could study it and waited for him to explain his latest brainwave.

"It's really quite ingenious," he started without modesty. "When you ask people living in a big city anywhere in the world, but specially here in Canada, a cabin in the country is on top of their wish-list, right?"

"Right".

"They dream of owning a place where their family can enjoy care-free holidays, go swimming and fishing and boating in summer, hiking and hunting in autumn and cross country skiing, snow-mobiling and ice-fishing in winter - in pure white, undisturbed snow, mind you - celebrating Christmas by the fireplace, roasting marshmallows ..."

"What about spring?" Daisy interrupted him.

"Are you serious?"

"You mentioned summer, autumn and winter. What about spring? The kids have spring break. What do you do in a country cabin then? The snow is melting but the lakes are still frozen. There is mush and mud everywhere and it looks totally unattractive."

"What do I know! Play in the mud maybe. Daisy, that's not the point. Cabin owners don't go there at every break. What *is* important to them is that they can call such a wonderful place their own. Family heirloom, so to speak. Passing it on from one generation to the next. Get it?"

"Not really, but if you say so."

He knew that she got it but only played the devil's advocate to uncover any flaws in his thinking.

"If you are right, country cabins in the mountains should sell like hot-cakes," she argued while she pulled a real estate survey from the top drawer of her desk. "However, the latest figures released by the Real Estate Board do show a fairly large inventory. There are plenty of cabins on the market in the Thompson-Nicola and Cariboo-Chilcotin regions. Average listing time is over nine months."

"Granted, compared to Vancouver that's a slow turn-over, but I tell you two reasons why this is so." He paused briefly for effect. "First of all, cabins at bargain prices are a thing of the past. Most of them are out of reach for families with an average income. And the ones with enough cash to make their dream come true often hesitate before spending so much money because they worry about the security of their property when they are away. Imagine, you lock up the place for three months or longer and there is nobody living there or looking after it. Which is a real concern, just like the caretaking such a second home needs. Who empties the mailbox? Who snowploughs the driveway? Who mows the lawn? When they come for their hard-earned holidays, they don't want to waste time opening up the cabin. Those people are not used to physical labour like snow shovelling or chopping firewood, they don't even like doing minor repairs or wasting their time on menial chores like cleaning or lawn mowing. They just want to arrive and enjoy their place." He paused again.

"So? You make it sound like owning a cabin is a nightmare. That's hardly an attractive sales concept."

"Quite the opposite. We will use those concerns to our advantage. Remember, people love the idea of owning a cabin – without the headaches. We will provide the service and security they crave. Our subdivision will consist of large parcels of land, so large that we guarantee nobody can even see his neighbour, yet we will have the whole 2000 acres fenced in, with a private road through it, protected by gates. We will have one or more caretakers employed by the Strata committee who look after the place. All the owners will be able to rest peacefully at night – no matter if they are in their cabins or their city homes – with the comfy feeling of having their families and their property protected. What do you say to that? Did I dazzle you with my brilliance?"

Daisy didn't even take one second to think it over. "You are nuts. Do you have any idea how much it costs to fence in 2000 acres?"

"It is already done, that's the beauty of it. Bob is a third generation owner. First his grandfather, then his father and finally him have used the land for grazing cattle and have painstakingly put in every single bloody fence post and stretched endless kilometres of barbed wire. Amazing, but of course in those days materials were cheaper, and their labour didn't cost them anything. Probably had nothing better to do anyway."

"It will be a lot of lots," Daisy said.

"Which makes each single one more affordable."

Daisy did a quick calculation. Subtracting the land needed for road building and communal property, there could be at least one hundred lots of between fifteen to twenty acres each. Dividing the development costs by such a large number resulted indeed in a low average price per lot. But there were servicing roads to be built. She had no idea how expensive this would be and mused over the unknown factor. She would need to check the terrain with experienced road contractors and get them to estimate realistically, and fast. With the purchase price of the land way over their limit they could not afford to dabble too long over plans and concepts. They had to get cracking right away. She would have to submit the requests for all the needed permits simultaneously to working on all the requirements as if the permits had already been issued. She could feel a headache creeping along her cranium. This project would be hell to co-ordinate because they had to push it through at high speed and there would be no room for errors. Even so, one year would be the minimum they were looking at before they could even dream of pre-selling, and more likely two years before the first money was coming in.

"Ah," Richard grinned, totally misreading her. "I have exhausted the opposition! You can't think of another argument against it."

She sighed, putting faint sarcasm into her reply. "Opposition can't do its job of cautioning and balancing if the party in power doesn't want to listen to reason. As it'll be my job to kick-start the sub-division process, you might as well fill me in on the rest of your brilliant concept." She bent over the map in front of her, so he would not detect her disappointment.

Richard Bergman was the boss and if he wanted to risk his company he could do so without her permission.

He pulled his chair closer to her desk. Heads together, they started to discuss how best to set the complicated subdivision process with all its governmental hurdles in motion.

7

In the past seven nights Martha had lost more than her innocence. She had lost her future. Her husband had abused her body in a way she had not thought possible until now.

He had hurt her physically, but the wounds he had inflicted on her went deeper than her skin and flesh, they penetrated her soul. They would never heal. She was bound to him forever, without the slightest hope to ever escape this humiliating treatment. He would do it again and again, until she died. She was now the property of her husband and he could do all those revolting and degrading things to her. He had invaded her most private parts, had pushed and shoved into her so forcefully and rubbed himself against her most tender parts with such crazed vigour that she would have screamed out loud in pain and shame had he not muffled her sounds with his hand over her mouth. So many times. *Again and again.* She finally understood what her mother had tried to tell her.

Her mother would be proud of her. Martha had been docile, letting him do whatever he wanted, but not by choice. Throughout the whole ordeal it had been as if she had been paralysed. She had been unable to move; a helpless animal hypnotized by a predator. Her body had refused to react. She only wished that her mind would have shut down the same way, ignoring the disgust which brewed and bubbled inside her like a poisonous concoction, ready to spill over.

She was constantly on the verge of being violently sick. For the past six nights she had barely been able to control the urge to vomit until he had let go of her, but tonight it had hit her so suddenly that she had violently thrown up right into his face When the revolting stream of sour brew had hit him, he had yelled out in shock and then stormed from the bedroom furiously slamming the door shut behind him.

The thought of what would happen to her now made her retch again, this time from fear not from nausea. She lay awake for the rest of the night, sick and scared, unable to get away from the stinking mess around her.

Anna arrived very early in the morning, carrying a bundle of fresh clothes. As soon as she entered the room and saw Martha, she quickly put her load down and rushed over to the bed. Only Martha's head stuck out from under the quilt. Her nearly translucent white face was as shiny and wet as a melting ice field. Fine copper strands of sweaty hair were glued to her forehead and ears. Below her chin vomit had hardened on the covers.

"I am so sorry," Martha sobbed, miserable and relieved at the same time. Thank the Lord it was Anna. "I was sick. I can't get up. It hurts so much."

It was true, she couldn't help it. As soon as she thought of her husband's fleshy mass squashing and invading her body with merciless brutality, it started again. Bile came up and she had to gag when the bitter fluid reached her mouth. There was nothing left inside her, but her stomach still revolted. Her body convulsed with the effort to cleanse itself from the memory of his repugnant presence.

Anna rushed out of the room in such a hurry she forgot to close the door. Maybe she is disgusted with me too, Martha thought. She couldn't blame her, the rancid smell was too horrible. For hours Martha had been lying there, breathing it in and wanting to move away from it, but couldn't. Because she had been sick many more times after her husband had left her, the revolting spot in front of her on the precious quilt had grown quite large.

Although the door was open now, she didn't consider getting out of bed. It was best to lie still, moving was too painful. Her body hurt so badly, especially the lower part where her husband had done such unspeakable things to her. It was all wet down there and she worried that she had soiled herself.

Anna came back. This time with a large bucket full of water and many towels. "Careful now," she said while she slowly rolled the covers down, making the offensive vomit miraculously disappear.

Martha was so grateful that she did not even feel ashamed showing her naked upper body. Anna dipped a towel into the water and started to clean Martha's face and neck with gentle strokes. The water was cold.

"There. That's better, isn't it!"

When she had finished, Martha started to cry again. It was so hard to explain that she was still dirty – down there. How could she tell the other woman that she consisted of two parts. So she only pointed between sobs to her lower part.

"I know, I know." Anna handed her a fresh wet towel and turned around so Martha could clean herself in privacy. When she sensed that Martha had finished, she turned back and handed her a dark green dress. "Can you put this on without help?"

Martha sniffled. She would try. Sitting upright made her head spin and she feared she would throw up again, but after a little while the woozy sensation subsided. Eventually, she carefully slid to the edge of the bed and lowered her feet to the floor. With Anna's help she stood up. Thankfully her dress quickly slipped down and covered her legs. She swayed.

"Are you still dizzy? Here, sit on the bed." Anna pulled the bed sheets from one corner of the bed and motioned her to sit down on the bare mattress. "We have time. I have to clean in here. Marion said I should get you ready to leave this room. Maybe she'll let you go with me to my hut when I have finished my work. So just sit here and take your time to compose yourself."

Martha's shaky fingers fumbled with the buttons in front of her dress. One by one she slowly slid them into the buttonhole. She bent slightly forward until she could reach another fresh towel and wiped her face and hair dry.

Anna watched her and frowned. "You must wash your hair. I'll give you some of my shampoo." She bunched the used bed covers and sheets together, placed them in a neat pile on the floor and opened the window. "He doesn't like it when we have greasy hair, so he lets his favourites have really nice smelling shampoo. It's quite expensive, you know, but he buys it at a discount shop in Kamloops. You can have a bit of mine, but only once. I guess he will give you some too, if you ever become a favourite that is."

Martha did not want to be a favourite. She was in pain and felt dirty. Washing her hair would not take this feeling away.

"Did you hear? You'll be allowed to leave this room. Our husband is done with you."

Martha finally registered what Anna was trying to tell her. She could leave this horrible prison cell! The fresh breeze drifting in from the open window made her feel a little less wobbly. "Thank you Anna, you are so kind." She took another deep breath to steady the quiver in her voice. "You are the only one."

"I know. It can be difficult here. I should not talk about it, but I must warn you. In this family, always be careful what you say and whom you trust."

"You mean the other sister-wives?"

Anna put her finger on her lips to underline her warning. "They are very upset that he has chosen another wife. They all thought I would be the last; even I did. It was a bit of a shock when they learned that you were coming, and even more so when they saw you."

"Why?"

Anna came closer and touched her cheeks. The tender gesture was so unexpected that Martha jerked her head back, fearful of being slapped. Was Anna now angry with her for not keeping still? Quickly she grabbed the hand of the woman who was her senior and put it back on her cheek. "I'm sorry. I didn't mean to pull away from you."

"That's alright. I only wanted to tell you how pretty you are. So pretty. That's why the sister-wives are upset. You are so young, your skin is fresh and soft like that of a baby. Your hair is so shiny, well, at least it was when you got here. They all worry that our husband will make you his favourite. I told you, he already neglects them and now they fear they will never get another chance to be with him."

That was bad. Martha remembered the time when her own father had brought a new young sister-wife home. Her mother had cried for weeks and all her mother's sister-wives had acted strangely. They had stopped talking to each other and had started watching one another with growing mistrust. However, after a few weeks the new wife had moved to her own home in the women's quarters and things had gone back to normal.

"They don't need to worry. I'll never be his favourite, I promise." If she was allowed to leave this room, didn't that prove that he had lost interest in her? Her nerves calmed down and her heart started to beat in a steadier rhythm. What had Anna said? *He was done with her!* "I can go with you now, can't I? I'll never have to come back here, right?"

"Oh dear, my poor little one." Anna stopped wiping the floor with an old rug and sat down next to her. "It's not up to me to decide. We'll have to ask Marion's permission. She is the first wife. We must all do as she commands. So you must try hard and not offend her, or she'll make sure that you are overlooked."

Relief flooded through Martha. With all her might she wanted to be overlooked. If she was obnoxious and somehow offended Marion, she might be considered undesirable and, as a punishment, would not be allowed to spend time with this terrifying man who was her husband. If she was allowed to leave the house now and move into the women's quarters, he might forget she ever existed. Without thinking she blurted out. "I don't ever want to see him again. He is disgusting and he hurt me. I hope Marion never ever chooses me."

Now Anna jumped up as if bitten by a poisonous snake. "May the good Lord forgive you! How can you utter such blasphemy! How will you become pregnant if you don't spend time with him? Do you really think those few nights were enough? I was quick, but it still took me two weeks in which he saw me every night. Every single night!" Her face had turned bright red with indignation and pride. "And if Marion would not hate me so much I would be with my second already. I know I can give him many more."

Slowly it dawned on Martha that the horror of his abuse was somehow connected to her getting with child. "What he did to me...," she hesitated, searching for the right words, "down there, I mean, the things ... you know, ...what he did, is that ... kind of ..., you know, did he do that to you too?"

Anna nodded.

"So, that is what he does to all ... I mean, to each of ..."

"Yes, that's how it's done. I know it is hard the first time. Specially as you are so young and so small. But it's necessary. You can't be his wife in the sense of the scripture if you are barren, so you must let him place his seed inside you. As I said, when I arrived I was with child after only two weeks."

Although Martha was still in pain and horrified by everything that had happened, her natural curiosity started to come back. As always in her young life, she just had to ask questions.

"Where are you from, Anna?"

"Utah. A small compound south of Provo."

"How old were you when you came here?"

"Not much older than you." Anna was all smiles again, remembering. "I was fifteen when the Elders chose me for our husband, but I had turned sixteen by the time they finally got me over the border."

"Did the Bishop ask your father to send you to him?"

"He didn't even know him. The Gatekeepers arranged it."

Martha had never heard of the Gatekeepers. She was intrigued and asked who they were.

"Oh dear, don't ask. It's a big secret." Anna loved the way the conversation had turned. She knew so much more than this young girl. In the back of her mind a warning signal went up - she wasn't supposed to gossip about such things but she was not willing to let an opportunity pass when she could impress somebody with her knowledge. "They are very important men. More important than the Prophet himself."

"My father taught us that the Prophet is not really God's mouthpiece. That he assumed his power over the Fundamentalists without the proper authority and that's why we mustn't listen to him."

"See!" Anna was a bit disappointed. "I told you. There are men so important, they're above the Prophet even. Nobody really knows who the Gatekeepers are, none of us women anyway. The Elders, like my father, have contact with them of course. Maybe my father is even one of them, I wouldn't know. All I know is that they have chosen me to increase our husband's family."

"Why did it take so long for you to get here? I was sent up in a matter of days."

"They had a problem finding the right girl to match me. The immigration laws here changed a few years ago. They used to be quite slack, you know, and suddenly it was much more difficult to send a single young girl to live up here permanently. Without the proper documents our husband can't collect money from the government, you see, so it would be pretty useless to send somebody from outside the country without having a trade in place. But once they had found a suitable girl from one of the Canadian compounds they smuggled me into the country. And in case you wonder, yes, the other girl was of course sent down south with my papers." Anna leaned forward, lowering her voice. "My name hasn't always been Anna. Do you want to know what I was called before?"

Martha nodded.

"Ruth. What about you?"

"Lillian." Martha thought back to the long drive from Arizona to British Columbia. Her parents had brought her into this country like a criminal. "They smuggled me in too. I wonder if the girl they exchanged for me likes her new name. And I wonder where the real Martha is now."

Anna smiled confidentially. "Well, I do know. But I won't tell. I can't. But trust me, the other Martha sure doesn't need your name where she is now."

"Oh, please, tell me," Lillian-Martha begged. Suddenly it was very important to her to find out more about the new Lillian.

Anna's face clouded over. "Forget it. We mustn't use our old names, never ever. It will only get us into trouble. Our husband has forbidden us to even think about them. Anyway, I am the wife that came before you, soon after Emma. She has two children already, but she is one year older than I am." Anna proudly straightened her back. "Emma and I were picked because we are young and can have many children quickly. The Gatekeepers told my father that the Canadian division of our faith needs to grow real fast. We must create a balance to the apostates who don't follow the old teachings. They must be outnumbered as quickly as possible. That's why we need to have many children quickly. We have to produce soldiers for the army of the Lord. Our husband is doing his best to fulfill the Gatekeeper's command, you have to understand that. And it's the Lord's command as well. I know it's not pleasant what he has to do to get you with child, but don't worry too much about it; it gets easier over time. And remember, once you have at least three children you will be rewarded. It is not so hard to do. Look at me! I have one child already and I'm on my way to becoming an eternal wife. As soon as I have two more children I'll be allowed to follow him to his kingdom."

"And you have your own house." Martha tried to hide that she was a little jealous of this fact, which seemed much more desirable to her than having three children. Hearing Anna so casually address their husband's horrific behaviour made her suddenly feel very embarrassed. She did not want to think about it and she was not really interested in her eternally glorious future while her present was so miserable.

"Yes I have. But I've got to rush now. Marion said I have to help in the field today. When I'm back, I will ask Marion if I can take you with me."

When Anna returned it was already getting dark, which meant it must be close to eight o'clock. Martha had spent another day in the room all by herself, but she had slept most of the day.

Anna lifted the cloth cover off the basket she was holding and said: "Look what Marion has given me. That's for us! I told her I only have enough food at my place for myself and my baby."

Martha wanted to jump out of bed but had to stop when a sharp pain pierced into her lower body. It felt like a knife slicing through her abdomen. She caught her breath and continued more carefully and slowly to get up. "Does that mean I can go with you?"

"This very minute."

Martha could barely move, but the walk down the hill from the main house was pure heaven. It was bliss to be able to take more than five steps in one direction before having to turn around. She treasured every single step that distanced her from the horrible house on the hill. Fifteen, sixteen, oh my, seventeen ..., Martha's legs were shaking and she had to pause. Eighteen, nineteen, twenty... She did not register that she counted out loud until Anna, somewhat bewildered, asked if the walk was too much for her. Martha shook her head. It was simply wonderful to be able to walk forward. One thousand-seven-hundred and fifty-three steps later they arrived at the bottom of the hill.

There were several small huts, arranged in two semi circles around the periphery of an open yard and divided by the driveway leading up to the main house.

The hut Anna had so proudly called her home was a ruin. The pigs at Martha's previous home were housed better than this. Martha tried to hide her disappointment, but the look on her face gave her away.

"It's only for now," Anna said defensively. "Wait until I'm with second child, then I'll move into one of the better ones."

When Martha's eyes adjusted to the darkness, she looked around. There was a makeshift bed in one corner. Several wooden crates had been turned upside down and tied together to support a thin mattress, a tattered pillow and a folded blanket. Another crate next to it had a candle holder on it, and yet another served as a cradle for her baby. That was all there was.

No noise came from the cradle. The room was dark and quiet; it smelled of mould and rotting wood. Martha's heart sank, but she quickly comforted herself. The living conditions in Anna's hut were much worse than in the main house, but at least here she was not locked in 24 hours a day – and she did not have to fear *him* appearing in the door frame.

Coming in, she had noticed a narrow bench in front of the house, next to the door. Would Anna let her sit outside for a while?

"Of course." Anna lit the candle and busied herself with her baby girl. "Go ahead. Take the basket with you, you need to eat something. I have to feed my little girl now, she has been alone all day."

Martha left quickly. Anna would give the child her breast and that must not be watched. Once or twice she had seen one of her mothers do this and was told that being able to feed a child this way was one of the Lord's gifts to women. "Every woman should be proud of this," her mother had explained, "but it is a very private thing and you must immediately lower your eyes when you notice it."

The memory of her mother made Martha sad. She sat down on the bench and looked at the cluster of huts on the opposite side melting into the forest behind them. Nothing moved and nobody was in sight. Dusk began to swallow the buildings and the trees. Their outline contrasted sharply against the lighter cloudless August sky, reflecting the bleak prospects of her future.

Burning questions rose inside her. Why was she sent here? Why did she have to suffer such pain? What would happen to her now? Would it always be so terrible? Was it worse for her than for her sister-wives?

Just thinking that the other women knew what she had been subjected to because they had experienced the same humiliating treatment made Martha cringe. Was it really necessary to do what he had done to get his seed into her? Did he really have to hurt her so badly? Was there no other way to get with child? If the other wives suffered as much, why were they so eager to spend time with him? Martha tried to stop the questions whirling around her mind. She was so confused.

She wanted to be back in her old home, where she knew everybody and everything. Was she supposed to spend the rest of her time here in Anna's dark and gloomy hut? What dreadful fate awaited her at the hands of her husband? Why had everybody abandoned her? Those questions were like a mud hole trying to suck her in. Their tight grip pulled her deeper and deeper into despair, where the questions became even darker and more dangerous. What was the sense of it all? Even living in Anna's hut, she was bound to her husband for all eternity. How could it ever stop? Why struggle, if nothing would ever change? She realized that her thoughts started to drag her into the forbidden zone of questioning her faith. It terrified her and she begged her mind to stop thinking altogether, but it was hard to get out of the whirling black muddle of rising doubts. Why didn't the questions stop torturing her? There were no answers, and it would not make her feel any better to try and figure it all out. She was all alone in her misery and she was so scared.

Through a veil of unshed tears, she saw a half moon rising above the tree tops. I must pull myself together, she thought. I must eat something or I will faint. She opened the basket. One apple, one peanut butter sandwich and a plastic container with eleven hard oatmeal biscuits. Thirteen items altogether. She bit into one biscuit, chewed slowly and looked around, focusing on the huts.

She could still distinguish twelve huts in the fading light. Counting them made her feel lighter.

Anna came out of the hut and looked down on her new sister-wife. "I've got to go now. Mustn't be late for evening work. Can you look after my child while I'm gone? She won't be any trouble, she's asleep now."

"Of course," Martha said.

"You should go to sleep too. Get as much as you can, we never have enough."

Martha nodded and when Anna had left she went inside and arranged the blanket Marion had given her on the bare floor, rolled herself into it and tried to fall asleep.

The floor was hard and cold. The summer heat was broken, just like she was. She could not figure out if it was the hard floor she had to lie on or the utter desolation she felt that made her toss and turn under the thin blanket.

Still, she must have dozed off eventually because a confusing array of strange pictures - close enough to grip yet too far away to shake off - drifted into her semi-sleep. *Marion gives her a glass of milk, watches her drink it and orders her to lie down. Immediately she feels nauseous and dizzy. Because she knows what is coming next, she fights her panic by counting the seconds. Goes through a sequence of numbers, one after the other, in a concentrated effort to dull her thinking and feeling. The numbers turn into crawling insects that swarm over her, creeping into every orifice of her body. Many, many numbers squirmed their way into her, so many that she loses count. She is so tired. Of course she is scared to let go because she knows the terror continues on the other side of sleep, looming there like a monstrous apparition, scaring her even more.*

Martha woke up shivering and sobbing. Reality filtered back into her consciousness, no less horrific than the nightmare. How could he do this to her? It was beyond Martha's comprehension. She was only thirteen and felt as if her life was over already.

8

"How did he take it?" Brother Lucas asked.

Brother Mathew shrugged his shoulders indifferently. "As expected. I talked to him last night again, for the third time now. I tried to reason with him to make him see his shortcomings and to warn him of further consequences if he doesn't adhere to our rules. All he did was rave on about the injustice of it all. That he doesn't deserve to be treated like any apostate. That, in his view, it was unjustified to cut his benefits so suddenly."

"After ten years?"

"He said it is not possible for him to make money with such a small family and under the harsh conditions he has to endure in his exile."

Brother Lucas studied the papers on his desk in front of him. "Now, let me see. With his latest wife, Brother Peter's daughter, he has fourteen wives altogether and, as far as we know, at least over fifty children. His oldest son must be about fifteen by now and there are several other boys approaching priesthood age. That is a bigger family than many of us have. What about you, Brother Mathew, how many wives do you have?"

The Gatekeeper sitting opposite him could not suppress a smile. "I must admit, I have just taken the daughter of my sister as a wife, so I have a few more than Brother Jacob has."

Brother Lucas smiled back at him. "That may be. You are a Church Elder of impeccable standing, you deserve to spread your seed for the

Lord's glory. I'm not so sure about our poor misguided brother. Does he at least understand why we have cancelled his monthly allowance?"

Brother Mathew shook his head. "Not in the least. He thinks it is simply an idle threat and believes he can persuade us to start sending money again. He doesn't even understand that we plan to excommunicate him if he can't support his family through his own endeavours. In fact, apart from asking for our continued financial support, he had the temerity to request yet another wife because the last one...," Brother Mathew cleared his throat before he could repeat the reason for Brother Jacob's impertinent request. "Because the last one is useless and all his other wives are too old."

"Shame on him!" Brother Lucas said quietly, but with enough emphasis to make Brother Mathew notice his contempt. "He should know that he has a duty to all his wives. It seems to me that he spreads his favours unevenly, merely to seek physical gratification. It seems to me he has not matured as we had hoped in the last ten years. And it seems to me that apart from his self-indulgent pursuit of pleasure, he is ungrateful and overly avaricious. Would you agree with my evaluation of his character, Brother Mathew?"

"Wholeheartedly."

"And it seems to me that our decision to stop financially supporting his compound has been just."

"All our brothers are in agreement."

"That is good to know. I would not want to seem unjust. Now, how long is it since we made the last payment."

"One month."

Brother Lucas stood up. "Excellent. So, he will feel the pinch already. Call him every month and keep me informed of his progress, if there is any. We must all pray for him to see the light." He walked Brother Mathew to the door of his office. "One last thing. Let us spare Brother Peter's feelings. He doesn't need to know that his daughter has been deemed useless by Brother Jacob. Has he mentioned what he plans to do with the girl?"

"I have not discussed this with him."

90

"Of course not. That's his own business. It is of no importance. May the Lord bless you."

After Brother Mitchell had closed the door behind him, Brother Lucas returned to his desk and to other pressing matters that needed his undivided attention. He had much work to do and he felt so tired. He ought to spend less time with his pretty twin wives Leah and Lorraine. He had visited them last night and they had drained his last reserves of energy. But it had felt so good. Even now, he savoured the memory of their hands massaging his tired old body into action. Who could resist one of the Lord's gifts in the shape of seventeen year old nymphs who were willing to the point of indecency. He had often spent part of his nights with more than one wife, but usually only until it was time for him to decide which one was allowed to stay and receive his seed. The twins however didn't mind sharing their most intimate moments with each other. He had never forced both of them to stay. He had also never demanded one of them to leave. To watch their near identical bodies moving in total harmony to heighten his pleasure - delicious, simply delicious. He liked to think the Lord had created them exclusively for him; as a premature reward for picking the truly faithful out from the hordes of make-believers and directing them toward the road that led to his throne.

Brother Jacob was one of those who had fallen by the wayside. It would do no good to ever get him back. When he had married his first wife Marion - how long ago was that now again? it must be nearly twenty years if he remembered rightly - he had not bothered to ask his permission, although he had been the head of the Gatekeepers already and Brother Jacob had been well aware that no marriage deal was done without his approval. Brother Jacob had been sneaky like a gentile in heat and had spoken to Marion's father in a way that the poor man had believed permission was already granted. Just like he had done recently with Brother Peter's daughter. He then had married Marion in a great hurry, in defiance of the rules. No, it would do no good to get him back.

Brother Lucas never wanted to see him in his realm again, not him nor the lovely Marion. But he could still remember her. Her heart shaped face with the pointy chin, the dewy eyes always searching to make out the contours of her surroundings, probably because she was short-sighted, her elegant movements when floating into the room to serve her father's guests. She had been so lovely to look at, he had been yearning for her company and had wanted to spend time alone with her. A lot of time. Even to this day he still assumed that she could have given him what he had been searching for in all of his wives. Companionship, someone to talk to in quiet moments who would understand him, someone to soothe his aching when the burden of responsibilities became too heavy to carry alone in the middle of a sleepless night. This thought had troubled him for a while, because he should not make himself dependant on a woman, but then he had stopped worrying because he would never know for sure if she could have held this power over him. Because Brother Jacob had beaten him to it.

May he rot in hell for this deception. May his damnation begin in this life already.

9

A week had passed since she had been allowed to leave the house up on the hill. One whole week filled with learning the rules and regulations of the household and with hard work. As Martha was still recovering from the physical wounds her husband had left her with, Marion had allowed her to join Anna in the kitchen. Weak as she was, she found the duty there exhausting, but at least she didn't have to join those poor women who were driven to the dumpsite outside Blue River every morning. The Bishop's eldest son loaded them on the back of his father's truck and picked them up again at nightfall. Usually they came back with a few orange coloured plastic bags full of old clothes, reeking of rotten garbage, just like Anna had described, looking dirty and depressed. Even their driver looked like he hated what he was doing when he helped them unload the bags. But he was the only one besides Marion and Katherine who had a driver's license, all the other boys were still too young. Marion had to supervise the whole compound and the Bishop himself of course had more important things to do than to drive his wives to work and back.

That would have left Katherine as a potential driver, but she couldn't be counted on any more. Anna had told Martha that the teacher mother's serious illness had disrupted the family's routine quite a bit. Marion was still looking for a replacement who could teach the children. "I'm no good at it," Anna had confided in Martha a few days ago, overjoyed that she was sent back to the kitchen, "to teach the scripture all day long gets really boring." She also hinted that everybody was now watching and waiting for their new sister-wife to take on her share of the work load. And that they couldn't understand why Marion allowed her in the kitchen and didn't send her to the dump. Obviously Martha was clearly pampered by the first wife.

Martha did not feel pampered at all. The days in the hot kitchen dragged on endlessly. She had to stand while chopping vegetables and preparing and preserving food and was not allowed to sit down except for the two meals, breakfast and supper, everybody shared in the community hall while listening to the scripture. After supper she had to clean the kitchen before she could join the other sister-wives and their daughters in the hall again. There they all sat on makeshift tables and benches, sewing small patches of material together until the sparse electric light in the community hall became too dim for the women to see much. Only then they were allowed to stop working and go back to their huts.

Martha and Anna were walking up to the main house at first light, as they had done every morning this week. Overnight moisture had settled in the trees and on the ground. The rising sun filtered through the misty fog, breaking it into patches, yet the driveway was still barely visible. They were both so tired they did not speak but trudged along like sleepwalkers.

By the time they reached the top of the hill they were breathing heavily from the exhausting climb. Some members of the family had arrived already, others were still making their way up. Marion stood in front of the community hall, a long wood frame structure connected to the main house, waiting for everybody to arrive. Martha and Anna were just about to enter the backdoor of the main house to start their duties in the kitchen when Marion called them back.

"All of you inside the hall please," she announced, ushering all the arrivals inside. She waited until they were all seated before she made a startling announcement. "My dear sister-wives, at our husband's request, only five of you will work in the fields from now on."

The room filled with anxious murmurs. All the women were stunned by this departure from the daily routine but one was bold enough to ask what many of them didn't dare to express. "Why? Only five of us will never get all the hay in! It will rot. And what about the vegetables?"

Marion pressed her lips together in a futile effort to hide her disapproval. Martha wondered if she disapproved of her husband's order or of the interruption.

"Who are we to query our husband's wishes!"

The murmurs died down.

"It is not our place. From today on, five will go to the fields, only one stays in the kitchen, and all the others will go to the dump to collect material for our handicrafts. Our husband wants us to increase our efforts to pile up as much material as possible before the snow comes. Three of the younger boys will build a shed behind the backyard where we can store it. Only by collecting enough can we keep ourselves busy through the winter months. You know how many old clothes are discarded at the dump. Most of the material is still good, we can pick it apart, wash it and make beautiful quilts out of it. Our husband says we need to become self-sufficient. We need to earn our keep. I don't have to tell you, we are a big family and we need many things to sustain ourselves. It is important for all of you to work together to make this project successful. I will be with you all the way. I will join you in the dump as often as I can. School will be suspended until I have worked out who can replace our dear sister-wife Katherine who is not able to join us in our blessed efforts. The ones who go to the field have to work doubly hard to harvest as much as they can. As I said, kitchen duty will be reduced to one. This week it will be Martha ..."

At this point in Marion's speech Anna clawed into Martha's arm. "Oh God, no," she whispered, "she will send me to the dump again!" And a bit louder, more than she had planned, letting go of Martha and staring at the first wife: "Why can't I do the kitchen? I'm senior to Martha."

Marion pretended not to hear. "It has come to our husband's attention that some of you think he favours Martha. This is not the case. We will rotate all duties. Next week Martha will be sent to the dump and another sister-wife will take her place in the kitchen."

She was lucky. For some reason it took until early October before Martha had to go to the dump. Working there was as brutal and disgusting as Anna had said, and she hated it from the first moment on. The sister-wives told her she should thank the Lord because summer was over and the cold northerly wind that increased in strength every day made the sweetish rotten stink a lot more bearable.

Martha couldn't even imagine how bad it must have been a few weeks earlier, she could only hope that she would gradually get used to it before the next summer arrived. However, what she would never get used to was sinking ankle deep into the indefinable mush that spilled out of broken garbage bags. Wading through the revolting mess of decomposing food, mixed with household trash like used diapers, broken bottles and even syringes, she often had to dig with her bare hands to free something that looked useful.

None of them got used to it. Martha noticed the disgusted expression on the faces of her sister-wives, noses wrinkled, lips tightly pressed together to keep their repulsion under control. They shuffled and crawled over the mountains of garbage, digging and rolling into the valleys of the landfill, sniffing and searching like rodents for anything useful.

They bundled up against the chilly autumn air as best as they could, grabbing any discarded jacket, skirt, coat, pullover and vest they could find and slipping them over their traditional dresses. The padded clothing worked against the cold and the stench.

Just like her sister-wives, Martha started to pray for snow. Snow would make it impossible to rummage through the garbage.

The good Lord must have listened to them. One day at the end of October it was sunny with the leaves on the deciduous trees around the dump site still golden and red, and the next day a blizzard-like wind from the North, carrying arctic chill, came up and blew them off the branches within minutes. Flurries quickly covered the ground, melting into the still warm earth until the many layers thickened enough to stay on top of each other.

Martha had never seen snow before. The flurries were now thick and fluffy, covering all the ugliness with a white blanket, making it disappear like magic. They all stopped what they were doing, straightened up and smiled. Some thanked the Lord aloud. A feeling of joy came over them. Now their hardship would be over soon. They would settle into winter, work in the heated community hall all day long, in clean dresses, with the smell of fresh air around them.

When the sun set, they heard their husband's son arrive. Only then did they dare to clamber out of the stinking hell hole to load their soaking wet trash treasures on the back of his truck and climb on top of it. None of them were permitted to sit next to him and he was not supposed to even look at them.

As often before, he ignored his father's rule, got out of the driver's seat and helped with some of the heavier items. He saw Martha dragging a large bag behind her, went up to her and took it out of her hands. Being suddenly so close to him, she sneaked a look to see if he was anything like her husband. His mouth was similarly fleshy but had a nicer shape and he seemed to be just as tall, but otherwise nothing reminded her of his father. His colouring was more like Marion's, with even brighter hair. Martha imagined that Marion must have been just as good looking in her younger days.

He didn't look back at her.

That night the temperature dipped well below zero.

As much as Martha had enjoyed looking at the snowflakes dancing in the headlights on the drive back to the compound, she did not care for the inevitable cold that came with the onset of winter.

Anna's hut was freezing cold, but she had no matches to light a fire in the stove. Waiting for Anna to come back, she huddled under the blanket Marion had given her nearly three months ago. All she wanted was to curl up and sleep like a dog, but the night was so cold and the blanket was just too thin and too short. Tucking her feet under the blanket only exposed her shoulders again. She constantly tried to cover her whole body, but couldn't get warm or comfortable on the hard makeshift bed.

Late at night, the door opened and Anna came in. She went to the small crate her child was sleeping in, noted that it was quiet, then fell on her own crate with a big sigh of relief.

"Anna?"

Anna's voice sounded impatient. "Martha, please leave me alone!"

"Sorry. Anna, please, I'm so cold, I can't sleep."

"Then get up and make yourself useful. Walk around with the baby, she likes it and you'll get warmer."

"Can't I light a fire?"

The tiny stove in the corner of the hut would warm the room very quickly. Outside, next to the cabin door, firewood was stacked up nearly to the eaves.

Anna sat up abruptly. "Don't you dare touch the wood pile. That's all we've got for winter. If we use it too soon, it won't last."

Martha wanted to cry. She wouldn't last that long. Why didn't Anna understand? "But I'm so cold," she complained. "I won't be able to work tomorrow if I don't get any sleep."

"It's not even November yet," Anna replied a little softer. "We have six months of winter ahead of us."

Now Martha did start to weep. "It's so awful. And it's always dark. When we walk up to the house it's dark, and when we come back here it's dark. I hate winter. I hate everything here."

"You'll get used to it."

Martha cried harder.

Anna took pity on her. "Alright then. Move your crate over here, next to mine. If we snuggle up we can warm each other."

Martha jumped up and carefully pushed the wooden crate over to Anna's. The young woman and the girl cuddled together and, as Anna had promised, quickly doubled each other's warmth. Finally Martha felt sleepy.

"Thank you, Anna."

She felt Anna nodding in the dark.

"Anna?"

"What?"

"How long did it take you to get used to the cold?"

For a while she could only hear Anna's breathing and waited patiently. "You know I'm from Utah. It's as warm as in Arizona there. The first winter here was terrible. I thought I would die, just like you.

But we don't die. We are sent here for a purpose and the Lord makes our skin thicker so we don't feel the cold so much. Every year it gets a bit easier."

Martha thought about it. It could be true. Some of her sister-wives had told her that mosquito bites became less itchy every summer, and back home she had watched one of her aunts collect snake venom as an antidote against the occasional snake bites members of her family suffered. Maybe the snow worked like that too. Would the snow make her more resistant against the cold? Should she rub herself with snow every day?

"I hate snow," she said.

"It's not the snow, it's the wind that is most dangerous," Anna warned her. "The wind is a killer. Last December one of the daughters, I can't remember her name, froze to death in her hut and there was hardly any snow on the ground, but the temperature had dropped to below twenty overnight and the wind was so strong it felt like minus forty."

"How cold is it now?"

"Don't worry, you won't freeze to death. It's barely below zero."

"You mean Celsius?"

"Yes, zero is when water freezes."

"It can't only be zero then." The nights in the Arizona desert very often dipped so low that frost covered the ground until the sun came up, but Martha had never felt so bone chillingly cold as she did now, on this still-October night in Canada. Of course, then she had slept in a proper bed, with a mattress and a thick blanket.

"Anna?"

"Go to sleep. I'm tired. I have worked all day chopping wood, and then our husband wanted to see me."

Martha immediately felt for the woman next to her and put her arm around her waist. "Did he …?"

Anna sighed. "What now?"

"Did he … I mean, did you have to…?"

"Of course we were lying together, what do you think? He will make me another baby."

"Can I ask you one more question? Please?"

Anna didn't respond, so Martha asked anyway. It was a question never far from her mind because she was still fearful that he might demand to see her again. In the last three months, the part of her that had been torn by him had healed, but she had not forgotten the pain. She took a deep breath and fumbled for the right words. "When he does those things, you know, I mean, when he is on top of you, and when he kind of goes inside you, does it still hurt you?"

Anna didn't answer for so long, Martha thought she had fallen asleep, but when she finally got her answer, she did not like what she heard.

"Don't be so squeamish. You want a child, don't you? I'll give you some advice. If you stop fighting him and tell him how much you like it, it will be over much faster. He gets too excited when you fight him. I guess men are like that. They can use their power any way they want, and if you don't give in quickly, they can feel their power growing. Just shut your eyes and think about the outcome. Smile and tell him you like it. To get pregnant is all that matters."

Martha wanted to blurt out how much she hoped that she would never be with child, but she didn't dare. Anna wouldn't understand, and somehow, buried deep inside her mind, she knew that she did need children. How else would she otherwise reach the eternal king-dom? And deeper still, nagging doubts were scratching on the surface of her faith. Was the dark abyss really so much different from the eternal kingdom on her husband's side? Instead, she asked Anna if she thought their life as it was just now would be going on forever and if she thought it was something to look forward to, but this time she got no answer.

Their hopes that rummaging through the dump would end with the onset of winter had been in vain. The next morning, their husband ordered that they must continue as long as the cold didn't freeze the garbage. He said they could still find many useful items to be stored in the makeshift shelter the boys had built near the community hall. It was already bursting with mountains of filthy rags, three legged tables and chairs, broken vases and flower pots, bent pots and pans and other household items. Anything that could be restored to its old shape by scrubbing and fixing, or made into something new by dismantling and reassembling individual parts.

So they continued to burrow through the filth, watched by a hoard of greedy crows and ravens as well as the occasional disgusted villager who came to the dump. Some of them thought it funny to target the bent over women with their garbage bags as they tossed them into the pit, hollering delighted obscenities when they succeeded.

Every now and then a small plane flew at low altitude over the dump, but none of the women ever looked up.

10

Since Richard had agreed to buy the land everything had changed. Time had developed a new quality, one that would expand and contract without being governed by the set rules of the clock. Sometimes Richard worked for a seemingly short period only to notice that a whole afternoon had flown by while, at other times, he felt like he had been working on the development project forever.

He was spending days and nights pondering over the plans to find the best layout for the subdivision, and only rarely met with his assistant. Daisy was flat out preparing all the necessary paperwork to make sure they would not waste any valuable time. They had one major hurdle to overcome, the meeting with the Advisory Planning Committee. If the APC voted against the project, it was dead. Should they approve it, the true fight to get the subdivision process going could kick in. Richard was hoping to clear this important barrier before the Christmas season started.

He looked at his desk calendar and felt a fleeting sensation of panic. Tomorrow was the first day of November already! Timing was crucial. To raise enough cash by the end of the year, Richard Bergman had put all his company's assets on the market. Sales were going quite well, and he was confident that he would be able to transfer the needed amount to the lawyers on the last day of December.

The panic subsided as quickly as it had hit him. Somehow he was looking forward to the challenge. Every subdivision was a unique experience because the twists and turns bureaucrats dreamed up to delay or even kill a decent development project were quite creative. Those government servants were like chameleons, changing the colouring of their rules as they went along, but that didn't worry him. It was a game, a give-and-take without a real loser, determined only by what degree one could win. The longer it took, the more it affected any potential profit, that was all.

Richard had been practically forced into this game over ten years ago by a cruel twist in his teenage life. When he was barely eighteen his parents had died in a horrific car crash and as the only progeny of two not very reproductive families, he had inherited all of his parents' wealth, consisting mainly of the family farm. He had hated this quarter-section of horse lover's heaven ever since his parents had immigrated to Canada. Being twelve years old at that time and suffering from an acute case of puberty rebellion, he had stubbornly refused to live in the new family home. His disappointed parents had reluctantly sent him back to Germany to finish his education at boarding school. For six long years he had grudgingly spent his summer holidays with his parents, hanging on to his childish resentment of Canada long after he had forgotten his original reasons. As soon as he had reached the legal age of eighteen he had left school even before graduation and gone to live with a friend in Berlin. Six months later, he was notified that his parents had died in a car crash. He had come to Canada only to deal with his inheritance, this hated ranch.

Ironically, horseflies and all, it had made him instantly rich. At least what an eighteen year old school drop-out without any prospects in life would consider rich. Once in British Columbia, he had immediately put the farm up for sale, had dealt with potential buyers and lawyers himself to save money, and had discovered that he liked being part of the selling process. It was exciting and exhilarating. He didn't even have time to grieve for his parents. Being good and successful at something for the first time in his short life had been such a rush, he had to do it again. And again, and again, like a gambler. Propelling himself from one deal to another, buying and selling, with a slowly growing stack of chips on the table, until he would finally hit the jackpot. By now he had already made a name for himself, but more as the underdog who had been lucky. The guy that was allowed to nibble off their spoils. Until now, neither the established big-time developers in British Columbia nor the top financiers considered Richard Bergman a serious contender in the game, and he detested their carefully hidden disdain. He would show them all what he was capable of. He was willing to work hard and his enthusiasm for the real estate market was as raw and intense as on his first day in the office. The past ten years had been good to him. He had been able to put his company on solid ground, something he was immensely proud of, and in this hectic and wonderful time he had gained the experience needed to tackle a truly big job. Yes, he could feel it in his bones, this new project was of a magnitude that could and would propel him into the upper echelons of developers' glory!

It was getting dark outside. Richard turned his desk lamp on and gave his eyes a moment to adjust before going back to the plans spread out in front of him. He leaned back, crossed his arms behind his head, looked out the window and watched the night life outside wake up, one light at a time. Metro Vancouver with its classy restaurants, top hotels and swinging bars was his for the taking. Soon. Soon he would be part of the elite crowd of entrepreneurs that made this town bubble.

The phone rang, catapulting him back into reality. It was Daisy, asking him if she should email him all the land development regulations of the Thompson Nicola Regional District she had finally obtained today.

"No need," Richard said quickly, being aware that the more stringent TNRD regulations would have to be adapted to suit their plans. They were specifically designed for urban areas like the large city of Kamloops and shouldn't really apply to the secluded mountain range north-east of Blue River where his sub-division was located, but who knew how an overzealous government agent might interpret them. Daisy was ideally suited to hold them at bay. "You handle it. You are so much better at that than I am."

"You're so right," Daisy agreed with him. "I just wanted to give you a chance to shine."

"Don't worry about me. I have enough on my plate to prove my worth." He hung up, meaning every word of it. His primary responsibility for now was to familiarize himself with the terrain as quickly as possible. How else could he come up with the best conceptual applications.

But it was such a huge area, and most of it was inaccessible. Studying the map, he could find only a few logging roads. He could possibly conquer them with an All-Terrain-Vehicle, but that would be a tedious process. On the spur of the moment, Richard opted for a faster and therefore more economical solution. He would hire a small plane and a pilot and spend a few days flying over the land. Together with the topographic map he had ordered at great expense from a company in Victoria, this should give him a good perspective of his land.

His pilot Andy was ex-Airforce but had never lost his enthusiasm for flying. He had his own Piper airplane and occasionally accepted paying passengers to supplement his meagre pension. Without those charters he would never be able to log in enough hours to keep his licence active, but that didn't mean he enjoyed doing them. As he told Richard even before take-off, he thought most people would be better off staying on the ground. He then proceeded to demonstrate his superiority in the sky. The stunts Andy flew were pretty scary at times. Richard did his best to hide his discomfort at some of the more risky manoeuvres and assured himself repeatedly that the guy had combat flying skills. And if nothing else, those daring escapades gave him a very close view of the landscape below. Often Andy flew so low that Richard thought he could touch the trees – not their tops, but the branches that whisked by next to his window. He could make out single pebbles in the streams, look into deserted eagles' nests and see deer bounding in front of the plane to take cover in the woods.

Each morning, they took off at Kamloops airport and flew along the Thompson until they reached Blue River. There, Andy would make a sharp right turn and drop his altitude. They stayed at a respectable height until they had cleared the Resort with its perfectly maintained cabins, gardens and walkways. Richard could see the workers busy winterizing the surroundings. Piles of raked leaves were loaded onto trucks to be taken to the local refuse collection centre, which was simply a huge crater in the ground where everybody living in the region brought their trash and dumped it. Although Richard was not overly environmentally conscious, such careless disposal did bother him a bit. He made a mental note to look into this once his subdivision was up and going.

Andy liked to drop really low when they flew over those mountains of garbage. Below, Richard could make out individual people sorting through the piles of garbage. When he wondered out loud why anybody would be doing something so gross, Andy snorted and said they were just dump rats. Just bums, too lazy to work. They liked to dig through other people's trash, *shopping at the mall,* you know.

Richard shook his head. No, he didn't know. Why the hell don't they find a decent job, he thought, anything would be preferable to that. But by then they had cleared the dump site, leaving any thoughts of trash behind.

Andy announced that he could smell snow coming. He told Richard that he had better take as many pictures as possible and study his land because soon he would not be able to fly over it any more.

11

One day at the end of November, Martha thought she could not endure the brutal work in the dump any longer. The next morning, as soon as the Bishop's son had dropped them off, she would run away. She would make a dash to the nearby forest and run and run until she would find shelter somewhere. She would probably not survive for very long, but anything was better than this life. Even the thought of being damned by the Lord for all eternity would not deter her, her decision was made. How much worse could the dark abyss be, compared to this!

That very evening, a miracle happened. After supper, Marion told her that she could go back to kitchen duty. Martha secretly wondered if the Lord had decided to spare her or to punish her. The kitchen was much, much better than the dump, it was always warm in there and smelled so good, but working there might also mean that she was being prepared for her husband again. He didn't like smelly women.

Since the weather had changed so dramatically four weeks ago, it had snowed a little every single day, gradually increasing the layer on the ground until it was nearly half a meter deep. As Martha never lost her fear of being noticed by her husband, she was always hugely relieved when she could leave the main house after she had finished her kitchen duties and wade through the deep snow back to Anna's hut. So far, the Bishop had always picked Anna.

She had looked forward to working with Anna, hoping for more of those brief moments when they had shared little stories about the sister-wives as well as the occasional giggle, but Anna had changed. Being her superior, she constantly gave Martha orders. How to perform her duties in the kitchen, how to look after her hut, how to take care of her little girl when she had to spend time with the Bishop. Anna was always bad-tempered and nagged about everything.

Martha didn't really blame her though. Anna's daughter was seriously ill and Anna must be fretting a lot when she had to neglect her baby for such long periods of time.

After another week of continuous snowfall, it took Martha twice as long to make her way down the hill, but as cold as she felt, she was in no particular hurry. By the time she arrived at the hut, her shoes and stockings were soaking wet. She sat down, took them off and rubbed her cold feet. She looked around the bare, ugly hut. It was always cold in here too. Cold and dead.

Martha got up again and peeked through the crack between the door and the door frame. Outside, the wind blew thick snowflakes sideways into the darkness. She hated snow. She hated winter. She hated being cold all the time. She had read about snow, and someone in her old family insisted that it had snowed in Arizona once, but not in her childhood it hadn't. Vaguely, she remembered that she had been curious about the white stuff that covered everything, thinking it must be so pretty. Now she knew better. Snow was not pretty - snow meant being cold and sad and alone and tired – and dead.

Martha really didn't want to look at the lifeless little figure in the cot.

She didn't expect Anna back until the morning hours and hoped that she wouldn't come back at all. If it continued to snow all night, Anna might opt to stay up at the main house. When Anna had left in the morning, she had been too exhausted to properly check on her baby and hadn't noticed that it made no sound and it didn't move.

Martha lit a candle, wrapped herself in the thin blanket, stretched out on the crate and tried to go to sleep. After several hours, she heard the door open. Anna came in, looked at the baby and seemed pleased that it was not demanding any attention. She fell on her crate, fatigued beyond words.

Martha was wide awake now, but couldn't find the courage to tell her sister-wife that her child would never need her attention again.

She should have told Marion about the dead child. If only she weren't such a coward. Last month, their husband had had one of his frequent revelations and had introduced a new rule. No wife should tend to the child of another. It was up to the Lord which one of the little ones would survive. He had explained to the women that the Lord wanted it this way, because only the strong must live for the glory of his future kingdom. To care for the baby in Anna's absence would be considered an act of defiance. Martha had felt sorry for the poor little creature, and even though it was against the rules, had sometimes dipped a piece of cloth in some milk and let the baby suck on it. The child had been so weak, it had barely had the strength to suck a few drops of milk from the rag. Looking at its wasted body, she had remembered what her mother used to say. *Those too weak to fight life should die quickly. Don't prolong the agony by feeding them.* And now there was no need for it any more.

Anna was moaning in her sleep. It sounded like soon, soon, soon. Then the wind outside strengthened his icy breath and spat wet mist through the cracks in the walls. Inside, the mist settled and turned to crystals, covering everything. Soon the whole hut was white.

Anna suddenly woke up and seemed to remember that she had not yet fed her baby. Still moaning, she got up and stumbled over to the cot like a sleepwalker. Martha watched her pick up the lifeless body and tuck it, wrapped inside a small blanket, tightly to her breast to give it milk and warmth.

"Come on, come on," she urged, but of course the baby did not drink. Anna tightened her grip, pressing the little body even closer to her own. It did not move. Anna started to cry silent tears; they dripped on the baby. Even the warm salty fluid did not make it move.

"You must let go." The child was dead, but for some reason Anna did not want to understand. "Please, Anna. Please, you have to let go."

"No! It's just cold. I have to warm it." Covering her daughter with the blanket, she rocked it back and forth.

When daylight filtered through the cracks in the walls, she stopped and placed the body back in its crib.

Martha and Anna left the hut together and joined the other women as they made their way up the hill. On their long walk through the knee deep fresh snow no one asked Anna about her baby. Somehow they looked at her and knew. It was only a matter of time until Anna would accept it herself.

When their husband had finished his breakfast, which he usually enjoyed by himself in his private quarters, he joined his family in the community hall and told them that they were snowed in. Nobody could leave the compound. It had snowed so heavily overnight that all the roads leading to the highway were closed. It could take up to a week before they were cleared. All the wives and daughters should now work in the kitchen and the laundry. They should start sorting and cleaning all the wonderful material the Lord had left at the dump for them. It had to be carefully cleaned and washed and dried and ironed so they could make pretty things out of it.

Immediately everybody's spirits lifted and over the next few hours the general mood seemed light hearted. Every now and then Martha noticed subdued laughter in the kitchen. One woman would make a silly or funny remark, and everybody would quietly chuckle. Martha adored this. It reminded her of her old home; of the times when her father had been away and the bigger boys were at work. When there was no one around to chastise her mothers and siblings for frivolous behaviour. Now, for the first time since she had arrived last summer, it was the same here. Even Marion had lost a bit of her sternness. She never laughed aloud or joined in the banter though; that would have been inappropriate. After all, she was the first.

In the early afternoon Marion abruptly turned to Anna and told her to go down to her hut and bring her child up to the main house. Anna frowned in confusion but only hesitated for a second before she ran out of the kitchen.

After she had gone, nobody giggled or joked any more. Everybody busied themselves with chopping the cabbage that was to be pickled, making dough for baking and doing some of the other things necessary to feed a large family throughout winter. Everybody seemed to be waiting for the inevitable.

Feeling cozy and content, both physically and emotionally, for the first time in many months, Martha was suddenly so sleepy she could hardly keep her eyes open. Just when she thought she could not hold herself upright any longer, Marion touched her back and ordered her to go to the steam room in the laundry. There was a pile of dirty clothes to be attended to. Martha considered this to be the best duty in the whole household. She would be by herself for an hour or two, and all she had to do was stay next to the large steaming bucket with a tall wooden paddle. Quickly, before Marion could change her mind, she rushed off. As long as she stirred and turned the clothes at regular intervals, she could rest in between and revel in the sensation of being completely, totally warm. The steamy heat would comfort her, penetrating her skin and her muscle tissue right down to her bones, right into her heart. The mood in the kitchen had turned so restrained, it would be a blessing to be away from the gloomy women.

When Martha arrived in the laundry, she went straight to the steam room and quickly closed the door behind her. She turned the soggy mass in the bucket once, then could not resist the mountain of dirty laundry waiting to be washed, bedded herself down on it and immediately fell into a deep sleep.

High pitched shrieking woke her up. A woman's voice, wailing uncontrollably! Martha jumped up, confused and dazed. Where was she? There was mist all around her, like fog in the morning. Her heart was drumming away. Strange noises, as indistinguishable as the contours of her surroundings, wafted through the haze. Loud, angry shouting and yelling – coming from a woman! Martha was stunned. That was impossible. Women stayed quiet, talked in hushed voices and suppressed their emotions; they did not yell or scream. They kept sweet.

Now there were other voices mingling with the crying and shouting. What was going on? Nothing this exciting had ever happened in Martha's life before. The cacophony definitely came from the kitchen, drawing her to it like a magnet. All tiredness gone, she raced out of the steam room, through the deserted laundry, up the steps and down the hallway. At the open kitchen door, she froze. All the sister-wives and their daughters who worked in the laundry and the kitchen were crowded in between the two long working benches, forming a semi circle but keeping a safe distance from the single lone woman in their midst. Anna! Some of them tried to calm her by begging her to listen to them, but without any success. Anna screamed at the top of her lungs. Martha listened, fascinated, to the bizarre accusations and swear words flying out of Anna's mouth. They were as foreign and incomprehensible to her as the chaos in the room.

"Bitches! Fucking bitches! Rot in hell!" Anna held a knife in her hand and was lunging at the women. "Give me my little girl back. You fucking jealous whores! You killed my child. You begrudge me my luck. I am his favourite. I will have all his sons and daughters. You have killed my child. He will kill you all. Satan will destroy you. Whores. Whores. Wicked women! You will be destroyed."

Nobody dared to move any closer. Looking around, Martha could see horror in every one of their stricken faces. Horror and disbelief and disgust. She was not so sure what the word *whore* meant, or *fucking*, only the word bitch was familiar to her. Why did Anna call the others female dogs? Of course Anna was very upset for losing her child, but she had no right to say such ugly words and accuse her sister-wives of murder. Anna was confused, surely she did not mean it. Still, this was so exciting! Martha's face was flushed from the heat in the steam room and from watching the wild exhibition of Anna's open rebellion. All the bad thoughts she had ever thought and tried to suppress were nothing compared to this. Anna was acting out something so unimaginably rebellious, it made Martha delirious with pleasure to realize she was not the only one behaving like a sinner, having secret thoughts of running away! There it was – out in the open. Anna screaming, accusing, forgetting every single rule they had to abide by - how wonderful, how satisfying was that!

Martha pushed through the wall of women and girls to get a closer look. Anna was still hurling profanities at them all. Most gave way to Martha's gentle pressure and before she knew it she was standing in the front row, watching the raving mad Anna crying and wielding the knife in wide circles, threatening to cut anybody who came close, and demanding to see her daughter. Martha was shaking like a leaf herself now; but more from exhilaration than distress. Even though she was a bit frightened, she knew Anna would not hurt her. Poor agitated Anna suddenly noticed Martha and stopped swearing and whirling around. Standing just a few feet away from Martha, she stared at her and her expression lost a bit of its harshness. "No, Martha. Not you."

Anna let her eyes wander over to her sister-wives, scrutinizing them as if she had never seen them before, then she turned back to Martha, the only face that seemed to make any sense to her. "Not you, Martha. It's not your fault. Go away now."

What did Anna mean? What wasn't her fault? That the baby was dead? Of course it wasn't. Anna was confused and that was a feeling Martha knew very well. How often had she been confused, not just since she had become part of her husband's family, but all her life, as long as she could remember. All those rules. Her whole life had been governed by rules she could not understand. Surely Anna was only looking for answers. Why was her child dead? Why did she never have enough time to look after it? Why were the others not permitted to take care of it? Why did she have to leave it alone all day in the cold hut? Anna needed answers to those troubling questions to find some kind of solace. Martha didn't have the answers, but maybe she could make Anna calm enough to let the others explain all those things to her. Martha held out her hand, feeling quite brave. "Please Anna, give me the knife."

The young woman and the girl stared at each other for a brief moment. "No...".

Martha smiled at her. "Please Anna, give it to me. I want to help you. You don't want to hurt anybody."

The caring tone in Martha's voice made Anna crumple. Slowly she lowered the knife. Her shoulders hunched over and her crying turned into hushed weeping. "No, no, no…"

The knife fell on the stone floor with a harsh clatter. Martha was elated. This was like a miracle. Hadn't she just saved Anna and everybody present from harm? Perhaps she was an angel! Angels did things like that all the time, the book was full of amazing stories just like this. She turned around expectantly, looking for approval and possibly some praise from the others.

After Anna had dropped the knife the room had become very still. The faces of her sister-wives did not mirror the same joy she felt, in fact they did not even look at her. All heads were turned toward the door. Everything was fine now – why wouldn't they acknowledge her? Weren't they at least a little bit grateful? Martha could still feel her skin tingle and wanted to hold on to this precious moment of glory. Because she was much shorter than the others she did not see what they were looking at until the crowd parted. Their husband had entered the kitchen and was walking towards her and Anna.

Martha tried to melt back into the crowd, but this time the women closed ranks and nobody let her hide. Her husband was coming towards her. She had not seen him since she had been sent from his bedroom in disgrace. You are disgusting, he had said, when she had thrown up all over him. But she couldn't help it; that one time it had come up too fast. As soon as he had lifted the covers off her naked body her stomach had contracted. She had tried to move away from him, but he had pinned her down with his weight. The milk Marion had made her drink earlier that evening had come up so fast, she really had not had a chance to avoid him.

Seeing him now immediately filled her with nausea and shame and fear again, but he did not even look at her. His eyes were fixed on Anna.

"What's going on here?" He sounded perplexed, yet his voice carried so much authority that every single woman in the room shrank into herself. With their heads bent, looking at the floor, they tried to make themselves invisible.

"Marion, what is this?"

Marion was just as terrified, but had to answer. " Forgive me, but I have bad news. Your child with Anna died two days ago. We are so very sorry. Anna did not understand that the child was dead and did not want to let go of the body, so I had to send her back to her hut this afternoon. It is unhealthy to keep the dead so long among us living and I was only trying to do what is right. I am so sorry for your loss."

"What about her?"

Martha stiffened. He meant her. How many months had it been? Four at least, and she was still as scared of him as the last time he had touched her. She hated him. God forgive her for feeling that way. She hated him passionately, and she feared him. She wanted to grab the knife on the floor and stick it into herself to stop him looking at her. May the Lord punish her for her thoughts.

Marion moved a little in front of her. "Your wife Martha only helped us to avoid bloodshed."

Their husband frowned hearing her name. Had he not recognized her? Martha was petrified that he would now punish her for her old sins, but his glance passed over her and he focused on Marion again. He contemplated the situation briefly then gave Marion his orders. "You have done right. You will not be punished. But the Lord has shown his displeasure with my wife Anna who has disgraced me by producing a weak offspring. Take the body of this poor soul and bury it. We will all pray together tonight for his deliverance to the Lord's doorstep. May he forgive the child's sins and send it on to my kingdom. I shall accept this child when the time comes for all of us to rejoice in our rightful place in heaven. All except this one!" He did not need to point at her or Anna. Martha knew he would now condemn them both. "Anna has wanted to shed innocent blood. She has sinned in the name of the Lord and it is my duty to destroy her in the flesh."

A tiny cry escaped Martha. Her hands flew to her mouth, but it was too late. Her husband had noticed it and shook his head. "You need not be frightened." Now he pointed to Anna again. "None of you, except her! I forgive you all for idling away your time, giving in to jealous satisfaction, letting one of your own sink so low. I know you like a father knows all his children. You are only women, you are not perfect, so I forgive you your sins. You should have told me about the dead child before it came to this. You should have let your master handle this. All of you are forgiven – all except this one who has cast a shadow on our everlasting glory. She will be dealt with in the manner the Lord will reveal to me after many prayers. Marion, take her away, you know where to. Get her out of my sight."

Anna slumped to the ground, crawled toward him on her hands and knees and grabbed his ankles, pleading desperately. "Please, forgive me. I will be with child again, I swear. I can give you many. You are my husband, I need to go with you to your kingdom or I will rot in the darkness of hell. I need a child. Give me a child! Please, please, give me another child."

Lips curled with disgust, he freed his ankles from her grip and took a step back. "Marion, take her away. I don't want to see her again."

Anna started screaming, violently resisting Marion. He signalled to three other wives to help subdue her. She would be taken away to the place nobody ever mentioned. It was a small hut far from the main house, way up the mountain at the farthest corner of the property. Martha had been there once when she had to bring food to one of the boys who had been locked up there for a month of solitary punishment.

All the women started scurrying around, either trying to help forcefully remove Anna from the kitchen or pretending to get on with their work as if nothing had happened. Their husband left the room after ordering that they should renounce supper to stay focused on their all night prayer session.

Martha was so confused that she remained standing on the spot while her surroundings exploded in frantic activities. He had overlooked her! She did not exist for him. That was good, wasn't it? Anna was being punished for losing her child, but why was that her fault? She hadn't killed her daughter. Would Anna have to die now? Then she would never have another child, never in all eternity, and she would finish up in the dark abyss reserved for apostates. But then, so would she. If her husband was so disgusted with her that he didn't even recognize her, he would never want to be with her again and she would not get with child either. She would also go to hell when her time came! Women without children were refused entry into his kingdom.

Martha could not figure out what exactly she, or Anna, had done wrong to deserve such a punishment. She remained standing where she was for a long time and nobody told her to move. Would they all now follow his example and ignore her?

Marion came back, saw her still standing in the middle of the room and whispered to her. "Go down to Anna's hut and stay there. Go quickly. It is yours now. Don't come back here tonight. Stay away until you hear from me."

Martha hurried from the room. All she could think of was that she would have the hut to herself now. The bed and the extra bedding!

12

The Bishop was asking for divine guidance on how to treat Anna's scandalous violation of proper conduct. Some of the wives had been ordered to the main house to pray with him. It was a privilege to be called to this duty. To be at his side when he was inspired by the Lord was a blessing. Each of the sister-wives who were not permitted to spend the evening on their knees in the community hall were expected to pray in solitude in their own huts.

Martha wasn't quite sure what to do, but thought it would be best to follow Marion's implicit instruction to stay in Anna's hut. Maybe she should have been praying too, but it was so comforting to have two blankets for herself, she just couldn't find the willpower to kneel down on the cold floor. Suddenly, she heard a noise outside and was immediately alarmed. Anybody could look through the cracks in the wall and see that she was not praying because she had a candle burning. Quickly she slid to the floor and pressed her hands on her chest. Her heart was pounding deep and fast from the sudden threat and stopped altogether, or at least missed a few beats, when she heard the door hinges creak.

One of her sister-wives entered the room and walked right into the cone of the candle light. Martha remembered seeing the intruder in the kitchen earlier today and a few other times before then, but she did not remember her name. The familiar but unknown woman was still very young but much taller than Martha and even skinnier, just skin and bones really, and she had burning eyes that were quite small but still managed to glimmer in the semi-darkness like red hot coal in a fireplace.

"I'm Emma-Elisabeth," she said, settling on the crate-bed without waiting to be asked. "But you can call me Emma. Everybody does."

Martha stayed on her knees, waiting.

"Oh come on, get up. I know you didn't pray. Neither did I. Some of the others didn't either, but I am not telling you who."

Martha was totally taken. What a ludicrous statement. This could not be! The woman was testing her. She quickly defended herself. "I did pray! It is our duty to our husband. How can you say I didn't?"

"I saw you through the cracks. You were stretched out on the crate. I bet you ate something too!"

"I did not."

"Yes you did! There are crumbs, I can feel them. See!" Emma ran her hands over the thin mattress, found what she was looking for and triumphantly held up her thumb and forefinger. Martha could not see if there was anything in between.

Maybe there was. Still on her knees, she nearly cried in desperation because the woman was wrong, she hadn't done anything bad. At least not this time. "That was from before, when Anna was sleeping here. I didn't eat anything."

Emma did a patronizing eye-roll. "Oh, don't be such a scary cat. I don't care what you do. Actually, do you have anything to eat in here?"

Anna stored the rations for herself, the baby and for Martha in a basket hanging from the ceiling. Marion had handed out the weekly rations only two days ago, so there must be plenty left. Martha finally got up and obediently pulled the basket down because Emma was older than her and had been married to their husband before her, giving her seniority.

Emma jumped up and came closer. "My, there's quite a stash! Look, you have half a loaf of bread left. And what is this? Milk?"

Martha was fascinated by the open delight Emma displayed. If this was a test, would the other woman go as far as eat or drink anything on a prayer night when it was forbidden? "Do you want some?"

"May I?"

When Martha hesitated Emma quickly pointed out that Anna would not be coming back to this hut ever again. The two girls looked at each other. Martha broke some bread from the loaf and handed it to Emma. If she takes it she will forgive me because I shared it with her, she hoped. She will not tell the others that I have failed our husband.

Emma greedily stuffed the bread in her mouth, hardly chewing before she swallowed it, and asked if she could have some milk too. Martha thought of the dead baby girl who had been the reason for the trouble Anna was in now and handed Emma the bottle. The dead child didn't need it any more, and she herself wouldn't drink it either. Ever since she had vomited so violently, she hated the smell of milk. After Emma had taken a long sip, Martha broke some more bread, sat down next to Emma and started to eat as well.

Emma, still chewing with deep concentration, arranged the blankets over both their legs. "I don't think Marion will remember that Anna's ration is still here. She often forgets such things. Once Sarah got twice what was due to her because she went up to the main house and stood in line twice. Marion didn't remember that she had handed the ration out to her already. That was lucky, but not for Sarah. It was a lucky day for us. You see, Sarah wouldn't have shared anything with us. When she came back with her second ration some of us had already taken the first lot. The best part was that Sarah couldn't say anything because she would have been punished for tricking Marion as much as we would have been for taking it away from her."

"But that's stealing!"

"No, it's not. It's fair distribution. You are so silly, you don't understand anything. We wives have to stick together, don't you know? Some of us know how important it is to help each other."

Martha could not remember when she had heard anything that outrageous. The bread in her stomach and Emma's amazing claim of women bonding together made her feel all warm inside, but she didn't really understand what it meant. Nobody had ever spoken to her like that. So open, so personal … as if she was a real person, deserving to be taken into confidence. Telling her secrets, sharing tales of disobedience, theft and lies. No, nobody had ever considered her worthy of such trust. She wanted to prolong the moment, know more about the wives who stuck together and helped each other.

Martha moved closer to Emma. Her body radiated such warmth. "What about this Sarah? How did you know she wouldn't have shared her ration?"

"She is not one of us." Emma crossed her legs and tucked them in again where the blankets had slipped. "Do you want to know who belongs to us and who doesn't?"

"Yes, yes, please."

"Well, I can't tell you. We talked about it walking down from the house tonight – you know I was one of those who had to go to that boring prayer session – and we agreed that we must wait and see how you turn out. We can't trust you yet, you know. That's what they said. But I don't agree. I know what you've been thinking, ever since our husband banned you from his bed you have thought about running away from here, right?"

Martha couldn't believe it. How could Emma know what she had planned on that last desperate day in the dump? She frantically tried to think of something to say.

"See, I'm right! You have that look on your face."

Martha blurted. "It would do no good. There is nowhere to go to."

Emma pursed her lips. "I guess you're right, but you can dream about it, can't you? Sometimes I picture that we live on a small plate and when I run far enough I fall off the rim and I land on a much larger plate underneath. It's always sunny and warm on that big plate and the people smile all the time and lots of fruit and veggies grow there and we all have plenty to eat. And all the men are nice to their wives and look after them and their babies. Nobody tries to climb back on the small plate, ever. They are too happy and laugh about the people above their heads who are so miserable. And you know what I dream next? One day, somebody takes a huge shotgun and blasts up there and the small plate shatters into a million pieces and they rain down on us as big snowflakes. Everybody dances in the snowstorm and then builds big snowmen that look like ugly fat men, and then we all blow those to pieces too. That's the most funny part of it all - I have to laugh every time I see that happen."

Martha shook her head. The picture Emma had painted was delightful. Funny and wonderful – but impossible! Best not to even think about such a wonderful world. It was not permitted to think like that! Suddenly Martha got worried again. She must not encourage Emma's fanciful ideas. "You said you were at the main house. How come you are back already? I thought this was to be an all night prayer session."

"Oh right, you don't know yet what happened. This is really exciting!"

Emma chuckled. "We were in the middle of our first long recital – the one about the husband's duty to punish his wives if they sinned and how the blood atonement is a righteous punishment and how he will be rewarded in heaven for it – and my knees were hurting so much although we had only been at it for an hour or so when there was a small cry from Marion. She turned all white in the face and lost the words of the prayer and started to mumble incoherently. She is always the one who prays aloud to guide us along. And she always feels our husband's revelations coming, even before he does. When she started to act funny our husband went over to her and they whispered together. I was right next to her and I could hear what she said. The Lord wants you to wait if she is with child, she said to him really softly, but I still understood. Then he went back to his chair, you know he can't kneel because of his bad joints, and the praying went on a bit longer and then suddenly he had a revelation. He said we must all go back and wait; Anna may be with child. And that means he can't kill her, at least not right away."

Stunned, Martha hung on to Emma's words. "Do you think Anna has to die?"

"Oh sure. But if she is pregnant, she can stay on until after the birth and then he will kill her. Sarah said he can't let such things go unpunished. What would it come to if he lets disobedience like Anna's go unpunished, she said, but I told you, Sarah is not one of us and she always makes comments like that."

"How would Anna be killed?"

"Who knows. When I was with my old family in Utah the women would be taken to the desert and left behind without any water, but here? Last time he shot one of us because she tried to escape, and I guess he had no choice, he had to stop her somehow. We all heard the shot but we didn't see what happened, so I can't say if he killed her. As far as I know, there has been no blood atonement apart from that incident, but I have only been here a few years. I came just a year before Anna." Emma pulled a face. "I can't say I feel sorry for Anna. She's always been greedy and tried to get our husband's attention away from the rest of us. Anyway, in Utah it was easy to get rid of women like her. Rita thinks Anna will be butchered like the pigs, but I don't believe that because he doesn't like blood and guts and stuff. He always goes away when we have slaughter day and the blood starts running."

"Who is Rita?"

"One of us … ouch, now I said it!" Emma bit her lip, indicating that she shouldn't have been so careless. "Please don't tell anybody that I mentioned a name."

"No, I won't, I promise."

"Swear by the name of the Lord."

"I swear."

Now they truly shared a secret. Martha was grateful for this, but she was also confused. One of the sister-wives had been killed by her husband – one that had tried to run away? She asked Emma about the dead wife.

"No, you got that wrong, I didn't say it was a sister-wife. It was only one of the girls, Katherine's daughter actually. That's why Katherine's gone mad. She can't handle it, although the girl deserved whatever she got. She was practically asking for it, always misbehaving. I saw it for myself, I witnessed her bad behaviour lots of times. Well, they say, the apple doesn't fall far from the tree. Katherine has always been a bit odd, and her daughter was too."

Martha was shocked. "My father never killed anybody. Are you sure our husband would do such a thing?"

Emma laughed. "No, I'm not. I told you, we only heard a shot. But after that, we never saw her again. Still, maybe he only sent her away."

That was how it must have been! Martha didn't want to think about blood-atonement. She wanted to ban such thoughts from her mind altogether, because, based on her own experience, she actually considered the Bishop capable of administering such extreme punishment.

"Katherine would have gone crazy anyway. I've heard stuff about her from the other Alberta wives you wouldn't believe..."

Emma proceeded to share some of the stories she had been told about Katherine and about some of the sister-wives with Martha. The two girls huddled closer under the blankets and giggled and gossiped. It was the most wonderful time Martha had ever had and she was disappointed when Emma announced she had better go. She was one of The Chosen Ones, having two children with their husband, who now needed her attention. "Two is enough to go to heaven with him," she grinned. "For the others it's three, but our husband said I won't need to get another one. He doesn't like thin women, it's been a burden for him already to give me those two." She playfully slapped her own cheek. "Oh dear, I'm sorry, Martha. I forgot you don't have any yet."

Martha didn't want to dwell on this complication. One day she would have to face the consequences of being barren, but please not now. Emma shouldn't spoil this perfect moment by reminding her of her shortcomings. "Don't worry, I am young, I will be fourteen next month, it can still happen."

Soon after prayer night rumours swirled around the compound that Anna had indeed been lucky enough to conceive before she had lost her firstborn. Martha praised the Lord for doing the right thing and sending a child to the woman who needed it most. She did not consider her evaluation of the Lord's good judgement arrogant; in fact, she thought she should make it clear to him that she appreciated his wisdom. After all, she could have been upset with the Lord because she was still outside the circle of The Chosen Ones. Deep inside however, she was grateful for his oversight. He might have a lot more possibilities in store for her to get pregnant, but for now, she gladly accepted to be left out.

For the duration of her pregnancy Anna was confined to the prison hut, which meant Martha had the hut to herself. Nobody bothered her there as long as she showed up in the kitchen every morning and did her chores to Marion's satisfaction.

As winter moved slowly forward without her being summoned to her husband's bed, Martha began to relax a bit. Since Emma had come into her life, she felt much better. It didn't occur to her that, day by day, week after week, month after month, she found life more bearable because she was continuously lowering her expectations. Her rations were never quite enough to make her feel full and seemed to get smaller as the months went on, but she had something that helped her forget how hungry she was. Emma! Most evenings, when they had finished their duties, they sat together, either in Martha's hut or, when Emma needed to stay with her children, in hers, sharing a few peaceful moments. Often one of the sister-wives – those who belonged to this secret group of *queer-thinkers*, a phrase coined by Emma and happily accepted by Martha – took charge of a small group of children to give the other mothers a little respite. It had to be carefully organized, to make sure the followers of the faith did not get wind of such disobedience. From the information Emma accidentally let slip, Martha had already figured out that there were at least five wives who did not follow the word as it was written. When she asked Emma about their identities, Emma refused to answer. It was a great risk to oppose the Bishop's rules in the slightest way and Martha still had not earned their trust.

All those conversations with Emma made Martha even more aware of the forbidden thoughts brewing inside her. Hidden within much of Emma's harmless and innocent sounding chatter Martha detected a message of rebellion. Everything – whatever they had to do, how they spent their days, where they had to live, what was being said - was scrutinized and ridiculed by Emma. Martha secretly questioned many of those things too, but would never have talked about them had

Emma not asked her opinion on many occasions. Imagine, the older woman wanted to know her opinion! To come up with a halfway intelligent answer, Martha had to sift through her memory, digging deep into her minimal life experiences. She knew so little.

By spring time, she had so many things to think about, she started to forget counting her steps when she walked up to the main house.

13

Mouschi-Bar was a classic pick-up joint. Richard had noticed it a few years back because the name had intrigued him. In the German language Muschi was an endearing synonym for the female private parts. Much nicer than the four letter English word that was commonly used, he thought.

The bar lived up to what it's name promised. Richard had often found willing partners for a quick evening romp there. Aside from the single women who frequented this bar looking for the same uncomplicated transient connection, some of the barmaids had, once they got to know him, indicated their willingness to serve him more than a cold beer in the backroom. When he was particularly stressed out, he liked to make use of their offer. Rosy and some of her like-minded servers only expected a small donation toward their income of course - no need to flirt and chat and laugh.

Today was one of those days. He had never had to worry about cash-flow before, but now money was rapidly drying up - and on top of that, he had to deal with a lot of bureaucratic nonsense that spelled trouble down the line.

By early afternoon he had had enough of it. Without giving Daisy any explanation other than that he would be back soon, he left the office and headed straight for the Mouschi Bar. At this time of the day it didn't surprise him that he was the only customer. Rosy was polishing beer glasses behind the counter. He was so eager to distract himself that he didn't bother to order a beer but indicated to Rosy how he would prefer to spend the next fifteen minutes. She went around the counter to the front door, locked it, came back to him, took him by the hand and guided him to a small office and storage room.

Sensing his eagerness, she expertly handled him, and he, still standing up, pushed her against the wall as soon as she had rolled her mini skirt up high enough. Then disaster struck. His stupid, overloaded brain refused to give in to his need for physical release. It just didn't want to shut up. He had come here to forget all the goddamn problems he had to deal with throughout office hours, but now a multitude of calculations, arguments and counter arguments didn't know their time and place, like so often nowadays. As if they had a right to control every waking moment of his life! As if they had a right to control his basic desires!

He tried a few desperate thrusts to get things upright again, but to no avail. Rosy made matters worse by reminding him that he had ten more minutes to get his act together and that he had to pay her regardless.

Ten minutes!

The harder he tried to switch off his racing mind, the more pushy and vivid the worries became. They had finally off-loaded the last condo. This morning the realtor had confirmed the final sale. Now his company had only one asset left – one that was becoming more of a liability every day.

God, Rosy, don't just stand there. Do something.

Damn it, he had put all his eggs in one basket. That was a pretty scary thought. In fact, it was so scary, it made him very nervous. He should stop thinking about it. All his cards on one bet, what if it didn't pan out as he expected?

Goddamn it, it made him too nervous. That was the problem. He should stop worrying.

Things were not going as smoothly as he had hoped. Although they had been able to come up with the purchase price at the end of last year and had sailed through the process of getting approval from the local planning committee, the following three months had been an uphill struggle.

Stop worrying. There is nothing you can do right now!

All those delays started to annoy the hell out of him. Maybe the sheer magnitude of this development worried the government departments involved, they had never been so slow before. Every single application Daisy had made took twice as long as usual to be processed and was apparently scrutinized through a gigantic magnifying glass. Some days he was so frustrated over the unnecessary delays that he blamed Daisy for it. Totally unfair of course, but she took it with stoical equanimity, which made him even more frustrated. How dare she be so aloof when it came to his livelihood!

How dare she ignore his problems.

He had hoped to get the all-important preliminary layout approval, the PLA, by now, but as far as he knew, the Ministry of Transportation had not yet forwarded all their documentation to the Approving Officer who would preside over the whole development and watch every single step until all governmental conditions were met. He didn't want to think about how much every single month of delay cost him in interest payments.

He didn't want to think at all.

Daisy should be trying harder to push this process along. She just didn't care enough. He pushed harder, thinking about her.

Daisy. Gorgeous, long legged, detached, distant Daisy.

It worked amazingly fast. The erotic image of Daisy dissolved into a blurred rush. He managed to muster a semblance of hardness, enough to quickly release some of his built up tension. It was a far cry from what he was used to, but at least he had managed at all.

He straightened his clothes, took a few bank notes out of his wallet and put them on the bar counter before he rushed out into the street without saying good-bye to Rosy. He didn't think he would ever go back there.

Spring had arrived early. It was late March and the cherry trees along Robson Street were in full bloom already. Unsatisfied and angry with himself, he headed back to the office.

Daisy would still be there, working, and the best thing for him to do would be to join her and concentrate on the tasks that needed to be done. He slowed down his pace. Daisy! He had better collect himself before he faced her. She was too smart. He always suspected that she could read him like an open book. My God, she would be horrified if she knew what she had just assisted in. She would despise him. But of course, she would never find out because he would never tell her what part she sometimes played in his fantasies.

14

There had been so much snow this winter, it took until the middle of May before the soft earth had finally dried out. After that, it rained every day. Not all day long, but often and hard enough to soak the dust dry earth again. Hurrying up to the main house, Martha had to lift her long dress to keep the hemline out of the mud. Emma had told her that June usually was a wet month, and she had better enjoy it, because from July on it would be unbearably hot again. The climate here was such a nuisance. Either it was too cold, or too wet, or too hot.

Soon, in just a few weeks, one whole year would have passed since Martha had arrived at the Bishop's compound, and she had to be grateful for many things. Since Anna had been banned from her hut, Martha had enjoyed the solitude there, but her heart would have been heavy with loneliness had not Emma come into her life. Having light hearted chats and giggles with a woman close to her own age made her feel much less abandoned and, on the many occasions when Emma shared her innermost rebellious thoughts with her, Martha felt honoured. She was also grateful that she was allowed back in the kitchen. As long as she performed her duties diligently, Marion and the other sister-wives left her pretty much alone.

Not knowing how the life of a fourteen year old should or could be like, Martha was grateful for all this, but above all she was grateful that her husband had not asked for her again. She assumed the sister-wives did not burden her with extra tasks or torture her with mean, unreasonable demands because they had no reason to be jealous of her.

The days were long and full of work, yet she gladly accepted her fate as long as her husband took no interest in her. In the back of her mind, she always worried that this might change. Every new day more or less mirrored the previous one, and sometimes she wondered if it would be like this for the rest of her life.

One morning at the end of June, Martha was called into Marion's small chamber next to the pantry. It was a narrow room at the end of the dark corridor that led to their husband's private quarters. Marion's office was furnished with a small desk and many, many shelves full of books and folders. Marion spent a lot of time in there, but Martha had never been asked to enter. She searched her mind for what she might have done wrong but couldn't think of anything.

"You know where Anna is staying?" Marion didn't look up from the journal she was writing in.

"At the hut up on the mountain."

"You know the way?"

"Yes, I've been there once."

"Good. From tomorrow on, I want you to go up there every morning."

Martha could see that Marion was adding up some long columns of numbers. Even looking at them upside down, she could still differentiate them.

"Anna is due soon and can't move around any longer. Our husband is worried about the coming birth. Nothing must happen to this child as he has already lost one precious daughter, which saddens him deeply. Somebody needs to check on Anna and spend some time with her."

Two rows had already been added up, but one of the sums was wrong.

"Go there at first light. Take some food from the kitchen, enough for Anna and yourself. You can have your breakfast up there with her. She must stay alert until the baby has arrived."

And then what, Martha thought. This question resounded so loud in her mind, she got scared that it might have escaped her mouth. Marion looked up now, without any anger but with a suspicious expression on her face. To cover any further rebellious thoughts the older woman might notice, Martha concentrated on the numbers again. "That one should be eight hundred fifty seven!"

"I beg your pardon?"

Now she had done it! Marion would be furious with her and the Lord only knew what her penalty would be. "I'm sorry."

"What number did you say?"

"Eight hundred fifty seven."

Marion wrote it down on a separate piece of paper. "Do you understand what I have asked you to do?"

"Yes, I am sorry. I shall make sure Anna does not hurt herself until the child has arrived."

"I see you are not stupid. Go." Marion wiped her nose with the back of her hand. Walking out, Martha did not see the little smile the first wife was hiding behind this gesture. She also did not see the surprised look on Marion's face when she checked the column and discovered her adding error.

Now Martha had something else to be grateful for. To care for Anna was a duty that would allow her to finally sit down and chat with her former friend again. Martha was eager to find out how Anna was doing after being locked up in the prison hut all by herself for the past four months. Surely she would be delighted to have Martha visit her.

The next morning she was so excited, she got up even before the sun rose, went to the main house to pick up the food basket for Anna and hiked up to the small cabin in the woods.

Nothing had prepared her for what she found when she arrived there.

Anna's prison was a tiny room with a ceiling so low even Martha could reach it without fully stretching her arm. But this didn't matter to Anna because she was lying on the floor, on a worn-out mattress, unable to get up because she was huge with child and too weak to lift herself from the floor. Everything was covered with dust and grime. Within her reach was a dirty plate, a bunched-up towel, some paper bags and what looked like old rags with dried feces smeared on them. Anna was unrecognizable. Her hair was matted and had taken on a greyish colour; her skin was of a similar pallor. She had turned into an old woman. Even her voice was scratchy from lack of use. She sounded like a crow when she tried to say hello to Martha. After a few words she stopped her futile effort and stared at Martha with feverish eyes.

Martha knew that nobody had spoken to Anna since she had been banned from the community. The despair of her own loneliness shortly after her arrival at the compound, when she had to wait for her husband in that cold and lonely room up at the main house, counting the patches on the quilt, was still vivid in her memory. She had come close to losing her mind then – but that was nothing compared to Anna's suffering. It would not have surprised her if Anna had gone completely crazy by now. Martha quickly looked around. Was there possibly a knife hidden amongst the garbage surrounding Anna? She couldn't see anything that remotely resembled a weapon. The stink was unbearable. Martha went to open the door wide and tried to open the window shutters as well, but they were nailed to the walls from the outside.

She started to talk to Anna soothingly while she got busy. There was so much to do. Since Anna could not get up any more, she had not been able to lift the heavy lid from the hole in the ground in one corner of the room that served as a septic pit. Martha shivered. Did they really keep Anna in this room, which was nothing better than a large outhouse? Only when Anna whispered yes, did Martha notice that she had murmured this question aloud. Martha did not care. But she kept the next thought that flashed though her mind buried in silent bitterness. Who was *them*? Who would do this to Anna? Only her husband and the first sister-wife Marion had the power to exercise such cruelty! This was neither the time nor was it Martha's place to put the blame on her superiors, so she bit her tongue.

But she would tell Emma!

Martha had to leave Anna by midday, otherwise she overstayed and risked not being allowed to come back. Anna begged her not to go – and Martha remembered how grateful she had been for Anna's stolen conversations when their roles had been reversed. "I promise I'll be back tomorrow," she said. Anna's pleading farewell echoed in her mind all the way back down from the mountain cabin. It broke her heart.

With summer solstice barely passed, daylight still lasted until after ten and all the sister-wives continued to work long hours. Martha could hardly wait until the day's activities had settled so she could sneak over to Emma's hut. She had to curb her patience until it was reasonably dark.

Her sister-wife was feeding her children when Martha knocked on her door. She stuck her head in and asked if Emma had time for her. Emma knew already that Martha had been assigned to look after Anna and told her impatiently to come in. She slipped in and sat down opposite the slim woman who was feeding her youngest with a wooden spoon. The other child was sitting on the floor, playing with a doll made of twigs and rags. Both children were too young to understand anything.

"You must tell me all about Anna," urged Emma. "How is she doing?"

Martha had a hard time to describe the indescribable. "It was so disgusting," she said, "it took me all morning to get the filth out and some fresh air in. Tomorrow I will take some clean towels and a blanket with me. I can take them from the storage room at the main house, can't I? I don't care if Marion finds out. I think Anna has lice. I need to shave her hair off and see how I can wash her. Why didn't the sister-wife who brought the food up to her every few days look in on her and help her clean herself?"

"Because unless you have permission from Marion you're not allowed to enter the cabin. And she didn't give it to anybody until now, you know that!"

"How can Marion be so mean?"

"Anna was our husband's favourite. As soon as she came into our family I was forgotten, which suited me just fine as you know, but

Marion and some of the other wives who still need more children were furious that they were ignored too. He spent all his time with Anna and did not want to do his duty to the others. You know how jealous they can get. He always respected Marion as the first; until he got smitten with Anna she had ruled the house. Marion always made a roster every month so every sister-wife would have a chance to get pregnant, but when Anna arrived he refused all the others. Anna was trying to take Marion's place and she nearly succeeded. But when she fell pregnant with her first child, our husband lost all interest in her, as is the normal way with men, and he decided to ask the Elders for a new wife. A young one like her. I bet Anna told him we are all too old for him. Then you arrived, but that did not work out as well as he had hoped, I guess." Emma poked her playfully in the side. "You little puke-baby."

Martha turned crimson. Did all the sister-wives know? "But still, how can they do this to Anna? What has she done that was so terrible?"

"Our husband has condemned her, that's all we need to know. Don't meddle, Martha, but if it makes you feel better, try and make Anna's last days more bearable, that's all you can do."

"Can't any of us help her? You told me we must stick together."

Emma's face closed. "She hasn't made friends with any of us. Nobody will lift a finger for her. You are the only one."

Martha got up before dawn again and jumped from her crate bed. She had to rush up to the main house and try and steal a bar of soap and some towels. She planned to hide her loot outside the house behind a bush and then go back and pick up the daily food supply for Anna and herself.

The nights were so short, they never turned really dark. How could she manage to sneak into the main house without the protection of total darkness? Marion lived up there and their husband too; what if one of them got up early, looked out of a window and saw her approaching? What excuse did she have for being there before the kitchen opened?

She had to risk it, no matter how fast her silly heart was beating. Anna didn't deserve to die with festering boils on her body and bugs crawling over her scalp. She should be clean and peaceful when she left this world and entered the other. Martha was sure the good Lord on the other side would accept her, He would not be as cruel as the people on this earth. Her mother had always told her to remember that the joy of heavenly living was the reward for all the suffering one had to endure in preparation for eternity. But Emma had said *life in heaven* meant that women would have to serve the men there in the same manner as on this earth. Didn't this mean all suffering would continue just the same, here in this world and there, in the afterlife? What did one make of that?

Martha had been thinking about it a lot and last night, just before she was drifting off, the answer had come to her in amazing clarity. If living in heaven was the same as living here on earth – with their husband and Marion and all the other mean sister-wives - she did not want to go there!

She had woken up with the same thought still in her mind. There must be another heaven, one where people like Anna and herself could go. She would never be with child as her husband would never touch her again, and therefore she would always be a slave in his world – here and there. The Lord surely had a place reserved specially for wives without children, for the ones who died before they could get married, for the ones who grieved themselves to death like Anna did over the loss of her baby, … for all the innocent ones who had done no harm but were damned by the teachings of the scripture.

…and he that abideth not my law can nowise enter into my glory but shall be damned, saith the Lord …

No, not the Lord, she assured herself, sitting upright with inner excitement. Joseph Smith had said it! He had written down the doctrine and covenants as the Angel Moroni had revealed to him, but nobody else had ever seen or heard the Angel. Martha did not believe in Joseph's writings any longer. Not after seeing Anna like that – it was not right and could not be explained or forgiven; not by an angel or by a man who thought he had seen an angel.

Suddenly she felt calm and strong. They could not harm her. If they caught her stealing they could punish her, but she would always know their excuses for doing so were based on lies. They could punish her again and again but in the end she would escape them and while they would have to continue living in their own nightmare, she would move to another heaven where people like Anna were waiting for her.

When she opened her door she saw a parcel on the doorstep. Martha frowned. What was that? Who put it there? She bent down and untied the string around it. Rolled in two brown towels were a bar of soap, a bottle of disinfectant lotion, a comb, a razor sharp knife, scissors, a candle and matches, some bandages and – o wonder, where did the sister-wives get that? – a strip of Tylenol.

Martha nearly cried with gratitude. She gathered her treasures together and quickly went back into her hut, looking around to see if anybody was watching her. She still did not know for sure which sister-wife belonged to Emma's supportive circle and could therefore not trust anyone. Obviously they did not trust her yet either, otherwise they would not have put the gift for Anna anonymously on her doorstep. Never mind, she would soon be able to prove that she was one of them.

It took two weeks. Then Anna's body was clean and all the festering scabs had closed and were healing, her head was shaved and rid of lice, the mattress had been aired and washed and covered with fresh towels. Anna always waited until Martha could help her get to the toilet hole in the corner, and Martha always placed the lid back tightly so it did not smell too bad in the tiny room. She had managed to loosen the nails on one of the window shutters. The summer heat made it possible to keep the door and the window open all night and Martha had brought more candles for Anna to light at night because she was scared of wild animals.

Every morning she found a new parcel on her doorstep. When she asked Emma one evening how she had managed to collect all those precious supplies, Emma vehemently denied knowing anything about it. So Martha left it at that.

Then, after two weeks, everything changed again. Martha had no experience in childbirth but she happened to be present when Anna's water broke and, not understanding what this sudden wetness seeping out of Anna meant, got very worried.

Anna was in pain, holding her swollen belly and moaning. "You need to go and get Marion. My time has come."

"Your time? You mean the child?" Martha asked dazed. To fetch Marion and bring her here was impossible. Until now, it had not occurred to her that somebody would find out what she had done. In a mad rush she started to collect all the evidence she could find.

"Quick, go and get her, there is not much time." Anna was moaning louder now.

"Wait, not yet. I need to hide all these things." Martha tried as best as she could to grab everything that did not belong in the cabin. She ran outside and found a small rock formation behind some bushes where she buried them. She covered the spot with earth and small pebbles. Then she ran back inside to find Anna doubled over in pain. She had always been told childbirth was an enlightening and wonderful experience. One look at Anna told her otherwise.

"Can I leave you alone?" Martha was on her way out.

Anna pressed her next words out between laboured breathing. "Yes… go… the child… needs to be… taken care of. Go… they must… come…and kill me."

Martha stopped dead and swivelled around. Oh good Lord, she had forgotten about that. Anna was to die. "Don't say that, please."

Anna lifted one hand. Did she wave her good-bye? Martha stood still and was unable to decide what to do and how to react.

"Don't…worry…it will be over…soon… go."

Martha went. She raced down the hill. Her small feet flew over the narrow winding path avoiding air roots and rocks, until she arrived at the main house. What normally took her an hour going up and about forty minutes down was over in such a short time that she had no breath left to support any thoughts. She had switched her mind over to counting the first fifty or so steps, then it was not necessary any more to occupy her thinking – all she had to do was run and breathe and run.

She bolted into the main house through the kitchen entrance. Only two wives were busy in there. "Where is Marion?" Martha panted, holding her left side with both hands.

Marion appeared like magic.

"It's Anna. She is …" What was she to say? She is ready – to do what - ready to die? "She is…" Martha could not get it over her lips.

Marion immediately took over. She pointed at one of the women. "You, get Elisabeth. Tell her to come here." Then at the other. "You, go and tell my son to bring the pickup. We need to get her down here." Then at Martha. "You, boil some water and leave it on the stove here. Get fresh towels and sheets from the storage and bring everything into the birth room. Glory to the Lord for giving our husband a new child. Nothing must happen to it."

Martha still had trouble getting sufficient air into her lungs. "What about…Anna? …What will happen…to her?"

Marion's lips tightened. "Do as you are told. Then go back to your hut. Birth is not for you to look at."

When one of her mother's sister-wives had given birth, it had always been a special day. Usually the sisters who assisted told the others as soon as it was over, and except for the one time when a baby had been born half dead – it is malformed, they had whispered loud enough for little Martha to understand, one must wait for it to die – it had always been accompanied by quiet excitement and followed by a festive ceremony.

But nothing here was like her old home. There had not been a single birth since she had been here. Imagine, so many sister-wives and not one child in nearly a year! Of course, it should have been her duty to produce one and she had let down her husband and everybody in the community, but Martha did not feel guilty about that. With her sharpened understanding of how eternity was arranged and her belief that the balance was in her favour, she could not care less.

All she cared and worried and fretted about was how poor Anna was to be killed. Would they be merciful? Would they let her see her baby before they did it? Who would execute it? Surely her husband. He would have to do it himself because the scripture commanded it.

All the huts were deserted. The mothers had taken their children along to the fields for harvesting, where the ones old enough looked after the little ones. Martha was all alone. She sat in front of her hut on the bench and let the sun shine on her face until it got too hot. Then she went to the large tree next to the roadside and sat in its shadow. What would happen when Marion went to Anna's prison and found her well cared for? Would she suspect what she had done? Was that the reason why she had sent her away and not asked her to join the other sister-wives?

Martha was suddenly very tired. Nothing mattered any more. Marion would probably condemn her to the prison hut as soon as they had killed Anna. She would have to stay there until she herself would be killed. She had taken matters into her own hands, had made choices all by herself and had acted as she saw fit. Their husband would not spare her when he heard about her disobedience.

She promised herself to stay strong - she would not tell who had helped her! Martha smiled when she realised that she couldn't anyway. So clever of Emma and the others for not telling her. She could raise her hand and swear to the Lord that she did not know any of the names. She merely suspected Emma, so she could safely swear that she knew nothing - it did not mean she committed perjury.

15

Richard Bergman's mobile rang at seven am. Not a good sign!

He was not ready for more bad news and, trying to ignore it, continued to inspect his hairline in the bathroom mirror. What he discovered there did not help to lift his spirits. Plucking out the second grey hair in a week, he felt cheated. For Christ's sake, he was only thirty-two years old, supposedly at an age when a healthy male should be at his peak, sporting a solid crop of wavy black hair. He pinched the flab around his midriff, disgusted with himself. His fingers could grab several inches of fat, all acquired in the last year. If he was honest with himself, he had to admit that those signs of premature aging affected his self-esteem quite a bit. Obviously they were to blame for his diminished sex drive, which had led to the disastrous episode with Rosy. His weakened libido worried him considerably, but that was nothing compared to the grey reminder of his own transience on his head. That truly freaked him out. He knew, the urge to copulate would eventually come back, but he had never heard of the miracle of grey hair turning black again.

The phone stopped after five rings, just before his mail box could kick in, then started again like the bell ringing in the next round of a major championship bout. Only Daisy would do that, and as his assistant was capable of countless more rounds, he resigned himself to the fact that he might as well take the call.

He temporarily abandoned his grey-hair-search and its age-related depression, went to the kitchen and poured himself fresh coffee. Then he moved, phone and mug in his hands, into the living room to take the call.

On the third ringing round he had settled in the easy chair by the window, had placed his mug with hot coffee on the side-table and took a quick sip while pressing the answering button.

"The bitch is at it again!"

Trust his considerate Daisy, a name that was, as far as she was concerned, in all its sweetness and simplicity incredibly deceiving, to alert him with one word.

"Liebling, it's only seven o'clock and yesterday's meeting didn't even finish till midnight. Do you have any idea when I went to bed?"

"Sorry." Daisy's voice was dripping with satisfaction. She would never say *I told you so*. She did not need to. By now, he knew that he should have trusted her instincts when she had warned him of taking on the overwhelming task of such a huge subdivision; it might not have been too late to get out of the deal. But no, stubborn as he was, he had not listened to her. He should have kept his emotions out of such an important business decision – falling in love with a piece of land, how ridiculous was that? - and above all, he should have researched the potential deal better before he nose-dived into it with a big fat grin on his face. Never before in the past ten years had he let his heart rule his head to such an extent. He should have done his homework. If more trouble came his way, those bloodless condescending know-it-alls who come out of their safe hiding places usually only *after* something has gone wrong, would rub their hands and gloat *I told you so*.

Of course, Daisy was not one of those patronizing bastards. She had warned him once in the beginning, even before he had noticed that any problems even existed, and had then kept her mouth shut and switched to damage control. That's why he considered her not only his personal assistant, but also his business confidante, his shield and armour.

Since instigating the subdivision process, she had patiently dealt with the various government servants in charge of handling the different requirements. Unfortunately the three major players assigned to this subdivision were known to be overzealous, which made them exceptionally difficult to work with. And as Daisy, an ardent feminist, said, sadly they were all female. She called them the Killer Bee Commandos.

"Which one is it this time?"

"Jeanne d'Arc!"

He sighed. Daisy loved to give her opponents labels. It was her way of working off some of her inner frustrations while keeping her cool. Most people she had to deal with, as well as her colleagues in his company, were totally fooled by her flawless show of soft-spoken diplomacy and mild mannered diligence. Only he knew that she was even capable of bad-mouthing; and only he knew the deeper meaning of those nicknames. Jeanne d'Arc had been a famous self-appointed female soldier in medieval France who had a knack for convincing a hell of a lot of otherwise quite sane people, including the king himself, to join her lost cause because some strange voices had told her to. At least that's what Richard remembered from his history classes. Obviously Daisy felt that their very own Jeanne d'Arc, who was the Government appointed Approving Officer for their project, a vicious lady who delighted in creating unnecessary delays, was also a fierce fighter in a lost cause. At least he liked to think that his AO would lose the battle against him in the end. The thought alone made him feel better.

"What does she want this time?"

"It's bad."

He waited, still not overly concerned. In the past weeks, Jeanne d'Arc had come up with a number of totally absurd requests, designed to make him, the disgusting developer who was in the game simply to get filthy rich, suffer by the strength of her almighty power. Deep in her heart she probably resented being an indirect contributor to the land development process.

"She objects to us building a road over the easement."

"You must be kidding? For what reason?"

"She doesn't need one. She is the AO."

"But…," he stopped himself before wasting his breath on useless arguments.

An Approving Officer was a legal entity, outside the political arena. To ensure that the holder of this position would stay as incorruptible as a Catholic priest – an oxymoron of course, as if an ecclesiastical employee would not misuse his power, confidently hiding under his cloak of supreme holiness – the AO could do, within reason, as he or she saw fit. Unfortunately those boundaries were often determined by the degree of self-love or -loathing when waking up. Apparently Jeanne d'Arc didn't like herself most mornings.

"The mail came in yesterday evening, but I didn't want to disturb your meeting with the lawyers."

"You should have. Maybe there are legal grounds to challenge her on that one."

He could picture Daisy shaking her head with lenient patience. "Been there. The rules were changed about two years ago. No more subdivisions over easements."

Damn those new rules! Two sides of his parcel bordered on Crown land, but, as Daisy had discovered *after* the sale had gone through, the stretch between the southern border of his land and the only rural road in the area was owned by somebody else. This somebody had granted the previous owner of the land, Bob, his father, or maybe even his grandfather, an easement to make it accessible. Even when Daisy informed him of this not totally unusual arrangement, he had not been worried. All his previous subdivisions had had direct access, so the problem of access by easement over foreign property had never been an issue. The offending stretch of land in question was less than six hundred meters wide and his plan was to build a connecting road over the easement so the future owners could get to their lots. And now the law would not allow him to do so – effectively cutting him off from his own land and making it useless for any kind of development. That was bad, very bad indeed.

"So, what does she suggest?"

Daisy hesitated.

"The government does have a solution for such a case, right?"

"Actually, no!"

"What do you mean? They let us buy the land but refuse us access?"

"You have access! But you can't subdivide because it's only by easement."

"Goddamn the fucking government! Who makes those goddamn rules? Who do they think they are?" An unpleasant but very familiar feeling was rising inside him, like fog drawn out of a cold mountain lake by the upcoming sun. It was pure, still undefined anger and he knew he needed to suppress this surge of nebulous outrage before it could turn into threatening thunder clouds of uncontrollable and counter-productive fury. He regulated his breathing. "They can't make new rules without offering solutions for such cases." Actually he knew perfectly well that it was not the government's job to come up with an answer. It was his job.

"Daisy," he urged her, "I'm listening."

"As this stretch of land is privately owned, it is of no concern to Jeanne d'Arc. We should have considered this before we bought."

"Is that what she said?"

"Yes."

He felt like strangling her. The queen of the Killer Bees, not Daisy, the messenger.

"She also said we are welcome to send our complaints to the MLA, or the Premier, or whoever you think might listen to you; it is not going to change her mind and will not help us at all."

"Stuck up bitch!" Now he was really livid. They had been working this deal non-stop for nearly one year now and he had regularly emailed information on progress to the local politicians, just to make sure the various government agencies involved knew they were being monitored. Maybe that had not been such a brilliant idea after all. The AO's uncooperative attitude was her little revenge trip. "Somebody should cut her down to size."

"Maybe, but that shouldn't be you, my dear," said Daisy. She knew how quickly he could fly off the handle.

"Right. Okay, let me think about this for a while. I'll call you back."

"Good boy." Daisy hung up.

He carried his coffee mug back to the kitchen to refill it and returned to his favourite chair by the window. Sipping the steaming strong brew, he stared out the tinted floor-to-ceiling window without registering the spectacular view over a slowly awakening Metro Vancouver. He pondered his next move. Once his initial anger had subsided it made room for a weird feeling of disillusionment. It was not like him to be easily discouraged and frustrated. To purchase the land and set up the subdivision process had cost him all the financial resources his company had accumulated so far, and then some. To cover the shortfall he had called in the good-will of every bank he had ever dealt with. He had worked like crazy day and night to get the requested surveys done, archaeological, geological and every other *logical* the Killer Bees could think of; had aerial photos converted into three dimensional maps; had sweated over the best dividing borderlines of the many lots, considering the lake shoreline, the hilltops, the valleys, and had submitted near perfect preliminary plans. From the beginning everything had seemed more difficult than with his previous projects, but he assumed that was how it felt when you placed a high bet. You lose some of your appetite, you lose your urge to chase after every sweet smelling doe in the nightly hunting grounds, you stay in the office till midnight, go home without hitting the pubs, and then you can't sleep, because you can't switch off those twirling fragments of pros and cons formulated in endless meetings and conferences throughout the day. Not very pleasant, this obsessive contemplation, but necessary, he had thought. No pain, no gain.

After all he had already gone through, had Jeanne d'Arc now raised the bar again? Did this new turn get him not closer but further away from reaching the prize? How could he overcome an obstacle which was so obviously out of his control? To change a governmental regulation was pretty much impossible and if he could not find ways around it, it would not only jeopardize his whole concept, it would ruin him. A chilling thought, that made him shiver. He reached for his coffee mug again. The air-con in his penthouse was set at twenty degrees, just as he liked it, and he should not have felt cold. Maybe he was coming down with the flu. Maybe he should take a break. Go out and divert himself from this permanent fretting over *the deal*.

152

He shivered again. The deal that should be rock solid by now was turning into quicksand because he could not provide legal access to his land. His own land! While he pondered this thought with deep-felt indignation, a possible solution to the problem dawned on him and made him forget that he was cold and depressed. Of course, you fool, he told himself, that's it! It's *my* land! I'm the owner!

This sudden inspiration lifted his spirits, making his heart muscles contract faster, pumping blood through his veins, which in turn lifted the fog in his brain even more. He grabbed the phone and dialled Daisy's number.

She answered right away. "So, what have you come up with?"

"It's so simple, I wonder why you didn't come up with the answer."

Nothing. She didn't take the bait.

"How long will it take you to find out who owns the land between the road and our border?"

"Already did."

Sometimes she was so annoying, he wanted to shake her. Just as well she had spent most of the last few weeks in their Kamloops office to co-ordinate the subdivision process from there, while he mostly worked out of Vancouver. "And?"

"It's a registered farm belonging to a guy called Jake S. Law. He owns that stretch in question plus about 500 acres east of our land."

That's what he liked about Daisy. She called it *our* land.

"I got his address and phone number. He seems to live there and farm the land himself."

"Well, call him and make him an offer. Not for all his land of course, only for as much as we need to build a road."

"I knew you would come up with this. But I think it is best if I drive up and present the offer to him in person."

"If that's how you want to do it, sure, why not. Some people don't understand things on the phone."

"Exactly. I'll have the plans with me and can sit down and show him what we want to do. He should like the idea, it upgrades his own land and makes it more valuable. I've already made arrangements. I need to get things organized in the office first and thought I'd leave Friday morning. If you can wait that long."

"Go tomorrow. That has top priority."

She made him suffer on purpose. "Can't."

"Why not?"

"Personal reasons."

"*Daisy!* You've got no personal life."

She didn't reply.

He gave up. "What if he's not there?"

"Then I wait for him. He's a farmer, he won't be far. How high should I go?"

What a question. "As low as possible and as high as necessary. Our cash-flow is rapidly drying up, but we need this land."

"Done."

"And Daisy, remember, he is just a simple farmer, he won't have a clue how valuable this land is to us. Take a sales contract with you, fill it out as soon as you agree on the price and have him sign the damn thing on the spot. Call me as soon as it is done. We've got to push this thing through now."

After she hung up he felt a lot better. Being forced into a corner was not his favourite position. For a short while he had felt exposed and powerless and had not liked it at all. It would all work out now. Daisy would fix it. That's what he paid her for. She would get the job done.

16

All day Martha waited for news, her mood alternating from panic attacks to calm defiance. One moment she beat herself up over caring for Anna without permission, the next she congratulated herself for having done what was needed. For showing compassion. For acting like a human being. But it wouldn't be interpreted like that by her husband because he was not human – he was a monster! A monster with the power to destroy her. Oh dear Lord, she would suffer horribly! But had the Lord anything to do with it? Would he interfere and help her and stand by her in this dreadful situation?

All day long, she agonized, reassured herself, went into despair and back again. Finally, by evening, word came down to the women's quarters that their husband wanted the whole family assembled in the community room. Martha was unsure of what was expected of her, so she followed the others to the main house, driven mainly by her desire to finish the nerve wracking wait, but also out of unexplainable, self-destructive curiosity.

Tell me my fate and let's get it over with!

Marion seemed to understand why she had shown up because she acknowledged her arrival with a simple nod of her head which at the same time indicated to Martha to get in there and kneel down like all the others.

The community room was packed with all the sister-wives, except Anna of course, and all the children. Some were very young, like Emma's two toddlers, but most could already kneel by themselves

155

next to their mothers. All the older boys, those who were approaching priesthood soon, stayed at the back, leaning against the wall, overseeing the family. Martha stole a glance at them. The tallest of them was the Bishop's eldest son. He held a straw hat in his hand, fidgeting with it, turning it around non-stop. Martha noticed again how good-looking he was, and then she quickly added *for a boy,* although his face was quite manly. She wondered again why he had so little of his father. Slim and tall with gentle features that were well defined, not at all like …, she quickly turned her head to her husband who had just entered the hall. He briefly whispered something to Marion who was kneeling in the first row, before he positioned himself in front of his family.

"Glory to the Lord!"

All heads turned to him and all eyes looked up to him. Only the older boys remained standing, listening to their father pronouncing the law.

Martha wanted to be brave and told herself there was no point in being scared, yet she did not dare to look at the big round man with the red face. She stared at the floor in front of her, trying not to remember what he had done to her. She made herself as small as possible, hoping to disappear behind the shoulders of the kneeling sister-wives in front of her. If only she could evaporate into thin air and float out the open window.

"*I am the Lord thy god…,*" as always he started reciting a part of the scripture from Section 132, well-known to all of them. "*… and will answer thee as touching this matter. Therefore, prepare thy heart to receive and obey the instructions which I am about to give unto you.*"

Now he would tell them about Anna's death and condemn her soul to everlasting damnation.

"One of our own has sinned, and by the power of the Holy Priesthood bestowed upon me I have to restore things to their right order. But the Lord has blessed me. He has sent me a sign, and I must abide by the law which was appointed for this blessing. Therefore the sinner will be spared…"

A murmur went through the family, followed by an expectant silence. Martha looked up again. Could it be? Did she hear right?

"When a healthy child is born, I rejoice because I have done my duty to the Lord. I have brought a waiting soul into this world to add to the Lord's army of soldiers. Today, my joy has been doubled and my reward will be even greater. Not one, but two baby boys have been born today! The Lord has blessed me and the sign is clear. He has twice replaced the little soul we lost six months ago and has thereby cleared the mark of sin from Anna. She will be forgiven and will enter our family again. Praise the Lord!"

Another louder murmur rose. This was unheard of! Martha wanted to yell out loud *yes, thank you Lord*, but did not dare. Tears filled her eyes.

Their husband then went into one of his long drawn-out eulogies, explaining the ways of the Lord, the meaning of the scripture concerning his decision and the unwavering faith he demanded from them in order to be allowed to enter eternity in his entourage.

After a while, Martha's knees hurt like hell. The others also started to fidget and shift their weight a little every so often. Martha had never questioned prayer sessions before. Her father had also enjoyed preaching for long hours and she had always pretended to listen to him while allowing her mind to drift off because his teachings were always terribly boring.

Today was different though; she listened intently. Every word her husband said sounded contrived. He preached how they must live according to the holy doctrine and covenants, knowing full well that those had been written by another man, not a God. Why did he make them believe that they came directly from the Lord? Did he really believe this himself? Martha stole a glance around the room. All the sister-wives had their heads turned toward their husband. Did they all accept his words as if they were the Lord's himself, or did at least some of them harbour doubts? It was impossible to tell what they were thinking.

Suddenly, she realized that the Bishop had not mentioned her at all. In her silent dispute of the validity of his sermon, she had practically forgotten the reason for her fear. Was she now judged more leniently? Was she also forgiven, simply because Anna had had twins? Because she had comforted Anna and had thereby assisted to bring two healthy children into this world - would that now count in her favour?

Finally, he seemed to have exhausted his need to preach. After he wrapped up the session with a final encouragement to "go and keep sweet", some women had to bend forward and put their weight on their hands to be able to get up at all. Martha's legs were stiff from the long kneeling too, but she straightened up quickly and hurried towards the door.

"Martha!"

Marion's low voice behind her made her freeze. She would not escape after all. Some of the young children, excited that the long session was over, pushed by her, elbowing their way out, while she stood where the voice had caught her. When all had left the hall, only she and Marion remained.

"Martha, I know what you have done. Our husband is pleased with the blessing of the Lord. You have fulfilled your duty in this miracle and I have told him of your obedience, do you understand me?"

Martha bit her lip. Did she understand? Her mind raced through the options Marion's cryptic question could imply. It had been Marion who had entrusted her to look after Anna. She must have noticed that the caretaking had been excessive to say the least. Did she now feel guilty for choosing someone who had so clearly overstepped the line? Was she guilty by association? She had not told her husband the whole truth. Had Marion gone as far as lying to her husband to cover herself? Marion wanted her to keep quiet – that was the only possible conclusion.

"Yes, Marion. I have only done my duty."

"Indeed, and you have excelled in it and shall be rewarded."

"Thank you."

"Anna needs a place of her own again to recover fully and to take care of the twins. We will bring her back to her old hut, but there is not enough space for all of you. Our husband has agreed that you may move up to the main house."

"Oh my God!" Martha could not hide her instant terror over this horrible prospect, but Marion must have misunderstood her, thinking she expressed excitement.

"Do not expect your husband to see you soon. Although you are still without child, he cannot forget the disgusting incident last time he was with you. There is little hope that he will ever forgive you enough to want you near him again…"

Martha felt the blood rush through her veins, pushed by shame and relief, all in one.

"You have been taught to count well."

This sudden change of topic surprised Martha. Of course she could count, what did that have to do with her and her husband? "It came easy."

"Do you read and write as well?"

Martha had always been quick to learn and her mothers had chided her often for being too bright for her own good. She nodded.

"Good. I need help with my office work and with schooling the children. From now on you will stay close to me and I will instruct you in your new duties. Just stay away from our husband."

17

All day Friday, an infuriating sense of vulnerability took hold of Richard. Every slowly passing hour increased his level of suspicion and dread. What if Daisy could not persuade his neighbour to sell him the needed land? What if he wanted more than he could afford? What if it took too long to settle? What if the moon would turn square and the sun would spit black dust on him?

By late afternoon he was in such a state, he checked the clock every ten minutes and could not concentrate on anything. Why didn't she call? It was a three hour drive from Kamloops, maybe a bit longer, which meant she would definitely have been at the neighbour's farm before two. Discussions, documentation, whatever, up to three, maybe even four, then back south until she got cell reception again, about one hour, so she should have been able to call him well before five. Not after! It was now quarter to six. What on earth was she doing? Was it a bad or a good sign if the negotiations took so long?

He decided to go to the lobby of the Vancouver Hotel, have a drink, read the latest Newsweek and distract himself by watching the pretty girls flaunt themselves in their flimsy summer outfits. Just as he walked out of the office door, the phone rang.

"About bloody time," he complained while rushing back to his office. He needed the security of his desk, jotting down notes while listening. Never being one to multi-task, talking, thinking and walking at the same time.

Daisy's voice was as clear and sharp as an ice crystal on a winter's window. "Richard, something very strange has happened."

He did not give in so easily. "What took you so long?"

"It was nearly eleven before I got out of the office and I then stopped at the Heli Resort in Blue River for a bite to eat before I drove on. I do have to eat, you know."

"Sorry. Go on."

"From there it's another hour drive."

"I know, I know. Never mind. Did you meet with this Jake guy?"

She sounded surprised, puzzled, slightly shocked. "I called him this morning and left a message on his answering machine that I would drop by his place this afternoon, thinking I'll have no problem finding it. According to the surveyors' map there is only one road and the turn off after our easement had to be the driveway to his house."

"Right."

"You are not going to believe what happened next. I drove along the road - by the way, it's pretty scenery there, lots of poplars and willow bushes along the roadside - until I came to a white wooden gate. It was open, but a truck blocked my way. I opened my window, stuck out my head and wanted to ask the driver to let me pass, when two guys popped up behind the driver's compartment. They had guns! They pointed them at me! They threatened me! I thought this must be a huge mistake, a misunderstanding, and yelled something friendly at them, I can't remember what I said, something like 'sorry, but I'm here to meet Mister Law' or so, but they didn't budge. Gesturing with the barrels of their shotguns for me to move, to back out. One of them, a really young guy, yelled a warning and started counting, five – four – three - so I reversed and got the hell out of there like a flash. Seriously Richard, I was still shaking when I was half way back to Blue River."

He was stunned himself and muttered something like 'that's unbelievable'.

"You better believe it. Those bastards looked like they meant business, so I drove straight to the police station in Blue River to report it. But now the next incredible thing happened. The RCMP officer on duty said I should not worry about it. It is a known fact that nobody is allowed on this property without prior consent of the owner. They've had complaints before, but nothing serious has ever happened and bar somebody getting shot at, and not only that, the shot would have to at least maim if not kill somebody, there is nothing they can do about it."

Because Richard was lost for words, he did a quick time calculation, as if this would be important. Daisy could not be back in Kamloops yet.

"Where are you now?"

"I'm still in Blue River. Did you think I give up so easily? I've checked myself into the Heli Resort."

Lucky it was August. If this had been the winter season she would not have been able to get a room. The Blue River Heli Resort was world famous for providing Heli-skiing trips into the nearby Rockies. The fact that it was only one hour's drive to his development was supposed to make his project even more attractive to potential buyers.

Sure, there was no point in her driving all the way back to Kamloops and then up again if she planned to see the guy tomorrow. "So, now what? Have you called him and told him to whistle back his watch dogs?"

"Well, guess what, I managed to get hold of him after my little chat with the RCMP and introduced myself as one of his new neighbours who wanted to make a social call on him. He seemed very surprised to hear that I was so rudely turned away, the creepy bastard, as if he wouldn't have known, and said there is no need for me to visit him. He does not usually entertain female visitors. I stayed polite and proceeded to tell him that I am your partner. "

"Excellent."

"And then he said, he would see *you* tomorrow at ten!"

Involuntarily Richard's hand picked up a pen and he started to draw spirals on the empty sheet of paper in front of him. Tight, narrow spirals. "Don't be ridiculous. There is no need for me to drive all the way up there."

"You are not driving. I booked you on the first flight to Kamloops tomorrow morning. A helicopter from the resort here will pick you up once you have landed there. No need to hire a car and drive all the way up as I have mine here and we can drive back together."

His spiral had reached the point of no return and he started a new one. "Please, Daisy, you know how much work I have here. Can't you handle this?"

"The guys had guns!"

"I know. But nothing ever happened. The police officer said so himself."

"Jake S. Law only wants to talk to you."

"You can handle him. You can be a very convincing woman if you want to be."

Daisy seemed to smile, because her voice shifted from cool and professional to slightly amused and professional. "That may be so. But I have done a little research since I arrived at the Resort and the waiter who brought me my, I'm sorry to say, outrageously expensive room service snack, filled me in on the local gossip. I now know why Jake refuses to see me. Trust me, if you want to get that land to build your road and save your ass you better come up here."

What reason could anybody have not to deal with gorgeous, intelligent, reasonable Daisy, he was wondering, and Daisy must have read his mind.

"The locals all know that Jake never does business deals with women."

"Is he gay?"

"Quite the opposite. He is the leader of a polygamous sect and apparently he entertains a whole harem of demure women on that property, who think of him as Holy Law. The locals know him as The Bishop."

"Get out of here!"

"Seriously. Our neighbours are a bunch of religious freaks who believe in male supremacy and some kind of end game when the earth will be destroyed and only their followers will inherit heaven in all its glory. It's a bit like Bountiful."

"Like what?"

"Bountiful, you know. Down south, on the border to America. Don't tell me you never heard of what's going on there…"

His mind was racing. Religious zealots in the wilderness? It could be worse. Maybe it was a stroke of luck. How much would some *hinterwäldler* know about the value of his land! And surely they would be short of cash. Fanatics living on the fringe of society always needed money.

Daisy realized that his attention had drifted and that he was not listening to her any more. "I will fill you in on that sordid story once you get here."

Sure. He did not need to know any more now. He was already planning his strategy to outsmart the Jesus freak. This would be fun.

18

When the alarm went off he must have been in a deep REM phase. Probably an early one as he had not gone to bed until well after midnight. His whole body ached from lack of sleep and begged for a few more minutes of rest. Then his memory kicked in again and reminded him that he had to catch the early bird to Kamloops. It was already five o'clock and the paranoid security measures airports enforced nowadays added at least half an hour even to city hopper flights.

Driving into the early August dawn, he reached Vancouver airport and got through the checks just in time to grab a coffee and a donut form the Tim Hortons' shop that mercifully was just opening up.

On the one hour flight he fell asleep again as soon as he had finished his breakfast substitute. Five hours sleep just wasn't enough for him. The steward had to wake him after landing. He stumbled off the plane and on to the waiting helicopter from the Blue River Resort. Forty minutes later they landed on their Helipad and he was taken to the resort's impressive lobby. A massive post and beam construction of huge Douglas fir logs supported the high vaulted ceiling, emphasizing the solidity and richness of the resort's reputation. Unquestionable wealth and old world charm, that's what the patrons expected when they frequented this luxury hide-away.

Daisy was sitting in a deep, comfortable easy chair, reading glasses low on her straight, prominent nose, studying a newspaper. Her inbuilt radar must have been switched on, as she looked up as soon as he entered. Her coiffure was in uncharacteristic disarray, with unruly strands standing out from her crop of short brown hair. Those tiny rebellious feathers surprised him even more than the slightly smudged eyeliner around her hazel eyes. Daisy was not a classic beauty, for this he considered her a touch too tall. She also was too thin, specially where it counted when you were a woman, and too aloof to let inner beauty shine through. But whatever her faults might be, she usually was a picture of perfection.

He sat down on the sofa opposite her and moaned. "I'm tired and I'm hungry. But I'm not complaining, because we will nail this deal and it will cost this Jake S. Law dearly to deprive me of my sleep."

"Good morning to you too," she said and was not smiling at all.

"Yeah, yeah, good morning. You look terrible. What's the matter with you? You had a good night's sleep and you've probably had a delicious breakfast already."

Daisy stood up briskly and informed him that she had not eaten yet and that there was still time for a quick meal before they had to be on their way. They went to the resort dining room and he loaded up on the opulent buffet. Daisy came back with some fruit and a small Danish on her plate.

"Not hungry?" he enquired.

While he was enjoying his meal, she filled him in on some details. No, she was not hungry at all, she had been up half the night, doing her homework as a number of reports had to be filed today, and then she had done some research on this Jake guy. She was pissed no end about what she had found out and told Richard she could not wait to accompany him to the meeting. Richard had until now assumed that he would go to the meeting by himself and asked her if the guy would not object to her coming along. After all, on the phone he had refused to deal with a woman.

Daisy instantly got angry like he had never seen her before. She actually raised her voice. "I don't give a shit what he wants. He didn't say you have to come alone, and I will bloody well not stay behind. You need a witness, and he'll just have to accept that it's me!"

"Calm down." Richard tried to appease her without much luck. The deep furrows on her forehead did not smooth out and her chin stuck out resolutely.

"I'm calm."

"No, you're not. But never mind. Come along and hold my hand if you must. I just don't understand what's eating you."

"You will in a minute when I fill you in on what I discovered last night. Let's get a move on, it's already eight thirty."

Richard drove, of course. The breakfast had been all he needed to energize himself again, and suddenly he could not wait to get the negotiations with his neighbour started and finished. They drove in silence a short distance north along Highway Five until they reached the turn off to the tiny village of Deep Cove, which would eventually bring them to his and Jake's neighbouring properties.

After they had left the busy highway with its paved surface, he had to reduce his speed drastically to navigate the worst maintained gravel road in the whole Province of British Columbia. As soon as they had turned a few more corners, they both felt transported into another world. He knew from previous visits to his land that they most likely would not meet a single vehicle on their hour long drive.

He asked Daisy what she thought of the land, now that she had seen at least some of the surrounding area yesterday.

"Nice," she said, non-committal.

He smiled and let the landscape speak for him. Countless specks of red 'Indian Paintbrush' brightened the meadows on both sides of the road. Uncontrolled vegetation crept over the curbs of the dusty road, wanting to take possession of it. In some places high willow bushes bent their heavy branches so far into the middle of the road that they scratched the roof of Daisy's car. She pretended not to notice.

To interrupt her brooding mood he asked her to repeat exactly what she had told Jake on the phone. She confirmed it was next to nothing, which would make his game of persuasion a lot easier than if the guy already knew the full scope of his subdivision plan. Daisy snickered that the creep had not even given her a chance to explain what it was all about.

"Is that what's eating you?" he asked.

"No, of course not."

"Then what is it?"

With an impassionate voice she tried to explain to him what had upset her so much. After the phone call, she had spent hours on the internet and had discovered disturbing facts about their neighbour. Jake S. Law was not just a harmless recluse protecting his property against intruders by pointing a gun at them, as the police officer had suggested. No, this forty-five-year old man had been born into a powerful American Fundamentalist Mormon family who steadfastly refused to give up their right – given by God through his mouthpiece Joseph Smith - to polygamy. In 1890, Wilford Woodruff, the president of the Mormon Church, had been forced by the American govern- ment to issue a manifesto suspending the "earthly practise of plural marriage", in short "the Principle", and the majority of the Church members had followed his directive, but it had also effectively started a thriving underground cult of polygamous communities. A number of families refused outright to bend to the ungodly request for mon- ogamy and moved over the borders. Some went north, into Canada, some south into Mexico. Over several generations those communities grew in size by exchanging young girls from families who followed the doctrine to live the Principle in secret. A flourishing bride trade developed between the countries to keep the inbreeding to a min- imum. From an early age, Jake had been groomed to become a leader of one of those secret sects, but something must have happened and he had fallen from grace. About ten years ago he was exiled into the wil- derness of Canada to form a new compound; multiple wives and all.

At that point Richard corrected Daisy. All that was very well, but it was past history, and he couldn't imagine their neighbour had any- thing to do with it. No matter what she may have googled.

She impatiently asked him to shut up and listen. The Canadian part of the Church, she carried on to explain, had owned a 500 acre large property in the North – said parcel next to his development property - which apparently nobody had wanted to farm. Ten years ago, ownership changed over to Jake and his wife, most likely against a loan repayable to the Church, because that's how it was done for all their compounds. Jake must have been pretty angry about the double punishment. Being sent into the wilderness and having to pay for it.

"Why?" Richard dared to interrupt Daisy again. "This is a scenic part of the country, one of the most beautiful areas of the whole Province, and no hardship to be exiled to. Granted, the farms further south produce a better yield and one would have to work pretty hard in this part of the country to make a living off the land, but it's not like being sent to Siberia. And to spend your time with a few pretty girls tending to your every whim can't be so tough either."

She shot him a glance that would have scared a lesser man to death. "Look at it from his perspective. By then he was already over thirty years old. He was demoted from being the groomed prince of his father's kingdom to an exiled pauper in the country, far away from the movers and shakers. That must have deeply depressed him. And you'd better keep comments like your pretty-girl remarks to yourself. Your male ignorance naturally assumes Jake must have been delighted to have a happy little harem joyously catering to his sexual fancies, but please remember, his wives are his property anyway, no matter where he is. Do you really think *that* mattered to him. That *this* is what he wants?"

"Well," he grinned, "I wouldn't mind. And neither would every other normal man who is honest enough to admit it."

"Don't you get it? Those women are like slaves!"

"Oh please! Don't give me that! This is Canada. They can leave if they don't like it."

Daisy rolled her eyes and sighed heavily in a deliberate attempt to ridicule him. "Sure. That's what everybody likes to believe. We live in an educated western society. Slavery and suppression of women do not happen here. They happen in Third World countries far away, hidden behind Burkhas and sanctioned by Sharia laws. It could never happen here!"

"Quite right! Talking about laws, *our* law happens to respect women's rights and gives them the means to fend for themselves. Don't give me that crap about slavery in the twenty-first century in British Columbia. What a load of nonsense."

His defence of the Canadian judicial system came out more forcefully than he had planned, so he took it down a notch. "Look, Daisy, I can accept that you resent being on our way to a Mormon splinter group you suspect of practising polygamy, and this is quite a mind bender for me too, but don't make me believe that their members, male or female, do not participate in this game willingly. Good on them! I wouldn't even call it perverted, it's just some form of sexual deviation from the norm. Maybe the women like it that way."

"Sure," she hissed. "They just love being raped and ..."

"Please, stop it! I am not trying to offend your feminist feelings, but I can't for the life of me figure out why you get so worked up about it. It's a religious sect, for heaven's sake, you said so yourself, that's all there is to it. Who cares? Who is to argue with religion? I sure won't, and that's not why we are driving up here. We want to get Jake to be a good boy and sign a sales agreement and be done with it, remember? At least that's all I want to get out of this trip."

Silence.

"Right?"

He glanced sideways and saw her nodding. Sulking and nodding.

"Fine. We've got our priorities right then. Once he has signed our sales agreement, you can slap him in the face if you like."

She tried not to smile.

"Honestly. Real hard! Slap the sonofabitch around in the name of all that is holy to you. Or better still..." now he was grinning with delight over a new vision tickling his imagination, but he was holding back until she got curious.

"What?"

"Better still, we kidnap our special friend Jeanne d'Arc and marry her off to him."

Finally Daisy saw the comical side of it and relaxed. "As crazy as this fantasy sounds, I must admire your criminally insane disposition.

The picture it conjures has merits, even if its social and humanitarian implications are totally unacceptable."

Thank God, Daisy was back to normal. Her sense of humour was a bit off the normal mark. She hardly ever reacted spontaneously, ignoring most of his many twisted and sometimes crude jokes. To acknowledge, albeit with a stilted comment, that indeed she considered his matrimonial punishment for one of the Killer Bees funny, was quite an achievement, for her and for him. His dear, unapproachable ice-princess Daisy.

There was a pickup truck waiting for them at the gate, but this time nobody was pointing a gun. The driver got out, walked over to the driver's side of the car and asked Richard politely to follow him. He was no more than eighteen and dressed as if he had jumped straight out of one of those old Norman Rockwell paintings, the ones depicting carefree, sweet country life. Distressed jeans-overalls with paint smears and rips that would cost a small fortune in an L.A. boutique, chequered shirt with rolled up sleeves, a straw hat with a leather rim band and a natural smile on his face that would instantly light up any grey city day.

The young man closed the gate behind them, got back into his pickup, turned and started moving up the driveway.

They followed him for at least five minutes along a straight lane until they came to a cluster of small, fairly run-down houses. Old dwellings constructed of rough wooden planks that had weathered over time, black in parts, showing open cracks between the horizontal beams. Richard counted at least ten huts, each one the same size and shape. Two small children, poorly dressed, were playing a finger game and were so engaged in their own little world, they did not hear the two cars approaching. Suddenly, a woman ran out of one of the houses and shoo-ed the kids inside. She wore heavy, clumsy looking boots and nearly tripped over her long skirt. When she balanced herself again, she threw a startled look in their direction. Realizing that they had seen her and unsure if she should react to their presence, she decided against it and disappeared into the house again as if she was scared of them. Other than her and the two kids, Richard and Daisy did not see anybody. The courtyard they had to cross was devoid of all human life. Darkness and decay had settled on it long ago, but some chickens picked on the ground, a dog was sitting in front of a door and a pig walked across the yard, carefully avoiding their cars.

The pickup drove on and Richard followed him until the mini-village had disappeared from his rear view mirror. It stopped next to a much larger house, which was obviously Jake's palace. Not that it was in any way prestigious. Quite the opposite. It was a fairly simple two-storey log home with a metal roof and a covered porch along the front, but compared to the huts they had passed, it was indeed palatial. It was quite obviously the official residence of the sect leader.

They all got out of their vehicles. The young driver walked up to the house and knocked on the door, with Daisy and Richard standing behind him. A big guy opened the door, filling out most of the space inside the frame. He was not grossly fat, but very fleshy, like a man who tends to obesity but has not yet lost all his muscle mass to the aging process. Big, bulky arms and folds on his neck like a grown up Shar-pei dog. He shoved his large stomach like a prized possession in front of him. This unnaturally blown up balloon stretched his shirt open between each button, drawing a chain of white underwear ovals along its middle, from the neck down until it went underground, to a secret place where his poor penis, which didn't see much daylight, as Richard suspected, was hiding. Richard also noticed a curious mixture of pride and ignominy in Jake's false welcoming smile. Quite understandable, if one considered that he must feel ashamed to meet sophisticated people like himself and Daisy under such depressing circumstances, yet at the same time feeling clerically and spiritually superior to them. Richard had him figured out in an instant. This man was a loser if he ever saw one. He should be no problem at all.

They introduced themselves. Jake shook hands with Richard and then with Daisy, making a polite remark about how lucky he was to be visited by such a pretty lady. Daisy swallowed hard and made a real effort to return his courtesy by nodding gracefully in his direction without looking him in the eyes.

"Please, come in," he invited and they entered a room that was much brighter than Richard had expected. Yellow stained logs and large south facing windows dispersed the eerie uneasiness of doom and gloom that had taken hold of him since they had passed through the clutter of huts. The interior of the house smelled of and looked like basic comfort: pine scented cleaning oils, chocolate chip cookies, hand embroidered cushions, ruffled curtains and a heavy duty wood stove with neatly arranged logs in a basket next to it. Wood in summer? Well, maybe the evenings got cold here, Richard thought, after all, the altitude was at least 1200 meters.

Their host made a gracious gesture that looked uncoordinated and wrong. "Please, have a seat."

Guys with such enormous body mass should not attempt flowing arm movements, Richard thought, while he took his appointed place at one end of the longest wooden table he had ever seen.

"Can I get you something to drink?"

Daisy sat down next to him and declined the same instant Richard said yes, thank you.

"Is coffee alright? I have some freshly brewed."

Richard said yes again. Jake walked out of the room, into the adjacent kitchen, and Richard looked at Daisy, mouthing a silent *please, try!* She pulled a face and they waited in unison like school children for the teacher to return.

Jake came back, balancing a large tray. He carefully placed it on the table and was starting to arrange the empty cups and saucers when Daisy stood up and, with her best imitation of a demure *hausfrau*, politely asked him if he would mind if she took over. Not a flicker in her eyes betrayed her true conviction, she was all female servitude.

He went for it, liked it. Patted her hand. Yes, of course she could. Her hand did not twitch.

While she was pouring coffee and moving the sugar bowl, the milk jug and a plate of cookies into his reach, Jake was chatting up Richard. Did they have a pleasant drive, how he liked this part of the country, if he came here often, were they married, did he think the weather would turn – a strange barrage of questions, basically just small talk to make his guests feel more at ease.

The drive had been good. Yes, he liked it a lot in this part of the Province, he planned to move up here one day to retire. Until then, his office in Vancouver kept him busy. No, they were not married yet. Well, he hoped the weather wouldn't turn soon, it was one of those dry summers. Non-committal talk, good enough to throw Jake off track and eventually direct him his way.

Country life holds such a charm, he mused, that's why he had bought the property next door, and was he ever happy to finally meet his new neighbour.

Jake smiled and asked Daisy to try one of the cookies. His wife had baked them this morning. Of the chocolate chip variety, as Richard had assumed from the smell that lingered in the house.

Daisy took one, nibbled on it and muttered a compliment. Jake was beaming in her direction and Richard started the conversation again to distract his attention away from her because he suddenly feared that Daisy would lose her cool and ask him which one of his wives was so good at baking.

"So, Jake," he started, "I am sure you are wondering why we came to see you today."

Jake did not stop looking at Daisy. "Actually, I am wondering what your relationship is with this lovely lady, who mentioned on the phone she is your partner, if you two are not married."

Scheisse. Richard already knew that Jake's twisted morals forbade him to discuss a business deal with a woman. Would he judge him on the same grounds now? Would he object if he clarified that Daisy was his assistant? Better be safe. "Daisy is my fiancée", he said quickly, looking at her. She blinked ever so slightly while she bit a large chunk out of her cookie.

"Well, that's good to hear. Unmarried people should not travel together if they are not promised to each other. It happens all too often, don't you think? There is so much wrong conduct with the young ones nowadays, it is encouraging to hear that there are people out there aspiring to do what is right and healthy."

"Hmm, right."

"I don't get out to town as often as I used to, too much work you know, but I must say, I don't miss it. All that crime and noise and filth. Drugs on every street corner. Every billboard with half naked women and the ones on the street not much better. How could you let a young girl walk in a city without corrupting her for life. Our daughters are not even safe in bright daylight, and nobody does anything about it. The politicians look the other way. What am I saying, not only the politicians, it's the teachers, the priests, the lot of them, failing their duties to protect society from those immoral seductions on display everywhere."

Before he could ramble on, Richard agreed fiercely. "Indeed. Indeed. Daisy and I, we always say it's a shame how some people have their priorities wrong. As far as we are concerned, our future together is very important to us and we are working to make it happen soon." Was this enough? Should he lay it on even heavier? A fiendish imp inside him edged him on to explore the depth of Jake's antiquated conventions, to define the borders of his narrow-mindedness. "We would be married already, but I don't feel certain that I can support a family yet."

"That is important."

"And until such time, we just practise patience."

Jake smiled warmly. "Patience and renunciation, I always say, paves the road to heaven."

Jesus, this guy was not real. Richard returned his smile a bit helpless, lost for words.

Jake did not stare at Daisy any longer and turned his full attention to Richard. "But as much as I enjoy our discussion of spiritual principles, I am sure that this is not what you came here for."

"Right."

Suddenly his round, jovial facial expression changed from a happy bear to a sly fox. "So, my dear friend Richard, what is it that you want from me?"

In the next twenty minutes Jake and Richard looked at the map of their neighbouring land parcels and Richard slowly and carefully explained to him that he wanted to purchase just a small strip of land so he could build a road leading to his property. No more than 3 or 4 acres, and preferably where the existing easement was. Daisy sat stoically next to them, pretending to be disinterested.

Jake wondered aloud why the arrangement which had served the purpose of access since long before his time, was suddenly not good enough for Richard, who in turn elaborated and waffled on about how he was just one of those guys who needed to have everything in order. After all, it would not matter to Jake one way or another and he could make some unexpected money.

"How much would you pay me for it," Jake finally took the bait.

"Well, it is not really worth much," Richard opened the negotiations.

Jake belly-laughed out loud. "To you it is."

Richard joined his laughter good naturedly and felt he had the deal in his pocket. When people laugh together, a hand shake is not far off. "I thought of five hundred dollars per acre," he said, leaving room to negotiate.

More laughter. An attempt at humour with a fake Spanish accent. "No waaay José."

"Well, what's your idea?"

Jake shook his head, rubbed his stomach, burped quietly, did all the things one does when pretending to consider. Richard was sure he already had a figure in his head, maybe closer to a thousand.

"You know what, Richard, my friend, I guess I never really thought about the value of my land. It's all a bit rushed, and I need time to think and talk it over with my wife. She is an owner too."

Then he stood up heavily, still smiling and Richard's expression must have betrayed his total surprise at this turn of events, because Jake patted him on the shoulder and said: "Don't worry, I'm sure we can come to an agreement. Why don't you and your pretty fiancée go home now and we talk again next time you come visiting."

Richard had to swallow hard to keep himself from bursting into some of his favourite German swearword creations. This bastard! Come back next time? The creep had no idea how urgent this was for him. How incredibly important. Richard collected himself and stood up as well. "Good idea. We would not want you to feel pressured in any way. I suggest…"

Looking over his shoulder in the direction of the window something caught Jake's attention and he interrupted his opponent in mid sentence. "But before you go, I want you to meet my wife. I can see her coming."

Daisy and Richard turned their heads and saw a female figure approaching. Jake went to the door, opened it and called out to his wife. Seconds later she came into the room. Daisy was standing behind Richard and her silent evaluation of the woman burned holes into his back. The woman wore a floor length dress, her hair was tied back and her face looked so haggard, it was impossible to guess her age. She greeted them with a lifeless grimace that was nothing but the mechanical movement of her hollow cheeks, pulling the corners of her mouth upward, mimicking a smile.

"Marion, come, say hello to our guests before they leave."

She stepped towards them. "I am sorry I was not back earlier," she said, not explaining the reason for her absence.

They all walked outside, Jake with his arm over Marion' s shoulder. The guy has a thing about shoulders, Richard thought, which is not surprising considering his bulk. Patronising gestures probably made him feel good.

It was time for one last try. "Actually we are staying in Blue River tonight, and I don't know when we will be back next. How about we drop by again tomorrow? That would give you time to think things over."

"Hmm. Maybe. Yes, maybe."

They walked to the car together and Richard's whole body was aching to scream obscenities at him. *Maybe*, you asshole, you verdammtes Arschloch! *Maybe* I kick your brains all the way down into your fat ass!

"If I can spare some time tomorrow, you can come up here again and we will talk some more. Give me a call tonight after dinner, then we'll see."

"Great. Thanks. Bye."

Daisy must have known how shaken he was and automatically moved behind the steering wheel. They drove off, not saying a word, while Marion and Jake, standing side by side at the entrance of their house, waved after them until they disappeared from sight.

They drove through the depressing assembly of deserted looking huts again, down the driveway, through the open gate, until they finally reached the road. They could see how the guard, waiting for them to pass, closed the wooden gate behind them.

It was a big relief to be back on the gravel road. In a sense it was as if a pressing weight had been lifted off him. Daisy seemed to feel the same way. He could hear her breathing in and out as if her lungs were desperate for fresh air. He hit the dashboard with his open palm. "Jesus Christ, what was all that about? What the hell happened just now?"

Surprisingly she turned and snapped at him. At *him*! "Well, what do *you* think just happened."

"How should I know. I normally don't deal with idiots."

"Neither do I. But you underestimate him. He's no idiot."

"Oh come on, he doesn't have a clue. Didn't you hear him going on about the value of abstinence and the fading moral values of the young?"

"Of course. I heard a lot I did not like. And I saw a lot I did not like."

"Like what?"

"Like him playing you, stringing you along as if you were a beginner."

19

It was only noon and Richard briefly contemplated driving down to his Kamloops office, but decided against it. Everything concerning this project had come to a grinding halt until he could persuade Jake to sell him the few acres in question. What could he - and Daisy - possibly do in the office that was productive and constructive? Absolutely nothing.

They just had to meet with this obnoxious bastard again and make him sign those damn papers. Hoping to hear from him but fearing that he was simply stringing them along, didn't really lower their stress level. The empty afternoon loomed ahead of them like an unconquerable mountain. Daisy suggested having lunch at the Blue River Resort and then going for a walk along the Resort's private lakeshore that led to the banks of the Thompson River. They should hold back booking a room until they were sure that Jake agreed to see them tomorrow.

As both of them had little appetite they opted for a simple soup and salad combination before they started their walk. Up to this moment Richard had believed he knew his assistant quite well although he had never met with Daisy outside of their office environment. She surprised him with her energetic stride; he had not expected her to be so athletic. After a while, they fell into a comfortable pace and marched on, probably thinking along the same lines. *What will we do if Jake doesn't give in to our request?*

"He has to," Daisy started out of the blue. "It's only a matter of money."

"Everything has a price," he agreed.

"Well, actually not everything. But in this case it's correct. He is out to maximize his gain."

Her comment irritated him. "Of course everything can be bought."

"No, it can't!"

"Like for example?"

"You could not pay me enough to trade places with that poor exhausted woman he said is his wife."

"That is not a proper example."

"Why not?" she asked

"Because I didn't mean to put a price tag on human beings. Some people don't have a venal disposition. Like you! *You* can't be bought, we all know that, so in effect I can't trade you. I was talking about things, meaning objects, like cars, jewellery, paintings, things with material value. Or land."

"Oh, that! Sorry I misunderstood. Okay, we leave human resources out of it. Some people can't be bought, I agree on this. But there is a grey area in between the human and the material factor where it is very difficult to come to a financial agreement."

He really could not imagine what she meant.

After a while of contemplation, she continued. "For example, somebody owns an object that represents a certain spiritual or emotional value. Take the bracelet of a woman given to her by her beloved husband."

"He can buy her another one."

"He is deceased."

"Trust me, there would be a price for it. Maybe exorbitant, but nevertheless, if the offer is high enough to guarantee her a life style she could never otherwise afford, she would eventually part with the silly trinket."

"She is already eighty years old!"

"Oh Daisy, leave me alone! You win."

Daisy stopped walking and looked at him. "Good. Because I want you to realize that we may have a difficult nut to crack. Jake may only hold out for more money, but he may have other reasons for rejecting our offer. Like that old woman, he may not be interested in changing his life style. Money may not mean anything to him. We need to be prepared." She started to walk again. "Although I can't for the life of me imagine what objections he could have against us buying this land from him."

He remembered Jake's expression when enquiring about the price he was willing to pay. Pure, barely concealed greed! "I'm confident that he is open to another offer as long as he doesn't know our plans. That would piss him off no end. A high class country development right next to his property, bringing the evil temptations of modern life right to his doorstep? Wow, he would go berserk if he knew that, but he doesn't, so why should he refuse? I may just have to shell out more than I was hoping for."

Daisy nodded, but her mouth was shaped like the fat lips of a carp while she muttered hmm-hmm-hmm.

"Come on, make me feel good," Richard pleaded. "Tell me it will work."

At four o'clock they were back in the lobby, having coffee. Richard's legs were heavy from walking over three hours at a good pace. Even Daisy admitted that her feet hurt, but she said it was only because she did not wear the right shoes.

To kill time, he finally got around to asking her about Bountiful.

"What about it?" she said.

"You have mentioned it twice already and said you'd tell me about it when there is time. We've got plenty of that just now."

"What's the point? You're not going to believe me anyway."

He promised her he would, and she launched right away into a story that sounded so absurd that he forgot his promise on the spot. He did not believe a word she was saying. In fact, he started to doubt her judgement altogether, wondering why he had never detected the slightest trace of irrationality in her. What was suddenly wrong with her? Daisy liked some wine with her meals, but that did not make her a heavy drinker. Doing drugs was also out of the question. Had she started to take medication that did not agree with her? Was she distressed, mentally unbalanced or temporarily deranged over a personal predicament he was not aware of? She could not seriously expect him to swallow her absolutely ludicrous description of a village with the fantasy name *Bountiful*, right at the Canadian border to America, that could not be found on any map for British Columbia – at least not under this name - but that had existed since the mid forties. Run by an excommunicated Bishop of the Mormon Church called Winston Blackmore, it was, according to Daisy's amazing tale, a bastion of polygamy, where a bunch of fundamentalist Mormons exchanged under-age child brides with their equally inclined counterparts south of the Canadian border. All this not only tolerated but in part financed by the liberal laws of a civilised western society in the name of religious freedom. *Really*, he was snickering! Government sanctioned pedophilia? Male and female children apparently raised in total ignorance until they were old enough to work for the Church Elders. Slaves in an oppressive system, bred for the purpose of making their superiors rich and comfortable. Young boys pressed into forced labour as soon as they were able to walk, carry and lift. Young girls doing household chores until they menstruated the first time and could be allocated to a fine standing member of the Church as sex objects and breeding machines. Sick stuff like that happens in the world, sure, but not in Canada! It was just too far fetched to believe! Daisy was making it up to get back at his laissez-faire attitude toward his freaky neighbour Jake. She was just testing his macho level of tolerance. Very well, two could play this game.

"Stories like that go around the internet all the time, but that doesn't mean they are true. I can't believe you fall for such cheap sensationalism. If this Bountiful really existed, the authorities would have clamped down on it like a flesh eating plant on a passing fly."

"It's real name is Lister and it is close to Creston, in the south-eastern corner in the Kootenays, at a dead end road. If you want to go there somebody stops you at gunpoint, forcing you to turn back, just like it happened to me up here yesterday. And the authorities, meaning our Provincial Government, are well aware of some of the criminal activities going on there, like trafficking young girls between America and

Canada. It has tried to interfere several times, but every single Attorney General has failed to prosecute anybody involved in those cases."

"And why would that be?" he asked her, smirking like a lawyer who had ripped a hole in the opponent's defence. "If justice itself failed that miserably, our whole country would be in a sorry state. The law does not allow polygamy in Canada. No, no, no – it's all crap, all those stories about fundamentalist sects in Canada, America and Mexico you mentioned yesterday, that's all bullshit. Including that Bountiful rubbish! It's all invented by some sick minds."

Daisy was not impressed by his display of outrage. She carried on without reminding him of his promise to believe her. "Bigamy can easily be defined and is clearly against the law, but polygamy operates in a legal grey zone. How do you prove it? The law cannot barge into Bountiful and arrest the guys because they have multiple wives. Don't even ask why not. Every male in charge there is legally married only to one, his first wife, all the others are bound to him by a religious ceremony."

"There must be a law against that."

"Oh there is! But there is also a law *for* it! It's called the constitutional right to follow one's religious beliefs. As long as there is no proof of coercion or restraint, what is wrong with consenting adults sharing their lives together? Do you plan to arrest every single adult who chooses to live in a commune? What's wrong with several women or men living together under one roof?"

Nothing at all, he had to agree, but what about the young girls. If the stories were true, surely they would not pick such a life style willingly.

"No, I don't think so. But you have to find one first, willing to give evidence against their tormentor. So far, no luck."

"See!"

"Those girls have been brainwashed since birth. They are insecure, uneducated and scared. They wouldn't know how to escape and where to turn to if they did succeed."

This conversation was going nowhere. For a while it had helped to distract him, but now Richard was losing interest and started to be fidgety again. The problems of this world were not really his concern, after all, he had his own quite considerable difficulties to solve, and told Daisy so.

She took it good naturedly. "At least it is already five o'clock and I think you can call him now."

Was five not a bit too early? Would Jake sense and take advantage of his display of urgency? They contemplated the time aspect for another half hour, then he gave in and dialled Jake's number.

He answered right away, as if he had been waiting by the phone, sounding exceptionally cheerful. Sure he would see him tomorrow. Ten o'clock would be fine, if that suited Richard. And one more thing - he thought it was best to come alone. To leave the fiancée at home. No need to bring her along when grown men meet to discuss important matters, Jake said.

Dinner was quite a different affair from the hurried breakfast they had had that morning. It was served in the same large Resort dining room, but now the tables were decked with starched pink tablecloths and decorated with silver candle sticks and fresh flower arrangements. Soft background music floated from hidden speakers, absorbing the already muffled steps of the well trained waiters. All sliding doors to the patio were open but protected with mosquito screens to let the warm August air in without subjecting the dinner guests to the armada of little bugs that rose from the sprinkled lawns outside every evening.

Daisy had suggested going to one of the less expensive restaurants in town, but Richard had insisted on splurging this evening. He felt like celebrating already. Jake had caved in, he could feel it. The greedy bastard was eager to get his grubby fingers on his money. In hindsight Richard suspected Jake had been willing to entertain his offer this morning but had not been able to show his willingness because of Daisy's presence. When he mentioned this to Daisy, she reacted rather smugly, telling him it only proved her point what a macho pig this guy really was. Richard dropped the subject then as he did not want to risk a major argument with her about seeing Jake on his own.

They chose steak and salad for dinner, and he ordered a bottle of red wine he thought was of mediocre quality and superior price until he tasted it. Liquid velvet, worth every penny. It made him more mellow than he had felt in months. He made a mental note to order a case of this particular label and vintage as soon as his bank account had recovered from its recent nose-dive.

Daisy took the helicopter back to Kamloops first thing in the morning. There was no point in her wasting any more time hanging around until midday. Richard felt so confident that he would come to an agreement with Jake that they had decided over dessert last night she should brief Nigel, the surveyor, right away and start preparing a new submission to their AO. It would still take at least a week for the new plans to be drawn up and even longer for the necessary surveying to be done.

The sky was overcast with billowing clouds on the horizon. A summer storm was forecast for that evening. Richard was confident he would be back in the office by then, with the ink dry on the most important document of his career. He was whistling along with a happy tune on the local radio station while driving the same route as yesterday. In his mind he was rehearsing the arguments he would bring forward and did some calculations to see how far he could go without having to rob a bank.

When he reached Jake's property, the same young fellow waited for him at the gate and he followed him again. This time his guide stopped at the place Richard had secretly labelled the *Plaza of the Huts* on the day before.

Jake was standing in front of one of the run-down huts and beckoned him to come closer. Otherwise the place was deserted; not even a chicken was in sight. Richard parked his car, got out and went over to Jake. Up close, the hut looked even more desolate than he had expected.

Jake greeted him warmly, shook his hand and extended one arm in what he probably thought was a grand gesture.

Richard feared Jake would place his heavy paw on his shoulder again, so he quickly moved a step back. But Jake attempted nothing of the kind, in fact, he actually pointed towards the entrance of the ramshackle structure. Next to the makeshift wooden barn door was a small opening with shutters. Without glass, this window would hardly offer protection on bitter cold winter nights. It must be dark and damp inside. A young woman appeared in the doorframe, briefly blinking before her eyes adjusted to the bright daylight. She was tall and skinny, no more than twenty at most, and carried a toddler on her arm.

Jake beamed. "This is Emma. And Jake junior."

Richard froze. *Jake junior? What stupid game is he playing? Does he want to shock me by introducing his extended family to me – now that Daisy is not by my side? So he can watch my reaction and, if I don't have myself under control, bully me into a higher price because my reaction could be interpreted as insulting? Is he so sure of my moral integrity that he expects me to react outraged? If Jake is out to confuse, shock or embarrass me before we get down to business, he has a surprise coming.* Richard's mind raced through all those thoughts, concluding that Jake's tactics were a little too obvious to be effective with a smooth operator like him. But he could still hear Daisy's warning not to underestimate Jake. *Don't let him steamroll you,* he cautioned himself, *stay on top of it.*

"Well, it's nice to meet your wife," he responded casually to Jake's bait, who opened his eyes in amazement and stared at him.

"Hello Emma!" Richard extended his hand to her, but she lowered her eyes and did not take it. Maybe he was wrong and she was not Jake's wife after all. Maybe he had embarrassed her and, paranoid as he was, had stumbled into this one like a fool. To admit a mistake at this stage would be even more embarrassing, so he added boldly: "And little Jake. What a cute fellow. You are a lucky man, Jake."

"I sure am," Jake muttered. "With my children, and with my wives!"

So Daisy was right. There was more than one.

Then Jake broke into a laughter, immediately shared by Richard to hide his shock at Jake's sudden revelation, but not by the guy standing next to him, who had been his guide. For a split second Richard had assumed the attractive young man might be Emma's husband. The way he looked at her would warrant such a thought. He had hungry eyes. Despite his obvious youth and good looks, he seemed worn out and desperate.

"Let me introduce you to my other son, Jake the first."

Richard stayed cool. There was no way Jake would trick him into a reaction that might hurt his negotiations. "Your first born! Nice to meet you too, Jake."

Jake the firstborn and Richard shook hands too, then his father put his arm over the young boy's shoulder who stood next to Emma and said: "Well, Richard, just bear with me for a second. I have to instruct my son on the daily chores and then we can drive up to the main house."

"Sure, I'll wait in my car."

Richard went back to his car and settled in the driver's seat. The windshield was dusty from the long drive on the gravel road, but this gave him the advantage of being able to study the small group of people in relative safety. Jake the father was the only one talking. Jake the firstborn took a notebook out of his shirt pocket. He was nodding and writing furiously. Emma stood passively by her - well, he guessed her *husband's* was the correct term – side, rubbing baby Jake's back with one hand. She was not very pretty, but much better looking than Marion. Much younger too. Her brown hair was pulled back in the same curious upturned wave that ended in a tight bun on the back of her head, just like Marion had worn her hair. And her pale coloured dress was old-fashioned and ridiculously long and bulky. Both women appeared to work hard on looking as unattractive as possible to any other male in their vicinity. So, why did Jake the firstborn look so hungry? Were plain Emma and haggard Marion the only women here his lusty eyes could feast on?

The notes the younger son made must be a shopping list, because now Jake turned to his wife and she said single words that his son wrote down. Would he be the one to go to the supermarket in Blue River, and not Emma or Marion, or both of them? A disturbing thought crossed Richard's mind. Were the women not allowed to leave the property? Not even to go to the supermarket?

Before he could ponder such a ridiculous notion, Jake stroked his baby son's head and headed towards Richard's car. He slid into the passenger seat and, without asking if Richard would mind giving him a lift, ordered *lets go*. Richard started to drive up to the main house without making any further reference to Jake's strange family arrangements. He wouldn't give him that satisfaction.

They sat at the long dining table, having coffee like last time. But Jake had visibly changed since Richard's first visit. He was no longer the jovial guy, harmless and obliging, casually chatting while bringing coffee from the kitchen. This time Marion was present and she served them quietly, with not as much as a thank you from him. Richard could not help but compare her to Emma. She was considerably older, moving with deliberate caution like somebody who is sick or injured or just plain tired. She looked even worse than yesterday when she had joined her husband – yes, in her case it must be correct; she was senior to Emma and therefore surely the legal spouse – to greet his guests.

As if he could read his mind, Jake started to explain. "Of course Marion is my wife in the eyes of Canadian law. She was my first and will always be the first."

Richard glanced at Marion who finished setting the table, wondering briefly how she felt. Having her husband's lover living on the same property, acknowledging her in front of a complete stranger must be weird. If she tolerated this behaviour from her husband, she must be a masochist. What happened here seemed to be a classic S&M scenario to him, with Jake the sadistic master and Marion and Emma the willing sufferers.

"You don't seem surprised that I have more than one wife." Jake was either determined to make Richard lose his cool or frustrated over his nonchalance.

"Oh well, there has been some talk in the Resort where Daisy and I are staying."

"The Blue River Resort?"

"Yes."

"And what's the talk about?"

"None of my concern."

"I would not be so sure about it. If nothing else, satisfy my curiosity."

190

"I don't really listen to gossip, but if you must know, the waiter told Daisy that you are an American and that you are living here in some kind of commune."

"A commune, or a cult?"

I shrugged my shoulders. "Who cares?"

"I do! You see, Richard, there is a huge difference. A commune is a loose union of immoral people sharing intimacy without rules of proper conduct. A cult is a system of religious worship devoted to a principle, practised by faithful followers."

Why did he appear to be so desperate for Richard's approval? Well, if that's what he was after, he could have it. "Thank you for explaining this to me. I am originally from Germany, where we are more experienced in the system of communes, free love for all you know, not so much in cults. But I get it now, you are the leader of a cult, living your life the way you want to, and that's fine with me. I guess it has its advantages to have more than one wife."

Jake leaned back and folded his arms above his sizable stomach. Grinning. Enjoying himself. "Marion!"

The woman had just gone back to the kitchen and popped her head back through the door the second he was yelling for her.

"Marion, come and explain to our guest the principle of celestial marriage."

She looked astounded but returned to the table immediately and started to recite like a wound-up doll. "If a man espouses a virgin and desires to espouse another, and another, and they are all virgins and have been vowed to no other man, then he is justified, he cannot commit adultery for they are given to him by the Lord and they belong to him…"

Wow! This was getting a bit too heavy. Richard had not come here for a lecture on their twisted beliefs. "Excuse me," he started and Marion immediately went quiet. "I'd rather you don't go into details." As soon as he said it, he realized his mistake. Jake had finally called his bluff.

Pleased with himself, Jake raised his eyebrows and changed the subject. "All right then, if your spiritual well-being is of no importance

191

to you, let us discuss the ulterior subject on your mind. Marion, leave us alone."

She rushed away like a dog that is let off the leash.

"You want to know if I will agree to sell you the three acres you desperately need for your development."

Damn it, he knew. Richard swallowed hard and collected his thoughts, but Jake did not wait for his reply.

"Relax. Although I am somewhat disappointed in your deception, Richard, I understand that you felt the need for trickery. You do not know us and you do not understand us. Your values are goal oriented in this life only and you do not consider the afterlife. I will help you achieve your goals because I trust in your ability to eventually look beyond the obvious and seek the truth as The Good Lord laid down in His *Doctrine and Covenants*."

"I am sorry...," Richard stumbled, "I did not know..."

"Of course not." Jake proceeded to tell him that he had attended the public hearing on his planned subdivision held last winter in the community hall of Blue River.

Richard had automatically assumed that Jake had no knowledge of his plans because he was nothing but a backward farmer. Involuntarily he turned his head and there it was, a radio. He had not noticed it before.

Jake taunted him. "Did you think I don't follow what is going on in the world? Do you think I don't read books or newspapers? Do you think I don't listen to the radio, check the internet or watch television. Yes, television! We do have satellite reception here, in case you are wondering. For television and for the internet. Do you think I'm stupid?"

That was exactly what Richard had thought. He had considered Jake ignorant and uninformed, but the way Jake was talking now was no longer the language of an uneducated man. Richard's anger rose again, but this time directed entirely at himself, at his amazing and inexcusable stupidity. But Jake had indicated he would help him despite his arrogant assumptions. "You said you will help me?"

"Yes. I will sell the land to you, but there is one condition attached to it."

Instant relief flooded through Richard, washing away his anger. "Sure. What can I do for you."

Jake shook his head, making a disapproving hissing sound with his tongue protruding snakelike from his fleshy lips. "Tz, tz, tz … this is nothing you should do for me. It is something you should do for yourself."

Richard gave up playing games and told Jake whatever he wanted would be done. When Jake informed him that all he wanted was that Richard would visit him again, to spend some time with him and his family, Richard guessed immediately that he was meant to attend some of Jake's brainwashing lectures. He relaxed and agreed. No problem at all. Promises of this nature were not legally binding and he might even attend one or two before he would let them fizzle out. It all depended on his schedule, which would be very demanding as soon as this sales agreement was reached. But that was something he didn't have to mention now.

There was only one thing left to discuss, the price. "And did you think about my offer?"

Jake said he did. He told Richard that five hundred would not be quite enough, considering that he risked the privacy of his until now secluded estate, which was very dear and valuable to him.

"So, what price have you thought about?"

"Ten thousand!"

"Holy …," barely holding back a very unholy profanity, Richard tried hard to stay civil. "But that's unheard of. Ten thousand for three acres, Jake, please, you can't be serious."

"You did not understand me. It's ten thousand for each acre. And I am very serious."

20

The week had flown by. Richard had pressured the surveyors to drop every other job they had going and instead measure and stake the parcel of land he had agreed to buy from Jake. While they were recording its exact size, so the lawyers could draw up a final purchase contract, he had to persuade his bankers to extend his credit line beyond its original limit to cover the needed thirty-five thousand dollars.

That was a real struggle. Considering the size of the initial loan, the relatively small amount of money he now needed seemed insignificant. But it turned into a major issue for the prudent bank manager handling his account. Richard moved a step higher and met with his superiors. Unfortunately, even there the Bankers didn't see the bigger picture. Their narrow minded and overly cautious attitude made Richard so furious that he lost his temper and called the headquarter's manager a tight-assed queen before he stormed out of the meeting. After he had cooled down again, he realised that this unprofessional attitude had only created further complications and no solution. As usual when he managed to get himself into deep trouble, he called Daisy.

She was quick to get in touch with a private financier, a wonderful woman called Linda, who charged higher interest than the banks but understood right away the need for this transaction and acted with lightning speed to transfer the needed amount to them.

It was such a relief to finally get rid of this sword of Damocles hanging over their heads. Lately Richard had constantly felt like that ancient Syracuse courtier, who had to sit at King Dionysius' banquet with a sword dangling on a horse hair over his head. Of course this was only meant to be a symbolic display of the constant danger a ruler is exposed to, but even when Richard had heard the story for the first time in history class, he had considered it a ruthless and senseless demonstration of power – of the same kind Bankers seemed to enjoy nowadays.

Next morning, Daisy was back from Kamloops. She had not been as shocked as her boss about Jake's exorbitant demand, but she did beat herself up over the fact that she had not bothered to check the attendance list from the public hearing. Only three people had been present at this mandatory meeting, Jake S. Law, Jake Law – who they now knew to be Jake's son – and of course the surveyor Nigel, who had acted as Richard's agent. To pay attention to the fact that their neighbour was aware of their plans could have forewarned them and in turn might have saved them a bundle of money. If they would have come clean with Jake right away, he might have been more lenient towards them.

Daisy agreed with Richard that Jake's outrageous selling price was a penalty for trying to deceive him. Because she was so upset over this seemingly minor but very important oversight, he didn't even mention meeting Emma. He saved that for another occasion, one with enough leisure to sit down and discuss things without further aggravation.

Daisy came to his office just before lunch and suggested they go and have a snack at the Bread Garden restaurant which was in walking distance of their office building. You look like you've lost weight, she said.

On the way there they passed the Mouschi-Bar and Richard felt a twinge of guilt. Since that miserable experience he had not been bothered by any further sexual arousal incited by fantasizing about Daisy. Come to think of it, he had not felt any at all.

When they arrived, they were immediately shown to a small table on the outside patio and they both ordered a Chicken wrap and mineral water. The meal would be delicious and quick, and they could be back in the office in less than twenty minutes.

Now seemed as good a time as any to fill Daisy in on the sordid little details of his last visit. As casually as possible he mentioned having been introduced to Emma.

Daisy smelled the rat right away. "Who's Emma?"

"Jake said she is his second wife."

Daisy reacted shocked. "I knew it," she exclaimed a bit too loud and immediately lowered her voice. "The bastard! Tell me everything you have found out about her."

He did. At least as much as he could remember, but he could not describe Emma to Daisy's satisfaction. What was there to tell?

"She looked okay to me," he said.

"What is okay to you?"

"Just okay."

"Happy? Sad? Scared? Pleased? Worried? Disgusted? Cheerful? Depressed? Moody? Troubled? Content?"

"I don't know. She barely said hello to me and that's about it. How would I know what frame of mind she was in. She looked after her child and then Jake asked me to wait for him in the car."

"How old was she?"

"Young, maybe eighteen, definitely under twenty."

"And she already has a child?"

"Well, what's wrong with that? A lot of mothers are very young."

"How old was the child?"

He didn't dare to tell Daisy that the toddler must have been two or three already, so he just said, a baby.

"What did she wear?"

"I can't remember."

Daisy took a copy of *People* magazine out of her handbag and smacked it on the table in front of him. "Something like that?"

The cover page showed a woman in a light blue ankle length dress with puffed sleeves and a round collar. She had her hair swept back in a bun and if she would have been blonde instead of brunette, she could have been Emma. Two toddlers were walking on each side of the woman in the picture, but she did not hold them by their hands. She was looking down at the ground. The headline read: *Texas Polygamy Sect: Inside the cult.* Subtitles: *The wives, why they stay* and *What will happen to the 416 children.*

The picture jolted him badly. He experienced a mental roller coaster ride without shock absorbers. There it was, on the cover of a reputable magazine, a story about a cult he refused to acknowledge! In which world was he living? Why had he never heard about it? The woman and her kids looked like they stepped out of a past century, but the magazine was from this week, and the resemblance to the young woman with the child he had seen in flesh and blood was just too eerie. Was he so self-absorbed that headline-making stories rushed by him unnoticed? Did he only register what concerned him or his business and let everything else carelessly drift by? That was not good. First the slip with the public meeting, and now this.

Daisy tried to make him feel better. "I know its shocking to be confronted with one's inability to register certain things, but it can happen to anybody. It's called selective absorption. We only see and hear what we need or want to know."

"Come on, this is ridiculous. I must have walked past this cover on the news stands a million times."

"You had other things on your mind. But I am glad it got to you." Her face was stern but she leaned forward with a hint of a smile on her lips and a curious inquisitive look in her eyes. "There is hope for you after all."

The chicken wraps arrived. They smelled of jasmine and ginger and were microwave hot. He took a large bite, had to roll his tongue around the pastry to cool it down a little and was able to recover his composure in the process. With a full mouth he asked Daisy if he was really such a hopeless case.

"Yes," she said, toying with her still steaming food. "You are aggressive and pushy, which is good in business, but you lose your temper every time it really counts. You are clever, even intelligent, but you are arrogant and self-centred. You are well educated, but you don't do your homework. You are single minded, again a bonus in many instances, but you have no empathy and are incapable of showing emotion."

He smirked to underline his conceit. "Enough praise! I might fall in love with myself."

She returned his smile, but hers was more complacent. "You are such a disgusting person, it can actually be quite fun to be with you."

"You would be in love with me if you weren't my assistant." He laughed. "But you are too straight-laced to mix business and pleasure."

Richard had never made a joke about the possibility of them hooking up but she took it as a joke – of course - and laughed with him.

"If I had a stronger character I would tell you where to shove this job." Then she turned serious again and pointed at the magazine. "Take it with you. Read the whole article when you have time. What are we going to do now?"

He looked at his watch. "We do what we always do. Go back to the office and work."

"No. I mean with Jake?"

"That's a done deal. His lawyer returned the signed contract to us this morning."

"I mean with Emma."

"What about Emma?" Before she could reply, it dawned on him what she meant. "Oh no! No way! We are not interfering at all in Jake's marital arrangements. I don't give a shit how many wives or concubines or lovers he's got. That's his business and as long as he keeps to the bargain – which he has done by signing yesterday – we will stick to ours and pay him when the money is due. Committing to his additional demand was just a loose agreement on my part and I have no intention of following up on it." As soon as this had slipped out, he bit his tongue. Damn it, that was a big mistake.

"What additional demand?"

There was no point in trying to evade the issue, Daisy was not one to give up easily. "Jake attached one condition to his agreement. I am supposed to go and visit him a few times, I guess for religious programming of some kind. But, of course, nothing like that was written into the contract."

"You promised him?"

"Yes. No. Well, yeah, I said I would. It was just talk, the way one promises relatives to drop by for a chat soon."

"What do you know about that? You don't have any relatives."

"True. Friends then."

"I always keep the promises I make to my friends."

"Acquaintances then. And don't tell me you have friends."

"Don't change the subject. I think it is a great idea if you follow up on your promise." She was getting quite excited now. "It will give you the best excuse possible to research what is going on at his farm. Jake will misinterpret your interest and may even let you in on his secret. You've got to find out if the local rumours are true. There aren't just two wives, I'm sure he has got more."

"But I don't care." It sounded lame, even to himself. So he gave it another shot. "Stop pushing me to do something I consider an utter waste of time. How often do I have to tell you I don't want to interfere with Jake's business. I truly don't care!"

Her fingers were drumming a demanding staccato on the magazine cover in front of him. "What about that?" Tap, tap, tap on the blue dressed woman. "You were upset about this story!"

"Not about the story! I was upset about *missing* the story. About me being so goddamn inattentive. Christ, I have to start paying more attention to what's going on in this world. A lot of it is important to our business, but it's not up to me to change what's wrong with it. I'm not responsible for all the sick shit that's happening everywhere."

Daisy leaned back in her chair and gave him a disgusted look. "You are a creep." Then she started to eat her by now cold chicken wrap in silence.

He waited until she had finished, then took the bill the waitress had placed on their table and got up to pay.

Daisy was waiting outside the restaurant by the time he had finally been able to leave his money with the cashier. She tucked the folded People magazine into his jacket pocket. They walked back to the office like an old married couple seasoned in sparring practise, and he was wondering how long it would take to be forgiven.

The afternoon was uneventful until the phone rang. The receptionist, who screened all calls, told him a rep from the Ministry of Environment was on the line and wanted to talk to him. He told her to put him through to Daisy. She usually dealt with that type of bureaucratic stuff.

The receptionist had been with his company from day one. She knew who really held the reins in the office and was not intimidated by Richard's ownership status. "I think Daisy is pissed off with you. She refuses to take the call and said you will. It's on line two."

He had no choice but to answer and spend half an hour, quietly fuming, clarifying his plans to protect the raptors' nests Nigel had discovered when surveying his property. One was an Eagle's nest which was actually a great asset to the development as people loved to see those big birds soaring over their heads. The other was an Osprey nest, abandoned a long time ago because those two species did not get along. As soon as the Eagles had decided to make their permanent home on the highest point in the area the Ospreys had moved on. Meanwhile the tree had died and was in danger of falling over, but the Ministry refused to let them cut it down. They insisted the developer had to protect the tree in case the Ospreys came back. A radius of twice the height of the tree had to be secured with a no-build no-touch covenant. Eventually Richard gave up arguing and agreed to the restriction, although this meant he would lose a valuable building site. It was nearly four o'clock. No self respecting public servant would be caught working after duty and Richard didn't feel like starting the same fruitless conversation all over again the next morning.

Daisy's office was down the corridor. Still annoyed over her refusal to take the raptor protector call, he went straight over to see her. Most of the small room was taken up by a large chestnut coloured desk. There was only a lap-top on it, a note-pad next to it, a stack of files on one end and a forlorn crystal vase with a few roses on the other. Her chair was turned away from the door towards the high window.

She had put her feet up on the low windowsill and was gazing at the impressive mass of Metro Vancouver skyscrapers. Over time one after the other had been added in ever increasing size and height. Ten years ago, when he had rented this office space, he could still glimpse Coal Harbour, but now the view was blocked by impenetrable tinted glass facades. Some of them reflected the setting sun.

"Come on Daisy," he pleaded. "Stop being mad at me."

Her feet touched the carpet and her chair turned around slowly. She looked him straight in the face with as much disgust as she could express. He could have sworn he'd seen her nostrils quiver like a wild animal sniffing out an enemy. Or its prey. "Now, why would I be mad at you?"

"Emma?!" he guessed.

"Yes. Emma. Well, that's a thought. Why would it upset me that an eighteen-year-old with a child is introduced to you as Jake's second wife?"

"What the hell do you expect me to do? Grab her and drag her off with me? She may not want to be rescued."

"How do you know?"

"For Christ's sake, do you expect me to go back and ask her?"

"You could try."

"What? You want me to go up to her and say: excuse me, but can you please tell me if you are happy with your life, or would you rather be saved from your liaison with your lover? You want me to annoy the crap out of Jake, now that he has been cooperative? I don't get it! You're meddling in his affairs at a time when everything is starting to work for us again. What the hell is the matter with you?" It did not happen often that he got annoyed with his assistant but now she had really overstepped the line. Who did she think she could boss around?

"You could just go there, *like you promised*, and check out the situation. Jake doesn't need to know what you are after until we can confirm if the woman is held there against her will. And the others. There must be others!"

It really made him crazy how she brought his promise into the play. How dare she! Who did she think he was? A lying bastard? He had only agreed in the interest of their company to visit Jake. Didn't she know that? Their future had been at risk. She just didn't get it. Looking down her nose at him instead of supporting his decisions and covering his back.

Richard felt as if he was fourteen again. Just as helpless, unable to influence his parents' decision to take him away from his friends, his school, his first crush, his soccer club, his life as he knew it. Helpless, powerless, incapable, impotent. Yes, impotent. A scary condition, as he had only recently found out. He had just about had it with all those control freaks around him who constantly told him what to do!

"*Verdammte Scheisse!*" The crystal vase was suddenly in his hands and, without thinking, he smashed it against the wall. The bloody thing did not burst into a million splinters, as could be expected, but remained one solid piece and made an awful dent in the gyprock wall, spilling water and flowers before it fell to the floor and rolled unceremoniously under Daisy's desk.

They stared at each other. He knew that she instantly understood that he was sorry. He also knew that she had no tolerance for his violent outbursts. Daisy got up, walked around her desk and started to pick up the damaged flowers.

He stepped back, looking down at her. "I'll buy you new ones."

"Forget it."

At six o'clock he could hear the offices on the whole floor packing up. Laughter, conversations, office doors opening and closing, the elevator bell ringing every time it stopped. He made up his mind and went back to Daisy's office, half expecting it to be empty. She was still there, working. The vase was back in place but looked desolate without the roses.

He stopped in the doorway. Behind him some of his employees rushed down the corridor, greeting him cheerfully.

"As soon as the altered road designs are finished, I have to go to Kamloops to meet with the engineers to go over all the quotes."

Her face was a question mark. Why did he bother telling her? As far as she was concerned, they were not on speaking terms.

"It will take a while and I hope you understand that I have my priorities. But as it is so important to you, I promise that I will drive up to see Jake as soon as I can fit it into my schedule."

"So?"

"It might take a few months before I get around to it, but I'll try my best to find out what you want to know. You win! Happy?"

Daisy did not embarrass him further by gloating over her success. She didn't thank him either. She stayed where she was and simply told him with a very serious voice that this was not a game.

"I know," he said, desperate for the last word. "But neither is what we are trying to achieve here. So please be patient with me."

21

Summer began to lose its dry heat. Martha sometimes thought about the cold season ahead. If she was allowed to stay in the main house, her second winter in Canada would be a lot more bearable than those horrible months in Anna's draughty hut. Most rooms in the main house could be heated with electric baseboards, and the large room where the family met for special occasions had a huge cast iron wood stove as an additional heat source.

The room Martha was allocated to was nothing but a cubicle next to Marion's office and had no heating or electricity, but there were no cracks in the outside walls and even the window frame was insulated, and when she was allowed to retire to her room she snuggled under her thick blanket and felt warm and cozy. She usually had a candle burning and sometimes she stared at the round honey coloured log walls and day-dreamed for a while. Usually she wished for Emma to be there. The only chance she and Emma had nowadays to exchange a few quick words were when Emma picked up her children from school. Would they ever find the time again for long conversations? She missed Emma terribly, but otherwise she could not complain. The coming winter would be good. Just like the sister-wives, Martha never got enough to eat, but she had taken to supplementing her meals with little treats she stole from the pantry. It had its advantages to live in the main house.

She could move around freely without causing suspicion. Every morning, she instructed the children in the community hall on how to write and read and taught them the basics of mathematics. When school finished around lunch time, she prepared herself for next day's classes. Marion had given her a few books on different subjects so she could teach herself and expand her still quite limited knowledge. Martha hoped she would soon become a really good teacher to the children.

She liked her new responsibilities. Compared to the workload the sister-wives had to accomplish, she had it easy. Even the compulsive counting that had burdened her mind for so many months had stopped.

Next to her teaching responsibilities, she often had to help Marion in the office, administering the accounts or preparing schedules allocating chores and provisions for their large family. Martha soon found out that although Marion tried her best, her attempt at organisation often turned chaotic, mostly through no fault of hers. So far, Martha had never wondered how the family survived and where the money they needed was coming from. Most of the food they consumed came from the land. The women planted vegetables and kept farm animals. But there were many things their husband had to buy in town. Seeds, fertilizer and feed for some of the animals, light-bulbs for the house, pens and paper for the office and the school, clothes and shoes, and baby bottles, and sometimes medicine, although Marion kept a herb garden and made most tinctures and ointments herself. In their faith it was the duty of the fathers and the husbands to provide what was necessary for their large families, and Martha had not thought about it until she started to add up the columns for Marion. The money coming in and going out needed to be recorded meticulously. Even with her limited accounting experience Martha realised very quickly that there was more money going out – much more. In fact, lately no money was coming in except the pittance they got for selling some of their produce. She felt sorry for Marion when the older woman fretted over the results of Martha's accounts, but what could she do? And anyway, that was not her concern, was it? Their husband would have to take care of that.

Martha hardly ever saw him, which suited her fine, but she got quite used to his voice. By accident of course. One day, soon after she had been allowed to spend time alone in Marion's office, she had been there preparing a new lesson for the older children and needed to look up the meaning of a word in the encyclopaedia that Marion had told her to use. The volume she needed was standing on the highest shelf. It was a little out of reach for her height, so Martha moved her chair to the shelf unit and stood on it. Somehow she slipped just when her fingertips touched the book. She tried to balance herself by holding on to the row of thick books below while falling off the chair. Several heavy volumes fell down with her. It made such a thunderous noise that she expected Marion, or whoever was close by, to check what happened. Nobody came.

Martha waited and listened for a while, then got off the floor again and picked up one book after another to place it back where it belonged. That's when she noticed a hole in the plaster wall right at the end of the lowest row of shelves. It had been covered by the last book in the encyclopaedia collection, and Martha was just about to line it up again when she heard a door open and close and then a loud and angry voice. The adjacent room was part of their husband's private quarters. Martha froze where she was standing, not daring to even move the book back into its old position.

"What do you expect me to do?" she heard her husband shouting. "They're all old and ugly. They should not complain; I've done my duty, they all have children!"

Marion's voice trailed along his tirade, begging him to reconsider. He shouted at her while she kept insisting in a soft tone to please, please let her prepare a schedule again for some of the wives to be with him.

Martha was so engrossed in the exchange that she never considered her eavesdropping to be inappropriate. How exciting! That's how it must be to watch television shows on the big plastic boxes. Her father had one of those. Sometimes, as a small child, she had caught a glimpse of the moving pictures when her father had forgotten to close the door to his room. Pictures of people moved over the flat surface and she had quickly lowered her eyes, pretending not to notice what she was not supposed to see. But she could still hear the voices coming out of the box. It had fascinated her to hear them talking to each other like real people - and that's exactly how it was now.

Her husband and Marion had no idea that she had her ear close to the small hole. It was perfectly placed for her height, she did not even have to stand on tip-toes to be able to look through. Unfortunately, she only saw one corner of the room – which was quite boring - but that also meant that they wouldn't suddenly spot her roving eye. She put her ear back in position, feeling quite safe to listen in as she kept her eyes on the door to her own office.

Only when her husband finished the argument with a final *suit yourself, but don't expect me to dance to your whistle* did she place the volume W-Z carefully back on its old spot.

After that, she made a habit out of moving the book to its side whenever she was alone in the office. Sometimes she could hear them talking again. What surprised her was how often they argued. Marion stood her ground firmly in defending her schedule for the other wives. And she chided him when he let a woman wait in vain for him all night. It is not right, she said, they want so much to be with child again.

From the fragments of gossip Martha overhead when the sister-wives chatted in the kitchen or when they brought the children to school she knew that they all considered it Marion's fault that their husband ignored them. The first few years after the Alberta wives had joined his compound he had still taken care to give each of his wives more children, but then he imported Emma and soon after that Anna and then herself. All were young and naturally had held his attention for a while, but all the sister-wives were aware that by now he had lost interest in Martha, and as far as Anna and Emma were concerned, well, everybody knew that Anna had fallen from grace and that Emma was not his favourite either because she was so skinny. So it must be Marion's doing to keep him from the rest of the sister-wives. Quite a few of them started to be very agitated over their husband's refusal to see them. They picked Marion as the culprit and started to accuse her of misusing her first-wife's power. They had no idea how forcefully Marion stood up for their rights.

One day late in August, when a sudden thunderstorm made it impossible for most of the mothers to pick up their children, Emma arrived just before the downpour started and was waiting for the storm to subside. She pulled Martha to the corner of the room, away from the few other grown-ups present, and talked to her in a hushed voice. Finally they could chat together again like they used to. Emma told her in detail how angry the sister-wives were about Marion. Martha, to her own surprise, defended Marion. "It wasn't Marion's fault at all that the wives got ignored," she said. When Emma asked how she got such a ridiculous idea, Martha confessed to her secret pastime of listening in to the private conversations between their husband and his first wife.

Emma was delighted. "You are too much," she giggled. "Aren't you afraid they will find out?"

Martha told her that she was not scared at all any more; of nothing and of nobody. What could they do to her? When it was time for her to leave this world she knew she had a place secured in a much better world. She could read in Emma's expression that her friend didn't really understand what she was talking about, so she asked how Anna was doing.

"She is the one yelling loudest how unfair Marion is. She wants to give our husband another set of twins, greedy as she is. The others hate her."

"And you?" Martha asked. "Do you long to be with him too?"

Emma came very close to her. "Sometimes I skip a meal to make sure I don't put on weight," she confided, and Martha thought how wonderful it was to trust each other with such dangerous confessions.

Martha sometimes wondered if she should do the same as Emma, just in case. Their husband did not like skin and bones! But she must have disgusted him pretty badly as he never took notice of her, not even when she was in the same room with him. And she was always hungry and wouldn't have the willpower to starve herself unnecessarily.

So she snatched whatever she could get her hands on, although there was less and less food around.

She was fourteen now, would turn fifteen soon. Last year she had not really gained any weight, so she felt quite safe from him, even as her childlike body was developing into that of a woman, making her dress too tight around her chest. She wondered what she looked like. Just like in her father's home, there were no mirrors anywhere in the house. The sister-wives usually asked each other if their hair was in order or if their faces were dirty; anything else would have been an improper display of vanity. Martha had never seen her face except as a fleeting distorted reflection in the water, on a window pane or on a shiny cooking pot. She wanted to know what she looked like. Now that her body had changed so noticeably, she wanted to see if her face had adapted to her new look. When she mentioned this forbidden curiosity to Emma, her confidant told her about the pond on the compound. "Go there," she advised her, "and take a good look at yourself. Nobody will disturb you there." She herself had done it several times when she still had been curious about her appearance.

Lately Martha had taken to sneaking out of the main house at night quite often. Marion seemed to totally trust her and hardly paid any attention to her. Martha liked instructing the children, she enjoyed doing the accounts and she loved studying, which meant Marion never had any reason to complain.

Once Martha had discovered how easy it was to sneak away, she had taken up visiting Emma as often as possible, sometimes even falling asleep next to her friend while chatting and giggling, waking up with the sick feeling that she may have overslept. So far she had always managed to get back to the main house before anybody was on the road.

The pond was a different matter. If she wanted to see her image she had to go there in daylight. Emma had described the way; it was the same route as to the prison hut, but half-way up she should turn into a heavily overgrown and therefore nearly invisible path just past the large Douglas fir tree. With all her duties, Martha had practically no spare time during the day, but she promised herself to find an opportunity soon to escape for an afternoon.

She had just about given up hope of ever getting there when she overheard a conversation between Marion and her husband through the listening hole. They argued over money. Marion said, there was none left in the account since she had paid the property tax. Her husband accused her of being stupid. Why did she pay the tax when she knew there was little left? Marion said, if she hadn't paid the property tax, the government might come and ask questions about why there was no farm income if they claimed to have a farm, and maybe even why so many single mothers with children lived there collecting social security payments. That made her husband think it over and after a while he said they would both have to go to town and register a few more children. Marion should take Anna's twins with her. "But we have registered them already," Marion said. "Who would know, they all look the same," was his answer. "This time, just sign them up as your own!"

They decided to drive to Kamloops the next afternoon. Although Martha had been living with them under the same roof for over one year now, she had never been alone in the house for so many hours. Of course she would have to do the schooling in the morning but the afternoon would be hers alone to do as she pleased.

Marion didn't give her any extra work to do - she must have assumed that it would not be necessary – before she left the house in her good lilac coloured dress with the pleats in front, her hair braided and meticulously pinned on the back of her head. She got into her husband's car, and they drove off. Martha was a bit bewildered that they did not have Anna's twins with them. Maybe they picked them up on the way down.

For a second, Martha considered going into the private quarters and snooping around. Maybe her husband had a mirror there. She got to the door, had her hand on the handle already, when the courage needed for this intrusion left her again. Maybe there was a hidden sign that would tell them that she had broken in. Marion could have left a hair sticking somewhere that fell down when she opened the door. No, it was not worth it. Outside was a beautiful late summer afternoon, perfect for a hike to the pond.

It took her less than half an hour to get there. Once she had managed to run around the corner behind the house, nobody could watch where she was going. She discovered the trail after searching for it for several minutes and thought this to be a good sign. How had Emma ever found it? The trail was narrow and easy to overlook. One could not see where it was leading until it suddenly opened up to a clearing in the woods. And there it was, the pond, just like Emma had explained. It was the most magical sight Martha could have imagined. Crystal clear water sparkled in the sun, surrounded by sea grass gently wafting in the breeze. A duck swam leisurely from one end to the other. The sky above was cloudless, reflecting its deep blue eternity on the water surface. Gentle waves were crowned by tiny silver drops. The pond lured her closer, inviting her to its shore. She knelt on the soft ground and could not suppress the strong impulse to touch the pure water, immerse her hands into it, play with the waves they generated, destroying the image of the face she wanted to explore.

After a while, she had satisfied her need to feel its cool wetness and let the water come to rest. Then she leaned forward. Her face was slightly distorted, she could see that, but otherwise quite clear in its contours. It was round and white. Her eyes were blue like the water, and her hair had the colour of the earth, but lighter. There were spots on her face. Emma had told her she had freckles, and so far she had not understood what that meant. Freckles on her small nose and some under her eyes.

Martha was quite pleased. She was not ugly like some of the sister-wives and her hair was much thicker and plentiful. In fact, her mane was so voluptuous, it was nearly impossible to keep it tied behind her back in the regulatory braid or bun. After her hike and as she was now leaning forward, some strands were sticking out and falling over her ears. She automatically lifted her hands to pull them back.

Then she thought she heard a noise. Footsteps! Somebody was coming through the undergrowth behind her, carelessly bending branches that snapped back or broke with threatening force. Somebody was coming after her!

Martha jumped to her feet, gathered her skirt without noticing the dirty wet spots on her knees where the muddy ground had left its imprint, and looked around in panic. Where to hide? The tree, over there, quickly. While she was running toward it, some voice inside her told her that it was a waste of time to do so. She was already discovered and would be caught.

Her panting was giving her away, the pounding of her heart was leading to her discovery!

She pressed her hand to her mouth and tried to muffle her heavy breathing. Not a second too soon. Just two or three bushes away the intruder broke through the wall of branches and walked so close past her she could have reached him with outstretched arms. Well, maybe not quite. But still, he was so close – and he was oblivious of her presence. Martha craned her neck a bit to see better. There was an opening in the thicket, barely enough to allow her a partial view of the pond. She strained her ears to listen if others were coming. The man who had reached the water seemed to be the only one.

Martha's heartbeat slowed down – until she realized who the young man was and what he was up to.

Her husband's oldest son, the good looking one she had noticed on a few occasions, was standing with his back to her and started to take his shirt off. Her heart began to race again. His bare back became visible as he slipped the shirt over his head, exposing lean and strong muscles. Elongated muscle strands divided his back into two equal halves of sun-tanned hard tissue. Martha watched the play of his muscles on his wide shoulders and bulky arms in awe. His body amazed her. She had never seen an uncovered male torso. Her husband had never undressed himself fully, and she had spared herself looking at what he did expose of himself by closing her eyes. She had never imagined a man could be so beautiful. She knew she should lower her eyes, but she couldn't bring herself to stop staring.

Jake junior ruffled his hair with a big relieved sigh, staring for a moment at the peaceful pond. What was he doing here? Did he come here to get away from his younger priesthood brothers for a while? Did he feel the need for solitude, just as she sometimes did?

Martha watched him as he looked at the duck swimming into the high sea grass on the opposite shore. The sun was still above the tree-tops. Its rays travelled sideways at an angle that highlighted the mounds of flesh rippling along his back and upper arms as he stretched himself. Then he unbuttoned his trousers, bent forward and slipped them over his round buttocks before Martha could look away. But to see him totally nude, even if only for a split second, was too much for Martha. She cried out in shock and embarrassment.

"No!"

Jake pulled his trousers up as quickly as he had lowered them and spun around like a stretched coil springing back into its original position.

"Who's there?"

He fumbled trying to close the top button on his trousers and looked around, surprised and worried.

Was he also worried he might be discovered? Martha stood motionless behind the bush with her eyes shut acting the child's game *if I can't see you, you can't see me.*

"I can see you, come out of there!"

Martha refused to listen. This was too terrible. Not only was she caught at a place where she was not supposed to be, but caught watching *a man.* A young and good looking man. Not just any man, but her own stepson! And to make matters worse, she had watched him undress! No, she would not open her eyes ever again and would stand here until he was gone. She could not look at him, was not allowed to look anyway, but the notion that *he* was looking at *her*, suspecting that she may have seen him, was too much to bear. If he walked away now, without coming any closer, he might not recognize her and would never know who she was. If only he would go away.

"Martha, I can see you!"

Oh my Lord, please help.

"Martha, what are you doing here?"

214

Suddenly his voice was very close, and she knew he was standing on the other side of the bush she was hiding behind. She opened her eyes.

Jake's beautiful body was still not fully clothed. He had his trousers back on, but through the leaves and branches she could see the skin of his upper body gleaming and his golden hair shimmering in the sunlight. She lowered her eyes again.

They quietly stood on opposite sides of the bush for some time. Martha could hear him breathing – in and out, steady and strong - and began to fall into the same rhythm. Slowly her body let go of some of its tension and her erratic heartbeat became more regular.

From under her lashes she saw him moving his hands to divide the branches between them, slowly and carefully, so as not to frighten the trembling little creature hiding behind them into flight. He had an open view of her now. His breathing became stronger, more laboured. "Look at me," he ordered but his words sounded coarse and pleading.

She mustered all her courage and looked him straight in the face. It was gentle and hopeful, and there was greed… no, not greed, it was desire. She had seen that expression on small children when they wanted more to eat but were not allowed to take any food from the table. Desire and despair. An ache to get something and anguish over not getting it. Martha knew this feeling – she had just experienced it herself while watching him at the pond - but she could not understand why he would feel like that. He was a man, a priest, he could take whatever he wanted. All he had to do was to demand and everything was his. Everything, except… his father's wife!

Suddenly, she felt exalted. His eyes had locked into hers, forcing her to acknowledge what he silently told her. She did not, could not, break loose from this bond. He bared his soul to her without uttering a single word. There was approval and – yes, admiration. He was marvelling at the moment of unimaginable intimacy between them. There was also hopeless despair. He desired her, here and now, but he could not have her.

Martha's eyes grew larger in amazement. She was safe, for he could never tell about them meeting here like this. But the fact that she was not in danger paled against the revelation that he wanted her. Admired her. Thought her desirable. She could not explain why, but her whole being basked in his adulation. She wanted to come closer to him, melt into his open positive aura, enter her providence with one simple step, but she could not move. The shackles of her upbringing made it impossible for her to do what every fibre of her being yearned for.

She could not respond to his longing, but her expression must have betrayed her. He lifted his hand slowly and his fingertips touched her cheek. They were cold and soft as they gently moved down and traced the lines of her chin and neck, yet they left a burning hot trail on her skin. After an endless and at the same time painfully short time his fingers let go of her, and Martha felt abandoned. But she smiled. He smiled back and then he put his finger tips, the ones that had just touched her, on his mouth and kissed them.

With this gesture, with those fingers, he sealed an intimacy between them she had not believed possible until now. She was his and he was hers. He let go of the branches between them and watched them fall back into place. Martha knew he would want her to go away now and get back safely before anything could happen to her. He was protecting her. He would wait a long time before going back to his own hut – and he would come back here again and wait for her.

22

Daisy never reminded him of his promise, but she started to withdraw from him even further, becoming monosyllabic when he needed her input most, and he couldn't postpone the call any longer. But before he gave in to the inevitable, he wanted to be prepared. Jake would not catch him off guard again!

He read the story in People Magazine and surfed the internet, typing in key search words he had picked up from the magazine article: *Polygamy, the Book of Mormon, The Church of the Latter Day Saints, (LDS)*, their fundamentalist splinter group, the *FLDS*, and even the name of the founder of the Mormon Church, *Joseph Smith*. He even bought some books on the subject, namely Daphne Bramham's extensively researched book "The Secret Lives of the Saints" as well as heart wrenching autobiographies of ex-FLDS members like Debbie Palmer, Carolyn Jessop, Dorothy Allred and Martha Beck, who had all grown up in polygamous communities, and glanced through them.

He thought he knew it all.

If Jake was out to test his catholic boarding school beliefs, he would get a rude surprise. Just like everybody else who had been through such an education, he had developed a weird brand of pseudo-atheism. He deplored all religious activities that carried the stigma of extremism, counting the Vatican's interpretation of Christianity amongst those, yet he considered himself a Christian. He despised religious fanaticism and belittled excessively devout worship, but secretly offered

Saint Anthony a reward if he would lead him to a lost item and would rather bite his tongue off than defile Holy Mary's name.

After reading all the serious accusations the American State had compiled against the FLDS Texas cult, Richard had to assume that Jake's congregation was fashioned along similar fundamentalist lines, but his liberal thinking reasoned that everybody had a right to believe in whatever they liked, and deep down he had to admit to himself that he didn't really care. His internet research had made one thing clear to him: Jake was a liar, a fake. That made him chuckle. Jake, the Fake! In Richard's opinion, defending a polygamous life-style with religious principles reduced Jake, just like any of those old lusty guys, to a cheap cultist sex maniac. He was nothing but a dirty old man on a sexual power trip. *Wouldn't we all be, given the chance, if we had enough women willing to play our game?* When this thought crossed Richard's mind, the image of Daisy popped up. She would kick him in the groin if he as much as suggested her being subservient to *any* man. And apart from Daisy there wasn't a single woman out there in his world who would agree to share a guy with other women. So far he had got himself into deep trouble every time he had as much as double dated.

But he now had a better understanding where Daisy's suspicions were coming from. Although he still couldn't care less what went on in Fake Jake's little set-up, he decided it was time to give in to Daisy's silent demand. One morning in late August, he called Jake to announce his visit.

Jake reacted openly delighted and invited him right away to come for an early dinner. When Richard agreed, Jake chuckled and said *so, now you are finally ready; now you want to become a God.*

Richard made it clear to him that he knew where this notion came from. One of Joseph Smith's revelations stated in his *Doctrine & Covenants* promised any man who had more than one wife – he called them plural wives - his own heaven! Thanks a lot, Richard laughed, slightly annoyed by Jake's assumption, but I don't think I could handle more than one woman at a time. Jake then said a strange thing, one which Richard could not categorize as easily. Jake replied, *so you will have to be an angel servant forever.* Richard made a mental note to ask Jake about that when they met.

This dinner invitation had all the makings of turning into a freaky but fun evening. Jake would surely try some of his superior God-kafuffle on him, but thanks to his background research he would not have to hold back due to lack of information. To hell with Jake's feelings. Now that the land deal was done, he didn't have to be diplomatic. He had nothing to lose, but would gain back Daisy's trust and respect in return. That should make the whole visit a worthwhile exercise.

23

When Marion and her husband came home from town, Martha was sitting at her desk pretending to check the inventory of dried meat, wheat and other basic supplies the family had left in storage. Supplies were dangerously low and the count would not have taken her long had she not let her mind wander, savouring the precious moments with Jake junior.

Marion came into the office, saw her bent over some paperwork and asked her to turn the light off when she had finished her work. She would retire to the private quarters now and did not want to be disturbed unless it was an emergency. Martha nodded and then, once the door was firmly closed, got up and took the last volume of the encyclopaedia from its place. Maybe they planned another trip soon, giving her the freedom to spend time away from the house and visit the pond again.

Practically right away the argument started.

"You are messing up everything," she heard her husband complaining. "I told you to take the twins along. We don't have a birth certificate from a doctor, so how else are they going to believe you have children if they don't see them? Look at you! Who would imagine that a man would still touch you. Only when they see proof will they write those stupid certificates. You can't claim anything without it. Why do I always let you have your own way! I'm too lenient for my own good."

Marion said it was too risky. They had registered too many children already and eventually the authorities would wake up to it.

Martha's whole body did a little jump of joy when she heard him answer: "Nonsense! I'll prove it to you. We'll go to town again!"

"But my husband, forgive me for saying this again, it's not a long term solution. Two more child support payments will not get the family through winter. We need more money, soon."

"The Lord will provide. He always does."

Marion continued unwavering. "We have always supplemented the farm income and the social service payments with the regular contributions you received from the Gatekeepers, but since those have stopped, we have used up all the money. It is all gone now. The bride money to Martha's father has been the last they have paid for you."

Her own father had received money for her? She had been sold by her own family? Martha's stomach turned upon hearing this unexpected bit of information, but she recovered quickly. She would never have met Jake junior if she had not been sent here.

"What do you want me to do then? Maybe I should get myself another wife. One of those who pay me instead of me shelling out good money for a useless piece of meat. There are plenty of Church Elders who want to get rid of a stubborn daughter. I could take on one of those mules and break her in."

"No!"

"Why not! You and the others are too old to be touched. Of the latest ones Emma is so thin I would hurt myself on her pointy bones, and Martha, well, you can't really expect me to touch that disgusting girl."

"There is Anna, she is begging me all the time to let her come to you."

"Anna is still nursing, and I am not sure if I want her again. I would have to worry about her losing her temper and stabbing me in a fit of madness. No, no, it is best to call the Gatekeepers and arrange for a new one."

So he would get another wife! Although Martha felt sorry for the next one, she still savoured his comment about not wanting to touch her again. It was as if he had divorced her, an act that was rare but not uncommon in their secret communities and usually a terrible shame for the wife, who was, of course, always at fault. Divorce! How liberating and wonderful this word sounded. Martha barely listened to the rest of the conversation, as Marion went on about the bleak future they all faced, with no strong men to support the family through labour that could bring in money and with too many mouths to feed that could not contribute. Finally, her husband announced that he was tired of being told what to do. Marion should just shut up and wait. He had a solution which would bring a lot of money into his house. Surely she remembered the degenerate gentile who had been stupid enough to pay thirty-five thousand for a useless small acreage not so long ago. This fool had called him again and had begged him for permission to come back for a visit tomorrow, so she had better concentrate on preparing a good dinner for him and all the boys instead of wasting her time moaning and complaining. She should just trust him, he knew what he was doing. This time he would get a lot more money out of that idiot.

And this time, Marion said full of hope but with an underlying twinge of sarcasm that totally escaped him but was very obvious to Martha, maybe the bank will not keep all of it.

Martha gasped. With a bit of luck, she might be able to feast her eyes on her secret love again tomorrow. If there was a dinner, Jake junior would come to the main house, and she could try and steal a glimpse of him.

To save time, Richard had flown to Kamloops and taken a rental car.

He was fifteen minutes early. The gate was still locked and nobody was waiting for him. He turned the stereo up and the windows down and enjoyed the gentle breeze blowing through the car. Crickets announced with their noisy afternoon concert the coming end of summer. Their crackling sound was always a sure sign that the hot days were numbered. Where had the time gone?

Late afternoon was the warmest part of the day. Inside his car the temperature rose quickly and made him sleepy and relaxed. Finally he had some time to himself. Every single day in the past few weeks had thundered through his life like a freight train. One thing after another to deal with, one problem after another. His last meeting with the road engineers yesterday had not been pleasant and had confirmed what he had suspected already. Thanks to the constant delays from Jeanne d'Arc and her crew of busy Killer Bees, there would be no chance to build the road this year. Autumn in the mountains was short, and winter could set in as early as October. Construction of any kind would have to wait until springtime, and with the winters being so long this would not happen until next May. The really bad news about this was that he would have to carry his finance load for many more months, and the high interest payments were painful. The only consolation was that they now had plenty of time to get the subdivision plans finalized and approved. No more mad rush.

Five or ten minutes went by, then he could hear the familiar engine noise of a pickup truck.

The driver stopped, got out, opened the gate and waved Richard through without bothering to say hello to him. Then he closed the gate again, got in his truck and led the way. Richard followed him along the usual route to Jake's house and noticed a little more life along the way than on his previous visits. Several young men, boys actually, were walking next to the driveway toward the main house; greeting him with a wave of their hands. He suddenly began to wonder how many people lived there and how they supported themselves. Some of them looked quite strong for their age, but most of them were of average build and scraggy looking, the way growing teenagers usually do. The two cars drove through the *Plaza of Huts* which was also not as deserted as before. Several small groups of women, dressed as if time had stood still for them, were standing together, talking or chasing after some playing children in the dirt next to the gravelled driveway. Every time somebody put a foot down, dust rose from the bone dry ground. It had not rained in over a week. He hated to think what this place looked like after a soaking – and what it would do to those ridiculous long dresses the women wore. The mud would be ankle deep. Why didn't they put some road mulch or gravel on the ground? The women acted strangely. The did not look at him; in fact they purposely looked away from his car, but still, Richard was amazed at the unexpected activity. Jake's sect was obviously quite a bit larger than he had originally thought.

Father and son Jake were standing in front of their home and greeted him like a long lost friend. Marion stayed in the background, but he could see her clearly. She was dressed the same way as the other women he had seen earlier and the same way those women in Texas had been. Pale, clean, crisp. He felt transported back into People Magazine again. Jake had outdone himself for the occasion; white shirt, black trousers, a black vest – very formal.

Involuntarily Richard straightened his shirt, glad that he had opted for the plain blue one and not the Tommy Bahama style with the colourful design he usually favoured for casual summer events.

They walked into the house together. Inside was much cooler, like log houses usually were. What a shame to have to sit indoors on such a glorious evening. Jake sat down at the head of the long table which was set for at least twenty people and asked Richard to sit to his left, opposite his son.

"My family is large," Jake explained. "I want you to meet some of them tonight."

Great, Richard thought to himself, just what I need - a family affair! How on earth will I get out of this one?

It was extremely awkward for him to be treated as a guest of honour, being introduced to every new arrival. He was yearning for a cold beer. One young boy after another came into the room, greeted him respectfully and took his seat at the table. They were all dressed in plain working clothes but were immaculately clean. None of them was even close to twenty, in fact he guessed most of them to be around fourteen or younger. The room suddenly reminded him of the dormitory at his old boarding school. Rows of awkward looking boys full of suppressed testosterone.

The atmosphere in the room was stifling, and he started to feel more than awkward. He had a sudden premonition of looming disaster.

24

The excitement of preparing for a visitor had spread like wildfire among the sister-wives. All day long, some of them had been cleaning the main room, scrubbing the floor and oiling the wood, others had been busy chopping vegetables and meat, preparing a tasty stew that would stretch far enough to feed all without revealing how empty their pantry was. Martha had begged Marion to let her help serve at the table and nearly cried in gratitude when she was given permission.

The whole afternoon was a blur for her. She was constantly walking past the kitchen window hoping to see when the boys arrived at the house. Jake junior was the first, and she was fortunate enough to catch a glimpse of him when he crossed the backyard. He wore the same trousers and shirt as yesterday, and she forgot to breathe as the sweet memory of his forbidden touch flooded through her, making her blood rush to her face. She quickly checked to see if she was being watched. None of the sister-wives in the kitchen had the time to take notice of her, so she pretended to wipe the window pane to steal a few more precious seconds. He turned the corner to walk to the main entrance at the front of the house, then he was gone from her view and she rushed over to the stove to be one of the first allowed to serve.

After a seemingly endless wait, Marion came into the kitchen, announced that the guest had arrived and that all were now seated, and ordered the food and drinks to be carried into the dining room. Martha jumped to attention and wanted to grab the first plate loaded with freshly baked bread rolls, but Anna pushed her aside.

"Go away and let me do it," she hissed. Anna looked as if she had a fever, with burning eyes and blotchy red spots on her cheeks. Martha recoiled from her but did not let go of the plate. She clutched it for dear life while Anna tried to take it from her. "Let me have that!" Anna hissed again. "My husband needs to see me. I need to see him. Don't you understand!"

Martha could only think of Jake junior being in the next room. Anna had no right to push her away. Who had allowed her into the kitchen anyway? Martha hadn't seen Anna since she had given birth to the twins and had thought she would not be tolerated in the main house. "What are you doing here?" she protested. "You have no permission to be here!"

"Let go of the plate."

"No."

"Martha! Anna! Stop this!" Marion called out and everything came to a standstill. One look was enough for her to evaluate the situation.

Anna pleaded with her. "Please, Marion, please, I know I am not supposed to be in the kitchen, but please let me try and make amends with my husband. Let me show him that I have changed."

There was nothing Martha could say that would explain her eagerness to serve the men in the dining room, so she let go of the plate and waited helplessly for Marion's decision. Tears welled up in her eyes. Marion gave her a puzzled look and told her to go back to her work at the office. She was not needed here any more, Anna would take her place.

As soon as everybody had settled on the long table, some women came in, carrying jugs and bowls of food. The women were not expected to sit down – all the place settings were taken up - but busied themselves with serving. Each one of them knew exactly what their job was. One poured water in the glasses, another placed small baskets with bread on the table, yet another put larger plates filled with some stew in front of the waiting boys.

Richard pretended to innocently watch the activity while studying the women, taking great care to guess their ages. Knowing Daisy, she would pester him later on with questions. None of the serving women looked underage. There were no young girls there. Some were reasonably young, maybe just in their early twenties, with the woman called Emma, Jake had introduced to him as his second wife, probably the youngest of them all. Others were very mature, closer to Marion's age, and he guessed her to be around forty.

He did a quick calculation. There were twenty young boys there and nearly as many women, albeit older. None of the boys would be married already; so there was definitely an imbalance. And where did those boys come from? Where were their fathers? Why weren't they present at this all-male family affair? Jake couldn't be the father of all of them! But it certainly looked that way! If he really was, he would have to have more than two wives. All those women – they couldn't be... Richard was suddenly sure of it, but he suppressed his surprise and promised himself not to mention this sudden revelation to Daisy. She would freak out if she knew.

Slowly everybody was served and the women disappeared back into the kitchen. He could have bet his life on Jake grabbing the opportunity to give a little speech disguised as saying grace and aimed at the only heathen at the table. Before Richard could finish this thought, Jake stood up, opened his arms wide and bellowed so powerfully that everybody on the table, including Richard, jerked to attention: *"For straight is the gate and narrow the way that leads to the exaltation and continuation of our lives, and few will find it."*

Jake's face was stern, with eyes looking at nobody in particular but commanding attention from everybody present. Richard considered standing up and taking his leave politely and quickly but could not think of an excuse that was not insulting. All he could think was *this can't be real.*

Fake Jake was warming up. *"But if you receive me in this world, then you shall receive your exaltation. This is eternal life. To know the only wise and true God whom he has sent. I am he. Therefore, receive my law."*

Now Richard's psyche switched from uncomfortable to unbearable. Did the guy truly believe he was a God?

"Broad is the gate and wide the way that leads to the deaths, and many will go there because they do not receive me nor do they abide in my law."

That did it. He was not going to sit and listen to the ranting of a mad man. He tried to stand up, but Jake must have anticipated this move. He lowered one arm and rested it on Richard's shoulder, effectively pressing him down.

"So says the revelation God has given to Joseph Smith..."

Thank God, he had misunderstood. Jake did not really consider himself a God, or did he?

"It is written in Section one hundred thirty two of the doctrine and covenants, which we will now listen to while enjoying the food I have put on our table. Thank the Lord."

As Fake Jake the Wannabe-God took his seat, all the boys repeated his *thank the Lord* and started to dig in like starving wolves. Only the poor young fellow at the end of the table could not join in the feeding frenzy because he had to read aloud from a book. Apart from his breaking voice, altering between childish heights and adult depths, and the sounds of spoons scraping on plates there was total silence. This was not the right moment for an escape. Richard decided to eat whatever they had put in front of him, although not with the same desperate urgency. As soon as this crazy meal was over, no strong-arm in the world would stop him from making a hurried exit.

Section 132 had sixty-six paragraphs! When the reader finished with number sixty-six he closed the book, sat down and started shovelling in his by now cold meal. Isn't six the number of the devil, Richard wondered? How fitting to have double sixes! This text was sent straight from hell to punish him for all the sins he had committed so far in his life. Putting himself in such a situation was the biggest sin of them all, and he swore silently that he would never again let himself be dragged into something he did not want to do. Not even by Daisy's sulking!

He had firmly closed his ears to the reading, and in any case would not have understood many of the ancient sounding words, but he had still been able to grasp the meaning of it. It was all about giving men the right to have many wives and damning them if they did not exercise that right. Men without plural wives would still go to heaven, but there they would only be angels and would have to be servants to those men who had become Gods. So that's where the angel-servant Jake had mentioned came from! Richard could save himself the question, he understood perfectly what Jake had meant. He would be one of those unfortunate angel-creatures. Unconverted, he would have to slave away for the well-being of the polygamous God-men. But even if he joined the true faith, he would have to pray that the Lord, or his Prophet, or the Bishop, found him worthy enough to allocate more than one wife to him. If not, well, then he would be allowed to accompany them into Eternity, but would still be their servant. Nice plan! After all, one needs workers on the other side too. Somehow, the context of this whole weird concept annoyed him tremendously. He was itching to jump up and get out of this cold house. He promised himself that he would never come back here. As soon as he had left this place behind him, he would forget that Fake Jake and his strange brood even existed.

It was hard to tell if the boys at the table were really listening to the reading or if they just accepted it as inevitable if they wanted to be fed. They certainly were a hungry lot. They had shovelled the stew into their mouths with the speed of light and had helped themselves to more out of the large pots the women had put in the middle of the table until it was all gone.

Jake had been eating with similar gusto, every now and then wiping some drips off his chin. When all the eating noises, the scraping of spoons and greedy shuffling had finally died down, he looked at Richard and said. "Well, Richard, I hope you enjoyed the meal more than you enjoyed our prayers."

There were no pleasantries left inside Richard to reply to such a smug remark. In fact, he was so disgusted with the whole scenario that he had to force himself to keep some semblance of civility. "Well, Jake, the food is good. Give my compliments to the cook. But I could have done without your cheap attempt to convert me in one quick session. Quite frankly, I found it distasteful - which I am sure is the right word to use for a demonstration like this at a dinner table - to be forced to sit through a religious recital that offends my personal beliefs. You have shown no respect towards me, your guest, and therefore I have no qualms to inform you that I respectfully consider my visit over."

He got up. Slowly, deliberately. All the boys had turned their faces and stared at him as if he was some circus attraction with two heads.

Jake laughed. "Calm down Richard, I did not mean to offend you. I am sorry."

"So am I. The show is over!"

With this he moved his chair back and walked around the table towards the door. "Good evening, gentlemen. It was nice meeting you all."

"Stay!" Now Jake had jumped up as well, flabbergasted at his guest's behaviour. Obviously nobody had ever stood up to him like this before! His body was shaking with anger and his face had turned a bright tomato-red. "You can't leave here!"

Richard had reached the door. "You bet I can!" he hurled at him and left.

232

25

For one miserable lonely hour Martha lamented her fate, then she made a bold decision. She would risk going to the pond and hide there, hoping Jake junior would do the same once dinner was over. Anna's cheap victory must have upset the sister-wives enough that they would insist she stay on after dinner and help with the cleaning up. Martha also hoped nobody would expect her back in the kitchen or would look for her in the office. With a little bit of luck, she had the whole evening to herself.

However, she could not take the usual route up the hill, which was in plain view for anybody looking out the kitchen window. Therefore, she decided to sneak around the main house, crouching low when passing the windows, hoping that nobody would exit from the front entrance. Then she could race the short distance along the driveway and make her way back through the forest behind the house until she reached the path that eventually led to the pond. It meant a large detour, but at least most of the time she would be hidden from anybody's view.

It took her another half hour before she could muster enough courage to leave the house. Once she had cleared the open space where she could be discovered easily, she darted down the hill, making sure that she always stayed behind the row of bushes that lined the driveway.

Walking to the car, Richard suddenly felt odd. A sensation similar to fear, but not quite the same, crept up his back, tickling his scalp and forming goose bumps along the nape of his neck. Was Jake following him? Was he going to jump him from behind and force him to the ground? Maybe with a knife? Or would he aim a gun at him to stop him from leaving?

Maybe it was just the sudden temperature change, walking out of the cool house into the hot air, that made him shiver. The sun was setting, but it was not yet dark and no breeze dispersed the stifling heat.

He quickly turned and looked back. Nobody was following him. The interior of his car was a furnace, with the cheap plastic seat scorching his thighs and back as soon as he sat down. He ignored it and started the engine. He wanted to get away from this place as fast as he could. Driving down the driveway he kept looking in the rear mirror, expecting to see one of the young boys running out of the house with a rifle in his hand, aimed at him. Nobody came. As soon as the house had disappeared from sight, he reduced his speed a little, but promised himself that if the gate was locked he would crash right through it. To hell with the damage, the rental car was insured, and he would tell them he'd had an accident.

There was only one spot where Martha had to cross the road before she could make a beeline up to the nearby forest. She was so excited that she did not even hear the car coming down the driveway.

A gust of gleaming metal trailing heavy dust suddenly appeared on the driveway. The noise was murderous; Martha stopped dead in her tracks, knowing that her last second had come.

When Richard turned the last corner before the driveway straightened out, he barely missed hitting a shadowy figure amongst the bushes at the side of the road. He had taken the corner a bit too wide and stomped hard on the brakes and jerked the steering wheel to the left, trying to avoid whatever was standing there. Only at the very last second did he realize that the figure was human. A female figure. The woman was pressing herself deep into the willow branches along the roadside. His adrenalin was pumping even harder now than when he had left Jake's house. He had nearly killed a woman! Jumping out of the car as soon as it had come to a stop, he saw that she was no more than a young girl, fifteen or sixteen at the most, wearing a by now familiar long dress.

"Are you okay?" he yelled at her.

She stood frozen in shock but seemed to be unhurt. Luckily he had not knocked her over, although she had been nearly squashed between the willow bush and his side window when he slid by her. He let out an exhausted, grateful sigh. "Thank God, I didn't hit you."

She was still frozen in position, but now it seemed more in fear than in shock. Her big eyes kept staring at him in horror as he walked closer toward her. It was only for a brief moment that he saw her face. What he saw made him stop in his tracks. He stiffened and stared back at her. This young woman, or girl, was a sculpture chiselled by a master artist. Although tiny, her delicate body was already formed like a woman and could not be mistaken for that of a child. Her features were hard to make out, all he could see were her bright, bright pupils swimming in white circles. She looked innocent, lovable, adorable – evoking pictures of Disney cartoon figures in his mind. Pretty, perfect, dream-like figures, invented to be protected and adored. She could have been Snow White if her hair had been dark, but it was the colour of Sahara sands, surrounding her head like a halo. It blinded him to look at her and he had to squint, wondering if he saw a Mirage until he realized that the final rays of the setting sun were shining directly on her, blurring all contours and making it impossible for him to see her properly.

She still had not made a sound but now began to move. Her hands flew to her face, covering it for a split second. Then she lowered them again, grabbed her wide skirt and began to run. She fled from him. He did not attempt to follow her. She was unhurt, scared of him, the stranger who had nearly killed her – and he was in a bit of a hurry himself.

Martha had instinctively pressed herself deep into the willow bush and had thereby avoided being hit by the car. A man – whom she assumed to be her husband's visitor – had jumped out of the car and talked to her, acting all excited. She had not listened to what he said but had quickly scanned the car. It had been empty. That was a good sign. She had run away as fast as she could, hoping the driver would not turn back to the main house to tell on her. There was a slim chance that her escape might stay undetected.

All she could think of was that Jake junior might be already waiting for her at the pond.

Shaking his head without understanding why, Richard got back in his car and drove, slower now, to the gate. He got out again, listening briefly into the quiet dusk, hearing nothing but some mosquitoes getting ready for their busy twilight activities.

The gate was bolted but unlocked. He opened it, drove through and, like a considerate guest, closed it behind him again. It was a bit of an anti-climax. On the drive back to Kamloops he tried to recapture the scene over dinner, but all he could think of was the girl with the sand coloured hair.

He drove directly to the airport, deposited his rental car and waited to get on the last flight back to Vancouver. He had an hour to spare, so he settled into the licensed coffee shop and rewarded himself with a cold beer.

Daisy should be home by now, so he tried there first. The line was busy. He watched a football game on the TV screen above the bar for a while but it was not very interesting; the B.C. Lions were not giving their best. He ordered another beer and tried to call again.

This time she picked up the phone sounding not overly surprised to hear from him. By now it was nine o'clock and she must assume that he had left Jake's compound and was back in cell reception.

When he told her that he was already at Kamloops airport she reacted surprised, but put her finger in the wound right away. "I know they have early dinners in the country, but not that early. What went wrong?"

"Just about everything," he admitted. "But not through my doing. I was forced to sit with Jake and a bunch of young boys at that long table he has got and be subjected to the most insulting treatment you can imagine."

"Oh dear! You lost your temper?"

"No, I didn't for a change. But I was close to it. Jake pushed my buttons as hard as he could, but I am proud to report that I stayed calm and collected and told him politely that I would rather not meet with him again. My promise for future visits has hereby been negated." He proceeded to describe the surreal, all-male dinner atmosphere with the involuntary Book of Mormon education, but she was much more interested in the female presence – or non-presence.

"Where was Marion? Weren't there any women there? If there were twenty guys, there had to be women too."

"Of course. There were quite a few women there, but they didn't join us for dinner."

"Why not?"

"They were just serving."

"Oh shit!"

"I guess that's how it's done up there."

"I told you! Jake keeps them as slaves."

Contrary to his usual behaviour he seemed to be the master of his emotions today. He was really proud of himself. "Please Daisy, let's not start arguing again. There is a huge gap between being a servant or a slave, and at the risk of repeating myself, it's none of our business. Now more than ever."

"How old were the women you have seen?"

After a tiny hesitation, which hopefully she would not catch, he told her that none of the women present had been under-age.

"You're lying!"

"No, it's the truth. None of the women in the room were younger than maybe twenty. Honestly."

"What about the others? There must have been others! You said the boys were mostly very young. You know what that means."

"No, I do not, and I don't want to know!"

"Those boys were sons, not husbands. Which means all the boys there are Jake's sons and all the women are Jake's wives. I am sure there are under-age girls as well. Jake was hiding them from you. He has been playing you along again."

He had been doing so well until now. "Whatever happens there is totally not my concern. Stop pestering me! I've had it. After that little freak show today, I'll never set foot on Jake's property ever again and I can't help it if you are upset with me. You didn't have to subject yourself to such nonsense and you can't expect me to do more than I've done already. I only went to see Jake to make you feel better, but this is the end of the line!"

"Okay, okay, I understand. You're mad. You don't care. But I do! There must be something that can be done."

"If you want to carry on, be my guest, but don't expect me to join your quest. It's none of my goddamn business."

Daisy was unimpressed. "Fine, but you will create some bad Karma for yourself. If you know something is wrong and you won't at least try to do something about it, it makes you guilty by association!"

His hand gripped his mobile until his knuckles turned white. "You know what? You can shove your Karma. I make my own. Stop meddling! Just stick to your job and leave me alone!"

"Don't you worry, I will!"

They hung up on each other. He didn't know how righteous Miss Daisy felt at that moment, but her constant critique of his actions annoyed the hell out of him. After all he had done to placate her, was there no gratitude? Didn't anybody understand that he had tried as hard as he could? To hell with all of them. Jake, his boys, his women, even the lovely sandy haired girl on the side of the road. To hell with her too, she had been scared of him. To hell with Jeanne d'Arc who had got him into this stupidity in the first place. And to hell with Daisy and her arrogant demands. Especially Daisy!

26

When she finally got to the pond the sun was slowly setting behind the hill. Martha did not worry how she would find her way back in the dark. She did not worry about the black bears or moose or coyotes living in the woods. All she cared about was getting there so she could wait for the one person who mattered to her.

She sat on an old dried out tree stump, chasing away a few mosquitoes playing in the dusk. Not many were left so late in summer and they had no more real bite in them. The last rays of daylight coloured the puffy white clouds pink and the sky in different shades of purple. Martha had never had the opportunity to just sit and watch nature reveal its beauty with such dramatic and magnificent results. As she gazed into the shifting layers of air above her, observing how they now moved from red to blue, she nearly forgot the reason for being there.

Then her sharpened senses heard a noise that was not part of the natural surroundings. Above the hum of insects, the swirl of water flowing over pebbles, the blow of the gentle evening breeze and the occasional call of the loon was the minute sound of a human making a careful approach. Martha heard him immediately and jumped up full of excited anticipation. He was coming!

Her heart stopped altogether and she thought she would faint. Sudden panic gripped her. What if he was not expecting her? What if she had it all wrong and he was coming here every evening to get away from his brothers to take a swim in privacy? What if he resented her being here? Thought of her as an intruder – reported her to his father!

Then he broke through the bushes that hid the pond and stopped in his tracks. It was too late. He'd seen her. She quickly lowered her eyes.

He came closer, so close that she could smell his skin above the sweet scents of the wild flowers still blooming on the ground. It disturbed and confused her so much that she opened her eyes again. He was as close as last time, his body nearly connecting with hers, so it must be his skin and his hair she was smelling with such intensity. She could not name what his scent reminded her of, had absolutely no comparison, but smiled because it was so delicious. His hand came toward her face, again just like last time, and with it another waft of this unique fragrance. He smiled back at her as he touched her cheek. His fingers lingered on her skin, gifting her with another sensation. Martha started to tremble.

"You've come," he whispered coarsely.

She did not trust herself to speak, so she kept looking at him, which was nearly as daring. But he was not intimidating like the other men, and she did not feel threatened by his presence. She felt secure and protected.

He lifted his fingers from her face and searched for her hand. She willingly interlocked her hand with his, and he gently pulled her down to the ground. For a long time, they sat next to each other on the soft grass, looking at the pond. Slowly the sky turned as dark as the water surface, settling into a comfortable semi-darkness. A nearly full moon rose, its yellow light reflected in the pond. Martha wanted to study his beautiful face so she would remember every detail, but she did not dare to turn to him. She resigned herself to feel the touch of his fingers on her skin. They travelled along the palm of her hand, stroked her wrist and came back again to settle in her hand. She wondered if he would do more. Like her husband had done.

The memory of his father made her shiver involuntarily.

Jake finally spoke again. "What is it? Are you cold?"

She shook her head. He must never know what she had endured. What his own father had subjected her to. A painful truth spread inside her. Wouldn't he know anyway?

As if he could read her mind, he whispered so quietly that she had to listen carefully. "I know you don't belong to him. Not in your heart."

Martha nearly fainted. She nodded in agreement, then she took a deep breath and told him even more quietly that she was his and always would be.

After that, they sat and held hands and did not say any more until it was time to go.

"Tomorrow?" Jake asked when they reached the end of the path where they had to part ways.

Martha shrugged her shoulders. She did not know when the next chance to break away from the main house would present itself.

"Don't worry," he said. "I'll be here every evening. I'll wait for you."

The next morning hardly concealed gossip was making the rounds in the kitchen. Luckily not about her. Last night, some of the women had been waiting behind the door ready to serve the men and couldn't help but overhear how rude their husband's guest had behaved. They were still in shock over this sensational incident and told the others in no uncertain terms about it. The man had ridiculed their husband's sermon, had yelled at him, insulted him, and had then stormed out before supper was over!

Martha concentrated hard to hide her satisfaction when the women went on and on about this. The visitor, who had raced down the driveway and nearly killed her in the process, had been instrumental for her beloved Jake to get away early and meet her at the pond. For that reason she liked the man, although she had no recollection of what he looked like and would not have recognized him if he stood in front of her.

All day, she was in a heightened state of anticipation and could barely concentrate on the work to be done.

Late in the afternoon, she overheard another conversation between her husband and Marion through the hole in the office wall. Her husband was angry that the plan he had had with the visitor had failed, and accused his first wife of neglecting her duties. If the food had not been so bad, the visitor would have stayed. Martha knew that this was untrue, and surely Marion knew it too, but who could argue with their husband?

Marion reacted as she always did, she asked demurely for his forgiveness but defended herself. She carefully argued that there was not enough food left in the whole compound to prepare a better meal. There was no money in the bank account and very little supplies still stored in the pantry. She started crying when he slapped her in the face – Martha could hear it with horrible clarity and nearly replaced the book she was holding because she couldn't bear to listen to the unjust punishment – and told her from now on it would be her sole responsibility to take care of the household. He could do no more than he had done already, and if the wives were too stupid to make sellable things out of their dump collections and thought they could squander the supplies and live like there was no tomorrow, then so be it. Then he stormed out of his private quarters and Martha put the book back in its place and sat down at her desk, waiting for the evening to come.

Unfortunately there was no opportunity to escape unnoticed that night. It took another three days before she managed to get away and see Jake junior again. Full of anxiety and with a racing heart, she finally got to the pond – to find him waiting already. He greeted her with that enigmatic smile of his that managed to calm and soothe her immediately. How wonderful it was to feel so special.

They sat and held hands again. This time she did dare to speak to him, if only a few words.

That behaviour became a pattern over the next few weeks. Once or twice every week she got away, always undetected and always with the same level of excitement. Most of the time he was already waiting for her, sometimes she had to wait for him, but never for very long. They talked a bit more every time, telling each other little things, discovering how the other thought and acted, all the while avoiding any dangerous subject. They never mentioned that she was his father's wife, they did not discuss the future, or the lack of it, they simply revelled in each other's company. Martha was happy, and he told her he also had never

242

known a feeling of such immense joy. Every time he saw her, happiness flowed through him, he explained in his soft, warm, dark voice and he only lived for those moments when they were together.

That was all she wanted too.

As the food supplies dwindled, life became more challenging. Every week, Marion rationed the food more and more until it reached the bare minimum where everybody was close to starving. Martha knew why, but it did not bother her. She felt as if she could have survived on air and water as long as she could secretly meet with Jake junior.

She was securely lodged in the main house, safely tucked away from prying eyes. If she would have to live in the women's quarters she would not be able to disappear so frequently. Marion had told her that she was ideally suited to become Katherine's replacement, the children adored her and she was quick to learn, and that she should start studying for a teacher's exam. She gave her all the books needed to prepare for a home schooling course and allowed her to spend even more time in her office, so there was little danger that her permanent place in the main house was threatened.

But for the rest of the sister-wives, life was getting really hard. As soon as harvest was done, Marion sent most of the wives to the dump again. They went grudgingly and blamed her for the hardship they had to endure, but Martha knew the truth. She had listened to their husband's new directive. He now wanted the women to sift through the garbage and look for metal. He was convinced they would find gold and silver. Marion had tried to argue that it was impossible to find precious objects there, and that it would be better for them to concentrate on their sewing as the quilts created at least a meagre income. He refused to listen to her and became quite agitated when she started to beg on behalf of her sister-wives. It is so hard on them, she cried, and they are so weak.

Of course, over the next weeks they didn't find a scrap of gleaming metal. Their husband started to give new orders nearly every day. It seemed to Martha, who overheard most of their arguments, that none of his orders made any sense - in fact, they were becoming increasingly erratic. After the metal disaster, he wanted all his wives to concentrate on collecting old newspapers because he could make a fortune with them. Then, after the dealer in town rejected his truckload full of soggy paper pulp, he told them to stop this. They must now bottle the methane gas evaporating from the garbage. That was rapidly becoming a sparse commodity. As soon as the oil reserves in Alberta were depleted, everybody would run their cars on methane gas.

Marion didn't even know how to explain this to the sister-wives on dump duty. She just said at the morning meeting they should collect empty bottles and bring them back. A huge pile of empty bottles grew in the yard next to the storage shed. Their husband seemed happy to inspect his increasing stash of invisible gas every day.

Watching this madness going on, Martha had one brief moment of anguish when he told Marion that the school should close. All the children should start collecting as well. Marion was adamant that at least Martha must continue to keep a semblance of curricular activities going, just in case the government sent somebody unannounced to check on them. We need the grant, she argued, we can't risk being investigated by them. That seemed to get through to him – and as a result, Martha was the only wife who didn't have to go to the dump. She could disappear to the pond most evenings without being missed by anybody.

Just like last year, those poor women in the dump prayed for early winter, and again the Lord must have listened to them. Snow arrived at the end of October, on the day of Martha's fifteenth birthday and created a problem she had not considered before. Her footprints in the fresh snow would tell everybody where she came from and where she was going.

When Martha looked out of the window and saw the road blanketed with fresh snow it dawned on her that she might not be able to see Jake junior again until next spring and she started to cry.

27

Martha grabbed every chance she could get to look out the office window, neglecting her studies and her work. Since it had started to snow, she had trouble concentrating. All she could think about was spring time, and that was so far away that she thought she would die of despair. Sometimes, while staring out into the unforgiving white, she caught herself counting again. It was very difficult to count snowflakes falling from the sky. And it didn't make time move any faster.

The snow had kept her apart from Jake too long already when, one afternoon, she heard a pickup truck in the driveway. Her heart jumped a little as it always did when there was any activity outside. She quickly stood up and went to the window.

Today her luck had changed. It was him! Jake junior was clearing the yard with the snow-plough he had mounted on the front of his truck. She could see his beautiful face clearly behind the windscreen. Every so often he looked up. Martha was overjoyed to catch a glimpse of him and thought he might have noticed her too, but could not be sure. Then the office door opened and Marion came in. Martha had to abandon her position and go back to her desk. There was no excuse for her to linger at the window. She pretended to close the window as if she had just aired the room.

Marion didn't stay but only picked up a book from the shelf and left again. With a huge sigh of relief Martha rushed back to the window. Jake junior was now ploughing the path that led away from the house and into the adjacent forest. Martha was not sure if that was done every year, but it made sense to her to keep this way free as it was leading up to the prison hut.

Jake junior was alone in the backyard. Martha opened the window to be able to see him better.

He leaned out of the truck window as if he was inspecting the path he was clearing, then he looked up to her and smiled. Then he slowly and deliberately turned his head back towards the forest and then back to her again, staring at her intently. She understood right away what he was trying to tell her. Stay away from the unploughed way, he instructed her silently, go up there in that direction and I will find you.

Martha nodded and closed the window again. Her knees were suddenly so weak, she had to sit down. She folded her shaking hands together, placed them on the desktop and rested her head on them. He had come! He had searched for ways to see her again. He couldn't live without her, just as she couldn't bear the lonely days without him. She was deliriously happy and knew deep inside that she would risk her life for a chance to see him. That very evening she would go up the snow-ploughed path. If no fresh snow fell until then, her foot prints would barely show on the frozen ground and the forever blowing breeze would cover them within seconds again.

She had to walk over half an hour in the bitter cold before she found him. He was sitting in his pickup truck, waiting for her, and when she was close enough, he leaned over, opened the passenger door and told her to get in and duck down. Once she was inside, he covered her with a blanket and drove all the way back again, past the main house and on to the small group of cabins the boys had built for themselves. Jake parked the pickup so close to the door of one of the cabins that she had no problem sliding over to his side, crawling out of the truck and into the cabin without the risk of being seen by anybody, even if they were close by. Her trust in him was so absolute that she did not hesitate to do as he asked.

Once he had followed her into the cabin, he quickly closed the door, secured it with a wooden plank and hung an old potato sack in front of the window pane. They were alone in the small room. Martha looked around and saw a bed with a blanket and a pillow on it, a table below the window with a chair in front, on it an already lit propane lantern and, best of all, there was a small cast iron stove that radiated warmth on the wall opposite the window. Jake busied himself adding a log to the fire and turning up the light a notch, then asked her to take a seat on the chair. She did, feeling terribly awkward. This was different from being at the pond with him. It was the first time ever she was alone in a room with a grown man that was not her husband.

Either he felt her nervousness or he was sharing it. He started to talk more and faster than usual, without looking at her. He proudly told her he had built the cabin for himself because he hated spending time with his brothers. They were noisy and rude and boisterous. She noticed that he did not mention if his father had given him permission to do such an extraordinary thing. So far, they had avoided mentioning his name altogether, but then he suddenly explained that he was in charge of his younger brothers and that none of them were allowed in here. They had to do as he told them. Those comments implied indirectly that his father did not know or care about what any of them did as long as his oldest son kept his siblings under control.

Finally he looked at her again. "You are safe in here," he said, although in a very low voice for the benefit of anybody walking by. "As long as we don't make any noise, nobody will know you are here. I hope you don't mind me bringing you here." His eyes were pleading with her to accept this hide-away – and whatever came with it.

Martha was surprised at how worried he was about her opinion. She had come with him without hesitation, had put her life in his hands, why would she now feel bad about it? Of course, she had to get used to being alone with him in a confined space, but, as it became clear to her now, it was also something she had dreamed about. All her life she had been lonely without realizing what was missing. Now, that she had spent every waking moment of the past few months yearning for him, she revelled in his company and gave no thought to the consequences. There was no future to consider. Only the present mattered.

Before she thought about what she was doing she stood up and walked over to the bed. "Come and sit with me," she invited him. "I'm glad you brought me here."

He was more nervous than she was. His hands were fidgeting and his eyes were darting around the room, but he sat down quickly, leaving a little space between them. "If you want to come again, I must pick you up directly at the kitchen entrance. As long as there is snow, it's too risky for us to walk anywhere. I can back up with the truck really close against the door. If you see me moving snow in the evening, and you have a chance to hide next to the wood pile, I'll look for you there and you can hop inside the truck just like today. Nobody will see you getting in. That's the only way we can meet until the snow is gone."

This had been his longest speech so far. Martha had listened with growing delight and nodded enthusiastically while he spoke. He already planned to see her again. He wanted her here, or anywhere, wanted to spend time with her! He was willing to take big risks just to see her.

"Thank you for putting yourself in danger because of me," she said, hoping this was enough to show her pleasure.

"It's far more dangerous for you," he answered.

She saw a shadow fall on his face, dimming the brightness of his blue eyes. They now searched hers, full of concern that she might not understand what her fate would be if discovered. "Don't worry," she made light of it. "I don't want to live without seeing you again. But what about you? If you are caught, what will happen to you?"

She really didn't know. Men didn't get killed, or did they? There had been a few incidents when she had been living in her family's compound in Arizona. Once, a boy from a neighbour's family had been caught doing something indecent with his half-sister. Martha had not been told what had been going on, but her mothers had warned her that she would be killed like the girl if she was found alone with a boy. The boy did not have to die, but he was sent away. Another time, one of the older men who already had a number of wives, had taken a young girl to his house without her father's permission, but that was solved quickly. The girl had been only twelve then, not ready to be married, so the Elders had granted the man exemption from the rule. He married the girl on the spot, but she died soon after. Martha's mother told her that the girl had been guilty of seducing the man, and therefore the devil had grabbed her and made her jump off the barn roof. No, nothing ever happened to the men; nothing would happen to Jake junior, unless the fact that she was betrothed to his father made a difference.

Jake smiled at her. "You amaze me. Aren't you scared at all?"

She vehemently shook her head to make it clear to him how little she cared about herself. "No, I'm not."

"Not even if you think of what will happen later on?" He was talking about the after-life. About the threat of eternal damnation that held all the others in its iron grip. Could she tell him what she really thought about it? Would he despise her for throwing off the shackles that bound him to his family and his faith?

His face was so open, so anxious to take away the fear he assumed she must feel, she decided to give him an honest answer, even if her confession was nothing more than a faint tremble. "I don't really believe what the scripture says."

There it was! Never before had she articulated her doubt in what was written. To hear herself say the unspeakable, no matter how shaky her words sounded, was liberating beyond imagination. So she added, a touch firmer: "I don't believe what *he* says either" – meaning her husband and knowing that his son understood – "I don't believe that I have to be bound to him for all eternity. I don't even believe that I belong to him now."

For a terribly long time he did not reply. His eyes searched over every square inch of the cabin, wandering from the table to the chair, along the walls, sliding up and down as if he was seeing all of it for the first time, and she was getting very worried until she realized that he did not consciously see anything. He was deep in thought.

Martha could not stand it any longer. "I'm sorry I said anything," she begged. "Do you hate me now?"

He shook his head and she regained some of her courage. "It's just that I can't believe in anything any more. I probably never did. Nothing makes sense to me. Why should I try so hard in this life to conform to the scripture if all I get is more of the same later on? I'd rather go to the deep abyss than stay his wife for ever and ever!"

Jake slowly took her hands in his and looked at her. "You are so incredibly brave. You are a girl, and yet you say aloud what I don't want to admit to myself. I too have often wondered about all the strict rules we have to obey, but I have never dared to question them openly. I'm the first born, so I have more rights than all my brothers, but what did I do with them? I have closed my heart to all the things I consider unjust and pretended not to see them. When I listen to my father's sermons or when I see him administer punishments, I often think he is wrong. It is unfair for one man to hold all the power over so many – even if he is my father. Why is my mother worth nothing? Or her sister-wives? You are one of them. Why don't you have a say in how to live your life? I don't understand most of what is written in the doctrine and covenants. I have been trying hard to accept what is written without questioning it, but it's been a real struggle. And now you make it sound so easy. All I have to do is admit to myself that I don't believe. That is the only way to come to terms with it. I realize that I have to make my own decisions now. I can't let others rule over me any longer. Because I don't believe, and because I feel deep inside how wrong all of this is, I must be allowed to change it. I'm my own man! From now on, I will shape my own future, and so will you!"

Martha stared at him, speechless. He not only agreed with her apostate judgment of the faith, thereby sharing her deepest and darkest secret, he went one step further. He concluded that, if he didn't believe, he had a right to shake himself free of the unwanted faith that had been forced onto him. The sheer magnitude of this realization was earth shattering. It made her tremble. They both did not believe and according to him, they were free to think and act accordingly.

But could they really?

Until now, the future had been elusive. Her current existence had been ruled entirely by the desire to see him, to be able to exchange a few words and maybe even touch him briefly, and that had been good enough for her to take her from day to day, filling her existence with joy and satisfaction. But now he had opened a door to her future, and she felt pressured to demand more from her life. She wanted the right to break free from all constraints and to have a choice. She yearned to be free - but to do what? To live where?

It was impossible.

What had come over her? What was she thinking?

Martha was suddenly terribly confused and started to cry softly. There was no freedom, no future. Not for her, not for him. They were doomed from the beginning, even if he or she did not want to accept this.

Jake's body stiffened, his hands gripped her tighter and he had a determined look on his face. She had never seen such deep lines around his eyes. When he saw the tears running down her face, he realized that his words had upset her deeply and he softened again. After he had collected himself, he put one arm around her shoulder and gently rocked her. "Shh, don't cry, please. I will figure something out. Don't think about it, all right? Please. I will protect you. Nothing will happen to you. Please, stop."

He soothed her until she felt calmer. Of course there was no hope for them, but she was here now, with him, and nothing else mattered. Nothing had changed, except she trusted him even more now that she had opened her heart to him.

Martha turned her face up to him and waited. He was so close to her. When his mouth finally touched hers, she closed her eyes. The most amazing sensation of softness gradually hardened to a greedy desire to dig deep into his mouth, a desire he shared with the same intensity. Her breathing became erratic. She threw her arms around his neck to keep his mouth tightly pressed against hers. He grabbed her by the waist, lifted her onto his lap and kissed her harder and faster, breathing just as heavily. They fell back on the bed. Without breaking the lock of their lips, they settled into a more comfortable position, him half on top of her, savouring the mind-blowing sweetness and sensuality of the first kiss both of them had ever experienced.

When their flushed faces hurt from the sucking and licking and probing, they slowly let go of each other. That was all they could do. Their bodies were screaming for release from the tension they had allowed to mount inside themselves, but an invisible, insurmountable barrier held them back.

They did not sleep all night. It was too wonderful to cuddle up close, feeling the warmth of the other's body, whispering gently into each other's ears and letting their hands innocently stroke and explore the shape of their fully clothed bodies.

When it was time to go, Jake whispered into her ear that he must take her back now, the morning light would come up soon. It would not be unusual for him to drive up to the house still in darkness to bring firewood or attend to some other chores. This way she could sneak inside before her sister-wives showed up for kitchen duty.

When he used the term 'sister-wives' she hated him for a second, wanting to scream *I am not his wife – I have no sister-wife!*, but it was the truth and she could not blame him. So she gave him a final kiss, got up and braced herself. All life inside her would stop until she could see him again.

It was much more difficult than they had anticipated. Many times, he had to drive the truck around the backyard in vain. She only managed on very rare occasions to leave the main house at the right time for him to pick her up. In between those glorious moments full of barely contained passion were days and nights of aching desire. Martha longed every breathing moment to feel the touch of his hands, hear his voice, look deep into his eyes and smell his scent. When her senses finally got the satisfaction they craved, she always stopped short of allowing herself to give in to her desperate need to have more of him. She knew what a man could do, how ruthless he became when he took possession of a woman, and how much shame and pain this forceful act inflicted on the submissive part. Martha had never experienced the tenderness Jake junior offered her while they were lying on his cot, nor had she imagined that she herself would pant and wriggle in the same hot desire, but she was petrified that his passion would ultimately culminate in the same cruel activity his father had displayed, and thereby destroy everything they had. Every time they met, it became more difficult to stay firm. He pleaded to let him touch her. She opened the front of her dress, and when she felt his hand on her exposed breast she nearly died of pleasure, but she did not let him go further. Not yet. She wanted to indulge in the unbelievable sensuality she experienced and savour every pleasure-filled moment before it inevitably turned into suffering. Jake did not understand this as he had never been with a woman and only acted on his instincts. He promised her he would be gentle, but she knew that was impossible. No man could do what her husband had done to her without inflicting excruciating pain.

She knew, eventually she would have to give in to him. He had turned eighteen last month, and his growing manhood could not be denied much longer, but she was hoping to delay the inevitable as long as possible.

28

After surfing through all the channels without finding anything interesting to watch, Richard settled on a reality show about the daily antics of a punk tattoo artist. It was a repeat. Halfway through, he realized he had seen it before but was too lazy to do anything about it.

When the oven beeper announced that his frozen pizza was ready for consumption he got up, loaded it on a plate and grabbed another beer on the way back to the TV. Another boring night at home. Like so many nights before, he ate, he drank, he watched, until he was tired enough to go to bed. Would he ever get the energy back to resume his normal life? To do what? His small circle of friends did not exactly beg him to come out of hiding and his larger circle of acquaintances had given up sending him their occasional invitations as he had ignored all of them in the past year – ever since *the deal* had taken possession of him.

Being so busy for so long, he had not noticed how loneliness had slowly crept into his private life until his socializing had come to a complete standstill. As busy as he had been before, he now had a lot of spare time on his hands, waiting for winter to pass, counting the interest payments accumulating every single idle day. He could have revived some of his old contacts but could not get his act together. It was a bit like those awkward situations when one had done something wrong and had missed the first opportunity to apologize. With every passing day it gets harder to explain the delay, until it becomes practically impossible.

It was as if he was sitting on the sidelines, waiting to be called back into the game. Until he could start to build the road and get the final approval from Jeanne d'Arc, there was little to do. There was also no point in premature celebrations, even with Christmas around the corner, because his company had reached a financial breaking point and he could not afford the slightest thing to go wrong. Already he had reduced the office staff dramatically and as of January it would be only Daisy and him handling the precious little work there was. He briefly thought about the coming festive season. Realising he would be spending the holidays in his flat all by himself, he decided to give the third beer a miss and get into the Scotch.

He must have drifted off for a while. Waking up, his neck was stiff and the tattoo artist was replaced by an overweight chopper designer yelling at his sons in a spotless workshop. Did Daisy have any plans for Christmas? He rubbed his neck, rolled his head around and considered pouring himself another whisky. This was stupid. Daisy had limited her conversations with him to the absolutely essential business communication ever since he had stormed out of Jake's idiotic sermon. Why on earth would he ponder over how she spent her holidays? Probably with some friends, drinking eggnog until she was tipsy and tired, and then she would go to bed, probably not wearing pyjamas. Snuggling under the duvet, totally naked.

He pictured Daisy's lean body with those endless legs... oh no, forget it! He would not go down that road again. What was the matter with him? Had his voluntary sexual abstinence since the disaster in the Mouschi Bar sunk to a new disgusting low, getting a cheap kick out of imagining his assistant asleep in the nude? This was sickening! Quickly his developing hard-on died on him again and he poured himself another large shot. He just had to do something about his sex life.

Whisky didn't go so well with beer. The next morning, Richard did serious penance for his drinking excesses by quietly suffering on the treadmill until his headache subsided. A little worse for wear he made his way to the office around eleven.

Driving downtown, he made a decision which he knew was pitiful because it was born out of last night's confused loneliness. If Daisy was in, he would ask her point blank what her plans for Christmas were. If she didn't have anything lined up already, and somehow he was confident she didn't, he would ask her to accompany him on a skiing trip somewhere. If she hesitated in the slightest before she dished out a story about a family reunion or some other merry get-together, he would know that she was lying. Then he would tell her that he missed their friendship more than he had imagined and that he thought they should just forget their differences over something so silly that he had already forgotten the reason, go somewhere and have a hell of a good time together. She could ski, he was sure of that, she was athletic. But if she would prefer a trip to New York for some of the famous Christmas shopping or to Las Vegas for some shows, that was okay with him too.

In his mind, he gathered all the valid reasons to convince her. As far as he knew, she had spent her past Christmases at her parents' house in Calgary and on her return had complained about the boredom and the superficiality of the whole exercise. Every year, she had got into arguments with her brother and sister-in-law who, according to her, were conservative fools, and had subsequently announced that this had been the last time. He imagined the real reason those visits had been so ill-fated was her frustration over her love life. He was pretty sure she didn't have one. Maybe he should proffer his services in that respect. Here we go again, he cautioned himself, don't think along those lines!

Maybe he should offer to accompany her to Calgary – but then he would have to endure those dreadful family affairs which had never been his cup of tea, or eggnog in this case. Anyway, wasn't she old enough to skip visiting her relatives altogether? She would be much better off enjoying some fun times with a good old friend like himself who shared her inborn dislike of forced celebrations. In his youth, he had spent most Christmas holidays with a handful of other leftovers at boarding school. The two week break was hardly long enough to warrant the long journey to Canada to see his parents, and he had told them every year that they needn't bother to fly over to Switzerland as he did not want to see them. He was happy with his few friends who were just as lonely as him and just as determined to hide it. God, they had been a sorry lot. Every year he had been glad when this warm-and-fuzzy-feeling holiday was over, and it still puzzled him why so many people were so crazy about keeping up the appearances of enjoying it.

Surely Daisy did not have many friends; she was always working and never mentioned any friends. So, apart from her family, whom would she see? She might actually like the idea of spending time with him, strictly on a friendship basis of course. But did she consider him a friend?

Daisy was sitting behind her desk, talking on the phone. She was smiling like Mona Lisa. Secretive and knowing – conspiratorial even. Looking at the painting of Mona Lisa, he had pictured her listening and talking to a person opposite her in total confidence about something truly delicate. Just like Daisy now on the phone. As soon as she saw him her smile faded, and he felt at a disadvantage, not knowing what she had discussed with whom.

She quickly said good-bye and hung up. Where the crystal vase with the roses had been was now an elegant seasonal arrangement of genuine fir branches and glass balls with a candle in the middle. Daisy's arm shot out and moved the décor to safety.

"You don't need to do that. I come in peace."

She was not in the least embarrassed by her gesture. "One never knows with you. What do you want?"

He realized he had not been to her office since their last fight. "Can I sit down?"

"It's your office."

"No, Daisy, it's not just mine, it's yours too! Don't start like that." He checked his tone and reminded himself why he had come. "I have a question and I want you to tell me the truth."

"Ask."

"Am I your friend?"

She looked at him quizzically, contemplating her reply like a chess master his next move. Then she crossed her arms in front of her, not a good sign, leaned back in her chair and said very slowly. "I don't know. Are you *my* friend?"

Now, that was easy. "Yes, I certainly am."

"Well, then I guess I am too. And now tell me, what has reduced you to this kindergarden level of questioning. Do you want to exchange friendship rings next?"

"Don't make fun of me! I'm serious. I want to know because you certainly haven't behaved like a friend lately."

"If you say so."

She did not make it easy for him. But he would not get angry with her. He definitely would not! He had everything under control. "I know you're still mad at me, but I honestly don't really know why any more."

"Shall we call it a slight difference of opinion on moral matters?"

"Oh please, don't call it *moral!*"

"I thought you don't remember? Never mind. We will not reach a consensus on that one anyway. You are entitled to your opinion, we don't need to agree on everything."

"Exactly. Can't we put this whole stupid, ridiculous incident ..." she tried to object to his choice of words but he silenced her with an impatient gesture. "Yes, I know, it was not just that one isolated incident you are angry about. You are mad that I refuse to get involved with Jake's crazy set-up. But can't you respect my decision on this? Can't we agree that we have different objectives and opinions and put our differences behind us? It's not really something that should stand between us."

"So, friendship rings after all?"

No sign of that Mona Lisa smile returning, but he was working on it. "If you want one, I will run to the nearest bubblegum machine."

Now a glimmer of amusement danced in her hazel eyes. "You cheap bastard. I want a nice silver ring with turquoise stones. Southwest design."

He sighed in mock resignation. "Done! How about we consider it a Christmas present."

"No, I want it as an admittance of your failures as a human being."

"So you shall have it now." He pretended to have a sudden brain wave. "But how about Christmas? If you have nothing important planned we could try and spend some time together. Maybe a few days in the mountains?"

"First you give me a ring and then you ask me on a romantic getaway. Do you want to marry me?"

He burst out laughing. "No, don't worry. I know you are only interested in my fortune and not in my brilliant brain, good looks and chiselled six-pack."

Daisy finally smiled. "Actually, if you continue to guzzle down so much beer and don't start exercising soon, your midriff will resemble a barrel and not a six pack."

"Ouch! So, what do you say?"

"About what?"

"Christmas in the mountains."

"No."

Her answer stunned him. What can you say when you get rejected without even the pretence of a gentle let-down? Best to just leave the battlefield without a further attack. "Right, okay, well then, I'd better go and get you this ring."

"Richard," she called after him and he turned around at the door.

"Yes?"

"I've made some prior arrangements I can't really cancel. But I'm not seeing my family. I'm staying in town and maybe you'd like to come over to my flat on Christmas day for lunch."

"Hmm." Playing hard to get is not easy with one foot out the door. It didn't leave Richard much time to be persuaded.

"I'd really like you to come. There will be others too, so it should be a fun afternoon. Would eleven be too early for you?"

"No, that's fine." Going back to his office he felt quite pleased with himself. He had at least weaseled himself into a lunch date. Taking care of Christmas day had been the main hurdle to get through the holidays - and who knew, maybe he would meet somebody there who would distract him for the rest of the festive season. Daisy had said there would be others.

As it turned out he did not have to wait that long for some desperately needed female companionship. As long as Richard had lived in Europe he had always disliked Christmas Eve. The major event for Germans was Christmas Eve when the kids got their presents and everybody developed this cozy family feeling. Without family around, it can be a very depressing evening. All the pubs and restaurants were either closed or catered to a few unsociable drunks, unable to hold a reasonable conversation. In Vancouver however, the shoppers were rewarding themselves for their last minute gift buying successes by painting the town red, and he knew he would not have to face another boring Christmas Eve at home.

He left the office, picked up the necklace he had ordered to match Daisy's ring and felt so proud of finding the perfect Christmas present for her that he dropped into the nearest sports bar. It was over crowded with young and carefree adults out to have a good time. Soon he was leaning against the bar, squashed between a group of noisy Nordic sounding European tourists and a couple of females who must have just left a beauty parlour. They were immaculate. One of them had long hair which she occasionally flipped right into his face. The bar was boisterous and smelled of wet clothes because it was pouring with rain outside, but he could still catch the almond scent of her mane. In the subdued light under the bar spotlight it looked like copper. A fleeting image of a frightened young girl next to the road side crossed his mind. Then the redhead turned around and one look in her face made him forget the idea of young girls. Here was a woman who knew everything they both needed to know. For the first time in ages, he felt the urge to try his luck with a female again.

Two hours later, they were both very drunk and he suggested going to his place. The excessive amount of alcohol in his body however took its toll. Luckily she must have felt similarly incapacitated. Finally undressed and on his king size bed, his new found sex drive quickly turned into a pretty limp affair. After some desultory petting that culminated in a mere pretense of intercourse, they rolled away from each other and fell asleep.

It was still raining on Christmas morning, but the rain was mixed with flurries. A few degrees colder and it would be the real stuff befitting the season. As snow in a city can get quite annoying, he was hoping the thermometer would not plunge down further during the day. It was nine o'clock when he turned his percolator on to make his first cup of coffee. The woman from the bar who's name he had forgotten – if he had ever known it – was in the shower. He had told her that he had to get to a lunch on time – a family lunch he had added, just in case she was hoping he would suggest that she tag along. On reflection, he told himself that although he had not exactly covered himself in glory last night, she was no New Year's eve material either.

It was nearly half past eleven when he arrived at Daisy's flat. He had underestimated the length of the drive from his place in North Vancouver to hers on Nanaimo Street. He had to cross the Lions Gate Bridge and drive through Metro Vancouver, together with a million others on their way to their respective families. Instead of warming up more, the weather had done one of those quick turnarounds this coastal region was famous for. Now the flurries had turned into heavy wet flakes making the slushy roads treacherous for driving. He always marvelled at how many Vancouverites had the wrong set of tires on their cars. After barely avoiding a minor crash on Georgia Street he was relieved when he finally reached Daisy's address.

The house was an old three story commercial building close to Hendry Park but unfortunately right on the main street. He turned into one of the side streets and had to circle the area a few times before he found a parking spot. Then he had to brave the icy wind and the thickening snow to walk back to where Daisy lived. He had never been there. Coming closer, he wondered if he paid her too little. This could not be an address of her choice. East Vancouver with all its troubled residents was too close. Just a few streets down, he had seen droves of junkies hanging out in front of the soup kitchens and the shelters, the Salvation Army and Mission buildings. He wondered if his car was safe. When an undistinguished group of passers-by appeared out of nowhere he checked that his wallet was still stowed safely in the inside pocket of his coat. They were huddled under two umbrellas but made way for him, laughing and shouting Merry Christmas into the heavy snowfall, and he felt like a fool.

Daisy opened the door on the first buzz. She wore an oversized knitted pullover with a moose design on the front and tight red pants. The moose had blinking eyes.

"Where have you been? I've been trying to call you."

"The weather!" he explained and held out his gift to her.

She took it without any visible sign of surprise. "Thanks. Come in and take your wet coat off. We are starving and are already half pissed because of you."

After getting out of his coat and boots, she opened the door to a tiny living room crammed with people and announced him simply as *that's Richard*. Nobody present seemed to know that he was her boss and, if they did, they certainly were not impressed. Daisy introduced her friends also only by first names and without any further explanation. There was a balding short guy with over-compensating broad shoulders engrossed in an animated conversation with a pretty blonde. Plus two other couples - all four of them rather ordinary at first glance - who also continued their lively discussion as soon as they had greeted him; and then there was a single male sitting in the corner of the sofa with headphones over his ears. Richard found this a bit odd, but the guy was visibly younger than all the others in the room. Did Daisy have a brother? He looked up and acknowledged Richard with a brief nod. The fact that his arrival had not interrupted the other guests made Richard feel less conspicuous.

He followed Daisy into the kitchen which was twice the size of the living room. Somewhat relieved, he noticed the large dinner table with ten settings on it. As usual he did his math. There were three couples and none of the women looked attractive enough to warrant any effort on his part. The outsider who preferred music to their company was male and therefore also of no interest to him. There was one woman short.

Daisy had told him that it was self serve and he poured himself a glass of white wine, pledging that this would be the only one today. "Anybody else coming?"

"I had invited a nice girlfriend of mine with you in mind, but she had to cancel at the last minute. Looking outside, I can't blame her if she prefers to stay home with a good book instead of meeting my pock-marked, salacious boss."

"I have no pock marks!"

"But you are salacious?" she taunted him.

"I certainly hope so!"

She unwrapped her present. "Wow, this is nice. It matches my ring!" She held up her left hand to show him that she was wearing the jewellery he had given her last week, came closer and gave him a peck on the cheek. "Thanks boss!"

"Hey, stop this boss thing. At least for today."

"Ok, but everybody here knows who you are. There's no point in hiding it."

"So, who is everybody?" He asked casually, trying to make it obvious that he was not really interested. Being a bit moody since he realized that he now was stuck in a party that would be pleasant but not exciting, he felt let down by it all and blamed Daisy for not organizing it better.

"Just friends. You will get to know them. Go and talk to them while Jenny and I get lunch ready." She yelled into the living room. "Jenny, let's get started!"

Blonde Jenny came and he traded places with her, getting involved in a conversation with the stocky guy who turned out to be a medical doctor and quite interesting. He specialized in sports medicine, which explained his muscular build, and told Richard about all the good advice he gave to a select group of athletes training for the next Olympic games. Richard became uncomfortably aware of his soft stomach muscles and straightened up a little to hide the developing bulge around his midriff.

Daisy's call to the table rescued him from further discomfort. As soon as everybody sat, he forgot his previous reluctance to have a good time. Everybody was witty and entertaining and they drank lots of wine. Everybody except the young kid of course. Minus his headphones, he must have shut his ears down because he was not listening, and subsequently his mouth because he did not contribute one word to the conversation. Richard started to think he was deaf and dumb until he watched him lean over to Daisy – they were well into the turkey by now – and whisper something to her. She had placed the young guy next to her, which practically confirmed Richard's assumption that he was a relative. She laughed out loud. And then the strangest thing happened: Daisy put her hand on his cheek and let it rest there a moment too long. The way her face lit up when she laughed and the tenderness of her gesture was no sisterly behaviour. Bewildered, Richard began to watch her closer, all the while disguising his interest with clever contributions to the gradually deteriorating table talk. What was this supposed to be? The kid was barely of age! The more she drank, the more she demonstrated her affection for this toy-boy. Why was she acting like this? She couldn't possibly be serious? Attracted to a young boy barely out of puberty. That didn't fit. He was no match for Daisy. With a little twinge of guilt, Richard remembered last night. The redhead had been a stunner, but she was not his type either, way too bosomy and direct.

Daisy's toy-boy did not drink a drop and never loosened up. Richard did catch on that his name was Adam. Weird name for a weird guy, Richard thought, but Daisy seemed to feel totally different. She was more gregarious than ever, laughing and chatting with everybody and every now and then turning to whisper to Adam as if she had to translate what was being said and joked about by her other friends. It was sickening to watch. Adam was smitten with her too, of course. Any guy his age would be delirious with pride if a mature woman like Daisy paid attention to him. A mature woman for heaven's sake. She was making a fool of herself!

Richard had no desire to leave any more, being way too engrossed in this childish display of affection going on across the table, but eventually dessert had been eaten, coffee had been served and taxis were called. Richard didn't raise his hand when Daisy asked who needed one, but she ordered one for him anyway.

People began to make their farewells, politely exchanging phone numbers. Everybody got their coats and waited for the taxis to arrive. Everybody, except Adam. He had settled on the sofa again, headphones over his ears, feeling perfectly at home in Daisy's flat.

29

Adam! The first man created by God out of his own rib. A man created for Daisy? What on earth did she see in him? Richard sat at his desk in his office and shook his head in disbelief. He shouldn't be asking himself this. He should rather ask himself why he was stupid enough to hypothesize on the meaning of a name and associate the same with his assistant. But still, what on earth did she see in him? He was nothing but a snotty nosed teen hardly out of puberty! Maybe he was being unjust to the young fellow. Maybe he only disliked him so immensely because of Daisy's openly displayed affection. Because she had demonstrated so clearly at her Christmas lunch that Adam, being the young stag, could break into territory reserved for him, the one with the older claim to Daisy! Now, wasn't that a funny thought! As if he would lower himself to be in competition with a kid who had barely sprouted a few whiskers – over Daisy! *Please, Richard, don't be ridiculous. Don't behave like an idiot. She has never been interested in you and never will be, so what is the matter with you? Let her have her fun. She is not going to ask your permission, and in any case, she doesn't have to.*

But still, the picture of her being so attentive and caring towards young Adam haunted him all Boxing Day.

The office was closed until the beginning of the new year and he had too much time on his hands. He was so bored, he even considered going downtown to do some shopping in one of the overcrowded Malls. The rotten weather outside stopped this idea before he could degrade himself to partake in the after-season buying frenzy.

He usually shopped for clothes and shoes and groceries and all other necessities on the way to somewhere - a quick in and out without wasting any time – and here he was, actually thinking about strolling with the masses, looking for bargains. And bargains they would have to be. His latest personal bank statement showed an overdraft of such dangerous proportions that, if there was a thing called financial emergency, his account would be having an infarct just now. He had not paid himself a regular salary since autumn and realized he must transfer some money soon. He did not want to depress himself any further by checking if there was any money left in the company's account. Daisy had said they could last until summer, and that was all he wanted to know for the time being.

But what if she was wrong? He really should ask her. This was an important question and warranted disturbing her on her week off. Would she be upset if he called her while she was hanging out with this Adam toy-boy? Well, to hell with that, he really needed to talk to her.

He silenced his doubts by giving himself a legitimate reason: *A boss can do such things, it has nothing to do with me feeling rejected.*

When Daisy answered after two rings he thought he detected a playful swing in her voice. "Great minds think alike," she said, "I was just about to call you myself."

Some words have a tendency to smooth over little annoyances. He felt better already. "Really? Anything in particular?"

"Actually yes. When you left my apartment yesterday, I thought you acted a bit weird."

Now he felt bad again. "What are you talking about? In what way?"

"I thought you didn't really want to leave and I practically pushed you out the door. I'm sorry if it looked as if I wanted to get rid of you, but it just occurred to me too late that you didn't want to go home like the others."

"No, no, you got that wrong. I was fine."

"I don't think so. In fact, I am sure Adam was right. He made me aware of it, but of course by then it was too late."

Adam again! Damn Adam. "Listen Daisy, I told you I was perfectly fine, and I am sure you and Adam have better things to do than worry about me."

She gave him one of her quiet chuckles. Tiny pearls rolling over her tongue, telling him that he amused her. "Hey boss, are you jealous?"

"Of course not, don't be ridiculous."

"You couldn't be. Not about Adam."

"Why not?" He was getting very annoyed being the source of her amusement. "I mean of course I'm not, but in theory, strictly hypothetically speaking of course, why shouldn't I be? He is a guy and the way you carried on with him could certainly give an innocent bystander, or shall I say by-watcher, some ideas."

"Give one ideas? You sound like one of the Bronte Sisters!"

"And you, *sister*, sound like you are justifying something you are doing that is out of character. If you want it without the Bronte bullshit, let me tell you, I don't give a hoot whom you screw."

"So, what exactly are you angry about then? No, don't say it, I think I know!"

"Ok, give it to me." Maybe she could tell him what he could not grasp himself.

"It's not the fact that he is a man ..." she started.

A man? Please, don't insult my intelligence. He had to bite his tongue to keep quiet.

"...you have not met before. It's his age. Like every man on this planet, you believe a woman should be younger than the guy she goes out with."

Sure, that was it. As usual she was spot-on, and he had to agree with her. "Yes, I guess I found it a bit revolting to watch you making a fool of yourself."

"I'm so sorry I offended you." The pearly laughter again.

"Oh go to hell."

"But apart from having to point out to you, *dear boss*, that it's none of your bloody business, I can assure you that Adam and I are not an item. You got that completely wrong, and I wonder how you could even consider it. Didn't you always suspect me of being frigid?"

"Until now I did. Actually I still do. But I guess you have forgotten yourself temporarily."

"Forgotten myself? Aren't we poetic today!"

"Come on, you did snuggle up to him."

"A little, yes. But it is very different from what you think. Call it motherly love if you want a label for it."

Suddenly he saw it in a different light. It was true, she had never kissed Adam or anything like it. "My mother never displayed her affection that cuddly, but let's leave it at that. Can we now come to *my* reason for calling you?"

"Sure. What did you want?"

He talked to her about his worries over the accounts. She gracefully accepted his excuse for disturbing her and gave him a quick run down of their financial situation. It was bad, but not hopeless, she said, giving him permission to transfer a small amount into his personal account.

"Thank you, your Royal Highness," he said.

"Don't hang up yet. Apart from worrying about you, there is another reason why I wanted to call you."

"Shoot."

"I was thinking about that offer of yours to go into the mountains for a few days. Does that still stand?"

"As long as I can pay for it with that miserly amount of pocket money you have just granted me, then yes, I would be delighted."

"I've got a small savings account. We could deplete that and live it up."

"No way. Where shall we go?" He suggested driving up to Jasper but she said she would like to go to the Kooteneys. She had never been there. Personally, he didn't care where they went as long as he could get out of his flat for a few days, so he said yes, fine, let's drive east, but allow me one more question.

"Are we going plus or minus Adam?"

"Oh shut up, you creep! When shall we leave?"

"How fast can you be ready?

Daisy had asked him to give her until the next morning. Richard arrived at seven, circling her block five times before she came down schlepping a gigantic suitcase. He double parked, jumped out and heaved the monster into the trunk of his car.

"What on earth are you planning?" he asked. "I thought we're only staying until after the New Year." That was three days away.

"A girl needs to dress for the occasion."

The driver in the car behind him blew his horn impatiently, and Richard indicated with a popular finger signal to shut up and wait. An hour later, they were on Highway One past Chilliwack already, driving east. The Christmasy promise of snow had changed back to solid rain which had then turned to drizzle and eventually fizzled out. With the ominous heavy sky brightening up rapidly, it looked like a good day for travelling. Lighter clouds travelled with them and accumulated on the mountain barrier before Hope. The sun broke through them every now and then to spread the illusion of spring by warming the inside of the car through the glass.

Another hour later, the weather changed suddenly and furiously, reducing them to the speed of a turtle on four wheels. Creeping along Highway 3 at less than 50 km per hour, they passed a number of cars in the ditch and one semi-trailer lying sideways. Once they reached the end of the mountain plateau, the heavy snowfall subsided and the sun presented a gorgeous view over the Okanagan valley.

Richard could have driven all day long, listening to music and to Daisy's companionable silence. At four thirty it turned dark and he had to concentrate on the icy road to make sure they didn't finish up like those poor bastards stranded on the mountain highway.

When they finally reached the Hotel in Nelson he was feeling as if he had chopped wood all day or done some other strenuous physical labour. His eyes were strained, his back hurt and all his muscles felt like jelly. Daisy stretched like a cat when she got out of the car and said it was great to be here and that the air tasted like champagne.

Richard had booked two single rooms which were prepared for them already. They quickly freshened up and met in the lobby again. The hotel dining room looked too formal, so they decided to have a quick bite to eat in the local pub. After a fast beer and a huge plate of cheesy spicy tacos Richard felt a lot better, but the second beer hit him like a hammer and he had to admit that he was dog tired.

That night he slept as deeply as a child with no worries in the world.

The weather was on their side. It was cold in Nelson, but sunny. They rented cross country skis and spent the next two days on beautifully maintained tracks in the surrounding hills, coming back to the hotel only when twilight made it difficult to see the trails. Tired and exhausted, they replenished themselves with hot spiced wine and enormous meals which made them even more tired and totally relaxed.

New Years Eve was not going to be any different. There was no way they would make it till midnight, so they decided to give the Hotel dance a miss and only show up for dinner.

Daisy came down to the lobby wearing the same black slacks and grey sweater as the previous evenings. She had pepped it up with a silky blue scarf and wore – Richard guessed, in his honour – the silver and turquoise necklace and ring. Their activities in the fresh air with all the temperature changes had given her complexion a rosy glow and made her dark eyes shine. She looked exceptionally attractive.

"This outdoor life does wonders for you," he complimented her, "but what did you pack in your suitcase? You wore that same outfit yesterday."

"How observant of you! I could explain to you that a woman needs to be prepared, but it would be a waste of time. Men don't get it. Now come on, take me into this fabulous dining room and spoil me with a lavish dinner."

He did. The food was first-class. The wine list was not quite as extravagant, but at least it offered a choice of really good Okanagan labels and he picked a sparkling wine that was, to his beer drinking knowledge, an excellent choice because it was the most expensive.

Daisy took one sip and said: "Quick, ask if they have another bottle. We must reserve it right away. This is delicious."

Of course the restaurant had more than two bottles in stock, but they only drank two. To be exact, Daisy took tiny sips and Richard drank most of it. After dinner, they went to the hotel bar where sensible Daisy ordered a coffee for herself. Richard had an Irish coffee for a nightcap, followed by a generously poured double scotch.

On the first day of the New Year, Daisy called his room at seven in the morning. "I can't sleep."

His head was pounding a well known warning. Do not attempt sudden moves, only speak in a whisper. "Good God, tell someone who cares! Go away!"

"We're supposed to leave today."

"Check out is not until noon. Go away."

"I want to go for a drive."

She had the second set of keys in her handbag. Why did she bother him? "Fine. Knock yourself out. And don't call me again until ten to twelve."

At a quarter to twelve the phone rang again, but it was housekeeping, reminding him to get ready for check-out. He asked if he could delay it for half an hour and if he could have a large pot of coffee sent to his room. Both posed no problem, they must have heard those requests many times before.

Daisy called exactly at noon, just after he got out of a life-saving ten minute hot shower, feeling still not very fit but at least human again.

"Are you ready?"

"I will be in ten minutes, but only if you promise to drive the first part of the way. I need to check my snow vision first. Somehow I dread to open the curtains."

"I have checked us out and am sitting behind the wheel already. All you need to do is drop your room key off at reception and come out to the parking lot. I'm waiting at the back entrance."

"I've ordered coffee!"

"And I have told them not to bother."

"You what? How could you do that? I need my coffee! What's the rush?"

"We should make use of the short daylight hours. We can stop at the next Tim Hortons and you can have all the coffee you want."

Richard was not in the mood to argue with her. All he wanted was a cup of hot coffee and his chances of getting one were better if he left the hotel quickly than if he re-ordered from the restaurant. "I'll be down in a second."

"Oh, and Richard, I have a little surprise for you. Don't get mad at me."

His fragile state did not like surprises so he asked what it was, but she had hung up already. Oh well, it couldn't be too bad. As long as she let him sleep for a few more hours he would be fine.

His BMW was hidden behind a black SUV with a Washington licence plate. He nearly did not see it and had to walk straight across the parking lot searching for it. When he approached, Daisy was sitting in the driver's seat as promised and started the engine before he even got in. He slid into the passenger seat, flung his small travelling bag with an unceremonious thump behind him on the backseat and had barely closed the door when she sped off.

"Hey, what's the hurry?" he asked again. "We won't make it back home before dark anyway."

No answer. She concentrated on turning into the main street, and he let her get settled and waited until they reached the Highway.

"Okay, where's my coffee?"

"Coming up. The next gas station with a Tim Hortons is yours."

He sighed. "And what's my surprise?"

"Don't get mad."

"You said that before."

"You have to promise."

Normally he wouldn't have, but he was in no mood for silly games and just wanted to close his eyes. The brilliant sunlight was reflected by the undisturbed snow, hitting his poor besotted brain with a thousand sharp needles. He turned and reached back to get his sunglasses out of his bag. Before he could touch it, the bag moved. It jumped as if the car had hit an obstacle on the road, but it hadn't. Then it slid sideways and the blanket on the backseat moved like a camel's hump.

"Holy shit, what's that!" It really scared him to death. What kind of animal would hide out in cars? They were in the wilderness. Did bears really sleep through the whole of winter? City guys like him did not like unexpected movements under blankets.

"Something's moving! Stop the car! Daisy, stop the car!"

She didn't. Not right away anyway, and what made it worse, she didn't seem surprised.

"Daisy!" He unbuckled his seatbelt and was practically on his knees, leaning over the back rest and staring at the hidden camel. Nothing moved any more and he gave total abstinence some serious consideration.

"Stay calm, I can explain."

He sat back in his seat again, not wanting to look back. His future as a teetotaller loomed around the corner. "You can explain what?"

She didn't answer for about a minute. When the sign she had been waiting for came up, she indicated, turned off the highway into the next rest stop and brought the car to a halt. Now it was her turn to look back and glare at the blanket. "Okay guys, come on out."

He followed her glance. The blanket moved in several places at the same time and he nearly screamed again. *Schlappschwanz!* He was such a coward when he had a hangover.

The black sea of blankets parted and out popped two heads, no, first four hands, then arms, then the faces of two scared young boys. If a movie studio ever auditioned for two urchins for a Charles Dickens novel, those two would be the perfect choice. Tussled hair, hollow cheeks, long scrawny necks and wide, wide eyes. The misery of an abusive childhood personified.

Richard's jumpiness was replaced by blank astonishment. "Jesus, what is this?"

Daisy was more concerned with the well-being of her passengers who crawled from under the blanket into full view. She tucked their bare arms back in. They wore short-sleeve T'shirts! "Don't worry, he doesn't bite. I told you he would be a bit startled." Then she sighed deeply and turned back to him. "Richard, these are two boys I picked up this morning. This is John and that one is Matt. We are taking them back to Vancouver with us."

Sure, why not! He lost the last sense of reality, wondering who was more mad, her or him. "So now you are into picking up young boys. Does Adam know this?"

"Of course. They are friends of his."

He waited.

"Don't be daft, Richard. Haven't you guessed by now? They are just like him."

He waited some more.

"They belong to the Lost Boys!"

The term Lost Boys triggered some vague memory of Daisy mentioning something about boys being kicked out of polygamous communities. But Richard was too flabbergasted by the presence of her precious load on the back seat to accept her explanation at face value. He needed more detailed clarification, so he waited for her to speak.

"Okay," she resigned herself to the fact that he would just be sitting there and staring at her dumbfounded until she elaborated. "Adam had to leave Bountiful when he was fifteen. He had begun to ask questions and rebelled against the system. They dumped him at a gas station in Kamloops. Normally, boys like him have little chance, they have no education and no means of supporting themselves. A lot of them finish up in the drug scene, selling themselves for something to eat or a hit, and many die before they are grown up. There is an underground organization which has dedicated itself to helping them. Unfortunately, a lot of the Lost Boys don't know about it or get in touch with them only when it's too late. By then they have developed terrible psychological scars and are often beyond help." Daisy looked behind her apologetically and had lowered her voice to spare her passengers' feelings. "So it's important to get to them fast. Adam was lucky, he found out about the organization by chance and contacted them. That was three years ago. He has managed to overcome most difficulties those Lost Boys face and is now actively involved in trying to rescue others. He told me about Matt and John. I drove to Creston this morning to pick them up. We need to take them to him."

Okay, he understood that. At least some of it started to make some sense. It also slowly dawned on him that Daisy had taken him for a ride, literally speaking. "Why didn't you tell me about this? Why the secrecy? You never planned to take a few days off to relax and have a good time with me, right? This whole trip was organized to pick up those guys. You really didn't need to fabricate this elaborate cover up."

"True, I could have come here all by myself, and I would have if you hadn't invited me for a little vacation. It felt like doing the right thing; you were a bit depressed around Christmas time, weren't you?"

"And now, thank you very much, I feel much better finding out that you didn't trust me enough. I don't get it! Why couldn't you tell me? What's wrong with picking them up and giving them a lift? I wouldn't have refused it."

Daisy said, she had not just picked them up. The boys had not been kicked out by the Church elders. They were runaways and it was dangerous to be seen with them. That's why they had stayed under the blanket in the parking lot while he had taken his sweet time getting ready. It had been a nightmare for those poor boys, she said, having to wait, expecting the car door to open any second, being discovered and carted back to their compound.

"Are you telling me you kidnapped them?" Richard blurted out. "Are you out of your mind?"

"See, that's why I kept it a secret. And anyway, I wasn't sure until last night that it would happen. The boys took a great risk and had to wait for the right moment to escape. They got out with just what they're wearing and nearly froze to death waiting for me at the arranged spot."

The car was getting cold by now. He looked at John and Matt. Their skinny shoulders covered with only thin T'shirt material stuck out from the blanket. The expression on their faces took him by surprise. There wasn't a hint of curiosity, anticipation, hope or desire, as one would expect from teenage runaways after bolting successfully. He could only see dread, anxiety and genuine alarm. They were intimidated by him! His presence scared them out of their wits and he didn't feel good about this. He was angry with Daisy, but he could see her point now. No way would he have played along had he known. What was she thinking?

"What were you thinking? How is this supposed to work? Their parents will look for them. When they find out what we have done, they are going to sue the pants off us."

Daisy leaned over and gave him a quick peck on the cheek. "Thanks!"

"What the hell was that for? I have not agreed to this madness!"

"Yes you have, you said *we*." She opened the car door. "Come on, let's get them some warm clothes before we drive on."

She went to the rear of the car, opened the trunk and rummaged through her suitcase. When she came back with two fleece sweatshirts and two padded jackets he finally understood the reason for her excessive luggage. He felt like such a sucker. But he did not object to driving on to Vancouver. Those boys with haunting fear in their eyes were not his responsibility, and unless he had a car crash on the way to their destination, they had nothing to do with him.

30

Daisy was in a real hurry to get out of the Kootenays. She did stop once for Richard's desperately needed coffee fix, but her nervousness reflected on him and he quickly dashed into the gas station to reappear after less than a minute with a large plastic cup in his hands.

On route, they stopped at a McDonald's drive-through in Osoyoos where he could get more coffee. The two kids on the back seat looked so under-nourished that Richard wanted to order two Big Mac meals for each of them, but Daisy stopped him. Junk food was completely foreign to them; one would have to ease them gently into it or they would be sick. She only allowed him to get one serving of hamburger and fries each. When the order was ready, they drove to the parking area, stopped there and she handed them their meals. They ate like pigs.

"That's normal in the beginning," Daisy whispered to Richard after he shot her a reproachful look. "Adam told me. It takes some time."

They didn't say thanks either. In fact they had not spoken one word since Richard had found them on the backseat.

Daisy got rid of the empty McDonald's bags, and they were on their way again. By now, he had recovered enough from his New Year's Eve hangover to take over the steering wheel. He turned back on the Highway, direction Vancouver, feeling rejuvenated and ready to talk. As he didn't want to discuss the boys' lack of good manners right in front of them, he changed the subject to a more interesting topic - something he was dying to know and had not asked because he had pretended to sleep while Daisy had been driving.

"So, this Adam of yours, how did you meet him?"

"Through my research."

A large truck was racing in front of them like a freight train on wheels. Richard had to wait until they reached a steady incline leading up to the plateau before he could overtake it.

"Go on."

Daisy checked on the boys. The food must have made them tired. "They are asleep now, thank God. The poor things, what they had to go through today." Daisy moved a bit closer and lowered her voice to make sure they would not hear her. "Basically it's all your fault. You made me angry when you refused to find out more about our neighbour Jake. You said it's none of your business, that I only imagined things and would be on my own with my concerns. So I wanted to prove to you that something very fishy is going on there and started to research the Bountiful compound in southern B.C. I figured Jake's set-up must be very similar to this Canadian epicentre of fundamentalist Mormonism, so it made sense to start gathering information about that place."

His foot pressed down on the gas pedal.

"You don't need to speed! Killing us is not an option."

He lifted his foot again slightly and put the car in cruise control.

"I managed to get hold of a few people who are involved in trying to convince our government to do something about what goes on in Bountiful. One thing led to another and in the course of it I found out about an organization which is trying to help the Lost Boys. Adam being one of them is a great advantage to them. The runaways and the ones who are expelled trust one of their own more."

"So you met Adam and shacked up with him?"

"Please! Don't degrade yourself with absurd assumptions."

"What's absurd about it? He did look quite homey in your place. Headphones and all."

"I told you, those Lost Boys have a lot of catching up to do. Adam is crazy about music, he can't get enough of it. And yes, his conversational skills still need some improvement."

"So he doesn't live at your place?"

Daisy shook her head.

"In that case, can you please tell me where we deposit those precious uncut gems on our back seat?"

"Adam is staying at an old farm house in Fort Langley."

Great, at least that would not require him to take a huge detour. "What will happen if their parents start looking for them? Aren't you worried about that aspect at all?"

Daisy settled back in her seat. "They have no parents."

It was nearly midnight when they took the highway exit to Fort Langley. Daisy directed him to the farm house. The old fashioned street lanterns in the historic Fort settlement shone their light on empty winter streets. Mounds of forgotten snow, brown from exhaust fumes, had frozen on the sides of the pavement. Rows of deciduous trees with bare branches lined the main street. All the daintiness of the pretty houses, each different in design and many of them painstakingly restored to their former glory, was lost on a night like this. Apart from a small group of people who bundled up in the icy wind on the short way from the pub in the centre of town to their car, not a soul was in sight.

Richard could hear the boys stirring and briefly saw one head in the rearview mirror. Daisy talked to them, telling them they would soon arrive at their new temporary home.

They drove to the outskirts of Fort Langley, over the railway tracks and then quite a way more. Finally Daisy told him to turn into a driveway hidden behind a thick evergreen hedge. At the end of it was a rancher that looked quite small until they got to it. Richard noticed light in several windows. He parked the car in the driveway and got out.

Adam must have been expecting them. He came rushing out of the house, raced straight past Richard, opened one of the back doors and helped the boys out. Richard mumbled something to the effect that he was well aware that all Lost Boys had bad table manners, but why the hell did they all have to be rude on top of it.

Daisy lifted the suitcase out of the boot. Two more guys came out of the house, both of them around thirty, and rushed to help her, but she had been too quick for them. One of them then held out his hand to Richard and actually thanked him for coming. Sure thing, Richard grumbled and stepped back to let them do whatever was necessary so he could be on his way again. Adam disappeared into the house with the boys and Daisy followed him with the suitcase.

"Please, come in," offered the friendly one.

"No, thanks, we must be on our way." Why did he still mumble?

"I insist. It must have been an exhausting drive. Come, meet the others." He went back into the house, and if Richard didn't want to be left standing all by himself in the freezing air he had no choice but to follow him. To get back in the car and wait for Daisy to appear was the other option, but who could say how long she would be. He decided to go in as well so he could urge Daisy to hurry and then get the hell out of this whole mess.

They had to pass through a large mud-room cluttered with piles of coats and hats and gloves and boots to get to the next room which was a combination of kitchen and living room. There was a cooking stove in one corner and a wood stove in the other. A conglomeration of tables, chairs, easy chairs and sofas, none of them matching, furnished the place. Because the light was dim and there was a lot of wood in the structure – ceiling beams, siding, floor panels – it managed to look rather cozy in its chaotic comfort.

Some of the seats were occupied by the residents who apparently lived in the house. All of them were male, mostly young ones, well below their twenties. Daisy was the only woman.

The friendly one came up to Richard with a bottle in his hand. "I'm Ted, one of the handlers of this brood of fine young men," he introduced himself. He pointed to the other grown-up in the room apart from Daisy and Richard. "And this is David. He owns this house and has graciously consented to let us occupy it for a while. "Would you like a drink?" Ted held the bottle toward Richard. It was a soda pop. "I'm sorry I can't offer you a beer or a glass of wine as we have a strict no alcohol rule here. You understand."

Richard understood alright! The way Ted spoke made a few facts of life pretty clear to him. Ted and David, the loving couple who boarded young boys out of the goodness of their heart? *Come on, Daisy*, he thought, *grow up*. He had to get out of there.

"I'd love one," Daisy said, grabbed the bottle from Ted and sank into one of the beanbags close by. It made a rude sound, but she did not care and stretched her legs with a big yawn. "Come on, boss, sit down and relax. Nobody is waiting for you at home."

Adam came back, minus the two new boys. "I showed them where they can sleep tonight. Some of the other boys are already talking with them." He sat down on the floor next to Daisy, like a puppy dog.

"A miracle!" Richard couldn't help himself. "Adam can speak!"

Daisy didn't react to his sarcasm. She took a sip and then handed the bottle to her Adam-doggie. The familiarity of the gesture pissed Richard off no end.

Adam put the bottle on the floor without drinking and looked up. It was quite a feat to look up at Richard and make him feel insignificant at the same time. "Thanks for bringing the boys to us. I know you didn't really want to."

"You are damn right I didn't! It's kidnapping, goddamn it!"

"Please don't use swear words around here," David said. "We try to avoid anything that might offend the boys."

By now most of the kids had disappeared – Richard guessed they were checking out the new arrivals – with only a small group huddled over a board game on the other side of the big room.

"Really now, do you?" Richard asked, hoping the right amount of sarcasm in his voice would tell them that he was onto them.

Daisy smiled up at him. "Sit down, you fool," she ordered. Her next comment was directed at Ted. "He thinks you and David are gay and run some kind of pedophile organization."

"What?" David looked flabbergasted.

"Richard is a homophobe. In his book, just about everybody who doesn't fit his norm is gay."

"I am not!" Richard objected. "I mean homophobic."

"Yes, you are!" Daisy answered very gently. "I can assure you, Ted and David are not what you think, and this organization is as legit as the Salvation Army. So stop being such a blockhead and relax. Do you really think I would be involved if it was anything but?"

She had a valid point there. Nobody messed with Daisy, she was not the type to be deceived by anybody. Richard sat down, feeling mortified. "Could I have one of those delicious sodas now?" was his peace offering to Ted.

They chatted for a while about the drive Daisy and he had had and the weather that was to come until Richard, who was still hoping to get out of there as soon as possible without offending the hosts, made a bad mistake. He asked what would happen with the two boys from now on. Immediately David launched into a lengthy explanation about the difficulties such kids faced when integrating themselves into society.

"The organization needs to hide them from the authorities until they are old enough to be allowed to make their own decisions," he elaborated. "Once they are eighteen, nobody can send them back without their consent, but until then it's a dangerous business. No matter how strongly they object, they have to be delivered back to the com pound of their sect once they are caught by police. Some of the boys in our care have run away from our shelter because they don't understand the need for all this secrecy. Understandably, they are so greedy for their new life, they can't wait for it to start. As much as we try to stay in the background, I fear the police know about our organization already. We do harbour the Lost Boys outside of the law. That's why none of the boys should know the exact location of where they are kept."

"But it's only a matter of time until the authorities find out more about us here," David said. "The organization has different shelters. We have to keep moving every so often. It makes it hard to give the boys any sense of stability, not to mention giving them some kind of education. We can only do our best."

Richard shook his head. He was glad that this was not his problem. "You bet," he said. "But we really should be going now. Thanks for the drink."

This time Daisy did not object.

While driving Daisy back to her place, strange thoughts ran through his mind, stirring up memories and emotions he thought he had dealt with and discarded a long time ago.

Daisy did not say anything, but he had a hunch she was waiting for him to talk. After ten minutes of silently mulling over fragments of his messed-up youth and wondering why they muscled themselves back into his consciousness again, he gave up.

"You do know that this whole thing freaks me out, don't you?"

"No."

"Daisy, for heaven's sake, what are you doing? What are you trying to achieve by getting kids away from their families and hiding them for months or years from the authorities? You are bound to get caught and then what?"

"We are rescuing them so they have a chance in life…"

"Bullshit!" he interrupted her furiously. "You are trying to press your own conviction of how life should be onto them. You are judgemental. You can't comprehend that those people in Bountiful may like to live the way they do. It's their own choice, and you – granted, with the best of intentions – are trying to force them into your own mould."

Now she got angry. "No. We are not talking grown-ups here, we are talking kids! You don't understand how they have to live. Those boys never had a choice! Some of them don't want to live like that, they can't handle it and are desperate to find help outside. They have asked us for help – we don't *kidnap* them against their will."

Of course not. He knew how boys that age ticked; he remembered very well. "Ask any kid of thirteen or fourteen if they want to get away from their parents and they will jump at the chance. No more rules, no more restrictions. The hormones are flying wild, giving them a sense of infallibility."

"Is that what happened to you? Did you go back to boarding school in Europe because you wanted to get away from your parents?" As usual her sharp mind hit the bulls-eye of his current emotional turmoil. "Did you want to punish them?"

Why did he have to put up with this? It upset him to be confronted with the past, unable to shake the painful flashbacks, by somebody who had no right to meddle in his affairs.

Daisy didn't let go. "Forgive me if I look at it the wrong way, but I think you were just a mean and selfish little brat and your parents loved you too much to force you to stay with them, while those Lost Boys don't have parents who care about them. There is a slight difference."

Memories of his mother crying her eyes out at Vancouver airport every time he left after summer break suddenly overshadowed their argument. His anger at Daisy turned flat and sour.

"But they *do* have parents," was his weak reply.

"No, they don't! They have a father who has multiple wives and so many children that he forgets their names. Who doesn't let them go to a normal school but gives them the minimum of education in his own community school. Who works them like slaves as soon as they show a little strength until they enter the so-called priesthood. Who chases them out of their community once they demonstrate the first signs of youthful rebellion, simply to keep the male-female odds in balance for himself and the few other lecherous Elders in the different polygamous communities spread all over the continent. That's not a father, that's a monster!"

Richard's father used to look so sad and serious at the airport. Richard had always felt a surge of supremacy when he stubbornly refused to share his parents' farewell pain. It was a mask that did not shatter until he had passed customs and was well out of their sight.

"But they have mothers," he insisted weakly.

Daisy sighed. "When the boys are banned from their communities, it is usually the mothers that drive them to a remote place and abandon them."

31

He thought it best to distance himself from Daisy and her quest to save the Lost Boys. Eventually she would come around and accept the fact that those kids had little to do with her, or him for that matter.

Richard was glad the festive season had made way for the more sombre lifestyle a dull and grey January presented. Everybody was back at their offices, as usual regretting the over-indulgence of the past month, joining fitness centres, taking another crack at giving up smoking and trying to lose weight. Just like him.

With the completion of their big project still on hold and no other real project to work on, he had more time on his hands than he bargained for. Apart from occupying his mind with designing the entrance gates to his development or having meetings with representatives of the advertising agency he had commissioned and the realtors who would eventually market the project, he had nothing to do. All those things were way ahead of schedule and simply served the purpose of killing time more than anything else. He was in danger of getting overly sluggish from all those senseless activities and knew he had to do more than sit around the office. To make matters worse, the youthful and vibrant energy Adam had radiated inexplicably bugged him to such an extent that he finally overcame his inner *Schweinehund* and made a slightly belated New Year's resolution to take better care of himself. Like all the other hopefuls, he joined a fitness centre.

All through January and February he doodled on his desk like an imbecile until he could finally leave the office around four to join his personal trainer for heavy sweat sessions. Daisy never asked where he went and never commented on the already visible improvement in his physique. Richard prided himself in having an exceptionally good metabolism. Getting leaner had the additional benefit of getting stronger. All this exercise was very tiring though, making him fall into bed well before midnight. His abstinence from alcohol, which was a prerequisite for the three month intensive course his trainer had insisted on, did therefore not get jeopardized by any unnecessary pub crawling. Neither did his sexual abstinence. His only regret when he saw his emerging six-pack in the mirror was that he was the only one admiring it.

Daisy always seemed busy in the office. He knew she also had very little to do, so he assumed she was still nurturing her motherly instincts, probably raising funds for the care of Ted and David's protégées or saving a few new ones. He did not care as long as she did not involve him and as long as her work did not suffer. And that was no problem as they simply had nothing to do except wait for the frost in the ground to melt away.

Or so he thought, until one sunny afternoon when the February sun actually made a brief appearance in a windy sky, chasing some heavy clouds away and with it the downcast mood of the rain-soaked Vancouverites. He was just getting ready to go to his sweat class, when Daisy knocked on his office door.

"Come in," he said, thinking how silly this distancing effort of hers had become.

At least she sat down without waiting to be offered a chair. She crossed her legs and pointed to the chair behind his desk. "You'd better sit down."

He did.

"Remember our project? The one up north - our Rainbow Country Cabin Development?"

"Of course I do. Why?"

"Because I just got a call from our AO."

He groaned. Jeanne d'Arc again. That was usually a guarantee for trouble. But then he remembered that they had crossed all the governmental hurdles and were now already planning the road into and through the Development, only waiting for the weather to permit the start of construction. He relaxed. "What does she want? All is done and there's nothing she could want from us."

"You think?"

He did not like the look on Daisy's face. "Yes, I think. Now don't be a pain and tell me what she wants."

"She refuses to sign off the subdivision plans if we don't change our road design."

This was unexpected, but it did not totally shock him. In his experience bureaucrats usually didn't accept plans in their virgin form; continuous minor alterations to drawings were their favourite pastime. "I didn't know we had submitted the construction plans already. Shouldn't I have signed them first?"

"You're right, we didn't. Jeanne d'Arc called to tell me that she finally had some time over the holidays to consider our PLA and now feels it will not be possible to build a private road over the thirty meter wide corridor we bought from Jake because it cuts his land into two parts."

Daisy's explanation didn't make any sense to him, so he just opened his arms wide, with palms up, to demonstrate to her that he waited for further clarification.

"She now feels that she cannot allow this as our neighbour – meaning Jake - may not be able to subdivide any of those two parcels in the future."

"Why not?"

"Because of the access problem."

"I thought we agreed in the sales contract to give him an easement over our road? So, there is no question of access!"

"Oh yes, our agreement stipulates this quite clearly, but Jeanne d'Arc now thinks that's not good enough."

"Not good enough?" he repeated dumbfounded. "What's she talking about? I don't get it."

"She hadn't thought about the aspect of future subdivision before. Because of the steep hills this land cannot be accessed directly. The only way to get to future parcels is through the ravine, which we now own! If Jake wants to divide his two remaining parcels later on, it can only be done if we grant him an easement. She feels this solution is, again I use her own words, not good enough. It has to become a public road." Daisy crossed her arms. "Which means it has to be paved."

"Damn it, how much will that cost us?"

"I don't know. How much does 60 kilometres of paving cost?"

"You mean 600 meters", he corrected her.

"No, I mean 60 kilometres. If the road leading to our development becomes public, no matter how short this part may be, we have to pave it – there are your 600 meters – but we also have to pave the whole distance to the next paved road. And that, as you well know, is approximately 60 kilometres, give or take a few clicks. That's how far the highway is away from our development!"

He nearly fell off his chair. The reason why he had opted for a private road was exactly because of this particular legal requirement the Provincial Government insisted on nowadays. Any public road needed for a new development had to be paved. They could not afford to pave the whole distance. It would make the lots unsellable, way too expensive for the market they targeted. Or any other market, for that matter. If their AO insisted on this madness they would go under.

He was beginning to hyperventilate. "She's not serious?"

Daisy stared at him.

"She can't be serious. This is not something she can hit us with now! We've already got PLA. We ran it by her before we bought the land from Jake, didn't we?"

"Yeah, but she said she hadn't realized that we are only buying three acres, which effectively cut the land in half, rather than the whole parcel that runs along the road."

"Who cares? She agreed to it. She can't change her mind now. We bought the part we needed. We *own* it. It's ours. And it cost me a shit-load of money!" His anger level was rising but was not quite up to pre-training times – there was something to be said for mental and emotional leverage through physical exercise. "Has she gone completely nuts?"

"Yes and yes. Yes, that's why we bought it, but it's not enough for her. Unfortunately the law says it's up to the interpretation of the AO as to how she wants to handle this matter. And yes, she can demand it. And another yes you have not asked yet: yes, it means we are dead."

He deflated. Daisy's honesty poked a hole into his composure. All air flowed out of him, leaving him drained of all energy. He sagged in his chair like an empty balloon. "We're dead?"

"Yep."

They stared at each other. This could not be. There had to be an answer. Going to court? No, that would only be an additional expense – one he could not afford any more – and in any case it would not alter the outcome. It was all up to the AO, no court in Canada would help him there. This was a nightmare. But there had to be a solution! He could not think of one. Maybe Daisy could. "Can you think…?" He could see it in her eyes that she could not.

"There would have been a faint possibility to solve this crisis, but it's not an option any more."

He leaned forward in his seat. Hope. There must be hope. He was closing in on Daisy, looking at her like a bloodhound, sniffing hope. "Tell me anyway."

Daisy gave him a pitiful glance. "Forget it."

"No, come on, tell me," he insisted, now practically leaning flat over his desk.

"Okay, you asked for it. Under different circumstances the solution could be quite simple. We would have to do as Jeanne d'Arc says and buy one of the parcels, either east or west of the three acres. Actually west would be better, it is less acreage."

She gave him time to let the idea sink in. If he owned this part of Jake's land and not just the three acres that divided his land, they could run the road through their own land and keep it private. And they wouldn't have to pave it. Very simple.

"All you would have to do is persuade Jake to sell it to you."

He was sure Daisy did not say this to rub salt into his wound, but it felt like it. Even if he had the necessary funds to buy more land from Jake, the guy would never sell it to him – not after he had totally blown it at their last meeting. If that was what Daisy implied, she was entitled to a little sarcasm, he could not hold it against her. Why on earth had he picked a fight and walked out on Jake's religious sermon last summer? Why hadn't he bit his tongue and played along to make him happy?

"Jesus Christ, he'll never sell us this land!"

Daisy nodded. "And even if he would, we couldn't afford it."

"How many acres in the western part?"

"Fifty-two. He wanted ten thousand per acre, so we are talking over half a million. It can't be done."

Usually Richard gave in to frustration, anger or outrage very easily, so he was surprised that he was capable of feeling another, even deeper, emotion. Defiance! He would not give up what he had created over so many years! He would not let one single bureaucrat throw the book at him and senselessly destroy his life's dream in the process! He would do the impossible, achieve the unachievable, convince Jake and conquer fate. It had to be done, so it could be done. Searching for the last bit of faith he had left inside him and clinging to it, he told Daisy not to worry. He could do it.

"But how?" she asked.

"First, I'll get Jake to agree to sell us the land, then I'll make him agree on a more realistic price, and then I'll find the money necessary for it. There's no other way." His resolve nearly disintegrated into despair when he saw the hopelessness in her expression. Of course she did not believe him. "Trust me, Jake will be delighted if I crawl back and apologize. He is one of those guys who loves to feel superior. He won't miss an opportunity to teach me a lesson. All I have to do is swallow my pride and let him see me squirm. He is not really a bad guy, he is just a bit power hungry."

Daisy bit her lip, probably to stop a comment about how he was underestimating Jake again.

More than six months after their last meeting, Jake and he would start anew, and this time he would keep Daisy's warning clearly in his mind. This time Jake would not be able to play him – Richard knew what to expect!

32

To be blessed with many healthy children was a gift the Lord bestowed on righteous men. For them the door to their celestial kingdom opened a bit wider every time they enabled one of God's little soldiers to enter this earthly battlefield. When Brother Lucas died, he would leave over one-hundred-twenty descendants, the oldest of them already in their sixties. He wasn't quite sure any more how many soldiers he had created, it didn't matter to him if there were a few more or less. The Lord would welcome him with open arms anyway.

This morning, his first wife – who was actually his third, having moved up the ranks after the first and then the second had died – had told him that one of the twins was expecting. It had not pleased him. Those two had been his only distraction in the current difficult times. He had actually looked forward to the nights when he had ordered them to his chambers. Now one of them would have to be moved to the women's quarters, out of his sight until she had given birth. What good would the other one be to him now? Not pregnant herself, she would be miserable and desperate. What he had liked about the twins had been their carefree enjoyment in each others' company while doubling his pleasure. That was gone now. He would never find a worthy replacement for them. The news of Leah's pregnancy had made him so angry that he had told his wife to ban the other twin from his sight until her sister had given birth. Nine months at least before he could make use of them again. He wasn't sure if he would live that long. Already his body was frail and he needed to replenish his frequently dropping energy level through regular naps. His skin had become translucent and was covered with large, dark brown age-spots. The few strands of hair on his head were white and thin, while his body hair had become coarse and long in some parts and had fallen out in others. Time was rapidly running out. Why couldn't the Lord let him enjoy the last few years of his existence? What was wrong with making the twins massage his limp body parts with fragrant oils and entice him with their youth, their firm nakedness, their willingness to submit to all his demands! Why did the Lord take this away from him? Hadn't he done enough to increase his glory?

His wife had asked him if he wanted to choose from one of the sister-wives again and had shown him pictures to refresh his memory. He had barely glanced at them, had shaken his head and left for the office. He mustn't question the Lord's motives, but he could mourn for a while to show him how he suffered over his loss. Those twins would one day be allocated to another man, one within his inner circle no doubt. That thought annoyed him even more.

When Brother Mathew arrived in his office for his daily briefing, Brother Lucas was still in an unforgiving mood.

"Has there been any progress with the Canadian compound?" he asked, once the routine part of the meeting had been dealt with.

Brother Mathew sighed. "None whatsoever. Brother Jacob constantly calls all the Brothers, except you of course, and demands that we reinstate his allowance. He claims his family is working hard and he is making some money, but he refuses to give us monthly statements. Unfortunately, he is wearing some of the Gatekeepers down. Some of them have already asked openly if we shouldn't support him again and one, Brother Ervin, even suggested that we bring him back here so he can flourish under our supervision. After all, he is our own flesh and blood, he argues, one of us who has suffered enough in exile."

Brother Lucas looked around for his pen to hide his agitation. Brother Jacob to come back here? To sponge off the Church, disrespect his Elders and benefit from their hard work? Not in his life! Suddenly Brother Lucas had a vision. Brother Jacob standing at his coffin, lovely

Marion next to him, looking down at him, bending down toward his corpse. What did he whisper into his ear? *And next I'll take your twins!* Brother Lucas picked up the pen and a piece of paper. Poised himself to start writing. Looked up at Brother Mathew.

"And what do you think?"

"I trust in the Lord to give us guidance. I had hoped for a sign from Brother Jacob that would give us an indication we could act upon, but I have not seen one. I fear nothing has changed since last year."

"So we should continue to wait?"

Brother Mathew was cautious. He wasn't sure where this conversation was going. It could be dangerous to read Brother Lucas wrong. As frail as his body was, it seemed to house an iron will. "Maybe a bit longer, but not too much."

"But he is annoying our Brothers."

"Yes, very much so."

"We have a duty to protect them."

"Yes, we have."

Brother Lucas smiled benevolently. "Then it would be best to act soon. I think we should call an extraordinary meeting to discuss our possibilities. There are several options. I do not favour bringing Brother Jacob back here, but understand the concerns our Brothers have. One option could be to bring his family back, without him, to make sure they survive. Of course then we will have to excommunicate him, but that was a proposal brought forward last year already, wasn't it?"

Brother Mathew agreed quickly. Rarely had Brother Lucas been so direct in stating his wishes. He would spread the word to make sure the other Brothers understood. "I believe most of us agree with this course of action. It should not be too difficult to pass the motion."

"For excommunication we need the decision to be unanimous."

"Only Brother Ervin might oppose. I believe he does not understand the complications if Brother Jacob was indeed to come back. Where would he live, what position would he hold, how could we control his ego. All those problems."

"Didn't we plan to send one of our Brothers to the mission in Europe?"

"Yes."

"Well, why don't you give Brother Ervin the good news that I have chosen him for this post. I should like him to leave by next month."

33

The danger of losing his company had a surprisingly electrifying effect on Richard. Since Daisy had hit him with Jeanne d'Arc's ruinous demand to make his private road public and have him pave it, his mood had changed. He suddenly felt alive again, invigorated, full of energy. No way would he give in so easily. Just thinking about this anti-development bitch gloating that she could trick him into bankruptcy made his blood boil. Except this time, he would not let his anger get the better of him.

Daisy reacted quite the opposite. She was devastated, and he could not shake her out of her depression. She was convinced that there was no point whatsoever in his even trying to meet with Jake S. Law and even less of a chance to convince him to sell his land at a bargain price. They had had their run and now it was over. It did not surprise Richard when he saw her at her desk about a week after the fateful call, scouring through the classifieds, looking for a suitable position.

"The rat is leaving the sinking ship?" he asked.

His attempt at being funny was greeted with an icy reception. "Even a rat has to eat."

He sat down opposite her and looked past her shoulder out the window. He could glimpse the harbour in a narrow blue corridor between the dark grey high-rise buildings. A large vessel sailing by on the horizon broke the blue strip of water and sky into two halves. She moved elegantly along until she disappeared behind the building to the right.

"Nice view, isn't it?" Daisy said. "'I'll miss it."

"Don't be so negative."

"It's called realism."

He shook his head in honest dismay. That's not how he knew her. Daisy was invincible and indestructible. "Look," he started again, "this attitude of yours isn't helping at all. How do you expect me to pull us through this if you mope around like an unprepared school girl before a class test?"

His reproach infuriated her. "Stop it right here and now! Tell me what I'm supposed to do to pass this test! I would go and talk to Jake myself – and trust me, my powers of persuasion are a hell of a lot more refined than yours – except the bastard refuses to deal with me, a mere woman! Or should I try and coax you into finally calling him, after you have wasted another week without making the slightest attempt to contact him! You have not made a single move in seven days, and the clock is ticking so loud even you should be able to hear it. Tell me what do you expect me to do besides sitting here and wasting my time like you do so brilliantly and, if it makes any sense to me, I'll do it!"

She was right about the week, but he had had his reasons. He hadn't just wasted his time fuming over the unfairness of the Approving Officer, he had tried to use his grey cells to come up with solutions. She started to seriously annoy him. "Don't be like that. It'll work out, trust me."

"Trust you to, as you call it, *pull this off*? Knowing full well that you blow your top every time something doesn't go to your majesty's desire? Heavens, you've had your chances and you screwed up big time. There are no more chances coming your way, and if they did, you'd manage to blow those ones too. Trust? Ha, I have trust in you. I totally trust you to mess it up even more, given half a chance."

How could this woman bring him so close to boiling point every time they had an argument? Because she was right. With superhuman effort he let the rising anger subside until it was no more than a minor hotspot in his brain. "I hear what you are saying. You have every right to be angry, and I admit I've made a lot of mistakes. I'm not infallible, but I'm trying to change. In case you haven't noticed, I'm working out now and I've stopped drinking altogether."

She frowned at the alien in front of her and – to his secret delight – busied her fingers with folding the classified section of the newspaper and putting it to one side. "What's that got to do with it?"

He quickly continued. "Just to prove that I haven't been sitting on my bum. And I haven't been inactive in the office either. True, I haven't called Jake yet, but, as you know yourself, it is only the end of February and we still have a few weeks before we can start with the road."

Doubtfully, she asked the reason why he had not called Jake yet if he was so confident that a miracle would happen. Wouldn't Jake's lousy piece of property be instrumental in securing their future?

"I've been talking to a few private investors. No point in making Jake an offer if we can't back it up."

"And?"

Their friendly Kamloops investor Linda had, after much persuasion, agreed to extend her loan by another hundred thousand. Richard was quite proud of this feat.

Daisy shook her head when he told her. "That won't get you anywhere."

"Granted, it's a long shot. Why should Jake lower his demand? I've given this problem some thought as well and have, after much consideration, worked out a proposal he can't refuse."

Now he finally had her undivided attention. "I really want to hear what we have left to offer in our situation."

She had said *we* again – thank God!

"We still own the 2000 acres. I've worked out a deal where he gets the hundred grand first and a share of our profit later on when the parcels are selling."

Daisy jumped up. "No way! You want to make him a partner? What on earth has got into you? Have you totally lost your marbles? Never, not in a million years, will I agree to that."

Did he need her permission? She must have realized instantly that it was not her call and sat down again, defeated.

"Daisy, I understand that you have strong feelings about Jake, but this is business. Emotions don't come into it."

"It's your company."

"I know, but I want you with me on this one. What's so bad about paying him some money later on? Consider it a deferred purchase price."

"You're inviting him on board."

"Only as a minor partner." He should not have used this word. He bit his tongue, but it was too late. This time Daisy got up and remained standing behind her desk. In fact she started to open the top drawer of her desk, taking out stuff.

"It's your decision. If you want to partner with the devil, you're welcome to it, but don't expect me to be there and watch you lower yourself to such a level."

"Daisy, I…"

"I am done here. I resign with immediate effect."

He closed his eyes and took a deep breath. This was not supposed to happen. "You can't. You have six months …" he stopped. Was it six months or only three?

"Who's counting? You haven't paid me in two months, so I have every right to leave immediately. Which is exactly what I am doing right now!"

"Isn't there anything I can say to change your mind?"

"Yes, tell me you refuse to deal with Jake."

"You know I can't do that. It's our only chance. If I don't, I lose everything."

She punished him with a dagger look, then turned her eyes back to the desktop. Her face set into a granite mask.

Richard knew he had lost, but struggled to accept it. "Well, you have to do what you think is right. I'm sorry that it had to come to this." She continued to ignore him and carried on emptying her desk of all personal belongings. He did not hang around to watch her and stormed back to his office to nurse his injured pride. All the suppressed anger had twisted his stomach into a tight knot and he did not seem to be able to untangle it. Again and again he told himself to stay calm and focused. *You may have lost Daisy, but you have not lost your company. Not yet, anyway.*

That evening, he fell off the wagon. Considering that he was not an alcoholic, this phrase was not quite appropriate, but after three neat scotches he wallowed in his misery and wanted to punish himself even further. Above and beyond the fact that he was on the brink of losing his livelihood and had no learned profession to fall back on, he had lost the respect and trust of the only person who's opinion counted to him. And to crown his misfortune, he could do nothing better than sit at home and cry in his whiskey glass! Didn't have the backbone to stick to his promise of abstinence. Feeling sorry for himself like a miserable wino just because one employee left! The wimpy owner of *Richland Ltd.* deserved all he got.

When he got tired of feeling sorry for himself, his fighting spirit returned. How dare she reduce him to this pitiful heap of self-accusations! For what? For some silly misguided conviction? Who would get hurt if he sided with Jake? It was a straight-forward business matter and had nothing to do with how he or she judged Jake's lifestyle. Didn't she see that? She was probably regretting her rash action by now but didn't know how to tell him. An idea popped up in his booze fogged mind. He would prove to her that he was a changed man. A guy that had his emotions under control and was in charge. He would not wait until she was ready to apologize and make amends but would take the first step. He would call her and let her know that he understood her overreaction and forgave her, that they were a team and that he needed her. If he could admit to that and beg her to come back, she would give up her hardened stance and let him handle the problem his way. Give and take, that's what it took to get people to cooperate. There was the telephone, it was really quite easy.

After two rings Adam picked up and Richard was so surprised he asked for Daisy without any introductory politeness.

"She's not here," Adam said.

"Oh." Richard waited and when Adam offered no further explanation he caved in. "Where is she?"

Adam stayed gracious. "She drove over to Ted and David's place. Should be back soon. Shall I ask her to call you."

"If you don't mind." Somehow Richard needed to hear a human voice so he wouldn't fall back into a miserable void that demanded to be filled with alcohol. "How are the boys doing? I mean the ones we picked up after Christmas."

Adam chuckled. "I know which ones you mean. They are doing fine."

"Nobody ever asked for them?" Richard could not remember seeing any missing persons alert on TV.

"Of course not. The Church has too many boys to get rid of. Most of them are kicked out, but they don't care much about the runaways either. It only makes our lives a bit more difficult because they are so young."

"Yeah."

Obviously Adam had learned to talk since he had seen him last – or was he only so loquacious when it came to a topic close to his heart?

"On the other hand," Adam continued his lecture, "being a bit younger usually means they are less damaged and therefore more responsive to our efforts. They stand a much better chance of integrating themselves into society later on."

"Like you?" Richard baited. He had no idea what Adam did for a living. The thought of him sponging off Daisy infuriated him suddenly. She had given him the boot, didn't want to see him any more, but Adam was allowed to hang out and freeload at her place. "Surely, you'll be able to teach them a good deal about how to survive in the strange land of the hard-working taxpayers. There must be loads of organizations catering to those who can't go out and do an honest day's work."

"Are you referring to me?"

You bet your ass I am. "Well, I don't know what you are doing," he stated pointedly, feeling quite clever.

"I'll tell Daisy you called."

After the line went dead Richard considered filling his empty glass again, but he was so mad that he decided to be sensible, take a shower and go to bed. He would not give Adam, or anybody else, the satisfaction of losing his cool again.

The hot shower intensified the alcohol level in his bloodstream to a point where he practically passed out as soon as his body stretched out on the bed. The phone never rang.

He slept like a log for a few hours then woke up, startled and sweating. The digits on the alarm clock were glowing red in the dark, showing 3.16 am.

All the frustration and distress he had experienced the day before had left him drained and susceptible to all sorts of weird butterfly thoughts. He stared into the darkness, trying to coagulate the wildly fluttering memories of past and present but without much success.

In his fevered mind, Adam's Lost Boys looked at him with wide eyes in blank faces. No parents were looking for them. Nobody missed them. Not knowing what to expect from life, they must be scared to death of the future. They had been scared of him. Him, who had also been a lost boy! His parents joined the dance of the butterflies. Richard was at the airport again. This memory was turning into a nightmare. His parents were standing there, watching him leave, but he refused to turn and look back at them. He caught their images reflected in the glass doors that opened and closed to the customs area. For a fleeting moment he saw his mother break down in his father's arms, sobbing desperately. His father holding her tightly with hanging head, pressing her against him in an attempt to reduce her grief and give her some comfort. He could feel his parents' sorrow intensely. He wanted to turn around but somebody pushed him forward and when he took another step the glass doors closed behind him and he was too proud to call out and run back to them.

The whole scene played over and over again in his mind. He wanted to catapult himself out of the butterfly nightmare and tried to alter the memory. He forced himself to turn around and run out of the customs area, toward his parents, and stopped dead in his tracks. His mother was on her knees, opening her arms wide and two boys, those two Lost Boys, threw themselves into her welcoming arms, nearly knocking her over. Everybody was crying and laughing and totally oblivious of him standing there. Nobody took any notice of him, he was invisible to them.

Then he screamed and his own cry finally woke him fully. He sat up, wiped the nape of his neck, where sweat had accumulated, and switched the light on. It was 4.15 am now. For the rest of the night he kept the light on, laid back in bed and let the dream walk by him again and again, until he understood. Then, for the first time ever, he truly, honestly grieved for his parents, and for himself. It was too late to tell them how sorry he was, but by finally acknowledging the hurtful mistakes of his youth, he started to feel at peace with himself. Only by recognizing his faults could he avoid hurting people that badly in future. His parents were somewhere out there, they would forgive him. He could let them rest in peace now.

He got up at 6 am, made coffee, went to the fitness centre for an early workout and felt quite human again by the time he got to the office.

Today he would call Jake!

34

Winter refused to give up its icy grip. Marion told Martha one day in February that she had never experienced such terrible cold since she had arrived in British Columbia. Usually the coldest part of the year was January; after that every day got longer and there was plenty of sunshine to warm the air. As if to mock Martha this year, it stayed brutally cold. She thought the snow would never melt and she would forever have to live from day to day, waiting for night to settle and hoping Jake junior would drive into the backyard and look for her.

Although she didn't have to attend the evening work sessions in the community hall because Marion thought it more important that she stayed in her room to study so she could one day soon take Katherine's place, she could not sneak away easily. Many evenings, she stood by the window in vain, waiting for the women to leave the hall, counting each one of them until they had all gone back to their huts, and even then she could not be sure if Jake junior had found a reason to show up just around that time. But they had made a pact that she would always go down to the yard, hide behind the wood pile and wait up until midnight. She should have been tired from the permanent lack of sleep, but the bitter cold and the fear of being discovered kept her awake during the wait and afterwards, when they did meet, she was so full of love and energy she could have stayed up all night. They managed to meet about once a week. She lived for those moments with him.

If only it wasn't so bitterly cold. Tonight, she had waited nearly an hour in the freezing cold before he finally appeared. Even after they had settled in his warm and cozy cabin, it took her a while to stop shivering. He held her close to him, cuddling and kissing her until she thawed under his caresses.

All their secret rendezvous started and finished like this. They tried to placate their insatiable need for each other that had grown unbearably strong while being separated by touching and exploring each other's bodies as much as their inner barriers allowed them. Always stopping before they totally lost control. It was sweet torture that gave them a sense of togetherness, but being physically close was not the only comfort they could give to each other. Their mutual trust was so deep by now that they could bare their innermost thoughts. Once they had started to communicate on such an intimate level, it was as if floodgates had been opened.

They were sitting on the cot, facing each other. Martha told Jake junior what she had heard earlier. Katherine had died that morning and had been buried without a ceremony. She had never really known Katherine but was aware that she had been the children's teacher and didn't think it was right to just dig a hole somewhere and throw her in like a decaying animal.

Jake junior told her that there wasn't even a hole. The ground was too badly frozen, and his father had decreed that she should be taken deep into the forest by two of his brothers. Nature would take its course.

"That's disgusting," Martha whispered. They were always aware how easily they could be detected.

"Apparently, Katherine wanted it that way. She had said many times that she wanted to be with her daughter."

Martha frowned. "I know her daughter died before her, but she surely wasn't just taken to the woods?"

Jake junior assumed Martha knew about the other Martha. "Of course she was. An apostate doesn't get a proper burial. And I've heard that Katherine renounced the faith in her last hour as well."

"How could her daughter have been an apostate? Anna told me she was my age. You can't reject the faith when you are so young."

Jake tried to change the course of the conversation. "You did."

"But not openly! What did she do to be considered an apostate?" She pondered the consequence of this for a few seconds. "And how exactly did she die?"

Jake squirmed. He couldn't lie to her. He also couldn't tell her. He had been one of the boys helping his father to dispose of Martha's body. "Please, drop it. Please, don't ask further. It's been horrible, and I'll never forget poor Martha."

"Martha?"

Oh dear Lord, not another slip. Now what?

"Are you telling me they named me after her?"

He nodded. "You got her identity. Nobody knows that she is dead. Officially you are Katherine's daughter. He's collecting social services money for you."

She stared at him intently, trying to figure out if he was making it up. No, of course he wasn't. She had become a dead girl. A Martha.

"I hate that name," was all she could whisper. "My name is Lillian."

He was glad she didn't enquire into the circumstances of Martha's death any further, at least for now, but feared her natural curiosity would not let it rest. "That's pretty. Do you want me to call you Lillian?"

Martha thought about it. She wasn't sure. Lillian was so far away by now. Everything was so confusing, she needed to think about it. There was so much to think about.

Since she had started to question the scripture, more and more of the written words sounded fake. She had already convinced herself that most parts of the *Doctrine and Covenants* were wrong. They had not been dictated by God but had been made up by Joseph Smith with ulterior motives in mind. All the strange rules and commands of the Bishop – she never allowed herself any more to think of him as *her husband* – solely served the purpose of allowing him to control the weaker members of his congregation. She could clearly see that now. How dare he make her change her identity so he could extract money from the Canadian government. How dare he make her his wife while officially declaring her his adopted daughter. He made a mockery of the faith as it was originally intended.

Martha told him so. "Everything he does is a lie! And everything that is written in the scripture is a lie, every single word of it."

Jake shook his head. "I don't think so. Those holy words have been twisted and bent out of their original meaning until they suited the unholy purpose of some very unholy men, but not all of the scripture is a lie."

"And who can tell me which part of it is true? I think even if only part of it is a lie, none of it can be true."

Jake junior breathed a silent sigh of relief. Martha was on her favourite topic again - the scripture. He had to encourage her to talk more about it so she would forget about Katherine and her unfortunate daughter. Quickly, he named some examples of covenants he thought to be correct. All of them had to do with trying to be honest and good and hard-working. It only gave Martha more reasons to argue her case. How could a man be honest and good and hard-working and at the same time have many wives, starve them, work them to the bone, steal their identity, bury them without dignity? How could a man treat another human being like dirt and expect to get a heavenly reward for it? They both knew who she was talking about.

Jake junior could not give her a satisfactory answer. As so often before, he had to agree with her. There was no possible explanation that justified the actions of his father; he couldn't even understand the structure of their faith which permitted such crazy behaviour. They continued discussing it. Slowly, without realizing it, they walked along the path that led to apostasy. They were bonding over this shift in their belief, dramatically increasing the speed of their individual convictions. Joined together in heart and soul, they were fast becoming agnostics.

Suddenly, all too soon, Jake junior cocked his head as if he wanted to ask her forgiveness, and she knew their time tonight was coming to an end. Soon he would have to take her back. They stopped talking and began kissing again.

When they finally managed to untangle their hot bodies, daylight crept through the tiny gap between the potato sack on the pane and the window sill. They reluctantly got up. He went to the table, opened the drawer, took three thin slices of dried meat out of the small tin box he stored in there, and handed them to her. "I'm sorry it's so little," he apologized, "but the rations for the boys are so inadequate nowadays, and our stash of dried meat is really shrinking." Martha knew of the covert hunting the boys had done in autumn to supplement their ever dwindling food supply. She felt guilty about accepting what they needed so badly, no matter how small it was. The few teenage boys in Jake's care still got more than the women and the younger children because they needed to keep their strength up for the hard labour they had to do, but she knew that they didn't get enough to sustain them over a long period of time. In the last few weeks she had seen Jake's face turn gaunt and his muscular body become lean. Still, she took the small parcel, quickly slipped it into the pocket of her skirt and tightly wrapped her shawl around her shoulders, before he ushered her into his truck after checking that nobody was around.

He drove very close to the wood stack which so late in winter had shrunk nearly to the ground. By now, she needed to crawl if she wanted to use it as cover.

Jake junior looked around again and then nodded to her. Seeing him signal that the yard was empty, she opened the door only as much as she needed to slide from the floor of the passenger seat to the ground. He closed the door again, expecting her to disappear behind the low wood stack, and drove off.

But Martha didn't. For some reason she couldn't really understand herself, she suddenly didn't want to crawl over the frozen yard like an animal. She straightened herself and watched his truck drive around the corner. She wanted to walk with her head high into the house. At least for this moment she didn't give a damn who might possibly see her.

She entered the house through the back door. It was still quiet. Nobody was in the kitchen yet although the first light of dawn shone through the window and filtered into the hallway. She decided to go straight to the small office and wait there until the house woke up. Most times she felt safe there because even while being idle and daydreaming, she could pretend to be studying one of the books for her teaching course.

When she opened the door she got such a scare, she nearly screamed out loud. Marion was sitting behind her desk, also suppressing a muffled sound when she saw her. Both recovered from their surprise quickly.

"Where have you been?" Marion said.

"Outside. I couldn't sleep. I went for a walk."

The notion to walk around outside in those temperatures was ludicrous, but Marion didn't seem to care. "Neither could I. It's the full moon that does it."

Martha just stood there, waiting. She noticed that Marion's eyes were swollen and red. The silence between them dragged on until Martha couldn't stand it any longer. "Are you all right?"

Marion placed both hands over her face, hiding it. Then, after another long pause, she started to weep.

"Are you sad about Katherine?"

The first wife nodded, then shook her head. It was very confusing. Martha came closer to the desk. She was so shaken by Marion's loss of composure, she didn't know what to say or do.

Marion sobbed on and started to whisper, barely audibly. "I'm sorry, I can't help it. Katherine is gone, but it's for the best. I'm just so …, upset…, I don't know what to do any more."

Martha saw her struggling, trying to stop herself talking, to no avail. "We will all die," Marion suddenly burst out. "We will starve to death. Katherine was the first one, we will all follow." Marion moved her hands from her face and looked at Martha. "Did you know he refused to give her food? He said she is no use any more. Can't work, can't teach."

"Oh dear Lord," was all Martha could say. "What are we going to do?"

Marion slowly stood up and straightened her dress. "I don't know yet. I'll think of something. Don't worry. I didn't mean to upset you."

She walked past Martha without a glance, just as the unapproachable first wife of earlier days would have done, but Martha could see that she was trembling. She wanted to take her in her arms and comfort her but didn't dare.

That morning, teaching the children was very difficult. Martha could not concentrate. She wanted to tell the older children to use their own minds, to scrutinize the contents of the prayers and to object to the most ludicrous rules they were subjected to. If she could only place the seed of doubt in their minds. But she was too scared to deviate much from the rigid format of the classes. The righteous sister-wives who entered the classroom at odd hours to pick up their children might detect it and tell on her.

Emma still refused to point out which of the sister-wives could be trusted. In fact, Emma herself had caught her once straying from the original scripture and had warned her severely to be careful. Strangely, Emma had said the sister-wives were not to be trusted. She had not said *some of them*.

By midday, Martha gave up trying to teach her pupils anything. She told them to read quietly in the holy book and sat down behind her small table pretending to study.

Last night she had not slept at all. Her mind was confused and she wanted to forget all the dreadful things she had learned, like her becoming the other Martha, poor Katherine being starved to death, or Marion worrying about all of them dying. It was too much to bear.

She looked up again. The faces of the children were emaciated, just like those of the sister-wives who started to trickle in. Most didn't even acknowledge her with more than a faint nod. They had no energy left and were just looking out for themselves and their own.

Emma arrived last and came up to her. Her expression was serious. "Well, what's for lunch today?" she asked blandly.

Martha was aware that Emma was jealous of her. She had mentioned several times before that Martha was lucky to be living so well at the main house, insinuating that she got more than her share to eat there.

"Please Emma," Martha tried to assured her, "we are not getting more than any of the others."

Emma then asked how it came that she was so unperturbed by the famine that had come upon them.

Martha frowned. How could she explain to her friend that she never felt any hunger pains. That she was more than compensated for the lack of food. She was tempted to let her old friend in on her precious secret. Sometimes the solitude in the house was hard to deal with and she desperately needed someone to confide in. Someone she could tell that she was in love! But then she would have to explain what it meant to love somebody so deeply. There was no way Emma would understand. The knowledge that Jake junior existed filled her with joy, and when she thought about the hours they spent together and how they delighted in each others company she could have burst with love. Yes, that was the love they were all supposed to feel. But they all only associated this wonderful word with the 'Love for the Lord', and that was a different thing altogether. None of them understood how it felt to be *in love*. It was best to keep this secret from Emma.

So she just said she had gone beyond hunger pains.

Emma scrutinized her and, realizing that Martha had become thinner too, relaxed a little. There was nothing else to say, so she warned Martha again. Some of the sister-wives thought she and Marion sided together against them, and it was not wise to give them grounds for condemnation. "You know how Anna had to live up there!" she reminded Martha.

A shiver went through Martha as she remembered the disgusting conditions in the prison hut. Anna's misery, which had catapulted Martha at lightning speed from a naïve child into a mature young woman, was still engraved on her mind.

"How is Anna doing?" she asked.

"I don't know, she has really bad luck. One of the twins is very ill again. Anna thinks her hut is cursed and is begging Barbara to do an exorcism. But our husband has not given his permission yet. I don't think the child will survive. And then she will probably go crazy again and will have to be put down."

Martha thought of Katherine. Did Emma know how she had died and how they had disposed of her? "To put down? You make it sound as if Anna was an animal."

Emma giggled quietly. "You should see her; she behaves like a fox with rabies. Forever going on about wanting to see our husband again. As if he would see anybody." Emma's voice took an even more hushed tone. "Is it true that he sleeps with you again?"

Martha nearly gagged. "What? Who says that?"

"There are rumours. You know, he hasn't sent for any of us, and Marion lets you stay at the main house. So it must be you."

So there was even more behind Emma's jealousy. "It is not!" Martha objected strongly. The thought alone made her skin crawl.

"Then what is he doing? The scripture says he must produce soldiers for the Lord."

"Oh forget the scripture! Maybe he doesn't want to do it."

"See, you are doing it again," Emma chided. "If anybody hears you, you are in big trouble."

Martha smiled and touched Emma's arm. "But nobody is here and you won't tell, right?"

Emma sighed heavily. "Oh my, sometimes I don't know what is right or wrong any more. All I know is that I am always hungry. Do you have any idea when things will change?"

"No". Martha had not been listening at the hole in the wall lately. She no longer cared what was happening between Marion and her husband.

"But you are still working in the office often, right?"

"I'm allowed to study there, yes."

"Well then you should listen in and try and find out what's happening. It can't go on forever, they must have a plan. We all need to know."

"What for?"

Emma quickly looked over her shoulder and put on her conspirator's face. "Because I, and some of the others for that matter, as you well know, don't want to starve to death. At least we should know what is coming, don't you think?"

Martha thought of Marion's desperation. What could she say to comfort Emma?

"Please? For me?" Emma begged.

"All right then. I'll listen in." Martha did not see any harm in it and promised to eavesdrop again as soon as possible.

The chance presented itself the same afternoon while Martha was bent over her geography book. The world was so big. So many countries! Couldn't she and Jake escape to one of them?

She had to learn the names of the continents, the different countries and cities. Not all of them belonged to the Church – in fact, Martha was aware by now that in Canada, and even in America, their faith represented a minority. Marion had told her to ignore all that false information and just memorize the facts she needed for the teacher's course. After passing the exam, she could forget all she had learned as it was not relevant for any of the classes she would be teaching. Unfortunately, the Canadian government insisted on a teacher's certificate based on their false textbooks, Marion had drummed into her, and if they were not satisfied that a teacher was qualified they would stop paying their home schooling grant and send all the children to one of their schools.

Martha had been tempted to tell Marion that she would actually love to see them go to a public school, but she did not even know if there was one close enough, and anyway, a comment like that could cost her the privilege of studying and, even worse, of staying in the main house. If she didn't live in the main house it would be so much harder to meet Jake. Here, she only had to deal with Marion, who was not very suspicious any more, and the Bishop, who never paid any attention to her anyway.

No, getting chased out of the main house was not an option.

A door was opening and closing.

Remembering her promise to Emma, Martha got up, went to the book shelves and removed the encyclopaedia. Almost immediately, she heard Marion's low anguished voice.

"Please, my husband, hear me out. I don't mean to criticize you, but we can't go on like this much longer."

Martha moved her ear closer to the hole to understand better what Marion was saying.

"The children are dying. We are all starving and cannot continue with so little food."

She heard how her husband answered in a tone full of resentment. "And what do you want me to do about it? If you're so clever, what is your solution? Don't come to me and complain all the time just because you have to make do with a bit less. It's good for your souls to cleanse your bodies. No need to panic like that. You're always exaggerating. Tomorrow is the first of March, then the social services cheques for the children will be in the mail. I'll buy some more supplies then."

"Those cheques are no use," Marion replied, and Martha knew already what she would explain next. "They don't cover the bank overdraft. We can't withdraw any more money. Not for many months to come."

"We have too many mouths to feed! I've always said that. I think it's time to get rid of some of them!"

Martha's blood froze. What was he saying? Did he want to kill some of the sister-wives or, more likely, some of the small girls to make ends meet? Did he want to starve them to death and throw them away like Katherine? She pressed her ear closer, not even thinking how it would look if anybody entered the office. The only two people who could possibly come in without knocking were on the other side of the wall, carrying on their deadly dispute.

"My husband, what are you saying? I don't understand."

"See, that's how stupid you are."

"Forgive me, I'm only a woman."

"Indeed, that is the only reason why I bear your presence. You can't help it. I don't have to explain to you what I'm doing, but I have a kind inclination toward you. You are my first wife and will be with me for all eternity. Now listen carefully, the Lord has presented me with a solution to our current misfortune. Ours is a unique problem as on the one hand we don't have enough men old enough to do the work that brings in money, and on the other hand we have too many useless females who can't do hard labour. I can't afford to send some of the boys away who are now maturing into priesthood. Most of them are respectful of our rules. I will just have to keep a close watch over those boys to make sure none of them stray from the faith."

An involuntary sigh of relief escaped Martha and she pressed her lips together quickly. Jake was safe! He would not be sent away!

"But some of the older boys need wives now. The sooner they start their families the better. We need many more souls in our congregation. They are old enough and if they have a wife for their personal use they will not develop unhealthy and sinful ideas. How many girls do we have here who are ready to enter marriage?"

Marion gasped. "But most of them are related! They are their sisters!"

"Tell me, woman, how many?"

"I am not sure."

"How many have reached thirteen?

Marion hesitated. She was possibly counting or only stalling, but eventually could not refuse her husband an answer. "I think twelve of them."

"Good, that should be enough. They will all be married off."

Suddenly, the implication of what he was suggesting hit Martha. Jake was the oldest son, he would be married first. And he could not be married to her. He would have to live with the first wife that was chosen for him by the Bishop, and then he would have to marry a second. And a third. And it would go on like that. He would never be able to spend time with her again. A sharp pain made her heart miss a beat before it thudded along with increased speed. This was the worst news she could have received. She wanted to throw the book back in place and slump down on the floor. Her knees were buckling and could hardly hold up her weight, but somehow she had to go on listening.

"Please, my husband, please consider if you understood the words of the Lord as he meant them. The scripture says to look outside the family..."

"Be quiet", he thundered at her. "How dare you question me! I know perfectly well what the Lord wants me to do. How dare you doubt me!"

"I am sorry, please be patient with me. Please make me understand. How would it reduce the mouths to feed if you marry brothers to sisters? They would still need the same amount of food to survive. How can this help us get more money to feed us?"

He let out a confident belly-laugh. "You really think I would marry them off inside our family? Stupid woman. No, I will call Brother Lucas today and offer our daughters to the Gatekeepers in marriage. There are Brothers in Utah and Arizona who need young and fresh blood. My daughters are brought up in the faith and will make perfectly submissive wives. Brother Lucas knows this and he will place them with men of good standing who can pay a handsome compensation for my efforts in raising them to respect Section 132."

"Praise the Lord. They will not be married to their brothers." Marion replied with audible relief. "And forgive my ignorance, my husband. I should not have doubted you."

"I forgive you."

Martha's mind silently and simultaneously asked the question that Marion now voiced.

"Thank you for your patience with your humble wife. But did you not say the older boys need wives to start their families?"

"Yes, and you did say twelve of the girls are ready. I will exchange four of them with suitable girls from the south. Jake junior must have a wife, and three who come next in line. The other eight girls will not be exchanged. They will bring in the money."

Now, having said it loud, it was an undisputable fact. Jake would be married soon. Martha's life drained out of her and everything went dark. She held on to the shelf, feeling faint. The book must be placed back in position. While she struggled to stay conscious, she paid little attention to the next sentence her husband chuckled.

"Actually, I should divorce the small one, what's her name, Meena or something or other, you know, the one that can't hold her food down. Then I can marry her off too. Somebody down there deserves her, for sure. Brother Lucas has lots of enemies, I must tell him about her. I'll throw her into the bargain for good measure."

With shaking hands Martha managed to place the book over the hole and slowly slid to the floor. Her own fate did not matter. If he wanted to get rid of her, it would mean nothing to her. If Jake were not part of her life any more, she would die for sure. And she had refused to give him what he yearned for so desperately! How would he be able to remember her now?

To stay conscious, she focused her eyes on the calendar hanging on the opposite wall. It had been a giveaway from the bank. Each month had its own page, with a picture of a representative of the Canadian wildlife family. Today was the last day of February. The month of the buffalo. Next month would be a snow owl, she had looked it up already. Very fitting, as March was not likely to be free of all snow up in this part of the world. This was her second winter here and childhood memories of sun and warmth had long ago faded into the pale landscape of her current existence. She didn't even regret this. Everything that made her life exceptional was here, personified by Jake junior. Like the buffalo who had only a small territory left to roam in, so was the radius of her existence confined to the small space around him. He, who gave her a reason to exist, who was the breath that filled her lungs and the touch that made her skin tingle.

Martha made a resolution and felt some energy coming back because of it. She slowly lifted herself up from the floor and straightened her dress. Tonight would be her last night with him, and she would make it count. It should be a night he would always remember.

35

He made two phone calls, one after the other.

First he dialled Jake's number and waited with bated breath for him to pick up the phone. He was lucky on his first try. More than lucky.

Jake seemed surprised to hear from him, but not as much as Richard had expected him to be. His greeting was jovial, mixed with a small dose of complacency, which was understandable considering how they had parted, and a larger dose of conviviality which Richard couldn't quite interpret. Jake acted as if Richard was a close friend he was eager to talk to after a long absence, and not somebody who had not once called to apologize for insulting him and storming out of his house.

Jake didn't even hint at Richard's hasty and inappropriate exit, but asked how he had fared since his visit last summer. Richard's internal warning system kicked in when Jake proceeded to ask him if all was coming along well with the development. He immediately wondered if Jake knew about his latest troubles or if he simply suffered a case of slight paranoia. There was no way Jake could know about the AO's recent request, and even if he did suspect it, it wouldn't really matter. Jake would grasp the reason for his call soon enough. Richard told him all was well, in fact so well that he was considering an expansion of his development and that he might have an interesting proposal for him.

"What kind of proposal?" Jake asked, not overly guarded.

"One that might be financially beneficial to you," Richard answered, using the old and worn-out phrase that always worked with people like Jake.

Jake said he would be delighted to meet, but Richard would have to come up to visit him again, if he didn't mind, as he had a lot of arrangements to make. An upcoming marriage in the family had to be prepared. They agreed to meet in two days, on the second of March.

Then Richard dialled again and waited. When Daisy picked up the phone, he launched right into it, fearful she might hang up on him.

"Daisy, it's me. Please don't hang up."

"Richard," she snarled.

"I have a proposal for you!"

"Let me guess, one that might be financially beneficial to me?"

Under normal circumstances he would have laughed, it was just too funny how similar their phraseology was, but that would have aggravated her even more, so he let her rave on.

"Oh wait, no, that can't be, you don't have any money left to make me an offer. Now I've got it – you want to make me a partner too. Great, except that this doesn't work either. I won't play along with Jake, and without him I'm of no use to you."

"Please listen to me," he pleaded. "I've just called Jake. He has agreed to see me the day after tomorrow."

"Congratulations, lucky you!" She meant to sound sarcastic but he detected a certain amount of curiosity in her pointed comment.

"I'm driving up tomorrow and I want you to come with me."

"Have you now lost it completely?"

"Bear with me. I want you to accompany me and be part of the negotiations. Just come and listen in on what I'm going to offer him, and if you don't like any of it we'll walk away and I won't do it."

"I don't like it."

"I've changed my concept. Jake will have no say in the company. He won't even be a silent partner. I will offer him a deferred payment, but such a high one, that he can't say no."

She seemed to retreat a fraction from her firm stand. "He'll refuse to see me. Remember, I'm only a woman."

"I'll insist on it."

"And if I don't agree, you'll drop your proposition altogether? One signal from me, and we'll get up and leave the table immediately?"

"Yes."

"Why? Then you lose your company."

He nodded eagerly. "I've thought about it. I don't like you being on the wrong side of the fence. It doesn't feel right."

A long silence followed. They were both thinking hard. *Why would I rather give up my company than have her consider me an asshole?* he contemplated, while at the same time she probably wondered why it made him less of an asshole if he took her along to deal with what she called the devil. The offer to give it all up if necessary felt right and he was confident that it was good enough for her.

"Alright, we can come to an agreement. You won't have to go and see Jake all by yourself. You'll have company, but I have one condition."

"Agreed."

"Don't you want to know what it is?"

"Whatever. I said I agree."

Daisy was a truly amazing woman. He should have expected to be blindsided by her. "I'm sending Adam with you on my behalf. He will be my representative, and if he doesn't like what is being said, he can call the shots."

"Oh shit no!"

"You agreed! It's not as crazy as you think. Adam was born into a polygamous community and knows what goes on there better than any of us. I want him to see Jake's set-up and analyze it based on his unique experience. Maybe I've been wrong all along and have been imagining things. I wouldn't want it on my conscience if you lose your company because I made unqualified assumptions. So it's a win-win situation for both of us. Only if the devil is truly the Satan I expect him to be, will we go under."

She had a very valid point. To agree to her condition was nearly physically painful for Richard, but it looked like this was the only solution to get her back on his side. "I'm not sure this is such a good idea. He has absolutely no experience in such dealings. If you insist I'll put up with him, but I will seal his mouth with duct tape."

"You will be civil to him and, even more important, you will heed his advice! That's what it's all about."

"Okay, okay, I said I'll take him along."

"I have to ask Adam first though. He may not want to go there. Too many bad memories, as you can imagine. Call me back in an hour."

Richard immediately crossed his fingers and hoped that dear Adam would be a coward and chicken out.

Adam had barely closed the car door on the passenger side when Richard laid down the law without giving much consideration to conventional politeness or to Daisy's instructions. "Just in case you plan to bore me with some sob stories about the poor Lost Boys, forget it. I don't like talking in the car and would appreciate it if you kept it to a minimum."

Adam had agreed to come along without needing much persuasion from Daisy, but Richard was quite worried. Of course Adam was heavily influenced by her and would be overly critical of what was visibly wrong with Jake's family. He just hoped that Jake wasn't out to shock again and was racking his brain as to how he could keep Adam out of harm's way.

For cost saving reasons he had decided to drive the whole way. Two plane tickets to Kamloops and a rental car for the rest of the trip were out of the question. It was bad enough that they had to spend one night in a motel because Jake had stuck to his usual 10 a.m. time for their meeting. On this trip it would not be the high-class Blue River Resort.

"I know you're not exactly overjoyed to have me replace Daisy," Adam replied annoyingly good-natured. "I just hope I can be of some help."

"You bet I'm not. But let's humour her, if we must. As long as you stay out of the conversation altogether you will be a great help to me and I won't mind having to baby-sit you. Your girlfriend's wish is my command."

The little sucker laughed. "I think you are jealous."

"What do you know about jealousy?" Richard demanded to know while he took the turn on to Highway 1 East. From now on they were driving straight to Kamloops which was about 300 kilometres away. With only two turn-offs along the route, even a half blind driver could find his way. He put the car in cruise control. It was early afternoon and the sun was out, reminding him to be grateful for small mercies. Mother nature sided with him and kept the Coquihalla pass free of slush and ice, which was not to be taken for granted. The first of March was meteorologically still winter.

"I am well versed with many emotions, but particularly familiar with a person showing signs of jealousy," Adam answered Richard's question.

Well versed? – where did this guy come from? Then he remembered. "So, you're saying places like Bountiful are a hot-spot of passion?! Who would have guessed."

Adam settled into his seat. "My mother had eighteen sister-wives, all competing for the attention of my father. Can you imagine the bitter intrigues, envious grudges and petty quarrels between the women? We children were in the midst of this, often being used as pawns. Trust me, I know enough about the good as well as - and especially - the bad side of human nature."

The idea of growing up in such an environment was too abstract for Richard to grasp, but for some reason it made him curious. Instead of reminding Adam of his initial demand to stay mute as long as he sat in the passenger seat, which he had voiced only a short while ago, he now urged him on to tell him more. "Why on earth do those women not feel humiliated being treated like animals?"

"You mean like chickens with one rooster, or a herd of sheep with one ram?" Adam asked very calmly.

"Yeah, it's not normal to live like that."

"It's normal to them. They grow up like that and have never known any other way."

"Come on – you can't believe that yourself."

"Think back to being a child. How do you gather knowledge? How do you form opinions? How do you see the world? Isn't it by being the centre of a gradually widening circle? If this circle is filled with people who behave in a certain way, you adopt their ways. And if those people keep the circle closed, you will never know what lies beyond."

"You broke out; why don't they?"

"It's difficult enough for us guys, but practically impossible for the girls to escape the system. They are raised under much stricter rules than we are. Compared to their lives I had quite a lot of freedom. You have to understand, boys will become priests after they turn twelve which means, if they abide by the rules of the Church and serve the Elders slavishly, they have a chance to eventually create their own kingdom. There are three tiers of kingdom, the "telestial" for the sinners of the faith who have to face the Lord's judgment, the "terrestial" for the good but not perfect, and the "celestial" for the most righteous."

Richard interrupted. "Sounds a lot like the Christian model of heaven, purgatory and hell to me."

"In Joseph Smith's cosmology no hell exists, only eternal blackness. An unimaginably terrifying thought for small children. I guess you could call it hell, just like the damnation of the not so faithful to act as eternal servants to the faithful could be called purgatory. In any case, if you do achieve the highest level you will be rewarded by your own planet and become a God. Most boys like the thought that they will eventually have their own flock to control, if they only behave and work hard until their Elders allow them to marry. They never think about being cast out of their community, which is inevitable for most of them because they eventually become a threat to the few Elders running the show. Let's face it, if one man has twenty wives, there will be nineteen guys missing out." Adam turned sideways and looked at Richard, smiling without malice but with playful mockery. "But forgive me, I must remember your rule not to mention the Lost Boys."

"Yeah, right", Richard agreed, because otherwise he would have contradicted himself.

"So let's go back to the girls," Adam continued with an even wider grin, and Richard did not interrupt his reminiscence, although he considered his sudden interest in Adam's insider knowledge to be slightly sick. But how often did one have a chance to listen to first-hand experience from a male bystander to a harem?

"The girls are much more demure to start with - no testosterone that makes them aggressive - so they are easier to mould. Their training starts very young and is rigorous, implemented by their many mothers who are devout believers in the righteousness of their husband's actions because they don't know any better. Most of them had experienced a short period of being a favourite, only to be discarded as soon as the next, usually younger, wife gets married into their family. After that, they are forever chasing those short moments of glory and would do anything to be desirable again to the only man they will ever intimately know. I have seen it happen many times. They look at the other women as competition, they are enemies, because they are trained to see it like that, and the children of the sister-wives pose a threat to them. All the bitterness and frustration has to come out somehow – and it is the girls from the sister-wives who bear the brunt of it. Often they are brutally bent into shape; there is no chance for them to develop naturally. Did you know that it is quite common in our compounds to use water torture on babies? They spank them and then hold their faces under a running tap until they have no more strength to cry? No, the women have no chance at all. They get *broken in* as it's called so early, they never start thinking for themselves."

Adam's sincerity and the horror of what lay behind his explanation killed the snide remark that had lingered on Richard's tongue. He had wanted to ask Adam why he did not feel inclined to shake some of the girls out of their stupor when he had still been living there, but it did not seem appropriate. After a short moment of silence, Adam surprised him with an unexpected depth of perception.

"I guess you're wondering what we boys did with our sexuality when we were growing up." Did the guy read his mind? "Of course, rape is not uncommon amongst the close-knit community with so many youngsters herded together. Again, the girls have to pay the ultimate price when this happens - the boys are just kicked out or, if the girl is not very valuable, simply get a slap on the wrist."

"The ultimate price?" Richard queried.

"Sure," Adam said, pressing his lips into a thin line. "When the attack happens, they may be badly damaged, or they are ugly anyway, in any case they are killed. What did you think?"

They drove straight through Kamloops. Richard wanted to drive all the way to Clearwater to check into a cheap motel there. It was getting dark quickly. He concentrated on the road winding along the Thompson River, every now and then overtaking a truck or a slower passenger car.

Adam's description of what he and his siblings had to endure while growing up had left a sour aftertaste in Richard. In the last three hours they had chatted a bit more, but they took great care to avoid the subject. Richard did not know what Adam was working over in his mind but could sense how he was drifting deeper into his, probably not very pleasant, memories. For himself, Richard started to concentrate on tomorrow's meeting. What happened in Bountiful had nothing to do with Jake's family, he silently assured himself whenever small doubts raised their pert little hand to ask silly questions like: *how can this be allowed to go on, why doesn't somebody do something about it, and, worst of all – why do you assume that Jake is not guilty of the same crimes?*

Soon after Little Fort brownish hardened snow accumulations appeared along the sides of the road. Sorry reminders that winter was not over yet. As they were gaining altitude, the piles were getting more voluminous and fresher, indicating recent snowfall.

The Motel parking area was covered with white powder. They checked into their rooms and Richard fell on a mattress so soft it must have been delivered from the manufacturer with a guarantee for backache. It was not even nine p.m. yet. He unwrapped the burger they had bought at the drive-through opposite the motel, turned on the TV and settled down for a quick meal while watching a re-run of Die Hard. And then Die Hard 2, which followed immediately after. Then he tried to go to sleep. There was no mini-bar, so he didn't have to fight temptation to get himself tired with the help of a potent drink. He really tried hard, but his mind was going in circles. What if Jake said no? What if Adam forgot himself and flipped out? But why should he? And back again to: What if Jake said no? He was tossing and turning in an effort to find a position to relax. Damn that mattress. Damn that regular ticking noise from the vending machine outside that got louder the more he concentrated on not hearing it. Damn the flickering neon light outside his window that penetrated his closed eyelids. Back to Jake again. Would he manage to convince him? Would Adam manage to keep his cool?

It was hell to get through the night, knowing he needed his sleep to be functioning properly at the most important meeting of his career. The more he forced himself, the wider awake he was. It must have been five in the morning before he finally fell into an exhausted sleep.

36

Martha stood by the window all night, waiting for the sound of his pickup truck. The silence outside was excruciating. Deadly. She was dying inside minute by minute. Why didn't Jake junior feel her anguish? He *must* know something was happening. He *must* know how urgently she needed to talk to him. Every fibre of her being was sending out signals, but he didn't come.

Night settled into impenetrable darkness, and she seriously considered sneaking out of the house and running through the forest over to his small cabin. But it had snowed lightly and was completely calm. Her footprints in the dusting on the frozen ground would give her away long after she had reached him.

When morning broke, she was still standing by the window, grateful that this night was finally over. Today was the first day of March, the month of the snow owl. Martha prayed that this animal's legendary wisdom would give her an inspiration. She just had to find a way to warn Jake junior of what his father had planned for him. Every cell of her being was urging her to hurry, telling her that there was precious little time left.

Teaching all morning was sheer agony. As soon as school was finished, all the sister-wives came to collect their children and Martha shuffled from one foot to another, impatient to get rid of them and rush back to the office. Maybe the Bishop and Marion were discussing his plans again and she could listen in – maybe they had postponed the exchange of the brides to a later date. No, not very likely. Something had to be done fast or the whole family would starve to death, therefore her husband would want to go ahead with those weddings quickly. Martha was desperate to find out how much time was left and if she and Jake could be together one more time.

She was trying to shoo out everybody quickly, insisting she had been ordered to go back to the main house. Emma was among the last to leave, scooping her pitifully scrawny youngest up in her arms, and looking at Martha with silent urgency. Martha whispered to her that something was happening, but she needed more time to find out exactly what was going on, and promised to tell her as soon as she knew something. Emma implored her to at least tell her if the food supply would improve soon when a sister-wife suddenly appeared behind her. Martha indicated with a nearly undetectable movement of her eyes that Emma should be quiet, hoping that her own anxiety would not give her away. Emma shut her mouth reluctantly and left with a very troubled look on her face.

Finally back in the office, Martha laid out some homework in case Marion came in, and then moved the book aside once again. Instantly she heard her husband talking on the phone.

"Yes, of course, I understand."

Pause.

"Of course, Brother Lucas, I am filled with gratitude to you for even listening to me. I am as always your faithful servant."

Pause.

Martha realized that the Bishop must be speaking to a high authority. There was only one person in the whole world he would treat with such reverence. He was talking to the leader of their Church, probably the leader of those mysterious Gatekeepers! Brother Lucas. Realising she now had a name for this person, a powerful surge made her body tremble. Her eavesdropping had now become high treason.

"But I do urge you to listen to me too. After all I've gone through, it is only befitting that I can state my case. Winter has been tough on us, you can't imagine how it is here. It's a hard life in the wilderness. But I've tried my best. I have brought my family through the dark cold

330

winter all by myself, without any assistance from the Church. I know you wanted to test me and I can assure you I have …"

Pause. He was listening. Martha held her breath so she would not miss a single word. The Bishop sounded not so demure any more, more like an obnoxious child, and she wondered how Brother Lucas reacted to that. She didn't have to wait long.

"But no, what are you thinking? Why should I fax you my account statements? I can barely scrape together a living here? Do you want me to …"

Pause again.

"No, of course not! That's why I want to send the girls down. Yes, to supplement my income. What's wrong with that? … Yes, naturally, I can vouch for each one of them. They are perfectly obedient. We have been schooling them ever since we arrived here."

Pause.

"Yes, of course we have a trained teacher among us."

Martha felt a sudden surge of pride, thinking he would now mention her name to the leader of the Gatekeepers! Telling him how well she was doing in replacing the deceased Katherine. But he didn't, he ignored her as usual.

"They are all ready for marriage… they are thirteen or fourteen, fifteen at most. Ripe as juicy peaches and ready to be picked by the brothers faithful to our Church and dear to your heart. They will be ever so grateful to you for presenting such delicious sweet young meat to them…"

He laughed. It was the same kind of superior snort she had heard when he had glared at her naked body. Martha cringed and suddenly did not feel proud at all any more. What had she been thinking? Why should she be proud to help the Bishop spread the lies of his Church to the little ones? Didn't that make her an accessory to their ill teachings? The Bishop, or the Gatekeepers, were not a mouthpiece of the Lord as the children were led to believe, they were just men, and thoroughly disgusting ones at that! One of them was offering Jake's half-sisters on the marriage market – what had he called them, ripe fruits, delicious meat? – while the other one was probably negotiating a good price for them.

"They are all attractive. The prettiest are the pair of twins ..."

A short pause now.

"Four of them I need to exchange for brides for my sons, but the other eight would be available for a certain fee to cover the cost of their upbringing and schooling. I would happily send them to you as a gift, of course, but everything is so expensive nowadays; to feed and clothe them cost me a small fortune. We do want to present them to our Elders in good condition, don't we? "

He snorted again, then listened.

"The twins? Oh, they are little beauties. I think they're about fifteen. Perfect for marriage. ... Yes, I can make sure those two will be among them. ... Yes, that would be very agreeable."

Pause.

"Sure, whenever you say. Next week would be perfect.... I am bound to you in the name of the Lord and our Church. Your word is my law.... Yes, yes, of course, cash is acceptable. Not through the bank. No need for anybody to follow such transactions.... American dollars will be fine...Yes, yes...."

Martha felt sick when she thought what those poor girls would have to endure. They would be carted off to one of the hidden compounds the fundamentalists ruled with iron fists, to be married to much older men who might already be in their seventies or eighties, in a quick and loveless ceremony similar to the one she had experienced two years ago. Their husbands could make use of them and dominate them for the rest of their lives, demanding not only their subservience but expecting their ever-lasting gratitude. They could inflict excruciating pain or soul destroying humiliation – all based on the promise of eternal salvation.

Martha had been lucky enough to escape her husband's attention. She would never have survived the past two years if he had carried on using her body the way he had in the first few nights. Many of the girls would not survive the ordeal that awaited them. Martha's stomach turned and she wanted to vomit, but she had to pull herself together and continue listening because she had to think of herself now. There was nothing she could do for those poor unfortunate girls, but there was a glimmer of hope for her to see Jake junior again. His father had mentioned doing the exchange next week! That gave her seven days – or nights – seven more chances to see Jake.

"Shall we do it like last time? We can bring all of them over the border on the old smuggler's route. It shouldn't be a problem to find suitable matches for most of them. The twins might be a problem …, oh, I understand, well, if you don't plan to have them registered it won't matter …, I see, you want them for your own family…, then there should be no delay. I will start to organize everything from here. Why don't you email the pictures of the girls you have selected to our dear and trustworthy John in Creston and I'll do the same with my girls. He will match up the passports to make sure we can keep them legal."

So that's how it was done! They prepared those documents through an agent called John who matched the girls that were exchanged one for one.

Her husband agreed with the Gatekeeper. "Sure Brother Lucas, if you want, we can bring the girls to the border tomorrow. All the paperwork can be done later."

Tomorrow already! Why the sudden hurry? The reason for this quickly dawned on her; the sooner he did the exchange the faster he would get hold of the money! But this urgency might be to her advantage. Surely he could not handle the transport of twelve girls all by himself. He would have to take Marion along with him to look after them. Martha's excitement rose until his next sentences squashed her hope to be alone in the main house for a short while.

"No, I won't come myself, but I'll send my eldest son, Jake junior. He is trustworthy and can take care of it. He is a good boy. And one of the brides is for him, so he can take his pick as soon as he sees them."

Pause.

"Forgive me, I was forgetful. Of course, he'll accept your choice in this matter. Your word is our command. He'll be grateful for your guidance. Yes, thank you. Thank you very much."

After a lengthy affirmation of his boundless loyalty and gratitude, the Bishop said his good-bye to the leader of the Gatekeepers. Martha's mind was racing. All she could think of now was how to get hold of Jake junior. She had to see him, had to talk to him, had to hold him one more time. Tonight! It had to be tonight; tomorrow he would be lost to her forever. She had to give him something that would remind him of her for the rest of his life, otherwise her existence had no meaning at all.

Far to the south, Brother Lucas placed the phone back in its cradle, stood up, took his white shirt off and placed it carefully on his desk. He sat down again, leaned back in his chair and let the warm spring breeze coming from the open window caress the parched skin of his exposed upper body. March was still cool enough to exist without the constant hum of the air conditioner. He swirled his chair toward the window, directly into the sunlight and closed his eyes. The warmth was comforting. The older he got, the more he appreciated those rare moments when he felt totally relaxed. Like the twins used to make him feel.

Brother Jacob was such a fool. He deserved to suffer long arctic winters, hardship and misery. The temerity of him, calling without making a prior appointment! Brother Lucas had been caught by surprise because today of all days he had been alone in the office – an exceptionally rare event - and had picked up the phone without thinking.

Brother Jacob had aggravated him beyond imagination, actually to the point when he wanted to blurt out his decision to excommunicate him, but he had held back. Brother Ervin had recently left for Europe, but the meeting with all the other brothers had not yet taken place and he must not be too hasty. So he had listened to Brother Jacob's proposal to send his daughters down to Arizona. He had briefly wondered if Marion had a daughter. If so, he wouldn't mind looking at her. But that had reminded him of his loss a long time ago and he hated Brother Jacob even more. No way would he agree to anything that insufferable, impertinent man proposed.

Brother Lucas had listened with grinding teeth, holding back all the spite he had wanted to hurl at the obnoxious self-proclaimed Bishop. Until he had mentioned the twins.

So what if he did that one deal with Brother Jacob! Get the girls sent down to the Church, and if the twins were really only fifteen and as pretty as promised, the least he could do was try them out himself.

His skin tingled in the sun. He could feel the warmth spreading. So the Lord hadn't punished him after all. He rewarded him again with a new set of twins. It could be expected that they would be even better than the old ones. Hail the Lord.

And damnation to the Bishop. Brother Lucas would not send any money to him. He would accept the girls, would not exchange any of them and would then proceed to punish Brother Jacob. He could make a decent case out of this. To instigate such a marriage exchange and demand money from the Gatekeepers for it was unheard of. It was not Brother Jacob's place to arrange something like this, it was the prerogative of the Church Elders – and Brother Jacob was not one of them. In fact, very soon he would not even belong to the Church any more!

37

Martha's mind was racing, trying to find an answer to her most pressing problem: how could she get hold of Jake junior?

The Bishop had ended his conversation and now addressed the first wife. Hearing his jubilant voice, Martha put her ear closer to the hole in the wall again.

"See, I told you so. Brother Lucas agreed without even asking the price. I'm demanding ten thousand for each of them and I'm certain he will pay. They have so much money down there, they don't care as long as they get something for it."

Marion seemed to be stunned by the amount. "Oh Lord, that is eighty-thousand!"

"Seventy."

"But aren't we sending twelve…"

"Yes, and we will bring five back," he confirmed.

"But only four of the boys have entered priesthood," Marion whined.

Her husband got even louder, thundering full of supreme reproach. "Are you questioning me again, woman? Do you expect me to justify my actions to you? You may be my first, but never forget that I can still divorce you and ban you from entering my celestial kingdom. Never forget, your exaltation is at my mercy."

"I beg your forgiveness," Marion said remarkably firmly. "You are planning to get another wife?"

"Yes, I am. You don't expect me to carry on like this, with a bunch of old hags that no decent man wants to touch!"

"They are all sealed to you by the Holy Spirit. The scripture says: *they shall receive your seed, the fruit of your loin, which is to continue so long as they were in the world...*"

He interrupted her recital, infuriated. "Stop it, I know what is written. I am your God, you will have to accept my will!"

"*Sarah's Law* says, your first wife must agree to any other wife you wish to bring into the family."

Martha was shocked. Marion had never sounded so daring. But her husband's reply to her amazing rebellion was surprisingly calm. As he recited a part of the second last command of section 132, he sounded smug.

"And it goes on saying: *If she does not believe and administer unto him according to the Lord's word, she becomes the transgressor and he is exempt from the Law of Sarah.*"

What could Marion answer to this? *Sarah's Law* demanded that the husband ask his wife's permission if he wanted to take on another wife; just like Abraham had done when God pledged Hagar to him through the hands of his wife Sarah. However, if the wife refused to give permission, this law became redundant because it contradicted the Church's rule that a wife had to be obedient to her husband. If Marion stood firmly, her husband would divorce her, and she would have to carve a self-sufficient life at the fringe of their family. Nobody would be allowed to even notice her, and she would soon starve or freeze to death. Probably not faster than the rest of us, Martha thought angrily. It was all a farce; a gigantic spider's web with sticky strings of covenants, woven by a master insect. The faithful were glued in this net of spiritual bonding. No matter how hard they tried, there was no escape for any of them.

Marion realized this too.

"I will give my permission," she muttered defeated.

"Fine. Then let's get on with the work at hand. Much needs to be done." He was like a different person now that he had got his way. "My dear Marion, don't cry now. I know it is hard for you to understand the

Lord's will. He has spoken through the Gatekeepers. The Lord wants me to have another wife, what can I do? Rejoice, the Lord has provided for all of us. We will have money soon, but I have some more good news, which will come as a great surprise to you. Remember the man who bought our land for his development, Richard Bergman? Well, the Lord has been guiding him toward me again. Guess what, he called me this morning and wants to make me another offer. What do you say to that?"

Marion still sounded very subdued. "Praise the Lord."

"Exactly! Soon we'll have enough money to satisfy the bank and will have plenty left over. I have plans for this heathen and can milk this particular beast for a lot more."

Martha understood his reference to *milking the beast*. It was normally used to describe the Church's practise of squeezing unjust welfare payments and any other possible social benefits from the government of their countries.

"He is coming here tomorrow at ten, so we must be ready for him. The women must not all be seen when he gets here. Make sure most of them stay indoors. There is much to do. We need to get the girls ready for the transfer. Jake junior will leave with them tomorrow, as soon as my meeting with Richard Bergman is over. Tonight, we'll have another prayer session to thank the Lord for what he has bestowed upon me and to ask him for further guidance. Make sure everybody over the age of ten attends. Choose one of the women to stay back to take care of the little ones."

An idea flashed through Martha's furiously racing brain. If she could somehow get close to Jake tonight, maybe she could slip him a note. It was a huge risk, for both of them, but maybe the only chance she had left.

Her luck was finally changing. In the early afternoon, Marion came into the office carrying a basket. She kept holding on to it while she asked Martha what she was doing. Her face was blank.

"I was studying my geography," Martha answered, pointing to the open book in front of her.

"Good, but I'm sure you know most of what you have to learn already."

Martha's pulse was rising. What did the first wife want from her? Had she finally realized that the hours spent hidden in the office were excessive? She struggled to see the older woman in the same authoritative light as two years ago when she had been a newcomer in their husband's compound. Marion had been lenient with her ever since she had moved into the main house – to a point where Martha had lost most of her fear and contempt. In fact, she had started to feel some sympathy for Marion, even pity her, because of the rigid position she was in. As the first woman of the household, she had to rule the others with a firm hand in order to convey their husband's commands, no matter what she thought of them. Martha had been told by her own mother that first wives must never be trusted. They tended to abuse their power and make the sister-wives suffer, she had said, and unfortunately her mother had been at the receiving end of her nemesis many times. If a first wife didn't like another wife, she could make her life a misery, even to the point of taking her children away from her and allocating them to another. As long as Martha's mother had been their husband's favourite she had cried herself to sleep often from sheer exhaustion because the first wife had made her work like a slave.

"I need you to do something for me." Marion looked her straight in the face, which was so unusual that Martha nearly lost her composure.

"What? Ah, well, yes, sorry … yes, of course."

"You were close to Anna, weren't you?"

"Yes."

Marion put the basket on top of the desk. "I hear one of Anna's little boys is quite ill. I want you to go down to her hut and take her some medicine."

"I'll go right away."

Marion hesitated slightly as if she had to muster her courage for what she had to say next. "Not now. Our husband is going to town shortly. Once you hear his car driving off, you can leave. There is no need for him to see you."

Martha waited, holding her breath.

"I have put some food in the basket, for Anna and her children. There is no need for anybody to see it, do you understand me?"

Martha nodded.

"I know everybody is starving. They may not like it when they see that one of their own is favoured. But I was told Anna's needs are most urgent. Don't worry, there will be plenty of food for everybody soon, but for now the little that is left here should go to Anna. I am told she and her boys are on the brink of dying."

Told by whom? Martha nearly asked, but instead she assured Marion that she would take the basket to Anna without stopping anywhere. She would not let anybody look inside. But on her way back she could stop at Emma's hut. As soon as Marion had left the office, she sat down and wrote a note.

Emma could give the note to her young son who could easily slip it to Jake junior when everybody assembled in the community hall tonight. This way there was no danger for Jake; not like if she was caught trying to give him a note herself. If one of the young boys was seen handing something to an older boy, nobody would think anything of it. And Emma would do this for her. She would want to know what it was about, but as long as Martha promised to satisfy her curiosity later on, she would agree to let her son do it.

Martha thought a long time about how she should phrase the note. Finally she settled on words with a cryptically religious meaning:

After prayer the Lord blesses those who wait for him with his presence. They do not need to walk far in the dark and will be protected by his angel of mercy.

She signed it with a distorted M, hoping he would recognize the letter and understand the meaning of the note. There was a miniature statue of the angel Moroni – the fabled angel who had directed the *Doctrine and Covenants* to Joseph Smith the founder of the Church – right behind the community hall. Jake would wait for her there if he understood her message correctly, and if it was discovered before it got to him, nobody would be able to connect it to him. Maybe not even to her.

Anna was very weak. The hut was even more dilapidated than Martha remembered. How Anna and her babies had made it through winter was a mystery to her.

She put the basket down and took out a small loaf of bread, a box with milk powder and a bottle of medicine which looked like cough syrup. Anna just looked at her with empty eyes.

"Shall I mix some of this with water?" Martha started to spoon some of the baby supplement into the empty bottle standing next to the water bucket. "Are you getting some help? Is the water fresh?"

Anna nodded and tried to sit up. "Elisabeth is coming every day. But it doesn't matter. Leave us alone, we will die soon."

Martha broke a piece of bread and took it over to her former friend. "Here, eat this. Hold out a bit longer. Soon there will be plenty of food, I promise. I'll prepare a bottle for the twins but I can't stay to give it to them. Can you manage by yourself?"

Anna nodded again. "I am so tired. Why did he do this to us? I hate him, you know."

There was nothing Martha could say.

"Why didn't she let me go to him? It is all Marion's fault."

"No, it's not. She understands how much you tried to get close to him, but he didn't want to be with anybody. There was nothing Marion could do about it."

Anna started chewing on the bread. A thin string of saliva ran from the corner of her mouth. "You are one of them now! Just as bad as his Marion is. Go away."

Martha filled the bottle with water and shook it until the milk powder dissolved. Then she put it next to Anna without saying another word. She had to hurry to see Emma and felt a twinge of guilt for not staying a bit longer. "Please, Anna," she pleaded at the door, not really meaning anything in particular. When Anna did not reply, she left quietly and started to run across the courtyard to Emma's hut.

The prayer session started around seven. Marion rang the bell, but it took longer than usual for all the women and grown children to assemble in the community hall. Everybody trudged along the driveway as if they had to use the last bit of strength left in them. When they finally settled in the hall, Martha could see the frightening signs of emaciation on every single face. They were all barely a few short steps away from total collapse. Not much better off than Anna.

She looked around to find Emma but couldn't see her. Emma was missing. Had Marion picked her of all the sister-wives to look after the children? Martha let her eyes roam over to the boys' side before she bent her head again. Jake junior was standing there! Leaning against the wall, magnificent as always, looking in her direction. At her! He unabashedly looked at her! Her stomach filled with butterflies of joy. He could not keep his eyes from her! But what if any of the sister-wives noticed? His expression was nearly blank, pretending to stare into the empty space above the women's heads, but she could read his face so well and detected a tiny understanding in his eyes. Was that Emma's young boy standing close to him? No, that was not him. It could not be. The sudden realization of her horrendous mistake hit her with a nauseating blow to her stomach. What had she done? How old was Emma's boy? He could not be ten yet.

Martha closed her eyes and prayed to her own Lord - the merciful one who would let her into his eternal kingdom, not the vengeful one who was a misogynist - that Emma had given the message to one of the other boys. But why hadn't Emma pointed this out to her when she agreed to accept the note? She probably had not been aware of their husband's order to keep the children under ten at home. But which of the other boys would she have trusted enough? Martha felt sick. Something was badly wrong. A threat of looming disaster was hanging in the air, mirrored by the many hungry pale faces around her.

About an hour into the prayers, which Marion initiated by opening the prayer book and making everybody read aloud, their husband entered the community room. He told everybody to be quiet and waited until total silence had settled. Then he opened his arms wide and thanked the Lord for the wonderful gifts his family would soon receive through divine intervention. Some of the women looked up.

So did Martha. She studied the bulky man up front with growing amazement. He did not seem to notice the pathetic condition his flock was in. With great fervour he went on and on about the Lord's mercy, reminding her of her father and uncles when they had been preaching with similar ardour. As a young child this had impressed her so much that all men had seemed God-like to her. Martha shook her head. The man in front there was no God! He was pompous; every word he said sounded false. Would she see her father and her uncles in the same light now? See them for what they really were – nothing but pretentious old men who dabbled in divinity but were condemned to hell for all their earthly sins. Martha toyed with this wickedly disrespectful thought, unable to stop the little smile that lingered on her lips. Her eyes darted left and right. All the women were looking straight ahead, so she dared another glance in *his* direction, still smiling faintly. Jake junior was staring at his father, who finally came to the point he had been approaching for more than half an hour.

"My family, rejoice with me! Twelve of our fine young women have been chosen by the Church elders to enter into the everlasting covenant of plural marriage."

A hushed murmur went through the lines of kneeling women. Some heads jerked up as if the news woke them from secret napping.

"Tomorrow, we will bid farewell to those lucky ones. It will be a day of celebration and prayer. I command you to pray and fast for one week…", he was interrupted by agonized groans coming from different corners of the room. But nobody dared to laugh, like Martha wanted to. She did not either, although a cynical giggle boiled hot as lava in her throat, wanting to explode out into the open. How brilliant of him to call the general starvation a religious fast!

" …to cleanse your souls," he continued, now with a deep frown on his forehead and a voice that demanded their undivided attention. "When the period of fasting and praying is over, milk and honey will flow. There will be bread for each one of you. We will celebrate the introduction of our twelve pure young women into the most holy and important covenant ever revealed to man on earth. And to those twelve I say, remember what the Lord commanded: *All those who have this law revealed unto them must obey, and if they do not, then they are damned; for no one can reject this covenant and be permitted to enter into His glory."*

Now giggles splattered out of her, sounding much like a suppressed cough. Martha doubled over, holding her hands over her mouth, gagging the treacherous hysterics, same as anyone would do who was caught up in a choking fit. Never before had his interpretation of the Lord's word sounded more arrogant and laughable to her. She knew he was selling the girls! Didn't her sister-wives, the mothers of those girls, at least suspect his true motives?

Nobody took much notice of her. She had successfully buried her laughter under coughing sounds and tried hard to regain her composure. The Bishop had finished his sermon and was getting ready to take his leave. On his way out, he stopped where his eldest son was standing and exchanged a few words with him. Martha had herself under control again. She pretended to be in prayer until most of the women had left, hoping she could trail out among the last. Her heart rate increased dramatically again, now that the time had come to find out if Jake was expecting her.

Marion came over to her and told her to wait until the room was empty, turn the lights off and make sure the doors were closed before going back to the main house. Then she rushed after her husband.

Soon after, Martha was alone. She let a minute or two pass, flicked the light switch off and waited a few more minutes in the dark, listening intently. All the sounds of the departing women had died down. They must have been in a hurry to get away from the main house so they could discuss the exciting prospect of getting fed soon and to try and figure out which twelve daughters would be sent away. There was not much to speculate, all they had to do was count their ages down. The twelve oldest girls would be the ones. Most of the mothers would be proud and happy, Martha thought, just as her own mother might have been. Or had the underlying sadness, which never left her mother on the whole journey from Arizona to British Columbia, possibly been a quiet mourning for a lost daughter? Martha had never suspected this, not until now. Wasn't her mother as much a victim as all of them? One day long ago, she also had been sacrificed on the altar of male dominance and arrogance.

Martha closed the door of the community hall and stepped into the backyard. No light was shining down from any of the windows. Her husband and Marion must be in the front living room. She quickly ran across the yard lit by a waning moon until she reached the safety of the tall trees.

And there he was! Not very hidden, right beside the angel.

She practically flew into his arms, hot tears flooding through a huge gate of relief that instantaneously opened up inside her. He folded her into his welcoming arms. Giant protective wings wrapped around her and pressed her so close to his body that she could hear his heart thudding and pounding at accelerated speed. He had pined for her as desperately as she for him. It had been too long. She lifted her head to reach his bare neck and sucked in his smell with her nose and her lips, hungry for more.

"You knew I would come," she breathed against his neck.

"No," he whispered. "I was just hoping. " His lips nibbled on her ear, sending tingling sensations through her whole body.

"Didn't you get my note?"

He shook his head and licked her lobe. How amazing, they had found each other even without a message. She sighed in wonder.

Quickly, he grabbed her by the waist, lifted her and carried her deeper into the darkness, just a few steps, but enough not to be seen even if a light went on in the main house. Leaning against a tree trunk, his strong arms lifted her up until her face was close to his. They did not speak, no words were necessary, but their silent communication was accompanied by loud and heavy breathing. The danger of being discovered was real to both of them, but they did not care.

Martha wrapped her arms around his neck, feet dangling in the air. One of his hands started to wander over her body while the other held her in position. She let him grab her skirt and bunch it up so he could reach underneath the billowing folds. Even in his effort to tear at her undergarment did he not let go of her. When he was not fast enough, she helped him slip it off with one hand while she hung on to him with the other. Everything inside her was screaming for more. More of him. More of his hands on her skin. Inside her skin. She didn't have time to rationalize that this was happening because he had wanted it so desperately and because she was finally giving in to him. Now *she* wanted it. *She* wanted *him*. She needed him, as close as possible. Closer, deep inside her. Now her busy hand tore at his shirt and fumbled awkwardly to open his trousers, trying to move everything that concealed his skin. Soon they had bared enough of each other to feel skin on skin. He lifted her higher so she could wrap her legs around his hips and settle on him.

With a lustful moan she accepted him into her, surprised by the sudden rush of blood rising to the top of her skull, flowing down again at rapid speed, heating her body and making her move with him. It didn't surprise her that there was no pain. It felt so right.

What should have taken forever lasted only a short time. After they had spent their passionate energy on each other, they came back into this world, still breathing heavily, smoothed their rumpled clothes and kissed each other gently on the mouth. Martha decided not to break this magical moment with words of warning of the inevitable. He would find out their fate soon enough, there was no point in sharing her sadness with him now. He should have one more peaceful night, going to sleep with her scent and her juice still on him, building a memory of their unforgettable ecstasy. The euphoria she had experienced had been absolutely unexpected and she was certain he had felt the same intense excitement. Surely he knew that this was not how it was supposed to be. This was her triumph over the painful, disgusting and degrading physical intimacy his father had inflicted on her. Now she knew how it could be, and so would he! When he had to lie with a woman the Bishop had chosen for him he would remember and would be yearning for her. Every time, and forever.

He wanted to say something but she caught him in time, put her finger on his mouth and smiled at him lovingly before she sneaked back the same way she had come. Yes, this would last forever.

38

Strange sounds penetrated her blissfully deep sleep. Shouting and slamming doors! Martha had trouble waking up. The memory of what she and Jake had shared last night was coming back to her and she wanted to hold on to it, but the threatening bangs and slams and screeches and roars grew louder with every second. Sudden fear shook her wide awake and chased away the last sweet traces of reflection.

She sat up. Somebody was running down the hallway. The door to her chamber flung open. Marion stood in the doorway, looking as white and drawn as a ghost.

"Come with me, quickly. Your husband demands to see you," she panted.

Martha jumped out of bed and straightened her night gown. "Why?" she asked, dreading the answer. He had found out about her and his son! It was all over. Now they both would be punished.

Marion seemed helpless and petrified. There was nothing the first wife could do to avoid the looming tragedy. "Quickly, get dressed," she ordered.

Martha changed into her day dress and tried to pull her unruly hair back into a bun. The pins didn't want to stay. Her hands couldn't stop shaking. All blood drained from her face and by the time she entered the living room she was as white as the older woman.

Her husband stood with his back to her by the window. When Marion announced softly *she is here now*, he flung around to face both women. A staunch figure of suppressed fury. He waved a note, *her* note, above his head like a white flag, except he was not the one to surrender. "Admit it," he bellowed. "You wrote this!"

Blood shot back up into Martha's head so fast, it made her dizzy. They had discovered her note. How? When? It could not have been last night. Jake junior had never got the note. If his father had found it sooner, he would have caught them, maybe even interrupted them while they were…, her mind refused to finish this trail of thought. The father discovering that his own wife made love to his son – no, that was too shocking. She winced and then pushed this image far from her. She didn't want to defile what she had experienced with Jake junior by letting his father become part of it. Not for one second would she allow him to have power over her mind! He was still waving the note. Why did he have it now, and not last night already? Martha looked at her husband in utter confusion, until she saw Emma appear behind his wide frame.

"Emma," she called out in total shock. "You?"

Their husband stepped aside to let his wives confront each other; like a lurking predator ready to devour his chosen prey. Let them fight it out before the final attack. Marion disappeared into the shadows of the room.

Emma stood solid, defiant.

"Why? Emma, why did you do this?"

"Why do you think?" Emma was spitting resentment. She swung her right arm through the air in a wide gesture to demonstrate the difference between those surroundings and what her usual dwelling was. "Look at this! You are nothing, you don't even have a child, but you live here like a queen."

"I was your friend."

"Liar! You never cared for me, or my children. Not once did you bring me anything from this house, not even the tiniest scrap of food. You knew how much we suffered but you couldn't care less. All you thought about was precious Anna and her babies. They got food, you told me so! You had the cheek to come to me empty handed, except for this note, after you delivered food to Anna. Not even a small token of our friendship did you bring, but you dared to beg me to cheat on my husband and on our faith."

"You are wrong. I am sorry if you see it this way, but I had nothing to give to you. There was nothing I could bring...," Martha could hear Marion in the background inhaling sharply. Careful now! If, in the heat of the moment, she would reveal what had been in the basket, Marion would also be in deep trouble.

"You told me you brought food for Anna. And nothing for me!"

"There was only medicine in the basket," Martha lied. "You are imagining things."

"How dare you!" Emma screeched in frustration. "I know what you told me! You are a heathen! A barren shell, not worthy to even live among us!" She turned to her husband. "My husband, please, believe me, she did say..."

He ignored her and thundered at Marion. "Speak!"

Both young women looked at the older one as she stepped out of the shadows and into the bright March light shining through the window. Marion's gaze was steady now, focusing on the wooden planks in front of his feet. "My husband forgive me," she started as always. "I did ask Martha to take medicine to Anna to make sure her sick children would survive. I know how valuable they are to you. There was nothing else in the basket."

He nodded. "You did right." His head swung over to Martha. "Did you steal any food before you went down to see Anna?"

Marion bit her lips, answering in Martha's place. "There is nothing left to steal. The pantry is empty."

Emma knotted her fingers together to stop the shaking of her hands. Her face flinched painfully. "But you told me so," she wailed at Martha.

Now their husband took charge. "I'll deal with you later," he addressed Emma. "You've lied to me to gain favour!"

"But my husband," Emma cried, "that is not fair. I have brought the note to your attention."

"Be quiet, woman! You didn't do your duty as you should have. If you would have brought the note to me right away I would be more lenient. Why did you wait all night? What else do you know that you are not telling me? Why would she give you a note without telling you what to do with it?"

Martha stared at Emma. She could feel her bitterness, despair, even hatred so strongly, she couldn't figure out why Emma had held back part of her betrayal? The most important part! Why had she not told that the note was meant for her husband's son? The answer to this riddle came to her as soon as she considered the consequences such an action might have for Emma. It was one thing to denounce a sister-wife, but quite another to point an accusing finger at the oldest son, the second most powerful man in the family.

"I told you," Emma justified herself. "She wanted me to keep it safe for her. I don't know why."

"I've missed the opportunity to check into the matter right away because you thought it better to sleep on it...."

"No, please, I couldn't speak to you after prayer. You left so quickly...."

"Quiet! Get out of my sight. I'll deal with you later!" He beckoned Marion to usher Emma out of the room. Once they were alone he poked his finger at Martha's breast. "Now to you!"

Martha felt a crushing burden lift from her soul. He had the note, but would never be able to connect it to his son. Jake junior was safe! Emma could never tell him now – not after her plan to ingratiate herself to him had failed. Poor Emma, all she had wanted was for her children to survive. Martha felt compassion for the misguided woman and chided herself for not taking her into her confidence. If she would have told Emma how close the rescue was for all of them, she might not have been driven to such a treacherous action. Nothing was achieved by it, except an unjust penalty. Hopefully Emma would not have to suffer too much. But Martha doubted it. Her husband was stark raving mad! But Martha could not dwell on Emma's unfortunate situation. Jake junior was not exposed to his father's lunacy, and that's all that mattered to her.

"What are you grinning at? Have you lost your mind?" His finger kept jabbing at her. Hard, painful, trying to prod the deranged delight out of her.

"What does this all mean?" … Jab, jab…"Why did you write this note?"…Jab, jab…"What was it for?" … Jab, jab… "Stop grinning, woman!" … Jab, jab …"I will teach you …"

He was repeatedly poking at the same spot just below her collarbone, really hurting her now. Finally she could stand it no longer and, without even thinking, slapped his hand. "Stop it!""

He turned pale. Then the colour came back in a mad rush, transforming his head into a fiery balloon. "How dare you!"

The slap she had instinctively dealt out had not only surprised him. After a short moment of stupefied confusion, when she didn't know how to react, she realized that she felt no fear and burst out laughing.

"Stop it! Stop it! I command you!" he yelled at her at the top of his lungs.

She could not stop laughing – didn't want to stop. "You can command nothing, you pitiful man."

"I am not a man to you. I am your God. Stop it this instant!"

She laughed even louder now, full of spite. "God? You are the devil! You are Satan's pitiful helper and you will rot in hell!"

"Apostate! You are condemned! You shall be destroyed!"

Martha kept on laughing while he tried to beat her into silence. What could he do to her? Threaten her with death? She would welcome it, much prefer it to a life in the shadows of the women's quarters, having to watch as his son, her only love, entered into plural marriages. She could never be part of Jake junior's family, but even if she were single and available to him, she would not want to become one of his wives. She couldn't bear the thought of having to share his affection.

She was his only one, for now – and until the day she died!

39

A restless night like the last one would have normally affected his ability to think straight, but as soon as Richard woke up from the few hours of troubled sleep he had finally succumbed to, he remembered that today was his make-or-break day and a sudden surge of adrenalin compensated for the missing sleep. He jumped out of bed, showered, dressed and left his room.

He knocked on Adam's door and asked him to join him at Danny's Diner next to their motel. After two cups of coffee and a hearty breakfast of bacon, eggs and hash-browns he felt even more awake. He was now physically and mentally ready to enter Jake's battlefield. In fact, he could not wait to get started.

After breakfast, they went back to their rooms and Richard was out again in a flash. Adam made him wait an agonizing quarter of an hour in the car while he finished whatever he was doing in his room – Richard pictured him on his knees praying for guidance, until he thought how ridiculous that would be – before Adam finally appeared at the door and went to reception to give back his key. The guy still didn't understand how the world worked.

"You could have left the key in the room," Richard complained, eager to leave Clearwater, although they were still way too early.

"That wouldn't be polite," Adam said.

They were silent for a while. Richard drove along the highway, taking his time now, because under no circumstances should they be early for their appointment. But driving was better than sitting around waiting; at least it was something to do. And the route was picturesque to say the least. A strong March sun was already above the mountain peaks to their east, bathing the meadows along the Thompson River in golden light. That was a good omen! Gold! Couldn't be better. Richard did a mental exercise one of his Chinese boarding school friends had taught him. Imagine that it is already done and that you have already achieved your goal. *Jake will be putty in my hands today – no, wrong, I must think in the past. Jake has been putty in my hands, all is well and I have saved my company from disappearing into oblivion.*

"What are you thinking?" Adam interrupted his pleasant day-dream.

He groaned. "You talk like a woman."

"Why?"

"Only women ask such questions. You've got a lot to learn."

"I know. The key stays in the room."

This made Richard laugh. He did not want to tell Adam what he had been thinking, but he also did not want to be rude on this gorgeous morning – another trick out of the Chinese wisdom treasure trove: *do not ruin the good vibes surrounding you by being nasty* -, so he asked him the first thing that came to his mind.

"Yesterday, you mentioned I'm jealous. Why?"

"You've really been thinking about that?"

"Yeah," Richard lied.

"Because you are."

"I'm not!"

"Yes, you are."

"No, I'm not."

"About me and Daisy."

"No, I'm not!" *Congratulations Richard, you have now successfully reduced yourself to the level of a first-grader.*

Adam must have thought the same. "I will refrain from insisting any further, but one final time, yes, you are," he smirked.

"Nothing is further from my mind than the concept of Daisy and me being a couple," Richard replied truthfully. "We know each other too well and respect each other too much to even consider such a notion."

"What notion? A love notion?"

"You know, Adam, sometimes you really piss me off."

"Oh, I'm sure I do. But maybe it's not me you are pissed off with. You act like a jilted lover. Maybe you are pissed off with Daisy because she lavishes more attention on me than on you. It's freaking you out that you can't get a handle on her. It's a control thing, you know."

"Bullshit."

"I have learned to recognize the signs, believe me. Our fundamentalist leaders are masters in this."

Here we go again, Richard thought. Another lecture from Adam's wealth of freak-experience. "Look, let's not spoil the nice day. We'll get to Blue River in an hour, have a coffee and wait until it's time to confront Jake. Then you can do your evaluation and it's judgment day."

"Do you want to talk about it?"

Richard thought it over for a few seconds. "The meeting? Yes, sure. You know how important this is to me, right?"

"Right."

"And to Daisy."

"You bet I do."

"Then there is nothing more to be said."

They drove along the gravel road leading to Jake's property when Adam surprised Richard with another question.

"Why exactly do we need to see this man?"

Was Adam more stupid than he appeared to be? "Because we need to convince him to sell us part of his land. Hasn't Daisy briefed you?"

"I mean, why is this land so important to you. I don't get it."

They were actually driving along the border of the offensive 600 meter stretch of Jake's land that lay between the road and Richard's development property. He stopped the car on the roadside. "Look at it, Adam. What do you see?"

"Hills, covered with remnants of snow which will melt away like crazy in this sun."

"Can you see the narrow valley between the hills up there?" Richard pointed to the indentation of the high rim that went all along the northern borderline. That was where he planned to build the connector.

"Yes."

"This valley is ours and leads to the development site. The hills left and right of it belong to Jake. You will notice the hills are way too steep to accommodate driveways. The only way he can get to this land is through the valley. We own it and we have granted him an easement ..."

Adam was getting impatient. "I know all this. I just don't understand the problem. And don't start on the subdivision rules. I know your Approving Officer says the owner can't subdivide the hills in future because each subdivision needs its own access, but quite frankly, that's nonsense. The fact is, Jake won't anyway. Nobody would want to divide those hills – ever! They are not suitable for smaller lots. She should know that."

Okay, so he was not a total moron. His uneducated mind had grasped the root of the problem very quickly. "Yes, she knows it and she could waive that rule, but she doesn't want to. And now don't *you* start questioning me on what benefit she sees in sticking to this silly subdivision rule. She has her reasons. Maybe its only to harass me, maybe she is on a cheap power trip, who knows. Whatever drives her, I can't challenge it. She holds the ultimate power of decision."

"It looks nice, though. The land, I mean. I wonder what's behind those hills."

Richard paid immediate attention to the signals of a bright new idea flashing through his brain. "You want to see it?"

Adam looked at the clock on the dashboard. "We don't have time."

"But you would like to?"

"Of course."

"We can drive through it after our meeting with Jake. I'll show you what we plan. It's amazing. You won't believe how beautiful the landscape is."

Adam was a lot more perceptive than Richard had realized. "Do you want to manipulate me in case I don't approve of your deal with Jake?"

What could he say to that? He grinned. "Yes, actually, I do."

At exactly ten, the pickup arrived at the gate. Jake's son got out and greeted Richard politely with a handshake. He looked at Adam, frowned and nodded at him. Richard did not feel the need to introduce Adam to Jake junior, although the boy was more mature than he remembered him to be. He had not noticed the determined set of his jaw or the bright and inquisitive look in his eyes before. But then again, he had not really paid any attention to him at all.

They drove up to the house. Richard also could not remember driving so slowly through the Plaza of Huts last time. Jake was going so slow that he nearly bumped into him twice. Adam jerked his head left and right with wide open camera eyes. Richard was certain he was trying to take in and remember every little detail, which in his opinion usually resulted in not really seeing anything of any importance. There were a few women walking on the side of the road. They hunched over and hid their faces as soon as the cars approached. No children or animals were in sight.

When they had passed the cluster of huts Adam muttered something to himself about the dresses the women wore. Richard ignored it.

They parked in front of the main building. This time nobody was waiting there to greet them, but Jake junior asked them to follow him into the house as his father was expecting them. All very polite.

They actually had to wait a few minutes until Jake came in trying hard to appear jovial and beaming. But his smile belied his body language which was tense and disturbed. His eyes shifted nervously from Richard to Adam to his son and back. There was an aura of haste and agitation about him, which was confirmed by his greeting.

"Well, well, well, Richard, so we meet again. Forgive me for making you wait. I had a few pressing family problems to solve."

"I hope nothing serious," Richard replied.

"No, no, nothing that can't be solved with a firm hand." He laughed without humour, sounding like a crow, and turned to Adam, looking him over with interest. "And who would this fine young man be? Another assistant maybe?"

"Indeed," Richard confirmed. "My last assistant decided to leave the company." Even as the words came out of his mouth, he cringed. He had forgotten about the fiancée story.

Mercifully, Jake phrased his comment more generally. "But privately all is well between the two of you?"

"Yes," he said quickly. If Adam caught on to him pretending to be engaged to Daisy, he would have a field day with this nonsense later on.

"Such a pretty young woman. But now to you, young man, what is your name?"

"Adam."

Jake nodded and extended his hand. "A good name!"

Richard cringed again. Adam, the stupid, stupid idiot, did not take Jake's hand but moved away from him as if he had not seen it.

Jake's arm went limp and his dark eyes narrowed. Then he got himself under control again and concentrated on Richard. "I am afraid I have little time today. As I mentioned before, some family matters."

Richard remembered. "Aren't you getting ready for a wedding?"

"Yes, among other things. But let me offer you something to drink. Coffee?"

Richard nodded. Jake didn't ask Adam. He went to the door and shouted into the hallway. "Marion!"

His wife must have been close by because she came in only seconds later. Richard thought he would remember her, but he had no recollection of the haggard woman in the doorway. Her face, her neck and her hands, the only body parts visible, had no flesh on them. The rest was hidden under a dress that hung so loosely on her frame that it was not difficult to imagine that underneath it were also only skin and bones. Richard was shocked. Jake did not seem to notice his reaction, nor did he show signs of concern. Maybe the woman was ill and he was used to her gaunt look.

"Marion, bring us coffee and some cookies."

She did not lift her eyes. "My husband, forgive me, there is no coffee left."

Adam jolted slightly when he heard her addressing her husband so demurely. Not a promising beginning.

Jake did not notice this reaction either. "Then get us some juice and some cookies."

"There is no juice left."

He sighed and then laughed embarrassed. "My dear Lord, if I don't check everything myself! But as I said, there's been so much to do lately. Some water and cookies then."

"Look," Richard interrupted after seeing the poor woman flinch. Suddenly he understood that there were no cookies waiting for them either. She just did not want to serve them anything. "I don't really need anything. We had a big breakfast and lots of coffee before we came here. It's not necessary."

"Very well then." Jake waved her away, and after she had closed the door they all sat down at the long table. Jake and his son on one side, facing Richard and Adam. However, Jake did not look at Adam, and Richard had the distinct feeling that Jake junior would not contribute much to their conversation either. "Let's get down to business, shall we? What do you have to offer me, Richard?"

Richard started to explain the concept of his development again, just in case Jake had forgotten it, and outlined the potential profit with supporting analysis and forecasts which he had not shown him last time. Jake glanced over the documents briefly and put them aside. Richard told him that he wanted to buy all the land west of his planned 600 meter road and, as expected, Jake asked why.

Richard told him the partial truth, hoping Jake would not be well versed in the rules and regulations governing subdivisions. "Because it will speed up the process tremendously. If I own it, I don't need to apply for all the different permits needed when building a road that cuts land in half not owned by me. It's just one of those time consuming things that might hold us up unnecessarily."

Some life came back into Jake's eyes. They glimmered with greed – now, that was a good sign. "And if you own one part of it, it will make all the difference?"

"Yes, exactly, you've got it! It is such a complicated system that many don't understand it at all. I knew you'd be smart enough to understand right away."

Jake folded his arms over his big stomach. He should give some of his weight to his wife, Richard suddenly thought. Maybe he bought his flattery, maybe he was only just plain greedy, in any case Jake said he would certainly consider his request. If he was willing to pay as much as before.

Richard felt entitled to crack a little joke at Jake's expense. "No waaay, José," he mimicked Jake's previous response while putting on his best poker face. "Last time I had to buy, this time I want to. If we don't come to an agreement, it will only delay the project for a while, that's all."

Jake didn't argue this point. Stroking his front he thought it over and Richard waited, trying not to hold his breath or seem too anxious over the outcome of his deliberation. Finally Jake stared straight at Adam, frowned as if he saw him for the first time, and then a devious expression flitted over his face. One he quickly concealed by breaking into a wide smile.

"Richard, why don't we let the young boys off the hook while we discuss the finer points of this deal. I am inclined to accept an offer from you," – Richard's heart made a quick frog leap of exhilaration – "but there are boring little details to work out. No need for the boys to listen in." – The frog leap plunged straight into a muddy pool. What was the guy up to now? – "So, Jake, my boy, why don't you take Adam here on a tour of our wonderful back country. Take the truck and drive him along some of our country trails. That should be fun. Say for half an hour or so."

Jake junior got up right away, but Adam stayed glued to his chair. Jake senior raised his eyebrows and looked at Richard as if this would make him get rid of his assistant. Actually, as much as this twist in their negotiation confused Richard, he secretly agreed that it was a good idea. Adam didn't need to know it all.

"Adam," he said, hoping Adam would jump at the chance to check out the compound for himself. "Why don't you let Jake show you around. You wanted to see more of the land and what's going on anyway. I can always brief you later on what we decide here. You won't ever get a better chance to see the surroundings."

For Jake's benefit he added: "Adam is still learning. He hasn't even seen my land yet and after the meeting I will drive him over there. It will be good for him to look at the neighbour's property."

Jake nodded and Adam finally got up too. He must have decided that it could be beneficial to snoop around outside of Jake's watchful eyes.

After he and Jake junior left, Jake and Richard worked out the deal. Richard offered him the one hundred thousand he could afford. As expected, Jake refused it and made a counter offer of three hundred thousand, which surprised Richard. He tried to hide his pleasure over the comparatively reasonable amount and said he might increase his offer to two hundred thousand, but only if Jake agreed to defer payment until the profits rolled in. Jake must understand that it would cost him a lot more than that in interest payments. They haggled for a while, both of them doing the usual financial hardship number, but Richard sensed that Jake's heart was not really in it. He fidgeted in his chair, every so often lifting his head to listen to the silence in the hallway, and eventually agreeing a little too soon. They settled on quarter of a million, with one hundred and fifty thousand in deferred payment, and drafted a basic contract to sign on the spot. When Richard finally put his name on paper and slid it over to his new partner, he could taste victory. Already, all the tension of the last few months started to dissolve, and he was close to liking Jake, had the sly bastard not hesitated for a well-planned pause. Just before scribbling his signature on the document, Jake said there was one minor detail he needed to add.

"What is it?" Richard asked as nonchalantly as he could muster. He had the sinking feeling that their whole negotiation had been leading to this point. He was the bull, fighting for his life, and Jake was the matador, toying with him, getting ready to plunge the blade of his sword into his unprotected neck.

"I liked you right away, Richard – nearly as much as I like my sons. And, as you can imagine, I suffer like any father would, knowing that his off-spring's soul is in danger."

Oh God, Jake was starting a sermon again. This time there was no escape for Richard, he would have to sit through it. Jake would make him pay for his hasty retreat last time, but if that was all it took, to just sit there and listen to his ramblings, Richard would do it. Honest to God, he would do it!

"Deep in my heart, I know you are yearning to find the right way. I cannot be around you all the time to help you find your path, but I think I can steer you toward it."

Richard made a demure face and studied the wooden lines on the table surface that had developed fine cracks through the changes in temperature the room was subjected to all year round.

"But if you had a virtuous and subservient wife to guide you in the ways of our Lord, it would assist you greatly in your search for celestial acceptance."

"Well," Richard said, not liking the direction this negotiation had taken. "Daisy and I will get married soon. She will make a good wife." He quietly begged Daisy's forgiveness for this double lie. She would never make a good wife in Jake's sense – and would certainly never be his!

"I am not interested in any wedding promise you make outside of the *New and Everlasting Covenant*," Jake smiled sweetly. "I believe you are ready to receive the Principle."

"The Principle?" Richard asked, wondering if he was losing his grasp of the English language.

"Our prophet Joseph Smith had inquired of the Lord concerning the principle of plurality of wives and he was told by the Lord that the principle of taking more wives than one is the true Principle!"

"You are not seriously asking me to ..." Richard had to swallow hard, "to take... to get this ..."

Jake carried on in his best preacher voice. "Our prophet Joseph Smith has received the Lord's commandment as it was recorded on July 12, 1843 and canonized in the *Doctrine and Covenants* as Section 132, being the revelation of the 'New and Everlasting Covenant of Plural Marriage'. If you do not wish to face eternal damnation, Richard, you must seek to enter the doctrine of celestial marriage."

Richard burst out laughing. "You want me to get married? To plural wives?" He emphasized the word plural, letting it roll over his tongue with obvious sarcasm.

"We will start with one. But she must be brought up in the faith, to make sure she permits the growth of your family as the Lord commands."

"Jake, forget it!" Richard's laughter died down like a fire without oxygen. "There is no way I would even consider this. No way! Not in a million years!"

Jake looked at him, and then at the hand written contract in front of him, and then back at Richard again. "It's not a request. It's a condition, Richard."

He could not be serious. A rapidly tightening knot in his chest told him that Jake was.

"It's not an unreasonable condition, Richard. I'm actually doing you a favour; one you will be most grateful for later on. I'm presenting you with a kingdom of unimaginable joy. That is worth many times what I'm asking for the land. So you see, I'm nothing but generous to you. How could you deny me such a small favour."

The guy was a control freak, just like Adam had warned him. Jake wanted his money *and* the feeling of having control over him. Jake must be bluffing. No way would he miss out on a quarter of a million dollars. Richard remembered their negotiations last summer. Jake had won that one by firmly sticking to his guns. What if he was just as uncompromising now? Then he would lose out because of ..., because of what? Richard didn't understand what Jake expected him to do.

"Are you telling me I have to become a member of your church?"

"Oh, is that what you are worried about? No, no, nothing like it. As soon as you enter into the Principle of plural marriage you are one of us."

It could not hurt to ask. "And what exactly is required to enter into this Principle?"

"Three wives at least. Once you have three, you can build your own kingdom."

"No big deal then, hmm?" This was getting him nowhere.

"You are probably wondering how to achieve this. Richard, nobody expects you to take three wives right away. You are young, you have time. But you must start with one now and I will provide you with your first bride. I have just the right one for you."

Wrong again, it did lead him somewhere. Straight into a marriage market conducted by lecherous men with a mind-set anchored in the deepest Middle Ages. Had he seriously considered Jake's proposal even for a second? Richard knew he should get up and leave right now, but his body did not listen to his brain. He remained slouched in the chair like a rubber doll, unable to move. The implications of Jake's insane suggestion were ludicrous, grotesque - and yet, to him, they were devastating.

"I will get her for you to look at. Martha is a bit of damaged goods" – at this point Jake chuckled - "having been married once before. She actually still is, but we'll get her divorced in no time and married to you. Don't you worry, she has not had any children yet and she is young and really quite pretty. Just the right one for you, trust my judgment."

Richard's brain continued to refuse co-operation. This was not happening! Not to him, not now, not when he had been so close! He still could not move, feeling an enormous burden weighing him down.

Jake took his numbness for approval. For the second time today he got up and yelled for Marion.

When the poor frail woman came into the room, he informed her that he had selected a bride for Richard and that they now needed to prepare for an immediate wedding. He was suddenly full of obstreperous energy, nearly frantic in his demand for urgent attention to the matter. The girl needed to get divorced, and Marion should better hurry to get her prepared!

All Richard could manage was to sit there and helplessly watch what was going on.

Marion stared at him, which was a shock in itself. The woman so far had never raised her eyes higher than to his knees. A tiny light flickered in her eyes which Richard first misread as hope. How could she hope for him to be part of this? Her intense glance was mesmerizing. She despised him! It didn't surprise him. Considering she was Jake's first wife, she must be agreeing with this way of life. To her, he must be an intruder who took one of her own, maybe even her daughter, to drag her into the hell of non-believers. He personified everything she loathed – and that was reflected in her face. He stared back at her, hurt by the silent accusations she hurled at him, but he could not phrase an appropriate answer as he had none. He did not know what to think, or what to say to her.

Jake was oblivious of what went on between Marion and Richard. He rubbed his hands full of glee, hopped around like a young goat, rambled on about this day of glory and the joy this union would bring to all of them, until he had enough of it and announced, beaming from one ear to another, that he would now go and take care of the necessary details. Richard should just stay here and relax and wait for him to come back with the bride that was chosen for him.

He ushered Marion out with him. Richard was still slumped in his chair, frozen. The contract was still on the table, unsigned by Jake.

Then, after several agonizing minutes had passed, he heard a car outside and the sound of the engine catapulted him back into reality. Adam! In a minute he would walk in here, and then what? Should he politely ask him to be a witness to his marriage? Daisy! What would he tell her? She would go berserk if she found out that he had entered into what would be the beginning of a polygamous career.

He had promised to leave the final decision up to her – or her delegate Adam to be more precise. Both of them would be kicking his ass. In fact, he was as good as dead. Sure, he could break his promise to Daisy, there was nothing written that bound him to it. Then Marion's puzzling glance came back to him. There was no way he wanted to deal with such misguided disgust. It freaked him out. He didn't want to have anything to do with this, even if it cost him his company! He could always work on building a new future for himself, one that did not have to deal with an ignominious decision that would make him cringe in shame every time he looked in a mirror.

Finally he reacted the way he should have done five minutes earlier. He jumped up, full of outrage and elation – yes, he felt elated, relieved, strangely happy even – grabbed the hand-written contract, bunched it up and hurled it away from him into a corner of the room. Then he stormed out, nearly running Adam and Jake junior over.

"Let's go!" he demanded. "There is nothing further to discuss here."

He turned to Jake junior who plainly considered him to be an alien from another planet. "Sorry, young man," he said to him. "Your father and I will never agree. Too bad, but in my books he is a stark raving mad lunatic!"

Hard words for a son to hear, but at that moment Richard didn't care about the feelings of anybody associated with this cult. He had just lost his company and needed a little satisfaction in attacking somebody.

40

They had locked Emma in the pantry, and Martha was confined in Marion's office. It seemed to Martha that she was forever condemned to await her fate in this small room.

When she heard the commotion in the hallway she braced herself. Now they were coming for her! Please Lord, she prayed, let it be quick and painless. Don't let them send me to the prison hut. I don't want to die all alone in that dark and filthy hole. She fully expected her husband to barge into the small office and beat or strangle her. Although she hoped for a quick death, she started to shake like a leaf. Since she had been ushered away into her temporary confinement she had promised herself to succumb to her fate with a smile on her lips, but it was not easy to keep a proud composure.

The door opened. It wasn't her husband. Marion stepped into the room and closed the door quickly behind her. "Hurry. Tidy up your hair. Here, take this." She produced a thin rubber band from her pocket and handed it to Martha. Her hands were shaking as badly as Martha's. "Whatever happens now, don't question it. Don't fight it, do you understand? It will be for the best."

Having spent the last three hours resigning herself to the inevitable, Martha knew that dying was the more merciful fate. To go on living without Jake junior and spend the rest of her existence watching this family grow would be far worse. It was only the fear of the unknown that made her tremble so badly, and no matter how hard she tried, she couldn't stop it. Marion looked so scared that Martha could not pretend to be brave any more. She pressed her hand to her mouth to stifle a cry, and Marion shook her head and muttered something like *no, no, it's not what you think*. But Martha knew better. Marion was merely a messenger who was supposed to calm her down, and indeed, the door opened again and their husband appeared behind her. He pulled a face when he saw her standing next to the desk, frozen in fear. She must be as disgusting as a cockroach to him.

"I've taken you as my wife. I've blessed you to become a Mother of Zion!" he said to her, his voice dripping with resentment. "But you're not worthy to share the company of the devout women in my family. You are not worthy to be my servant. You are barren and obstinate. In the face of my first wife Marion, I sever the celestial ties that bind you to me. I hereby divorce you!"

Martha's jaw fell; she gaped at the man who was supposed to be her executioner. Instead of killing her, he was setting her free? Was she dreaming? Was she hallucinating? He divorced her! With one sentence – four words, that were some of the most dreaded amongst the pious women of her society - he made her whole again.

I hereby divorce you!

The words reverberated inside her like a bright light and magical sounds twirled around and settled in her brain like humming birds drinking sweet nectar from flower buds. He divorced her! He cut the chain linking her to him – for now and all eternity. Martha had to hold onto the edge of the desk to steady herself. She was free of him! But was she free to go?

"You shall spend the rest of your life outside the grace of our Lord. When you die, the devil will be waiting to take you in his hairy arms and drag you with him into the deepest darkness there is. You will rot there for all eternity and never be free of him again."

Yes, she would be free! The thought of being expelled from the Church didn't scare her at all. Quite the opposite, it delighted her to know that from now on she would not be bound to him, the most evil devil she knew, any longer. There was no dark abyss waiting for her. There was no hell for apostates. He had set her free! She was free to go, he had just said so. Martha did not dare to smile at him, for fear that he might change his mind and take it all back. So she lowered her head. Jake junior! She could leave here, and he would go away with her, wouldn't he? Of course he would. She must send a message to him somehow, before she was kicked out. He would go with her, and she would not have to fear being all alone in the strange unknown world out there. No devil was waiting for her there. It would all be good and wonderful, as long as she could share her life with him.

"In this life you shall be bound by a new contract to a husband outside of the faith. This will be your punishment. You shall be the slave of a heathen and when you die, you will be the slave of the devil. For now and all eternity!"

What? What was he saying? Martha looked up again to see her husband – her former husband now! – leave the room after he bellowed a final order to Marion. "Have the other one sent to the prison hut, and this one here, get her ready in an hour. Make her pretty. We'll let Richard stew a bit longer, it will do him good, the arrogant prick." Then he was gone.

Martha did not understand anything anymore. "Marion, what is he saying? Please, tell me this is not true."

"I'm sorry dear," the older woman addressed her quietly. Even in all the inner turmoil she was experiencing, Martha noticed the term of endearment Marion had used. "But I'm afraid it is so. My husband has decided to divorce you. I know it is hard…"

"No," Martha interrupted her with deep resentment, "it's not hard at all. It's easy! It's wonderful. I love that part. I never wanted to be his wife and I am deliriously happy to be rid of him!"

Marion's already snow white face paled into a translucency. Her skin seemed to wither away in agony. "Please…," she whispered.

"Don't you understand," Martha continued. "I hate him with all my heart. So should you! So should all of you! He has no right to make us all suffer like this. Now that I'm free, I will go away and lead my life as it is supposed to be."

"Please, Martha, what do you know about life. We are all sent to this earth as servants to the men. Our only hope is the kingdom waiting."

"Oh leave me alone with your kingdom! Nothing but more misery is waiting there. I just know there is another life out there and I will find it."

Marion nodded quickly. "Yes, you are right, there is. That is what our," - she quickly corrected herself – "*my* husband has commanded. You shall be betrothed to one of the men from the outside. May the Lord be with you and protect you."

So it was true. "What man? I don't want any man he is choosing!"

"You will like him. He seems nice. I have met him and my eyes have begged him to take care of you. I have the feeling he understood what I was trying to ask of him. He will take you away from here and treat you well."

Martha stared at her, still utterly confused.

"It's the visitor from last summer. He shall be your husband."

The man who had nearly run her down with his car! "No!" Martha stomped with her foot like a small child. "No! He will not. I will not marry him. Not him!" She nearly called out what was on her mind. *I will marry only one, the one of my own choosing, and that is the Bishop's son!*

"You must," Marion insisted. "It's the only way you can leave here. Think of the consequences. You know, your life is in his hands as long as you are here."

Martha had to agree. She racked her brain for a solution. She must give in to the Bishop's final demand or die at his hands. What if she pretended to marry the stranger and fled as soon as they had left the compound? Was he as tough and stern as her former husband? Would he keep her imprisoned as well, using her body as he pleased? Tears of frustration welled up in her eyes. "When will it be?" she asked, half broken already.

"Soon. Very soon. He is here in this house already and you heard our – *my* – husband. In one hour." Marion tried to sweeten the deal. "Most likely he will take you with him right away. You can be out of here by this afternoon."

Martha sobbed harder. How would Jake junior be able to find out what was happening to her if she was rushed off in such a hurry? "Will the whole family be present? Who knows about this?"

Misunderstanding her question, Marion squashed her last hope. "Oh no, you don't need to be ashamed. Nobody knows. I'm not supposed to tell anybody; he said it has to be a secret."

41

For some reason Adam sensed Richard's need to get out of that cursed house. He held the door open without even asking what had happened and asked Jake junior if the gate was locked.

Jake junior nodded, walked straight past Adam at the door and jumped into his pickup as if he felt the same urgency.

When they reached the gate, Jake junior got out of his car and opened it. Richard drove through without acknowledging the young man. He was still livid and knew he just had to get some space between himself and old Jake quickly. Adam waved at Jake junior when he closed and locked the gate behind them. It felt final.

Not a word was spoken between Adam and Richard until they had cleared the property and were well on their way. "I guess this means I don't have to fight it out with you?" Adam asked.

"I guess not." Richard saw Adam digging in his trousers pocket. "In case you want to call Daisy, it'll have to wait until we get reception. It won't be until we are on the highway."

Adam's hand appeared again, holding the mobile. He looked at it slightly annoyed, then placed it on the backseat and started to rub the outside of his upper thighs with his now empty hand.

"Are you cold?"

"A bit. Jake and I walked around the property for a while. It's still pretty nippy outside."

Richard turned up the heat for the passenger side. They were driving along the steep banks of Jake's hills, approaching the cut that would have been the entrance to the Rainbow Development. Richard expected a painful stab in his heart, but felt nothing.

"I guess there's no point in driving on to your property now," Adam half asked, half stated.

"No point whatsoever!"

"What happened?"

Richard sighed. How could he tell him that Daisy had been right all along. That he had been wrong. That there were things going on at Jake's compound, which made him sick to his stomach. Especially now, since he had been exposed to Jake's disgraceful manipulations. Jake had thrown him into his own private cesspool, expecting Richard to drown in it. To admit to himself that he had misjudged the situation so badly and that he had closed his eyes until now simply because it had suited him and his cause was bitter. But in the end it didn't matter. He had made his choice.

"Game over!" he finally said. "I'll tell you what happened in a minute. I need some time to get my act together first. How did it go with Jake junior?"

Adam cleared his throat, frowned and huffed.

"What's the matter with you? Cat got your tongue?"

Instead of explaining what he had seen, Adam asked. "Did Jake refuse your offer?"

Richard thought back. Yes, in a way one could say that. "His demands were too steep," he answered vaguely. "They can never be met. Daisy was right all along."

"Will you try again?"

"No. I told you. There is positively no way for me to ever sit at Jake's table again. Come to think of it, I would refuse to even be in the same room with him for longer than it would take me to kick his fat ass out of there, *dieses widerliche Schwein!*" Ah, his German ancestry was showing some of its lately subdued aggression again.

"Wow, I don't know what that means, but I guess you're pretty mad at him, aren't you? I like that!" It suddenly crossed Adam's mind what the outcome of those bungled negotiations spelled for Richard's future. "I mean, I'm sorry. That's a big disappointment for you, for sure.

I would have been pleased had it turned out in a different way, but frankly, there wasn't a chance in hell. It makes it so much easier for me to tell you what I think of the place, knowing that you've come to the same conclusion anyway. "

"So, what do you think?" Richard was actually curious to know how Adam had reached his verdict. After all, he had spent only limited time with the two Jakes in the room, so Jake junior must have managed to mess it up pretty good all by himself. "Is Jake junior the same asshole as his father?"

"Quite the contrary. He is a pleasant young man …"

"Gee, you sound as patronizing as his dad."

Adam frowned and cleared his throat again. "Sorry. I didn't mean to. I still have to work on my communication skills. Hard to hide one's upbringing sometimes, isn't it?"

"You said it." Did Adam know he had the same problem? Had Daisy told him about his uncontrolled bursts of anger? Did she mention that he had himself pretty much under control nowadays? "In your case it may never work. Being catapulted straight out of a sect that rivals the Taliban slam-bang into the twenty-first century must leave its marks."

Adam ignored his remark, but sounded a touch more reserved. "Jake's son drove me around for a while and I got the impression that he was trying to go to places that were unobtrusive. Eventually I asked him to take me back to the small group of huts we had passed on our way up there and he did. I had some more time to look around and I am absolutely certain the set-up is very similar to Bountiful – or to any other polygamous society in North America for that matter. Except that the weather is colder here and that the people living in it are even poorer."

"Not poor enough for their leader to accept my money unconditionally", Richard said, not without bitterness.

"That is what I don't understand. I saw some of the women. They look like they haven't had a decent meal in months. Jake junior is pretty skinny too. In fact, only his father looks round and well fed. Why didn't he jump at your offer? All the Church Elders I know of are greedy. It doesn't make any sense to me."

Richard felt bad about snapping at Adam. There was no point in upsetting him further by telling him the gist of his argument with Jake. Plus, he didn't really understand it himself. "Sorry about my remark before. That was uncalled for."

"That's okay," Adam said graciously. But Richard was not totally forgiven. They drove on in silence until his mobile sounded a thin signal. Back in range. Back in the real world.

Adam immediately grabbed it and dialled. Daisy, of course. They talked for some time, with Richard listening in, quietly annoyed. *Wasn't he supposed to tell her?* Adam informed her that the deal had fallen through, that Richard had decided to call it off all by himself and that he totally agreed with him. Very truthful. Daisy then asked if Richard wanted to speak to her - *as if he needed comfort!* - but Richard was sulking by now and shook his head when Adam relayed the question to him.

Adam mumbled something about Richard having to concentrate on the road and that he would probably call her later. That he was fine – considering the circumstances – and that he would get over it.

Richard hated him discussing his emotional state with Daisy as if he was not present and snapped at him, saying it was none of his or her business and he would appreciate it if the two of them would not make unqualified assumptions.

Adam sighed. "Sure," he mumbled into the phone, "sure, he'll get over it."

Half an hour later his phone rang again, and Adam listened intently while going through his small bag until he found a piece of paper and a pen. He took some notes before he hung up, saying: "Fine, I'll discuss it with him. I'll call you right back."

"What was all that about?" Richard asked.

"How far is it to Kamloops?"

They had passed Blue River quite a while ago. "Maybe two hundred kilometres. Why?"

"So, we should be able to make it there by three?"

"Yes. Why?" he asked again.

"That was Daisy. She has made an appointment for you with a woman called Jeanne d'Arc. Strange name."

Richard had to laugh. "You never heard of the medieval female warrior?"

"No."

"Never mind. That's all part of the catching up you have to do. She is our Approving Officer. Why on earth did Daisy make an appointment with her? There is nothing more to be discussed."

"Daisy said it's a long shot. You should just go over everything with her again and see if you can make her change her mind."

Bless Daisy for not giving up, but didn't she know how futile this exercise was?

"I don't even know the woman. So far, only Daisy has met with her."

"Yes, and that's why she thinks you should give it a try. Maybe she will react differently to a guy."

"Maybe pigs fly backwards."

"What's wrong with trying?"

Richard's fingers drummed on the steering wheel. What's wrong with trying? A lot, if it builds up hope. He considered briefly how much hope there was. None! So, there was also no danger in him getting disappointed. Obviously, he was already weaselling his way back into Daisy's good graces and if he humoured her with this, they might get back to their old ways altogether. He would need a friend when he started all over again - it wouldn't feel so lonely then. "All right, let's do it. But you are going in with me. You might learn something."

"Really," Adam asked excitedly. "You'll take me along to the meeting? Won't that warrior lady mind?"

"Who cares?"

42

In the hour Martha had to wait for her second wedding in this house to be arranged, she stayed by the window, frantically hoping Jake junior's pickup would drive into the backyard and he would look up at her. Twice she heard a car coming or going, but the sound came from the front of the house. The backyard was deserted.

Then she heard the key turn in the lock. Marion came in again and announced it was now time to go. The ceremony would be held shortly. When Martha didn't move, Marion went over to her and tried to take her arm. Martha stiffened and vehemently shook her head.

"You have to come with me," Marion pleaded, grabbing her a bit harder. "The Bishop is waiting for you."

Martha's hopes died and she suddenly knew how a cornered animal felt. She hissed and spat at Marion and tried to wriggle out of her grip. Both women had very little strength left and were panting from the effort.

"Please, Martha, don't make it harder on yourself," begged the older woman. "Remember, it's your only way out. If you refuse, he'll kill you."

"I'm not going to marry anybody," Martha wailed, "he can't make me. He might as well kill me." But her resistance weakened.

"Once you are out of his reach, you might find a way to escape. Your new husband is not one of us, he can't hold you if you don't want to stay with him. Think about it. This is not a legal marriage, it is only a religious ceremony, so it won't count on the outside." Marion's voice was more than a whisper in her ear; it was a seductive breeze of fresh hope in the wake of the inevitable. She was right. It was the only possibility for her to stay alive, and with it came a slim chance to escape. Martha clawed her fingernails into Marion's arms. "Please, please, tell your son about it. Tell him I didn't want to do this. Tell him I will try and escape. Tell him to look for me."

Marion's face was so close to hers, Martha could see the white in her eyes as they rolled around before the older woman's body went limp. Martha tried to hold on to her but only had enough strength to let her slump slower to the floor.

"Marion, Marion, please!" Now she was the one begging. Begging the unconscious woman to understand and to forgive. What had she done? How could she have slipped the secret so carelessly; to the first wife of all people. Maybe Marion would wake up and not remember.

The older woman moaned and came to, shaking her head in a daze. Then her senses came back and she moaned even louder. "Oh Martha, what have you done?"

Martha helped her to her feet, not daring to answer.

Marion still shook her head, but now with clear and very sad eyes. "Whatever you have done, I don't want to know. Understood?" She did not expect an answer. When both women had collected themselves, Marion opened the door and nodded. They were ready to go, when a low pitched, thunderous scream rose from the living room, making them stop dead in their tracks.

"Maaaarion! Maaaaarion!"

Her husband howled so hard and loud down the hallway that their blood curdled and they both froze for a second before the older woman hurtled into motion.

"Maaaarion! Get here! Fast!"

Martha automatically followed. It was a reaction guided by instinct, nothing else. Something horrible had happened, and they needed to rush to find out what it was.

The Bishop stood in the middle of the room. "Where is he?" he barked at Marion as soon as he saw her. "Where did that goddamn bastard disappear to?" When he realized that she had no idea, he demanded that she had better find out fast, or else. Then he noticed

Martha's presence. "What is she doing here? Get her out of here! Quick, quick. Back to where she came from."

Marion ushered Martha back to the office. In her haste she only closed but forgot to lock the door. Martha listened to the footsteps running back to the living room and then opened the door a crack and peeked through it. Something had happened to the man who was supposed to become her husband. She had to find out what. It was not her fault that the door was unlocked. She assumed this minor disobedience did not matter any more now; not if the wedding was called off – and with it her only opportunity to escape - because the groom had disappeared. The glimmer of hope she had nurtured only moments ago had a hard time flickering on.

She could hear her former husband yelling obscenities at Marion, interspersed with slapping sounds. Then he screamed for his son Jake. Martha opened the door a bit wider. Her heart was hammering away, excited that she might get close to Jake junior after all. Yes, there was hope. Jake junior was summoned. He must have entered the house when his father started the commotion because she could hear his deep and melodic voice interrupt his father's ramblings. Both talked loud enough for Martha to understand every single word.

"What is it, father?"

"Do you know where Richard and his assistant are?"

"Yes, of course I do. They left here in rather a hurry."

"They drove off?"

"Yes."

"I thought I heard a car, but I thought it was you bringing the assistant back."

"It was. I did bring Adam back here, but then his boss wanted to leave and I escorted them down to the gate."

His father's voice rose. "How dare you? How could you do this! Let them get away before we finished."

"But father, I didn't know the meeting wasn't over. You weren't there and I thought..."

"Leave the thinking to me, you fool! How can you be so stupid? You should have called for me."

"Father, I couldn't have stopped them anyway. They were adamant to leave right away. I thought nothing of it."

"Of course not, you half-wit. Why did the Lord punish me by surrounding me with such idiots? Am I the only one thinking here? Do I have to handle everything myself, can't I rely on anybody?"

He carried on with his litany of accusations and exclamations of self-pity until he ran out of steam. His son kept quiet, probably like many times before. Martha was hoping against all odds that his father would storm away, leaving Jake junior alone with his mother and maybe even she would disappear as well. Then Martha could set her foot over the invisible barrier that was holding her back inside her cell.

"Just as well that we don't have to rely on his money for the time being! He will come back though, mark my words." Jake addressed his son in a calmer manner now. "Let's get to the business that will bring in the money. Jake, listen carefully. You were told at last night's prayer meeting that twelve of my daughters will be sent off to get married. Your mother will get the girls ready by first light tomorrow morning. I trust you with delivering them to your uncle Rob at the border compound. The usual precautions are necessary, of course. Come to my office this evening and I will give you driving instructions and money for the gas you need. I would go myself, but we must prepare for the weddings up here."

Martha heard him slap his son on the back.

"This is the good news I have not told you yet. You will bring back five girls and one of them is for you."

"What are you saying?" Jake junior shouted in a confused voice. "You mean I'm supposed to get married?"

"Yes, Brother Lucas himself has picked a bride for you, and I hope, my son, you will do your duty and get me healthy and strong grandsons soon."

"I will not!" Jake junior refused angrily.

There was an audible gasp.

"I will do nothing of the kind."

The pain in Jake junior's voice went straight into Martha's heart. Obviously, he was shocked by his father's demands and did not grasp how dangerous his obstinate reaction would be. Oh please, no, Martha whispered to herself. Don't be openly against him. He is stronger than you are.

"You will do as I command!"

"No!" Jake repeated and raised his voice to his father's level. "I'll do nothing of the kind. Neither driving my poor sisters to be married to old men, nor picking up some unfortunate girls to bring here into this desolation. I will not marry any of them! I will not marry anybody just because you say so. I will do nothing, nothing, nothing...do you understand me ... nothing of the kind!"

Martha heard a hard thud, a chair falling over, some scrambling and more muffled sounds she could not identify. Father and son were fighting and she held her breath. Jake junior's refusal should have made her happy, but she was too afraid for him to savour this moment.

"You will do as I say! I command you!"

"No!" More slapping sounds. Marion whining.

"I'll teach you. Raising your hand against your father. How dare you!"

"You're a coward." Jake junior screamed with open loathing. "I know why you won't take them over the border yourself. You want me to do your dirty work because you're scared of getting caught. You know it's illegal. They're all minors and there's a law against marrying under-aged girls in this country. You're guilty yourself. Martha was only thirteen when you raped her, you bastard..."

Martha's shocked loud gasp was swallowed by Marion's horrified scream. "No, be quiet. Please, my son, be quiet."

Slapping again, this time he hit Marion.

"Leave my mother alone, you monster!" Jake junior yelled.

"Go, get out of my sight!"

Martha heard Marion rush out of the room; obviously she thought this was the best for her son. She ran down the hallway and Martha did not manage to close the door to the office fast enough. While Marion frantically panted *quick, quick, get in there, hide, he is out of control,* she let herself be pushed back into the room. Only after Marion had closed and locked the door from the outside, did she realize that she was now effectively cut off from the only escape route that had been open to her.

"Apostate! Apostate! Apostate! You will be damned!"

The screaming continued, but only the father's voice could be heard now, followed by an eerie silence. Martha started imagining that the father had hurt his son to shut him up. Had he killed him? Or had the son done the unthinkable? When she heard the roar of the pickup engine she ran to the window but could not see which one of them was leaving.

She was locked inside the room with no way of getting out and no way of knowing what had happened. Terror gripped her soul as she collapsed on the floor and started to pray. Before the words could form sentences, she began to exchange them for numbers.

"Dear Lord in heaven … please… two, three… whoever you are, please help… four…wherever you are…five, six, seven… please stop this madness…eight, nine…" The counting soothed her. It slowly shut out all the insanity around her.

43

The Ministry of Transportation and Infrastructure, MOTI for short, was housed in a large brown building hidden inside a huge complex of different government departments, all of them with separate, not clearly marked office buildings. Richard and Adam drove from one building to another and entered three wrong reception areas before they finally found the right department.

They were sent to a small conference room and asked to wait there.

"By the way," Richard whispered to Adam. "Don't call her Jeanne d'Arc. That's not her real name."

Adam frowned at him, but there was no time to explain. The door opened and a woman floated into the room and introduced herself as Approving Officer Trish Michener. She was much younger and slimmer than Richard had pictured her. For some reason he had always thought of her as a self-loathing sour-puss with a matronly moustache and wet spots under her armpits. Seeing her gracefully shaking hands and apologizing for keeping him waiting, knocked the wind out of his sails. Her plain face could have benefited from a touch of makeup and her long dark hair was mousy at the ends, but she was very young, considering her position, and not entirely unattractive.

She settled in the chair opposite him and looked expectantly at Adam by his side. Now Richard detected a coldness in her expression that was more in unison with how he had judged her so far. Unapproachable. Unbending. He introduced Adam as his rookie assistant, explaining that the young man was accompanying him on a business trip and expressing the hope that she would not object to him sitting in so he could learn something. Her lips formed a crooked smile to let Richard know she was well aware of his real objective, the fact that he wanted to have a witness present.

She did not waste time on any further preliminaries but rolled out a large map of his subdivision plan, and they started to state their different positions. Richard said his piece without much conviction, considering this meeting to be a major waste of time, and she expressed her stand on it. As expected, there was an insurmountable difference of opinion, and Richard asked her politely, more as a closing statement than anything else, if there was any way to close the gap.

"I understand from your *other* assistant that you are looking into purchasing some of the land west of your proposed road," she said.

What a shame that Daisy had brought this possibility to her attention. Now he had to admit to her that this was not an option any longer.

She shook her head, smiling complacently. "Well, that's too bad then. I'm afraid that would have been the only solution to keeping the status of the road to your land private. You know that there is the issue of future subdivisions which can't be granted over an easement."

"I know," Richard sighed in frustration. "But I also know that it is up to you to make the final call on this. It is within your power to make an exemption from this rule."

At this point, she actually twirled a strand of her hair over her left index finger, indicating she was musing over his comment. It looked contrived, and she did not fool him for one second. "Yes, I guess I could, but my answer to this will have to be no. I cannot allow this."

"Why not?" he shot at her, suddenly angry again. "Where is the problem for you?"

"I have to act in the interest of the public."

"What's it to the public?"

She stiffened a little, but waved his question aside unanswered. "I appreciate your frustration. But it is not the end of the road for you – if you forgive me the figure of speech. There is always the option of making the road public..."

"...and paving it!" he interrupted her.

"I am afraid that will be the consequence."

Until now, Adam had been silently following this meeting. He put his elbows on the table and leaned toward her. "There are more consequences to this", he barged into their discussion. Normally Richard would have silenced him with one sharp word, but he was beyond worrying what Adam might say. In fact, he was curious himself what his reasoning would be, just like Jeanne d'Arc who lifted her eyebrows like a fastidious teacher.

"And what consequences are you referring to?" she asked.

"To pave the country road from the highway to his property" – when Adam said *his*, he pointed with one open palm toward Richard, in a gesture that could only be called regal – "would add a huge expense to the whole project. Every single lot would become proportionally more expensive."

"Naturally," she smirked.

Adam was unperturbed. "This price hike would catapult it out of reach for the general public. Only the rich would be able to afford it, and that can't be in the interest of the public."

Bless his soul for coming up with such an argument.

"That may be," she said, "but a developer doesn't have to increase prices beyond what the market value should be. He can always lower his profit margin."

Now Richard stepped in. "Only to a point where it is still economical. It doesn't make sense to sell at a loss."

Trish looked at Adam. "Is that the only reason?"

"Well," he answered without hesitation, "there is also the creation of jobs to be considered. If the developer goes bust, there are no jobs. And I believe the provincial government is trying hard to reduce the current unemployment rate, specifically in rural areas, aren't they?"

Bless his soul again for being so controlled and moderate in his approach. Richard wondered how far he could have gone himself, had he ever been able to control his emotions like that.

"Anything else?" When Adam shook his head, she got up and rolled up her map again. "I will consider those points. Thank you for bringing them to my attention. I have enjoyed our conversation."

"When will I...?"

"I will be in touch." And with that they were excused. They walked out of the room behind her and she looked back and smiled at Richard. "You will get my final decision by tomorrow."

Inside the car they understood without words that they needed to control their reactions and drove off. She might be watching them from a window. Outside the government complex, Richard parked the car on Seymour Street, thumped the steering wheel with both hands full of excitement and exhaled noisily. "Shit! I can't believe this!"

Adam was grinning from one ear to the other. "Do you think...?"

"I don't know," Richard said truthfully. "But she hasn't rejected it outright, has she? Jesus, you were good. How on earth did you come up with something like that? You were like an old pro."

Adam beamed even more. "Thank you. I hope it works."

"How am I going to get through tonight? The suspense is going to kill me."

"Sorry about that!"

There was no need for Adam to apologize. To be in with a chance again was the sweetest feeling in the world. "I owe you a drink, man, but I'm afraid it has to wait until we get back to Vancouver."

"I don't drink."

"Yeah, yeah, I know, Mister holy-poly little smart-ass. Anybody who can talk like that is grown up enough for a beer. I'll teach you."

Adam's mobile rang. Richard saw Daisy's number on the display and his euphoria dampened, but only very briefly. It was a pity she did not feel it appropriate to call him directly, but he could forgive her for that, he felt too elated. Adam was all generosity, told her nothing and handed him the phone, still smiling proudly.

Daisy listened to Richard's gushing. He wasn't holding back on praise for the rookie next to him, even if there was a danger of Adam bursting with pride - and elaborated happily on the when and how and who said what to whom. So it took a while for Richard to realize that she was distracted by something. He asked her what was wrong.

"Where are you just now?"

"More or less still sitting outside the lion's den," he joked.

"Good. You have to drive north again, right away."

"Why is that?"

"Ted called me about a minute ago. He got a call from a Lost Boy. You have to pick him up."

"Are you kidding me?" Now Richard was upset. Daisy had not called to find out how the meeting had gone, as he had assumed in his childish excitement. The real reason behind her call, and all she cared about, was saving one of her precious boys again.

"Richard, this is very important. The boy is in danger. He is scared and angry and confused. If somebody doesn't get to him fast, God knows what might happen."

"That's not really my problem. As you well know, I have problems of my own and nobody seems to give a shit about those." Richard cringed over his own words. What kind of selfish bastard had he turned into? "Sorry, Daisy," he relented, still with a bitter note in his voice "I know, I'm a grown man and can handle things better than those poor kids. Tell me where we have to pick up this poor little puppy."

When she told him what it was all about, the phone nearly slipped out of his hand. Adam's pleased expression also changed. He had been watching Richard's reaction and his sensors instantly must have felt the dark clouds brewing. After Richard promised Daisy to hurry, he hung up, looked at Adam and gave him the sensational news. "We have to drive back to the gas station outside of Blue River immediately. You won't believe who is hiding there, waiting to be rescued by us."

"Oh excellent!" his rookie assistant exclaimed. "He made it out. That's great news."

"Who do you think it is?" Richard asked incredulously.

"Jake. Right? It's Jake junior, he's waiting for us. Right, right?"

"And how the hell do you know this?"

"Oh, I didn't. I was only hoping."

For the moment, his answer satisfied Richard, but only until he turned on to Highway 5 North again and had a bit more time to reflect on this new development. There was something that didn't quite fit. It seemed unrealistic that Adam would have guessed so quickly who had called Daisy … and in any case, why and how did Jake junior manage to get hold of Ted? It didn't take Richard long to grasp the crux of the matter.

"You gave him Ted's number," he stated. When Adam confirmed this with a vigorous nod of his head, Richard continued his sleuth work. "You knew Jake junior was susceptible to your enticement, you could sense it. When you were alone with him, you shamelessly and without any regard to how this might jeopardize my agreement with his father, seduced him to join the elite league of Lost Boys."

"I did," Adam admitted, not in the least phased by Richard's accusations.

"Well done, my son," Richard grinned. *Jake, you fat old slob, I'll get you after all!*

"You mean it?"

"Sure. Even if Jake and I had signed the agreement, he would not have associated us with his son's disappearance. At least I don't think so."

"I didn't refer to that", Adam said, a lot more serious than before. "You called me *my son*. Did you mean that?"

"No, you little fart!"

Adam grinned, all happy again.

Two hours later, by now it was nearly seven p.m., they arrived at the Blue River Gas station. There was a McDonald's next to it. Richard stopped right in front of the garbage containers in the parking area of the fast food chain, turned the engine off and looked at Adam. "I don't know about you, but I haven't eaten since this morning and I'm starving. I'm going in there to buy us a huge meal." He checked that he had his wallet with him and got out of the car.

Adam got out too, all excited. "Where will we find Jake?" he asked.

Richard pointed to the containers. "Daisy said he is hiding behind the McDonald's garbage dumpster, so I guess you'll find him there. He's your friend, go and get him. Cheeseburger okay?"

He nodded, and Richard went inside and ordered three take-away meals. If anything unforeseen had happened with Jake and he wasn't waiting where he was supposed to be, he would eat two meals all by himself. And then he would drive back to Vancouver and that would be it. Tomorrow was his day – lovely Trish would finally see the light and waive her unreasonable interpretation of the subdivision-by-easement freeze, and he could carry on with his life.

When Richard returned, only Adam was sitting in the car. He slipped back behind the steering wheel. God, he was tired. " If you think I'm going to chase after a scared runaway half the night, you are mistaken!" After he had made his point he opened the brown bag and handed Adam a cheeseburger.

Adam nervously took the round package from Richard. "Can we leave right away? At least get out on the highway again and stop somewhere, where nobody can see us?" With this he pointed to the back seat and Richard got the message. After all, he already had experience in this kind of childish hide-and-seek game.

"You're kidding me?" Richard lifted the blanket on the back seat. Jake junior was crouched in the space between the front and back seat. "What are you doing there?"

Jake junior raised his head, so he could look him in the face. His eyes were alert. "My father knows your car. By now, he might be looking for me."

"How would he know you are here?"

"I parked the pickup truck over there, at the gas station. I had to get here somehow, and he'll notice it as soon as he drives by."

"How would he get here if you took the truck?"

"We do have several cars, you know."

Suddenly Richard did not feel so laid-back any more. Jake junior's anxiety was rubbing off on him. He pictured his father racing into the parking lot, coming to a screeching halt in front of his car and ripping the door open to drag them all out. Richard had an unpleasant flashback, remembering how the boys had greeted Daisy with guns. Guns! Jake wouldn't even have to open the car door to get them!

He didn't consider himself a coward, but he had never felt the need to play the hero either. Without raising another objection, he dumped the greasy cheeseburger bag on Adam's lap, turned on the ignition and sped off.

Soon after, Jake's ruffled head appeared in his rear view mirror. He settled on the back seat, looking behind him with a worried expression - reminding Richard again of a similar situation, when Daisy and he had rescued the two smaller boys. Which prompted him to make a slightly sarcastic comment. "How old are you, Jake?"

"I'm eighteen."

He looked even older. His face was mature beyond his age and his body had seen a lot of physical labour. "You're an adult. You can make your own decisions."

Jake junior didn't answer.

"Your father can't make you stay." Richard insisted. "Why are we supposed to pick you up and hide you? Forgive me, but I don't get it. You could have just walked out of there and stuck your middle finger up his ass."

Jake junior's face twitched and Richard regretted his crude callousness. But it was a fact! How else could he make it clear to Jake junior that he was his own man?

Adam answered for him. "Nobody leaves the Church that easily, unless he is thrown out. Jake junior has run away and his father will be furious. It's very dangerous for subordinates to take the initiative, and it's certainly not safe for Jake to stay in the vicinity of his father."

Richard remembered the guns. "Okay, I understand. We'll drive him to Vancouver and take him to Ted and David."

"Right. They can work on getting papers for him."

"I've got my birth certificate with me," Jake junior interrupted. "I knew where my mother had it for safekeeping."

"Oh excellent, you remembered." Adam turned to Richard, as if he was a bit backward. "I told him that this is important. Makes all the difference when we can prove who he is. We need to apply for all sorts of documents for him, you know!"

"It's okay," Richard said, "I got it. I'm not an idiot." A parking area came up and he drove in there. The burgers and chips might still be warm. All three of them grabbed the meals and devoured them in seconds.

"What about your mother?" Adam asked Jake junior, cleaning his greasy fingers on a paper towel. "Does she know you got out? Or would you rather not talk about it?"

Jake junior licked some left over ketchup off the empty wrapping paper in his hands. "I'm sure she hopes I got away. She won't know though. There has been a pretty ugly scene." His face clouded over. "I was fighting with my father. He hit my mother and … and, there have been other things going on, I don't really want to talk about."

"That's okay", Richard said again, like a broken record. "You don't have to explain. I had a pretty ugly scene with your father myself. He can be quite cantankerous. There's not much point in reasoning with him."

"I just hope my mother is alright. He is so unpredictable."

Richard started the car again and drove back on the highway. They settled down for the long haul, each one of them lost in their own thoughts. It was dark by now. Traffic was light along this stretch of the highway and few headlights cut through the night. Richard put the car in cruise and started to fight an overwhelming desire to sleep.

They would reach Clearwater soon. He asked if any of them wanted to take over the steering wheel.

"I can, if you want," Adam said.

"Can you drive?"

"All the boys learn it when they are still very young. The family needs us to earn money, driving loads when construction or harvesting is going on. There was always a lot to do." He sighed. "I got my licence when I was sixteen."

Richard started to look for another parking area. A road sign announced the turn-off to Wells Grey Park.

Before he reached it, Jake stunned him with a question, seemingly coming out of the blue. "How soon do you think I can go back there?"

"Are you serious? Why would you want to go back?" Richard asked him dumbfounded.

Even Adam was flabbergasted. "Jake, you can't. Ever! It's way too dangerous."

"But I must. I have to find out if my mother ... and the others... are okay. I won't stay there. I just need to get in there without him knowing. I mean, I should really ... well, you know."

His stammering was getting on Richard's nerves. "Jake, get it out of your system. What's bugging you?"

"I need to take somebody else out. I need to go back and ... you know... and save her."

"Your mother?" Adam asked.

"Ah, no."

His admission made Richard grin. So there was hanky-panky going on among them after all. Wait till he told Daisy that one!

"But who then?" Adam asked again.

"Oh, don't be stupid, Adam," Richard said. "His girlfriend, who else."

Adam was unwilling to understand. "But there is only family."

True. He hadn't thought of that. He joined Adam's incredulity. "Jake, who is it?"

Jake junior stalled. "She is alright for the moment. She's quite safe there. But I promised to get her out one day. She doesn't want to stay there. I can't leave her behind. I have to make good on my promise."

"So it is one of your sisters, right?" Adam asked. "How old is she?"

"No, not a sister. I don't really want to talk about it."

Richard's patience was wearing thin. There wasn't anything he could do right now anyway, so he lost interest in the conversation. He was worn out and didn't want to concern himself with other people's problems, but Adam insisted on finding out who Jake junior wanted to save. He argued they wouldn't be able to help if they didn't know the details.

"As I said," Jake junior finally gave in, "there is no urgency. It's a young woman my father married. She is fifteen and can't stand being his wife. Please, understand, she is not a bad woman." His voice became coarse. "She is good and beautiful and very, very ..." he cleared his throat in an effort to hide his embarrassment. "Her name is Martha," he finally said, as if that would explain everything.

Richard slammed on the brakes. "What did you say? Martha?" Of course he knew the answer already. Luckily, Adam was wearing his seatbelt, but Jake got flung forward and hit his forehead on the head-rest. Richard pressed the gas pedal again more gently. Further up was the Wells Grey Park turnoff sign. He slowed down and turned into the small parking area next to the Tourist Centre at the entrance to the Park. "Sorry, Jake. Are you okay?"

Jake junior rubbed his head and nodded.

The car was idling now, parked under a street light, and Richard looked back at him. What he had to say now was horrible, just horrible. "You said Martha is your father's wife?"

"Yes."

"And you are in love with her?"

Jake junior could not verbally admit it, but his pleading eyes told Richard the whole story.

"Oh shit. Does he know?"

He shook his head.

"Jake, you have to talk to me, this is very important. I don't care if you slept with her or not, but I need to know why you think she is not in danger."

Adam was listening with such intensity, Richard could picture his frozen face and knotted hands without even looking at him.

Jake junior finally pulled himself together. "I'm certain she is not in immediate danger. My father suspects nothing. He doesn't even take any notice of her. It's not what you think. We do love each other..."

"Oh, I'm sure you do. But what makes you say he doesn't notice her?"

"He just doesn't. Something happened two years ago, just after the wedding..."

Adam gasped. "Then she was only thirteen?!"

"Yes. And I'm sure his new bride will not be any older. Nor will the girl Brother Lucas in America has chosen for me. That's what the fight was all about. I refused to get married. I wouldn't even pick up the new brides. The girls are always so young. Anna and Emma, the wives before Martha, have also been barely, as the Church calls it, ready to enter celestial marriage when they were sent to him."

Adam stared at Richard. "A girl is deemed ready as soon as she has had her first menstruation," he explained, full of defiance and anger, as if it was Richard's fault.

"Damn it!" Richard said to both of them. But there was no time to contemplate the gravity of those accusations. There would be plenty of time for that later on, he promised himself. The bastard would suffer, he would make sure of that. "Guys, we have to turn back again," he groaned, wide awake again. "Martha is not safe at all." He hated to do this to Jake junior, who had paled at his words and now stared at him like a madman. "Jake, you are wrong if you think your father doesn't suspect anything. Martha is the bride your father offered to me. He said she would be divorced, and believe me, I had no idea that he was talking about his own wife. I was supposed to marry her on the spot, that was his condition to sell the land to me. But I didn't wait for him to come back with the girl he had selected. I stormed out, thereby rejecting his proposal. Which means, I've rejected her. He'll be furious, God knows what he'll do to her now. Your father is very much aware that Martha has done something wrong - he called her damaged goods."

44

Night settled in front of her window. Pale moonlight illuminated the landscape behind the main house. Martha stared outside with unseeing eyes, dreaming of sights and sounds that would never happen. He would not come for her. Several hours ago she thought she'd heard the noise of a car engine but it must have been her imagination. Since then it had been deadly quiet, inside and outside of the house.

The wind picked up speed and shook the branches of the trees. They were bending in the gusts, toward her and back again, inviting her to come on over. How nice would it be to walk out of here and join them in the grey night, not worrying if her footprints could be seen. Not worrying about anything. But it wouldn't be long now - soon it would all be over.

She closed her tear-filled eyes and opened them again with a sigh. There was movement underneath the trees, and she detected a shadow in the dark. All her senses sharpened. It was a human shape. There was a person out there, scurrying from one tree trunk to the next, trying to stay in their protective shade. The courtyard was only dimly lit. Martha pressed her face closer to the pane. It could be Jake junior! If he was out there, he would look up. She had to make sure he would see her.

The figure was obviously trying to hide his approach. But he would have to leave the protection of the trees and step into the light of the yard for a brief moment before he could blend into the safety of the house shadow. Martha hoped she was the only one watching and her heart stopped when she saw somebody rushing over the open yard.

Then she realized with crushing certainty that her hope it might be Jake junior had been in vain. The person she was watching was wearing a skirt. She was female. Martha squinted her eyes and tried to recognize who it was. It could be Anna. Of course, it must be Anna, who else was crazy enough to approach the main house like a burglar. How did Anna get the energy to do this? The little bit of bread she had taken to her yesterday could not have helped much. She must be desperate to be out there in the cold and gloomy night. Anna looked up at the window, saw her standing there and stopped in her tracks, probably devastated that she had been discovered. Then she must have realized who was watching her, placed a finger to her lips and sealed them with this simple gesture.

Martha understood and nodded her agreement. She would not tell on Anna; whatever the deranged woman was up to, it did not matter to her.

Anna lifted her hand as a thank-you and was gone.

The strange occurrence had sharpened Martha's senses again. She became aware of a low sound. Invisible to her, a car came up the driveway toward the front of the main house, its engine noise barely audible. Why had Marion locked her in here where she could not see anything except Anna sneaking around under the trees?

The car noise stopped. The main entrance door to the house opened. Somebody entered. Not the person she had hoped for – it was his father, stomping in as bellicose as a warlord. She could tell from the way he slammed the door and yelled for Marion, calling her names and threatening to kill her if she wasn't fast enough, that he was still highly agitated. Lights were switched on; Martha could see a bright beam shining through the crack underneath her door. Marion must have arrived from somewhere. Her husband was hurling insults at her. It was her fault Jake junior had disappeared. She was harbouring him and better admit to where he was. Or did she think it was very clever to make a fool of him? Making him run around Blue

River like an idiot looking for his own son. All this was her doing, and probably all the other wives were involved in the conspiracy as well. Like the one she was protecting in the office instead of sending her up to the prison hut like the other one, that Emma, or whatever her name was.

Martha went on her knees behind the door, pressing her ear to the keyhole, trying not to breathe so she wouldn't miss a single word. She was overjoyed to hear that Jake junior had managed to escape and stored this wonderful news in her heart, hoping it would comfort her in her final hour. His father was clearly working himself into a frenzy. He was out to destroy somebody to justify his hurt ego. Whoever was close to him now would have to bear the brunt of his madness – and that was either Marion or herself.

He would make an example they would not forget so easily, she heard him ranting, to make sure this kind of subordination would not set a standard among the other wives. His whole family needed to find out who the master was in this house.

"Get me my gun!" he yelled - and then everything happened at once.

They were racing through the night. Richard could not believe that he was driving the same route for the fifth time today. This morning he had been driving north after a nearly sleepless night, anxious and hopeful that Jake would accept his offer. At midday he was going south to meet with Jeanne d'Arc for a last minute pitch, then back again for the Jake junior rescue operation and then down south again after collecting him from behind the McDonalds trash bins.

And now he was driving with Adam and Jake junior up those very roads again to save a young woman from a fate unknown to them. This was utterly crazy. Maybe he only imagined the danger she was in! No way! His intuition rang alarm bells, loud and clear. Richard thought about Jake trying to organize a wedding. *For God's sake, my wedding! To his own underage wife!* The erratic behaviour Jake had displayed – Richard remembered him feverishly flapping around like an oversized turkey in distress, while ranting on about the Principle - was living proof of his madness. Richard shivered in disgust and pressed his foot down even more. Already the car was exceeding the speed limit and Adam cautioned him to slow down. No point in getting stopped by a highway patrol car.

Richard didn't think there would be any on the road at this hour. It was not late by city standards, just after ten thirty, but out in the country the daytime traffic had trickled down to the occasional car coming toward him in the other lane. If they were stopped by police, he suggested, they could always tell the officers why they were in such a rush and subsequently could arrive at Jake's place with a patrol car in tow.

Adam quite rightly pointed out that they had absolutely no proof for their suspicions and that the police, upon hearing their story, would certainly consider them nuts and lock them up until they got around to investigating their accusations – if they bothered with that at all. And even if they did, Jake junior threw in with a quivering voice, his father would know how to manipulate them and hide whatever he was planning to do to Martha.

Either way, they would be discredited, look like fools and achieve nothing. Richard slowed down a little, clinging desperately to the assumption Jake junior had made. They assured each other, against any rationale, that nothing had happened to Martha yet.

Adam's mobile rang. The three of them were wound up as tight as spring coils and jumped at the foreign sounding tone. It could only be Daisy. Adam said *hi* and then *yes of course he is here* and then handed his phone to Richard again. This was becoming a habit.

"Hi there," Daisy said, not very cheerfully. Richard knew right away something was wrong. She sounded apprehensive. "You should be past Merritt already, right? When do you expect to get to Vancouver?"

Of course, she couldn't know that they had turned around and were heading up north again. God, how could he explain this whole mess to her in easy terms? "Why?" he asked instead. "What's wrong?"

"Nothing."

"Daisy, you used to lie better than that. You haven't asked me if we found Jake junior."

"Did you?"

"Yes, of course we did. He's here in the car with us. Now, tell me."

She swallowed, collecting herself. The messenger of bad news usually gets the first blame. "There is an email from Jeanne d'Arc."

"Wow, that didn't take her long. She must have sent it as soon as we had left her office."

"Do you want me to read it to you?"

Driving through the night with a former Lost Boy and a current runaway on a rescue mission to save the life of a child-bride must have distorted Richard's perspective of priorities. The approving officer's email was currently positioned quite low on his list and he had little desire to burden himself with a written statement of her bureaucratic interpretations. "Not really. I think I know already. Your reaction makes it quite clear to me that she has rejected our final plea."

"I'm so sorry Richard. She wrote, I quote: although she appreciates your disappointment, she cannot bend the rule for you."

"She could, but never mind," he said, with amazing calm. He was back at where he had been at lunch time – but at least now he could say that Adam and he had tried everything humanly possible. Suddenly he had to laugh. It sounded a bit strangled and sardonic, but it still threw Daisy.

"It's not really funny."

"I was just thinking, I'm back where I was at lunch time, but actually, I'm not. Not physically I mean. Guess where I am just now."

He proceeded to tell her as best as he could why they were on their way back to Jake's compound. It took nearly half an hour and several lengthy interruptions by her, asking him to elaborate certain details - of course always those he was trying to disguise because his conduct had been less than perfect. In the end she forgave him for not sharing her suspicions and worries from the start, for not acting immediately on information presented to him, while conveniently overlooking the obvious. She forgave him because he was doing the right thing now.

They talked until he reached the turn-off from the highway. They could lose reception at any moment. As she hung up, she said he must call her as soon as they got Martha out, no matter how late it was. She would wait up for his call.

Driving along the gravel road that led to his father's property, Jake junior suggested they should make a plan. He had pulled himself together enough to make reasonable sense. A wooden building intensified every sound, specially at night when all was quiet. It wouldn't be easy to sneak up and into the house to get Martha out without his father or his mother noticing, he pointed out, and added with the same breath that he had no idea what the best approach would be.

They thought it over and discussed possible options. There was really only one possibility. Jake junior knew where the key to the gate was hidden. He would climb over the fence, open the gate to the property and they would drive, with headlights off, as slowly as possible up to the main house. Jake would get out of the car before they reached the last corner, creep around the house and wait in the safety of the trees. After waiting exactly ten minutes to give him a good head start, Richard would turn the headlights on and roar at full speed up to the house. Accelerating and racing on the still frozen gravel would make a sound like a jet plane taking off. With a bit of luck, Jake and Marion would wake up and be shaken up enough to run out to see what was going on. Jake junior would use this diversion to enter the house and get Martha out through the backdoor. They would run down the driveway and hide somewhere along the road in the bushes until Richard's car came back. Richard asked Jake junior if it was likely that his father had a gun. Jake junior said yes, he did have one, but expressed the notion that his father would probably only fire a warning shot in the air and would stop as soon as he recognized Richard's car.

Richard prayed that he was right.

Martha knew the Bishop was coming for her. His boots stomped toward the office, and when he unlocked the door, she moved back to the opposite wall, trying to melt into it. The room was only about ten feet deep, and he was threateningly close as soon as he had entered. She saw the gun strap slung over his shoulder. Marion was beside him, her face still wet from crying, but already setting into a mask of acceptance and denial. Empty eyes buried in a stone hard expression. With only minimal movement of her body, she looked like a motionless statue, placed there only as an accessory to her husband, an extension of his wrath, coming alive only to cater to his demands. For the moment, he needed nothing of her except to observe him in all his glory as the executor of the faith.

Martha was not scared of him, but she was terrified of the unknown. What cruelty had he planned for her? Would she have to suffer long? It would be easier to bear if she knew what to expect.

She didn't have to wait long.

"Get out of here, you worthless piece of shit!" he snapped at her. He slipped the gun strap off his shoulder and casually swung the hunting rifle around, holding it in front of his massive torso like a trophy. "Here, see this! Fear this! It is the Lord's instrument of vengeance. He has appointed me to be his executioner. Commanded me to exterminate filthy vermin like you. Get out, you slut, so I can punish you for your sins!" He came closer, lowered the weapon and prodded her thigh with the tip of the rifle. Martha jumped sideways and was forced to move forward and slide past him to the door.

He directed her with his weapon. "Bitch! Out with you! Outside! We don't want a mess in here. Out you go, you miserable creature! I'll show you who your master is. Move it, bitch, don't drag your feet."

Martha moved a little faster. She was numb, didn't even feel herself walking past Marion who remained grotesquely frozen in her stance.

The Bishop kept pushing her forward, down the hallway, to the back entrance of the house. "Go, go, go. Let's have a little target practise. You'd better move a bit faster, or it won't be fun at all. Outside you go."

He pushed her through the back door and out into the yard. "When I count to three, you run. If you make it over there, I'll let you live. The Lord will decide."

The distance from the house to the trees was much larger than she remembered. But it didn't matter; he would get her anyway. Best to go slow, otherwise he might miss and only injure her.

"One!"

Martha took a deep breath. He slammed his rifle painfully into her back. She nearly lost her balance.

"Two!"

She forgot her resolution to be an easy target and instinctively started to run.

"Threeeee...."

She ran as fast as she could, trying to get away from his horrible 'eeeee'. She practically flew over the ground, driven by her survival instinct, until she stumbled, lost her balance and fell face down on the ground. A sharp slash whipped viciously through her whole body, ripping her insides apart. She was surprised to hear herself groaning, although the excruciating pain of a moment ago subsided into shocked numbness. He had not finished her! Mixed into her total confusion of being shot at, lying on the ground and not feeling any pain, was the realization that something did not fit into the whole scenario. Something did not make sense. She had heard him counting and his final endless, blood curling "eeeeeeeee" still rang in her ears. She was on her knees now, slumped forward to steady herself with her hands, and turning sideways to look behind her.

He was also on the ground, holding his side with one hand, the rifle lying next to him. His "eeeeee" had evaporated into a whimper. At the same instant Martha saw the shape of a woman running away from him. Nothing but billowing skirts in a hasty retreat, impetuously heading for the protection of the trees. Anna! Already she had reached the trees. A safe haven for the fleeing Anna; as it would be for her, if she could reach it before he recovered from the injury Anna had inflicted on him. He was already shaking his head like a wounded bear, groaning in an effort to get the nasty foreign object that incapacitated him out of his flank. Martha did not see what had injured him so badly that the air had been knocked out of his lungs, but it must have weakened him considerably. He was wheezing, coughing and gurgling in his angry attempts to regain his stability and was slowly steadying himself.

If only she had not been hurt – if only she could reach the cover of the forest before he recovered from the surprise attack. She forced herself to try and scramble to her feet, surprised that she was still in one piece and not cut into two like she had thought. Where did it hurt? Even more surprised, she realized that she was not hurting at all. Her brain finally solved the mystery that had puzzled her before. No shot had been fired! On his last count she had only heard his scream but no shot - no bullet had been flying in her direction. She had stumbled and fallen, that was all. The pain had been imaginary.

By now her legs were firmly on the ground, holding her weight, and she started to run. She looked back once and increased her efforts to reach the tree line when she saw that he was already on his knees, groping blindly for his weapon. She literally flew across the yard, her skirt bunched up high, with her feet barely touching the ground. The forest. The trees. There they were. She ran past the first few trees, getting deeper into the woods before she pressed herself behind one wide trunk, panting heavily. She dared to look back. He was nowhere to be seen. He had moved. Where to? She knew her panting was too loud, but she could not stop it, her lungs were screaming for oxygen.

It was mercifully dark in the forest, but he only needed to follow the wheezing sounds she made to find her. Anger welled up inside her. She wanted to live! Why hadn't Anna finished him! She must have been too weak. If only she had a weapon. The frustration of being so helpless made her even more angry. I will fight him, she thought. This time, I will scratch his eyes out before he can hurt me again. Martha slid down the tree trunk until she cowered on the wet cold ground, making herself as small a target as possible. She concentrated on the sounds of the night. He was injured and furious, he would not approach like a seasoned hunter but would storm through the darkness in search of her. When she heard him coming, she could hide or run away from him. She wasn't quite sure what she would do, but this time she would not make it easy for him.

A moon-lit night in the wilderness is never a peaceful time. There were many sounds she was not familiar with. Small animal paws pattering, bird wings swinging, wind caught in the branches, howling and whistling – too much noise for her untrained ears. All she knew was that he was not close, and that there was a distant familiar noise she could not yet distinguish. It sounded like a car approaching, but that was impossible. Before she was able to pinpoint the source, the noise had died down again.

The moon was guiding them along the driveway. They let the car roll through the Plaza of Huts without detecting any movement there. Jake junior whispered that the women were trained not to react, so they needn't worry that they might be prematurely discovered by inquisitive eyes.

Well before they came to the last bend in the driveway, and still protected by the high hedge on the roadside, Richard stopped the car. Jake junior opened the car door, slid out from his back seat, closed the door as quietly as possible again and looked back into the car through Adam's window on the passenger side. Richard checked his watch, it was nine minutes past eleven, and nodded in agreement. The ten minutes started now!

It was an agonizing wait for Adam and him.

"What are we going to tell Jake when he comes out of the house and confronts us?" Richard whispered to him to break the tension. None of them had thought of that. They were some rescue mission!

"Hmm," Adam mused, "Just tell him you wanted to try once more to change his mind about the sale."

"At this hour?"

"Who cares. He'll throw us out anyway."

He had a point there.

"You could pretend to be drunk."

That might work. He would act all insulted and make a hell of a ruckus. As soon as Jake started to lose his temper, he would jump back in the car and drive off – hopefully picking up Jake junior and Martha somewhere on the way down to the gate. If necessary they would wait in front of the gate all night for them.

They sat in silence, staring at Richard's watch.

Finally the dial flipped to nineteen minutes past and he gave it a few more seconds. Had they really allowed Jake enough time? Richard's heart was racing and one look at Adam confirmed that he was experiencing the same anxiety. He was as pale as the moon outside. They both nodded at the same time and with the same degree of determination.

Richard turned the ignition key and the sound was so brutal, it made them straighten in their seats. He put the car in gear and slammed his foot on the accelerator to give his tightly stretched nerves some release. Poor Adam didn't have that satisfaction. The car reacted beautifully, as he had hoped, screeching on the gravel like a whole slaughter house full of pigs.

The fine hairs on his arms stood to attention. The adrenalin rush dramatically increased his sensory perception. He could distinguish perfectly between a number of things that were happening practically instantaneously as he raced around the last corner of the driveway.

First there was his amazement that some windows of the house he had expected to be quiet and dark were lit. Then he became aware of a bulky shadow illuminated by his right front light. He slammed on the brakes, having a perfect déja-vu of another near collision in the past, knowing with absolute certainty that, this time, he was powerless to avoid it. Then everything blurred and, to be able to cope, his brain switched to slow-motion. This way it could dissect the different actions of the moment better. Unfortunately it also burned every horrid detail of what was happening into his memory. He hit the bulky shadow of the body which did not even attempt, or did not have a chance, to avoid his car.

Adam had already unbuckled his seatbelt when Jake junior had got out of the car. The impact catapulted him forward and smashed his head into the windshield.

Richard registered the enormous flat thump when his car hit the body in front of the right headlight with no more than a disheartened cringe, steeling himself against the truly bone crushing horror that would follow when the front wheels would inevitably roll over the mass.

The car had already slowed down, making it agonizingly slow.

Finally, in the middle of rolling over the obstacle, the brakes brought the car to a final stop. The dashboard was slanted downwards to the left because the right front wheel had rolled over the body but was not touching the ground. Richard didn't need to check to know that he had pinned a body underneath the chassis. For a frantic split second he considered putting the car in reverse to get it off the body again, but he couldn't. He was shaking like a leaf. Adam was thankfully unconscious. Richard had visions of him trying to exit from his side, stepping onto and over the body that must lie underneath his door. This was a nightmare in slow motion.

Then the stupor that had taken hold of him finally let go and made him react in the opposite extreme. He quickly checked if Adam was still alive and as soon as he felt a pulse, he got out of the car, already yelling and screaming for help, ran around it and grabbed the front bumper with both hands. He wanted to lift it, knew he couldn't, got mad at the still unconscious Adam for adding weight, let go of the bumper and straightened up and yelled again. *Help, Help, Jake, come here, Jake, help* ... or something to that effect. He had no idea what he was yelling.

Nobody came.

The legs protruding out from under the car didn't move. Richard carefully stepped over them and opened the car door on Adam's side. Somebody had to help him. Adam had to get out and lift the car off the body. It only needed a bit of a lift, but he couldn't do it alone. He pulled on Adam's sleeve, yelling and begging. Adam was coming round now, moaning and rubbing his bleeding forehead. Richard pulled harder, practically hauling Adam out of the car and dragging him over the legs without consideration of any injury he might have sustained. Then, and again this happened in a fast flowing sequence but seemed like an eternity to him, Marion came running from the main house, flying down the long distance on the driveway to his car and Jake junior appeared from somewhere behind. Adam seemed to recover his senses even more.

When Marion and Jake junior reached him, they assessed the situation astonishingly fast. Jake junior went around the front bumper and waved Adam and Richard to his side. The three of them managed to lift the car high enough for Marion to drag the body from underneath. In what had to be a superhuman effort, this frail and fragile woman found the strength to pull her husband by his legs over the gravel until his head was clear, then the men let go of the car and went over to him. It was so important for Richard to have the car off the body, he sobbed with relief. It made such a difference, although the outcome of the accident was the same. The Bishop did not twitch. He was dead.

Marion and Jake junior stared down at him, incredulous and confused. Richard was still sobbing and shaking.

Adam was the first to react with a semblance of rationality. "He must have run straight into us," he muttered, explaining to himself more than to anybody else what had happened. "I didn't even see him approach. Suddenly there was this shape in front of us. There was no way to avoid him."

Marion kept moving her head from side to side, obviously too dazed to understand anything.

Jake junior put his arm out to comfort her, but stopped halfway and let it drop to his side again. "Mother…," he started.

That woke her up. "Jake? Jake! Oh my God, Jake, it's you! You're back."

Now he did take her in his arms; she was shaking badly and started to cry as soon as she felt his comforting touch.

That kicked Richard's brain into action, at least to the point that he could pull himself together enough to stop crying, but it was far from helping him to sort out the unbelievable situation they were in. He could not think of what to do next.

"We have to call the RCMP and tell them there was an accident," Adam said.

Yes, exactly.

Adam continued to give orders. "Jake, Marion, you have to go to the house and tell the police that he is dead."

Yes, they should.

"Richard, you'd better stay here with the, the …" Adam hesitated before he finally mumbled *the body*. "We can't leave him lying here on the ground all by him…it…itself."

No, no way, Richard thought, not me! He didn't want to stay here with the dead body.

"Yes, of course," he said dutifully.

Marion inched closer to her husband's body. "Is he really dead?" she asked and suddenly they all jumped out of their daze. None of them had really checked him until now. Remembering his first-aid course, Richard knelt down beside Jake's limp body and touched his throat. No pulse. He put his ear on his mouth. No breath. "I'm not a doctor," he concluded, "but I'm certain he is dead."

Marion inhaled sharply and placed her hand over her mouth.

Jake junior patted her gently on the shoulder, in an awkward gesture full of tenderness. "Mother, we all came back here for a reason. Let's go to the house and I will explain everything to you."

"Oh," she said. "I know. You came back to get Martha, didn't you?"

Her son nodded, speechless. Richard was also quite stunned by this comment, but Adam acted most surprised. He was staring over Jake junior's shoulder as if he was seeing a ghost. Richard followed his gaze and saw a girl standing in the shadow of a tree not far from their group.

"Martha?" Jake junior had also turned around. He let go of his mother and flew toward the girl as soon as he recognized her.

Martha opened her arms and they melted into each other. Then all her strength left her and she looked like she would faint at any second. Jake lifted her into his arms and carried her up to the house.

Adam took Marion's arm and placed it on his. "Here, hold on to me, I'll steady you." He was getting ready to follow Jake and Martha.

"Wait, I'm not staying here on my own," Richard complained with panic in his voice.

Adam barely glanced at the dead body. "You don't need to. There is nothing we can do. Let's all go back to the house. I'll ask Marion for a blanket and will come back and cover him with it until the doctor and the police get here."

The depth of Richard's gratitude must have been obvious to Adam. "Come on, Richard, you're in shock. You were driving, but you mustn't blame yourself. There was nothing you could have done. It was an accident. Nothing but an unfortunate accident."

45

They all sat down at the long table. Marion acted like a robot, asking if she should make tea. That's all she could offer. Adam asked her for a blanket, and they both left the room briefly.

Jake junior kept stroking Martha's hair and crooned in a soothing tone to the deeply disturbed young woman.

Richard just sat there, staring at the table top, contemplating getting up and leaving. If he could just get out of there for a while, he would be able to get his brain together. He had just killed a person and no matter how big a creep the guy had been, he was a human being and Richard was beside himself with remorse, going over the accident again and again. He should have been able to avoid it. But how? He hadn't even seen him approaching. He should not have driven so fast. It had been his idea to race up the driveway in the dark. It had been his foot that accelerated the car. It was all very well for Adam to say it wasn't his fault, but he knew better. Self-accusations and self-pity circled around inside his head until Adam came back and placed the mobile on the table.

"Somebody has to call the police."

"No reception here, remember!" Richard said.

Marion came in, holding a tray with a pot and several cups on it. She said there was a phone in the house, in *his* – she hesitated, not being able to pronounce Jake's name - in *his* office.

Richard didn't move.

Adam got up. "We can't just sit around here. We have to tell somebody that he's dead. The police have to come and write up a report or something."

Martha heard their mumbled conversation without taking notice of what was being said. It was difficult enough for her to understand that Jake junior had come back for her – practically out of nowhere. While she had been hiding under the trees, she had seen somebody running out of the house seconds after she had been jolted by a strange noise coming from the direction of the driveway. That somebody must have been him, but she hadn't noticed him entering the house and she was by no means sure that she wasn't imagining things. Half the time she had her eyes closed to concentrate on the hunter in the dark – his father - until she had heard car tires screeching on the driveway. Hoping that it might be Jake junior who had finally come to rescue her from the hands of his father, she made her way down in the dark, even though it meant that she might run right into her tormenter's arms. She had heard somebody shouting *Jake, Jake* in the distance and all she could think of was Jake junior. If it was him, he would protect her from the Bishop's wrath. It just had to be him! First, she had carefully manoeuvred her way out of the forest, then, once she had cleared the trees, she had run as fast as she could over the open field and across the meadows until she had arrived at the scene on the driveway.

Three people had been standing around the car – and one of them had been Jake junior, just as she had longed for. And she had seen a body on the ground which, judging from the enormous stomach protruding in the air, could only be his father. After that, everything went blurry. But Jake junior was here now, holding her hand, stroking it softly. And the Bishop was dead! She was sitting at the very table she had never been allowed to sit at before. The people around her were talking about what to do next. As long as Jake junior was with her, nothing else mattered. Except that they were talking about calling outsiders in to report the death of his father. That mustn't happen! She looked up and tried to focus on what they were saying. "The police? No, no, you mustn't call them. We must keep it a secret. Nobody needs to know."

Everybody stared at her.

"Anna couldn't help it. She is disturbed, ever since her first baby died, we all know that. Please, Marion, tell them. You know she couldn't help it."

"Couldn't help what?" Jake junior asked her.

"Please," she pleaded on behalf of her friend. "If they take her away, they will kill her." She was not sure what kind of justice system existed outside of her small world, but surely they would punish Anna severely for stabbing the Bishop to death. Most likely they would kill her.

"But why do you say that?" asked Adam now.

"Anna killed her husband. I know he is dead, I saw him on the ground. And I saw Anna do it," she whispered, and, as an afterthought, "if she hadn't succeeded, I would have tried myself."

Now it was Richard's turn. "No Martha, you are wrong. Anna had nothing to do with this. I have…, I have…, he ran into my car. I hit him. I was the one who killed him."

"No, you didn't. I saw her stabbing him. He was hurt badly and only got as far as your car. That's why he was lying there on the road. I saw her running away. She got him! It wasn't you."

Richard frowned. What was she talking about? Could the body have been lying there already? He looked at Adam who shrugged his shoulders, indicating that he had no idea.

"It's true," she insisted. "Marion, you were there when he chased me outside. Tell them what he wanted to do to me."

It was suddenly very quiet in the room. Everybody looked at Marion who firmly pressed her lips together.

"Tell them!" Martha demanded. There was no question of her being confused or even demented, as Richard had first thought.

"He wanted to use her for target practise in the yard," Marion breathed, barely audibly.

Jake junior jumped to his feet. Then he slumped down again. His immediate impulse must have been to protect Martha and to go after his father until he remembered that Richard's reckless driving had already taken care of his urge for revenge. Jake junior turned his attention back to Martha. "I'm so sorry. You must have been terrified."

She shook her head. "I wasn't. I wanted to die - until I saw what Anna had done. How courageous she has been. After that, I realized that I wanted to kill him, not die myself. You must not give her up, please, Jake, please, don't call the police."

Adam and Richard looked at each other and shared a silent understanding. *We have to find out exactly what happened before we contact the police.*

"Okay, Martha," Richard said calmly. "We promise we'll try to keep Anna out of it altogether, alright?" She looked at him, concentrating on his words. "Adam and I will go to the office now to make a phone call, but I will only speak to my assistant Daisy. She is waiting for me to call her and I don't want her to contact the police because she is worried about Adam and me. Okay?" Martha nodded again. "We'll be back soon."

Marion pulled a large key chain out of her skirt pocket. She picked out a small key. "You'll need this. The office door will be open, but there is a small lock on the telephone, so only he could use it. He wanted me to carry a spare key in case he had a heart attack and I needed to call for help. He was always worried about that."

This precaution wasn't too far fetched, Richard thought, considering Jake's unhealthy size, but he bit his tongue and accepted the whole key chain from Marion with a simple thank-you.

Jake junior got up as well, conspiring nicely with Richard and Adam. "I'll show you where the office is."

The three men left the room and walked down the hallway, waiting to be out of earshot before they would discuss Martha's confused recollections. It never came to that as they became aware of a faint noise behind one of the closed doors to their left. They stopped walking. Jake put one finger over his lips. They listened. There it was again, it sounded as if a person or an animal was moaning.

Jake whispered to the other men. "That's strange. There shouldn't be anybody in the house, except us." He opened the door to a small room with no windows and wooden shelves lined up along three of the walls, turned the light on and made a surprised whistling sound. The other two men were right behind him and could clearly see why

Jake junior was so startled. All the shelves were empty. In front of the shelf unit opposite them was a woman crouching on all fours on the floor. She was not much more than a skeleton, skin stretching over bones with hardly any tissue in between, and large wounded eyes. She moaned again and looked at the men like a rabbit would stare at a snake.

"Anna, what are you doing here?" Jake junior asked, totally surprised.

It pained Richard to see the woman on the floor being so scared of the men before her, and his anger at the old Jake flared up again. What had he done to those poor women?

Instead of answering, she only blinked rapidly, as if the sight of the intruders hurt her eyes.

"So it's true what Martha said," Richard hissed through his teeth, feeling helpless hostility toward the man who had driven Anna to such an act of despair. "Look at her. It must have taken her last bit of strength to come up to the house and attack Jake."

Jake junior and Adam went to her and tried to help her up. She had no strength left. Jake lifted her into his arms and they all went back to the living room. After Marion got over her initial surprise, she quickly cleared a bench to bed Anna down and covered her with a blanket.

"There is nothing else we can do," Marion said.

Martha was rigidly sitting on her chair staring at them with big eyes, only relaxing a bit once Jake junior took his place next to her again.

Adam suggested that their priority should be to organize some food for the starving Anna. She looked so feeble. He glanced at Marion and Martha and mumbled, slightly embarrassed, that he thought every woman, in this room and probably on the whole compound, would be in urgent need of nourishment. Marion shook her head sadly. "You've seen the pantry. There is nothing left in there."

"So how come Jake didn't look so thin?" he asked incredulously.

"He has his own supply stashed away in his quarters. But he never gave me a key for that."

Richard jumped up. "Oh damn that. Let's break it open. Come on you guys," he ordered.

"I'll get some tools," Jake agreed.

Now Anna lifted her head with a semblance of defiance and accused Martha in a flat voice: "See, I told you so. I knew he had some. But all the shelves are empty. I couldn't find any. Everything is gone. I have no strength left. Couldn't go all the way back to my children." She slumped back and seemed to drift in and out of consciousness.

There was no way this feeble woman, who had obviously fallen asleep in the pantry from sheer exhaustion, could have attacked a grown man of Jake's size. Absolutely no way, Richard insisted in a low voice.

Martha was the only one who didn't agree. She got up, walked over to Anna and willed her awake by talking loudly and staring at her face. "Come on, Anna, tell them. You came up here to kill your husband, didn't you?"

"No, I didn't. I only wanted food for my children. There is none." Anna didn't even have the energy left to cry.

Martha was startled. "But I saw you stabbing him. He was holding his left side."

There is no way to confirm if this was true, Richard thought to himself. Short of finding a broken blade inside Jake's bloated body, his tires would have destroyed any evidence of such an attack. His car had crushed Jake's midriff and any knife wound would have been squashed by the weight of his car.

"I came to get food," Anna's voice faltered, while she moved her head slowly from one side to the other. "Bread. Something."

Richard sighed. "This is getting us nowhere. Martha, come back here. You must have imagined it."

"No!" Martha stood her ground. "If it wasn't Anna...if I really mistook her for somebody else," her glance turned to Marion, "...then it must have been you! It was dark, I might not have seen exactly who it was and only assumed it was Anna because I couldn't imagine it would be anybody else, but it was definitely a female shape. So if it wasn't

Anna, it could only be you, you were the only woman in the house besides me."

An apologetic smile appeared on Marion's face. "Sometimes I wish I would have had the courage to fight him, Martha. But no, all I could ever do was trying to protect you young girls from the worst. I have never been brave enough to intentionally harm anybody. I don't have it in me."

"But you tried to kill me," Martha insisted stubbornly. "Long ago, after I had just arrived here. Remember the milk?"

"Oh, the milk," Marion took her glasses off and started to clean them. "Did you think that was supposed to kill you?"

"Admit it, you were jealous of me and wanted to poison me. I know that now."

"You are right, I put something in your milk, but not what you think. I made an infusion from the *Lobelia Inflata* plants I grow in my herb garden and mixed it with the milk I made you drink. It's quite tricky to get the mixture right; if you overdose it can make a person very sick. I did this for each one of you when you had to endure him, at least in the beginning, until you got used to it. The wives got younger each time, I just had to do something. Lobelia makes you numb and relaxed, and I thought then it would not be so painful for you. Anna and Emma had no problem digesting it, but you reacted badly to it. Maybe I judged the dose wrong for you, or maybe you are intolerant to milk, I don't know. I'm sorry, Martha, I tried to help you. I know it was not good enough."

Everything the older woman explained made perfect sense to Martha. She had not touched milk since then, the thought alone revolted her. Slowly everything else fell into place and also made sense to her. Marion, always pretending to be on her husband's side so she could protect the other wives. Always holding up the shield of her first wife status for the others to hide behind. No, Marion would never have done anything drastic to endanger her position within the hierarchy of the family. The support of her unsuspecting husband was her only weapon of defence – and Martha remembered many instances now, when

Marion had used her influence to ease the burden for some of the wives, usually so well disguised that most of them had not even noticed it. Anna on the other hand had surely wanted to murder him, but just looking at her, Martha knew with certainty that the frail woman, no matter how aggravated she was, did not have the stamina left in her needed for such a vicious attack. It wasn't Marion and it couldn't have been Anna either! So, the conclusion was clearly that she *had* imagined the shadow figure in the semi darkness. After all, the Bishop had made it all the way down the driveway. Maybe her mind had played a trick on her. Hadn't she also imagined being shot at, even feeling the pain of being torn into two pieces, if only for a brief second? Apart from a few scratches on her hands and knees, she had not been injured at all.

Martha shook her head, then nodded bewildered. Yes, maybe it was all in her imagination.

She sat down again.

The others could see how Martha was struggling to accept the fallacy of her memory, and Richard felt it was time to get back to the most pressing problems. Somebody had to start making decisions here. He told Jake junior and Adam to look for his father's hidden food supply, while he called the police to report the accident.

Marion directed him to the office, and Richard went straight to the phone, but he called Daisy first. He had to collect his thoughts before he could make any sensible statement to strangers, and Daisy was more clear headed than anybody he knew.

Once Daisy was over her initial shock – specially evident when he admitted the part when Jake had asked him to marry his youngest wife - she reacted amazingly rational, giving him a dry run of the potential police questions they had to expect.

"Make sure your stories match. You have to go over what happened together and get your answers in sync. What was your reason for driving to his place at this late hour? Why was Jake junior with you? What made you drive so fast? What made Jake run into your car? What was he doing on the driveway? Oh yes, and don't let Martha talk. Do not even mention Anna. They will only get confused by this crazy story. Best to get both of them out of the way when the police arrive."

They discussed in detail what he should tell the RCMP and what he should leave out to avoid unnecessary trouble for the family here.

"I wish you were here," he said truthfully after they had agreed on his course of action.

"So do I!"

Richard hung up and dialled 911. He reported that there had been a domestic accident. The operator asked if the person needed medical attention and Richard said no, the person he had accidentally hit with his car on the driveway was beyond help. He was then asked if he knew this person. Yes, Richard said, I'm at his home. His voice nearly faltered and the operator lost a touch of his professional distance. We need you to stay calm now, he said, take your time, but I need a few more details.

Richard reported as best as he could, and as Daisy had coached him, what had happened. The operator then told him he would dispatch an RCMP unit right away. As, due to the location, it would take some time for them to arrive, he also informed Richard that the body and the scene of the accident mustn't be disturbed.

Meanwhile, Jake junior had found some bread and cheese for the women. Even in his father's private quarters there was not much food left. After the women had eaten some of it, Jake drove Anna down to her hut with a small supply for her children and returned right away. Richard had promised Anna to organize food for all the women and children as soon as the supermarket in Blue River opened and once the police had gone. Martha was showing signs of fading fast, so Richard sent her to her room to get some sleep.

Once the two women were out of the way, Jake junior, Adam, Marion and Richard tried to get their stories coordinated. Then Jake junior drove first to the boys' and then to the women's quarters and told all of them to stay indoors until they got further instructions, before he made his way to the entrance gate to wait for the police to arrive.

Two RCMP constables and an ambulance arrived about three a.m., long before the first light of dawn would creep over the mountain top to the east. After the constables had secured the accident scene and set up lights, inspected Jake's body and taken some pictures and measurements, they allowed the ambulance to transport the corpse to the coroner, who most certainly would order an autopsy.

Richard had a brief vision of the examiner finding a knife blade in Jake's liver, but discarded that figment of Martha's overloaded imagination quickly and concentrated on his statement again. After the RCMP constables had verified Richard's identity and confirmed he was not out of Province, they checked him for evidence of impaired driving. The result satisfied them, and they began to interview everybody present to establish the chain of events that led to the accident.

Marion explained, visibly distraught, that she didn't think Richard was at fault at all. Her husband had been very agitated because he was under extreme financial stress, had been fighting with his son on that day and had thought his son had run away after an argument. That had been a terrible misunderstanding on his part, as Jake junior had only driven to Blue River and could not drive back home because the motor had died on him - proof of that was that his pickup truck was still at the gas station, and she hoped nobody would gauge the remaining gas in the tank. Adam and Richard took turns to explain how they had stopped at this particular gas station on their way north and had – what a coincidence – bumped into Jake junior there, who had had no money on him to call his dad. He had been hoping his dad would be looking for and eventually find him at the gas station. This part was a bit weak, but the constable just wrote it down and didn't even ask why the son hadn't simply borrowed money at the gas station to use the pay phone there. Of course Richard understood the constable's indifference to this tiny flaw in their story. Who cared why Jake junior acted so stupid? The only question that concerned the police was why Richard had been driving so fast up to the house.

"I was in a hurry to deliver the young man back to his home and get on with my journey," Richard explained.

One of the constables was scratching his head. "And you didn't see Mister Law at all?"

"No, I told you so," Richard said truthfully. "He must have been real fast, running into my vehicle from the right."

"But there is a hedge."

"Yes, but…" Richard didn't know what to say. The constable was right.

"And your car doesn't show any real damage. Hardly a scratch to the bumper. Could it be that he was lying on the road already?"

"No. Yes. Well, no, I would have seen him, wouldn't I?"

"Not if you were as fast as you said."

"Jesus Christ…" Richard shut up quickly.

Marion looked up sharply. "My husband often went for a walk when he was upset." She looked so miserable when she said this, Richard wanted to comfort her.

The constable felt the same way. "Sorry to ask, Madam, but did he have any health condition that may have caused him to lose his balance?"

"Health condition?"

"Well, yes. I noticed that he was quite a bit overweight. Has he had high blood pressure?"

"I don't know," she said.

"Well, we will certainly look into that. There will be an autopsy."

"Do I have to come with you?" Richard asked.

"No. Not now. We have all the information we need. There will be a report to Crown Counsel of course and you will be charged. Don't look so worried, in cases of vehicular homicide we always have to lay charges. It's not a conviction yet and the Crown may drop the charges when they are satisfied that it was an accident."

"Will you impound my car?" Richard ask.

"No, I don't see any need for that. It's not damaged and you are admitting to speeding and that you have struck the deceased. Please read through the statement and sign here."

"I can drive it back to Vancouver?"

"Just don't leave the country, as they always say in the movies," one of the constables chuckled.

"Yeah, hang around. There may still be a charge of reckless driving," the other one added as they were packing their stuff together.

He would accept that, Richard answered remorsefully – and he meant it.

Marion was holding up well, considering that she had had to play the grieving widow as long as the RCMP constables had been there. Richard, Adam and Jake junior sat around the table with her, unsure of what to do next.

The phone in the office rang. The sound was muffled by the distance it had to travel, but Marion got up quickly and went to answer it. She was so used to jumping to attention that Richard wondered how long it would take her to accept the fact that nobody bossed her around any more. Would she ever learn to relax a little?

She came back quickly, saying that it had been Richard's assistant Daisy who had called from Kamloops airport. Now Richard jumped up.

Marion asked him to sit down again. "She already hung up, but she asked me to tell you that she is on her way up here. She said she will get supplies from..." Marion frowned to remember correctly, "... from Costco for us. It's a big kind of supermarket where bulk food is cheaper," she added Daisy's explanation unnecessarily. Richard knew, and Adam probably too by now, what Costco was.

Bless Daisy's rational soul for coming here, and for thinking of arriving with desperately needed supplies! Now Richard didn't have to drive to Blue River and back. He could already feel the effect of his prolonged highly charged adrenalin level subsiding. By now it was seven a.m. and they were all totally exhausted. Soon tiredness would take over his mind and body to an extent that he would not be able to trust his decisions. He, they all, needed to take a break. It would take Daisy at least three hours to do the shopping and drive up here, so he suggested everybody should use the time for a much needed rest.

Martha had difficulty waking. She couldn't shake off her deep exhaustion. It took her a while to realize that she was on her bed and that it was daytime. The sun was up and filtered light into her small room. Then the sequence of events that had happened before she had gone to sleep started to trickle back into her consciousness, filling her memory pool, one drop at a time. Jake junior, she thought of him first. He was the first drop that started the flow of recollections.

He had come back to rescue her from his father.

The man – the car – the accident.

His father had tried to shoot her.

His father was dead.

Somebody had killed him.

The memories did not flow easily into each other. There was something wrong. Something she could not grasp right away. But wasn't the most important part of it all – the good part, that overshadowed all the other ugly memories - that Jake, her love, had come back to her? And that the Bishop was dead, never to harm her again.

Martha stood up and stretched. The short dreamless sleep had been good, but now she felt sticky and dirty after so much time without being able to wash herself. She opened the door, still careful not to make any noise. It was difficult to accept that she could venture outside without waiting for permission from somebody. The house was quiet.

She went to the bathroom, freshened up as best as she could in her old clothes and felt her stomach grumble. The bread and cheese from yesterday! How delicious that had been! Surely there wouldn't be any left.

The living room was empty and the kitchen was deserted too. There was no sound anywhere. Of course, none of the wives would show up today. Their master was dead. Then the strangeness of it all hit her. Why weren't they all here, mourning or celebrating his death, depending on their degree of loyalty to him and to their faith? Where was everybody? Where was Jake? Probably in the private quarters with his mother, where he belonged.

She felt forlorn and forgotten. To occupy her confused mind she made a fire in the kitchen stove and put the kettle with water on it. There was a bit of herb tea left in one jar on the kitchen counter – the only supply that had always been in abundance. It might settle her queasy empty stomach.

Waiting for the water to boil, she stood by the window and looked outside, studying the familiar view she had stared at so often that she knew every branch of every tree. The trees! Another memory drop reminded her of how she had pressed herself against one of those tree trunks, of the fear that had paralysed her, of the elusive shadow person disappearing into the forest, of the hurt man on the ground, of the pulsating vicious hatred she had felt for him – how could she have imagined such a vivid scene?

The kettle whistled and she forcefully shook herself out of the memory to quickly take it off the stove.

Richard was dreaming of a policeman chasing after some robbers. The guy was dressed in an old fashioned uniform with a steel helmet that had a pointy metal spike on top of it. He was overweight and could not keep up with the culprits, so he stopped, legs wide apart, belly hanging over his leather belt, and blew into his whistle. He was out of breath and could only get a few high wheezes out of it. That woke Richard up, and he instantly knew where the association with the policeman originated – an old postcard he had seen in his youth in Germany depicting a *Gendarm* as they were then called, chasing some fleeing *Ganoven* – and that his subconscious had nicely mixed this childish picture with the events of last night; obviously in an effort to make it more bearable. But he also knew the sound penetrating his dream had been real and had come from the kitchen. And at the same time he became aware of another sound, a car, coming from outside the house. Richard jumped from the sofa Jake junior had generously insisted he should rest on, while he himself and Adam were stretched out on the carpet in front of it. Those two were still in dreamland, not reacting to the whistling sound of a kettle that had filtered into his sleep.

He looked at his watch, it was already eleven o'clock. That could only mean it must be Daisy's car he had heard. He considered shaking the boys awake, but looking at their exhausted faces and listening to their deep regular breathing, he did not have the heart. He made his way out of the Bishop's private quarters and tiptoed into the hallway, then into the large main living room and out through the front door.

He was right. A car came up the driveway and stopped a few meters away from him. Daisy! She got out of the car, looked at him and took a deep breath. And then she flew with open arms in his direction and into his arms.

All he could think of was *Thank God she is here!* They hugged each other. Her hug was supposed to comfort him and tell him everything would be alright and that she was here and nothing could go wrong any more. And his hug was supposed to thank her and tell her how grateful he was and that it felt so good to have her back and that she felt good ... and somehow things got all mixed up and something went wrong with the hugging communication. He could feel her telling him that she had missed him and wanted him, as much as he did ... and suddenly their lips got involved in the hugging act and they were kissing.

That was the strangest sensation. Him being so needy for her and she allowing him to show his need. They kissed until they got their senses back and then they both felt extremely embarrassed. They could not even look at each other.

To break the awkwardness he quickly pushed her away from him – hoping it was fast and far enough so she would not notice how urgent his need for her was – and mumbled something about Adam waiting for her inside. "I'm sure you want to see him."

She pushed herself all the way free and gave him an offended look. "Will you stop this nonsense now! Why the hell should I be interested in Adam?"

Being a prize fool as usual, he couldn't stop himself. "You always phoned him, not me!"

A deep frown developed on her forehead and she squinted at him. "You are the biggest idiot I've ever come across."

The salty coolness of her lips still lingered on his. How could she taste so good and be so bad for him? "I apologize," he said, not understanding what he apologized for.

"So you should, you macho creep," she said. "What is it with you. If a woman shows any interest in you, you withdraw."

It was a touch annoying to be called a blockhead, but the implication of what she had said smoothed over his bruised ego. In fact, his heart was soaring like a skylark on a beautiful spring morning. "So you *are* interested in me?"

"Never have been, you fool."

"Why did you hide it from me?" he smirked, for once understanding what she really meant.

"There were a few things you had to figure out for yourself first."

He grabbed her and pulled her towards him again. "And I passed the test, right? You never gave up on me."

"I knew there was hope for you. Children need to learn some things by themselves," she smirked back.

They were just about to seal their new understanding with another kiss, when they heard a savage scream coming from the back of the house. They let go of each other and started to run.

They all arrived in the backyard just about the same time. Jake, Adam and Marion came rushing through the back door, alarmed from being so suddenly woken up by Martha's urgent call.

"Look, look, look!" she kept screaming, pointing to an object on the ground. When they all gathered around her, she went on explaining: "I saw it from the kitchen window, I just didn't know what it was. And in my mind I always wondered what was wrong. I knew this had something to do with it. Look, it's what she used as a weapon!"

A pair of dirty scissors lay on the muddy ground. The dark spots on it could be dried earth, or rust – or blood.

They all looked at it bewildered.

Jake put his arm around Martha. "It doesn't have to be what you think. It could be there by coincidence."

Daisy bent down unceremoniously and picked up the scissors. She let them dangle from the forefinger she had stuck through one of the loops. Richard had mentioned Martha's suspicions briefly on the phone and Daisy was first to connect the pieces of the puzzle. "Does anybody know who these belong to?"

Marion looked at them closer. "Of course," she said. "They are his. Everything is his."

Martha stomped her foot belligerently. "Nothing is his any more! Don't you get it? He's dead!" And then a sudden realization crossed her mind, draining the redness of her anger out of her face. "Oh Lord! Emma! We all forgot about Emma!"

"What about her?" Daisy asked.

"She is still in the prison hut," Marion explained with a sharp gasp, remembering where Emma was. "We have to get the poor girl down from there. No need for her to suffer any longer."

Adam and Richard looked at each other. Now what had that to do with the scissors?

"I really forgot all about her…"

Marion blamed herself for her inexcusable oversight, but was interrupted by the highly agitated Martha. "Those are the scissors I took up to the cabin when I had to tend to Anna. I buried them behind the cabin because I feared I would be punished for taking care of Anna…" She hesitated. "But how did Emma get hold of them? She can't get out of the cabin. I don't understand."

Marion paled as badly as Martha was already. "I didn't lock the cabin door when I put her inside," she admitted and actually looked over her shoulder while she did so, as if her husband's ghost was close by, listening. "I was hoping Emma would run away. I couldn't bear the thought of her suffering as badly as Anna had."

"And before that, when I visited Emma after I had taken the basket to Anna, I told her where I had been hiding those things. She must have remembered and looked for them after she got out of the cabin. She must have found them and…"

"…and come down here to kill him," Jake junior finished the sentence for her. "You didn't just imagine things, my love. You did see a woman trying to kill my father."

46

Daisy had gone with Marion and Jake junior to unload the food supplies from the trunk of her car and deliver them to the women and boys. It was by no means enough, but would take care of their most urgent needs.

Marion had begged Richard and Adam to stay behind. The women were upset enough by the arrival of the RCMP so early in the morning, which surely they had noticed, and subsequently the news of their husband's death.

Richard had to agree with her. The presence of two men who didn't belong to the family would disturb the women even further. He decided it would be best if he, Martha and Adam would start searching for Emma.

It didn't take them long to find her. Martha had suggested driving up to the prison hut because she had an eerie hunch that Emma might have gone back there – and she was right.

Emma cowered in one corner of the cabin, babbling to herself, taking no notice of them when they entered. Her eyes were clouded over and she was seeing things they could not. A little smile danced on her face, appearing and disappearing as her mood adjusted to the different emotions troubling her. They could only understand snippets of her aimless rambling. "No need now, … I did good, … mustn't hurt, … bad, bad girl, … the Chosen Ones, …so sorry, …"

Martha moved closer and squatted in front of her. "Emma, its me, Martha." Emma stopped talking, but did not look up.

"I know what you tried to do, but it's alright. You didn't kill him."

Now Emma's head jerked up. "Yes, I did! Yes, I did! Yes, I did!" She began to laugh, all confused, and then, to everyone's horror, she started to sing. "Yes, I did, I did – yes, I did, I did…." on and on she pushed the refrain, in a forever higher note.

Richard tapped Martha's shoulder and shook his head. There was nothing they could do for the deranged woman. But Martha did not give up so easily.

"Emma," she insisted softly, "I know why you told on me. You were upset with me and wanted me to suffer too. It's okay, I understand."

Slowly her low tone penetrated the high pitched singing and Emma let go of her litany.

"You are bad!" she suddenly yelled. "Bad, bad girl! Don't believe. We are the Chosen Ones. Apostates! Rot in hell! But you got favours. I believed. But I got sent here. He is bad. He lied. He lied. He lied to me…" Emma started to break down. She covered her face in her hands and wept bitterly. "He said he would reward me for telling him. He lied. I told on you, but he sent *me* away. Me! My children are suffering. They are his children too. He doesn't care. How can he go to his kingdom if he doesn't care for his family? He is a bad man. The Elders will assign me and my children to a new husband. I needed to do the Lord's work."

How she tried to justify her actions even now with religious motives got under Richard's skin. Could such a deeply ingrained pattern ever be replaced by a more rational view? How could one correct the fundamentally distorted faith those women had been born into? They had never known anything else.

Martha represented a glimmer of hope. As young as she was, she had been able to recognize the misogynistic attitude of the man she had been forced to marry. She had been able to break out of the iron grip of isolated indoctrination. So had Emma in a way, but for all the wrong reasons and in the wrong direction.

Richard tried a new approach. "Emma, your husband is dead. But you did not kill him. It was an accident."

Martha took her hand. "You and your children will be fine. Come with us. We will take care of you. We have food for your children. And he won't be able to harm you ever again."

"I know. I destroyed him."

Martha gently pulled her up. "Let's go to your children."

Emma withdrew from her. "No, I can't. The other women will kill me. And my children."

"No, they won't," Adam said.

"They will want to revenge his death. They will demand blood atonement."

Martha shot Adam a warning glance, but he continued talking to Emma. "They won't, because we won't tell them what you did. It's our secret. If we don't tell them, they will never know. We'll say it was an accident. You must never tell what really happened, Emma, do you understand?"

Emma cocked her head and seemed to ponder over Adam's words. Then a wider smile appeared on her face and suddenly she didn't look so crazy any more.

Not only Emma understood the meaning of Adam's suggestion, so did Richard. What Adam attempted there was an effective cover-up. The less questions were asked about the accident the better for them all. Adam obviously had experience in handling situations where twisted reasoning was used to justify unusual behaviour. He was perceptive and intelligent. Sharing a similar upbringing in a polygamous sect had given him valuable experience to provide Emma with a way out. It would protect her and her children.

When Martha helped Emma out into the bright sunlight both of them smiled and held tightly onto each other. Adam settled them on the back seat of the car. Before he and Richard got in, Adam whispered to him that Emma would come around. She needed time to absorb the truth, but she had shown signs of rebellion and had already made an effort to understand, which was as good a start as one could hope for.

Again, they sat at the long table. Emma had been reunited with her children and all of them were now cared for by some of the women

433

Marion trusted implicitly. The news of their leader's death had spread like wildfire and the mixture of confusion, excitement and despair in the whole community could be felt all the way up to the main house. It made Richard dizzy just to think about the countless problems coming Marion's and Jake junior's way from now on.

Jake junior was sitting next to Martha, holding her hand under the table, trying to hide what was obvious to everybody. Marion stole a glance every so often, and Richard could see her struggling to cope with this concept of affection so foreign and therefore disturbing to her. Actually, looking around, Richard realized they were all hiding something that should be out in the open. Martha and Jake junior were careful to keep the love they probably still considered forbidden from the others' eyes. Marion tried her best to hide her discomfort over it. Daisy and he were still embarrassed about their own intimate exchange earlier on – at least Richard hoped she was only embarrassed and not regretful. Even Adam seemed troubled.

Richard looked at him perplexed. Why him?

"This is a true nightmare," Adam started to explain. "What will happen now?"

To see clever Adam so lost made Richard feel more age-appropriately adult than he had felt in years. "Daisy, you and I will drive back to Vancouver. We will wait for the outcome of the enquiry and with a bit of luck nothing will connect Emma to Jake's accidental death."

"I didn't mean that!"

"I know," Richard said. "Marion and the others will look after her. You said yourself, she will recover."

Adam pressed his lips together. After a pause, he relaxed them again and exhaled deeply. "But how will they look after Emma? How will they look after each other? How long do you think these few boxes of food Daisy brought will last?"

Finally Richard understood Adam's inner turmoil. Yes, he was so right. How on earth would they? "I'm sorry, but I haven't got a clue."

While everybody started to ponder their immediate future Richard's own gloomy prospects came back to him with a vengeance. He sighed. "I guess we are all fucked."

Daisy showed her silent disapproval of his swearing with a facial expression that was so minimal it was only visible to him. Behave yourself, her minutely lifted eye lids and tiny pout said, don't use such a word when you are among straight-laced people.

"Sorry," he added honestly embarrassed, "I didn't mean to offend."

Daisy finally smiled at him. "We'd better figure out how we can help."

"I'm sorry again," Richard replied, "but as you know, my company is going under and I can't even help myself. I haven't got a cent left to my name."

"You're broke?" Jake junior asked.

"Yes, thanks to your dad!" Again, Daisy's look hit him, and he bit his tongue. Would he never learn? The guy wasn't even buried and he badmouthed him in front of his own flesh and blood.

This time Jake junior must have noticed Daisy's annoyance too. "No need to protect my feelings." He actually grinned when he said this. "I'm afraid we know better than anybody else who and what my father was. What did he do to your company?"

It was far too complicated to explain and Richard just waved it off, but Adam elaborated on the fact that old Jake had not signed a contract they had desperately needed to go ahead with their development. Richard noticed how he now always used the terms *we* and *our* and *us*, just like Daisy did.

Too bad, Adam grumbled, that your dad is dead. He wavered when he realized what he had said and tried to collect himself without much luck. Seeing him so befuddled, everybody on the table started to giggle. The ensuing laughter had a cleansing effect. They all knew the truth and shared the same feelings - there was no more pretence at piety.

Marion got up and the laughter died down. She went to the window, bent down and picked up a crumpled piece of paper from the floor. Coming back to the table, she smoothed it out with both hands. They all watched her, waiting for an explanation. When she felt satisfied that the paper was smooth enough, she held it up. "Is this the contract you are talking about?"

Richard squinted to see it. It certainly looked like the hand written draft Jake and he had prepared together – how long ago? It seemed like a million years though it had been only yesterday. He nodded.

Marion sat down and asked, without reading it. "Who has a pen?"

When Adam took one out of his inside top pocket and handed it to her, she signed the document.

Richard was dumbfounded. "What are you doing?"

She smiled at him. "I have just agreed to the sale of the land you need."

"But ...you ....can't..." He started to stutter.

"Of course she can," Daisy exclaimed. "She was his wife."

Jake junior nodded fiercely to his mother. "Yes, you can, can't you?"

"But...you ... she ..., I mean, what about all the other wives. Won't they object?"

Marion's smile grew bigger. "I am the first wife as far as the Church is concerned, but I am the only one as far as the Canadian government is concerned. The property was written into both our names and I assume I will inherit his half."

"Are you sure about that?" Daisy inquired. "About the joint ownership, I mean. It strikes me uncharacteristic for him to do such a thing."

"They all do that. It's for tax reasons. The Church Elders always take it for granted that the wife has no say in it anyway. When the husband dies, the first wife is usually married to another man of their choice and is forced to agree to any change of ownership the Elders feel necessary." Marion put on a brave face. "But I won't agree. Not to a new husband, not to giving up my right to this property. And my son will help me to fight them!"

Jake junior got up, went to his mother and put his hand on her shoulder. It was a simple gesture full of deeper meaning. "I'm proud of you, mother. You did the right thing. Richard deserves our gratitude. Without him and Adam ..." his voice trailed off, choked up, like they all suddenly were.

The full implication of the latest twist in his fortune hit Richard before any of them became aware of it.

"First of all, Marion and Jake," he said, deliberately avoiding the *junior*, "thank you from the bottom of my heart. You have saved my company, but in doing so, we have solved a lot of the problems plaguing your community. Not all, mind you, but the most pressing ones."

They waited for him to elaborate. He savoured the moment, gathering his thoughts to make sure he would not forget anything. "Marion, if you would have read the contract, you would know that I'm willing to pay $100,000 up front, and a lot more later on for this piece of land. My friendly private financier, the lovely Linda, has agreed to lend me the money, so on the strength of your signature I should be able to draw a small amount of this money right away, with the balance coming as soon as your legal claim is confirmed. But with the first deposit you can immediately take care of the members of your community here. I don't know what you all will do in the long run, and it's none of my business, but I could imagine that you will allow at least some members of your community," at that point in his little speech he gave Jake and Martha a meaningful glance, "to stay here and make a new and better life for themselves."

Adam jumped up, in total excitement. "Yes. Yes. Great! Wonderful! That's brilliant." Relieved beyond further words, he sat down again, eyes swimming with tears. The dire situation the community was in must have burdened him more than Richard could imagine.

Marion's first wife's sense of responsibility made her brood on the next set of problems. "Of course I want all my sister-wives and their children to stay here. I hope they will, but not all of them will share our rebellion. Because that's what it will be if I refuse a new head of the community to take over. There will be repercussions from the Church, they will try and pressure me into submission, but as long as I have my son, and hopefully Martha and a few of the other women by my side, I don't fear them."

Jake swallowed hard, then he announced with a steady voice. "Don't worry, Mother, I'll make sure they can't hurt you, or any of us. I've had it with them and all their rules, their *Doctrine and Covenants*!"

Those were strong words from an eighteen year old, Richard thought, but then he was much older than his age in certain ways, just like Martha. A girl of fifteen with a two year abusive relationship that included Church sanctioned rape behind her, she was mature enough to be considered a woman.

Jake junior made this point more than clear. "Martha will also stay here. She and I will get married as soon as it's appropriate," he announced proudly. "Is that alright with you, Mother?"

Martha gasped in what the others thought was delight, while Marion looked a little shocked. As always when she was stalling for time, she took off her glasses, rubbed them in the folds of her skirt and placed them on her nose again. They all waited for her reply.

"Mother?"

Marion looked at Martha and then at her son. "Only if Martha agrees. I would like this very much, but I think you should ask her, not me, shouldn't you?"

Martha stood up. "Before you say anything, Jake, I need to know what happened to the real Martha."

Marion and her son exchanged a quick glance. Should they tell? What would be served by the truth after the murderer had escaped his just punishment?

Jake junior felt confident to speak for his mother. "My father killed her."

Richard, Daisy and Adam froze in shock. Not more bad news! The family would have enough to handle to somehow survive and manage their future without having to deal with a murder in their community.

Jake junior directed his words solely towards Martha but they were not lost on the others. "Martha died far too young and totally innocent because the Church gave my father reason and permission. He murdered her, but they are as much at fault as he was. It's done now, we can't bring her back. We can only honour her memory by staying strong if they try to break us apart. We'll have to fight them for the rest of our lives and we'll have to work on helping all those who want to leave their oppressive system. Something must be done. We can make a start by assisting those who are too weak to stand up to them. We have to stick together to stay free. Martha, will you be on my side? Will you marry me and support me and share this fight with me?"

"No!"

Martha steadied herself on the table. She had little energy left. She looked at Jake junior pleading for his understanding. He was too stunned by her unexpected reply to react to it.

Martha looked around the table. She took a deep breath, savouring the moment that would cut her loose - for now and all eternity! "No, Jake, I will not agree to what you are asking. There is only one Martha, and we will place a cross for her and her mother somewhere on the compound so she will never be forgotten. If you want to marry me, you will have to ask again." Proudly she lifted her chin. "Me! Lillian!"

47

The drive back to Vancouver was uneventful. They took turns driving, changing places nearly every hour, because all three of them were beyond tired. When they got to Langley, Adam was behind the steering wheel, Richard was dozing next to him and Daisy was asleep on the more comfortable backseat. She hardly woke up to say goodbye to Adam who couldn't wait to get out of the car, presumably to tell Ted and David all the gory and glorious details of what he had experienced on this trip.

Richard formally shook his hand, but when he let go Adam flung his arms around him and gave him a genuine bear hug; one of the kind that is so heartfelt it makes one reciprocate with the same honesty.

"I'll be in touch," Richard promised before he slipped into the driver's seat.

He drove off slowly, hoping Daisy would go back to and carry on sleeping. Just before they got to her apartment complex she stirred and then popped up in the rear mirror, all tousled hair and bleary eyes.

"We're nearly there," Richard announced. The same awkwardness he had felt after their embrace this morning took hold of him. He didn't look at her but stared straight ahead.

Daisy wasn't very helpful. She kept studying him in the mirror and didn't open her mouth.

He drove into the side street where he could briefly stop without disturbing the traffic too badly and, like a miracle, found an empty parking space. He manoeuvred the car into it, switched the engine off, turned around to her and announced, brilliant as ever: "Here we are."

She grinned at him. "Aren't you going to ask?"

"What?"

"If you can come upstairs."

"Can I come upstairs?"

She did not answer and got out of the car. So did he.

Richard followed her like a puppy, constantly worrying that she might turn around and chase him away. They arrived at the building entrance, he held the door open for her – last opportunity for her to snap at his impertinence, which she didn't take – they both went in, and once they were standing in front of her apartment door, all awkwardness disappeared. He finally understood that she had let him into her life and didn't waste any time proving to her how important this was to him. They had barely closed the door behind them when he grabbed her waist with both hands, pressed her slender body against his and, feeling her respond with tremendous urgency, lost all control.

They only made it into her bedroom after they had satisfied their need for each other on the hardwood floor and craved more creature comforts. There, they cuddled together under a fluffy duvet, totally at ease with their nakedness and closeness. It felt as if Richard had known her all his life and he told her so.

"But you did," she said.

"Not all my life."

"Nearly. I have always been there, you just didn't notice."

"You were always so unapproachable. I thought you were frigid."

She just gave him one of her famous glances.

"No, truly, why didn't you encourage me a little? We could have had this much earlier." To demonstrate his point he stroked her in a place no boss would normally be allowed to touch.

"You had a different idea of what you wanted in life and weren't ready for me. So I bided my time. I have always loved you."

She said this so naturally, so sure of herself, that he gasped. "You did?"

"Mhm."

He stared at the ceiling. What kind of fool doesn't notice when a woman like Daisy is in love with him? "I have been a self-centred creep, haven't I?"

"Mhm."

Now she stroked him in a place no assistant was supposed to touch. He took hold of her hand to stop her. He had to think first. She looked at him quizzically.

"I've made you unhappy, haven't I?"

"Sometimes," she admitted.

Her. His parents. Who else? "I have made a lot of people unhappy in my life." That was a statement, not a question, so she didn't reply.

He thought some more. Adam. Marion. Martha-Lillian. Jake junior. Even Ted and David.

"This isn't over yet, is it?"

She smiled at him and shook her head. Of course it wasn't over, she said, it was just beginning. They were both up to their necks in this.

"What am I supposed to do?"

"Just be yourself."

"What? The usual egotistical, insensitive maniac?"

"That was the guy you thought you should be. But that was never you."

"But how do I know who the real me is?"

"Just be yourself, you big stupid softie." When she said this, he let go of her hand again, delighted that she resumed her previous activity. It also made him incredibly happy that she was right beside him, watching and sharing the awakening of his real self.

They had to wait two weeks before the results of the autopsy were made official. Richard got a call from the RCMP Sergeant handling the case. His hands became sweaty and his heart was pounding in his chest when the Sergeant told him the final verdict of the police enquiry. He was not to blame for the fatality. The deceased had been dead already when Richard drove over his body. He must have fallen on the roadside just as Richard had come around the corner, otherwise, if he would have been alive and standing up, the impact would have sent him flying over the hood. Or maybe even over the windshield, the Sergeant went on, considering how fast Richard had been driving. People underestimate the force of such a collision, he explained. No way could he have been pinned underneath the car.

So he had been dead already! That could only mean the pathologist performing the autopsy had discovered the knife wound. Richard was alarmed, and instantly worried for Emma, and Lillian and Jake, and Marion and the whole compound. His blood was pounding in his ears. His throat closed up. He wanted to insist that it had been his fault, that he would gladly accept being charged for reckless driving, that Jake had been killed by his car and not by a crazed woman seeking revenge.

Just as well he could only get a few scratchy words out of his parched throat.

"You can stop worrying," the Sergeant carried on, "Mister Law died of a massive heart-attack. Happens a lot with over-weight guys like that when they exert themselves beyond their capabilities. He must have been running down the driveway. One of the constables on site had suspected this right away, that's why he had asked the widow for the deceased's medical history."

Jake's death was officially declared an accident. Richard's driver's license was suspended for six months.

No hardship for him, as Daisy had moved into his apartment and she could drive him to and from work. She was his partner now, in life and in business and they made all decisions concerning *their* development together. It was still too early to start building the road into the subdivision because so far up north mud season could last well into May and the road building contractors still couldn't move the heavy equipment on site. But Richard had been able to streamline the company's financial arrangements thanks to the pre-sale contract Marion had signed, and had sent the first deposit of $ 20,000 to her.

Jeanne d'Arc seemed quite surprised when Daisy informed her that Richard had secured the needed land after all. She immediately thought of a few new hold-ups to antagonize them, which annoyed the hell out of Daisy, but Richard didn't care. With Daisy on his side he was infallible. He was convinced that this Approving Officer would eventually see the light and give up her lost cause.

Marion had been incredibly grateful when they sent Adam up to deliver the cheque. Adam was the new assistant at Richland Ltd. After Richard had lost Daisy in this capacity and with the subdivision soon to be in full progress, they certainly had enough work for him. There was not enough money to pay him yet, but he was so eager to join them, he promised to work for a *butterbrot*, as Richard called it – a slice of bread with butter on it – if he just took him on. Of course Adam was paid a little more than that, but by far not as much as he was already worth. Adam had a knack for real estate development, Richard could see that clearly, and he reminded him a lot of himself some years ago. Except that Adam was more diplomatic and had a lot more patience. Adam simply was a better person than he had ever been.

All was coming along nicely until, soon after the police had closed his file, Marion called, all in tears.

Daisy and Adam were in his office, so he put Marion on speaker and asked her what was wrong.

"This is terrible," she explained between heavy sobs. "They have come this morning and picked up the women and children!"

They all gasped in unison. "What?" Richard yelled. "Who? Why?"

"The Gatekeepers. They make all the decisions for the members of our Church. Some of their men came to claim what they believe is theirs. They picked up Barbara, and Elsie, and Deborah, and, oh, seven of my sister-wives altogether, with their children, nearly all their children. ..." she sobbed louder now. "We tried all we could, but we just couldn't persuade them to stay."

"Calm down, Marion. Daisy and Adam are here, listening in. Tell us exactly what happened."

"Oh, and Emma, of course. They took Emma with them too."

"Tell us what happened," Richard urged her gently.

She was inhaling deeply and they waited for her to collect herself. "They sent a delegation up here to take the women and children back into the Church. That's what they told us. They will reallocate them to another Canadian compound. When they heard that Jake had died, they knew our family was without a head. They wanted to send a new man up to marry me and all the others and take over his position, and his property of course, just like I had said, but I refused. I told them we don't want another man here, we would manage ourselves. But the women are not allowed to do that. They said it is not for me to decide what the sister-wives should do. So we had a meeting in the community hall last week to decide together." She nearly lost it again and Richard reminded her to stay focused, otherwise they wouldn't be able to help.

"You can't help anyway," she continued. "Half of our women and children are gone. They didn't want to stay here. They said, everybody who stays behind will go to hell and they don't want to be part of a community of apostates. You must realize, they are more scared of being damned in the after-life than of going into bondage with an unknown man for the rest of their lives here on this earth. It is so terrible. We couldn't convince them to stay, not even for a trial period. We needed more time, but it all happened so fast. Jake refused to open the gate when the church men came to pick them up, so they just crashed through it."

"That's kidnapping!" Richard said.

"No, it's not." Adam argued correctly. "They only picked up those who wanted to leave, right, Marion?"

She sniffled a barely audible yes.

Richard was unconvinced. "But how did they know the outcome of your meeting? They couldn't just assume that some wanted to leave."

"Emma called them and told them."

"Emma?" they all shouted together.

"Yes, it was her. She admitted it. She had always been the one spying on us and telling our husband what was being said amongst us sister-wives." Marion lowered her voice to a whisper. "She has spread lies about me too, so they would hate me. Poor Lillian was not the only one who trusted her and told her things that got herself or others into trouble."

It was quiet for a moment. Then Daisy asked how Lillian was coping.

"She's fine. We are all doing well. All who stayed behind. We must get over losing the others. There is nothing anybody could have done. I just wanted to let you know."

With this she said goodbye and hung up. The three of them sat there motionless for a while. In an effort to make the inexplicable a little more comprehensible to Daisy and Richard, Adam said, it was actually very encouraging that half of them had opted to stay behind.

"You really think so?" Richard sneered at him.

"Don't forget where they came from. They don't know any better. It will be hard enough for the ones who broke loose to adjust to their new freedom. In fact, some of them may not make it. You should talk to Ted and David about how hard some of their Lost Boys have to struggle to come to terms with the fact that everything they have been told and have believed in is an ...," he struggled himself now to find the right words, or maybe he could not get it over his lips to call it an *outright lie*, "...that what they believed in was only one of many religious interpretations of what we humans dream up to save our souls, and that a lot of it comes down to a very unholy greed for power and possessions. It's tough on those boys, and there is not much help they can get. Nobody wants to know about young people broken by the manipulations of fanatical fundamentalists."

"I don't know about that!" A sudden inspiration replaced the anger that had built up inside Richard while listening to Marion and Adam. It all became so obvious to him. The whole dramatic and traumatic experiences of the past months made sense to him now. "You are right, Adam, we need to talk to Ted and David. They can do with some help and I know exactly how we can show our support."

Daisy frowned in an effort to grasp his meaning. He smiled, loving the idea that he could surprise her.

"Our development will be taking off soon, right?"

They both nodded, bewildered.

"We will need a lot of help to log and clear the land, build driveways and cabins and later on, when the cabins are sold, they need to be maintained. We'll need cleaning and care-taking staff and so on, right?"

Daisy started to smile.

She was a little faster than Adam was to catch on to his vision of the Lost Boys and runaways, male or female, finding a safe haven in Marion's community, which was right next door to their development. A haven where they would find employment and a new purpose in life. They needed training and jobs and someone to mentor them so they could support themselves as soon as they were old enough, but until then they needed a safe place to hide. Wasn't that just the neatest idea ever? As Adam said, once he truly understood the beauty of it, Marion, Jake and Lillian would make the perfect leaders for this support system.

"What are we waiting for?" Richard grinned and picked up the phone. "There's a lot of organizing to do. Let's get started."

48

The call came through at 7 p.m. Brother Lucas had been waiting for it all day.

As soon as he got the news, he left his office and told his driver to take him to his main residence. The one he shared with his first wife.

Resting comfortably on the back seat of his Cartier coloured Lincoln Town-car, he called Brother Mathew. He was in a hurry to get home and wanted to keep it brief. As much as he was looking forward to the evening's activities, certain things still needed to be arranged.

"Brother Mathew, I know you have done your best to solve the Canadian crisis, but we cannot ignore the situation as it stands now."

The reception in the car was not very clear, and he had to strain to understand the Gatekeeper's response.

"Thank you, Brother Lucas, I have acted in good faith."

"Yet only seven of Brother Jacob's former wives and their children could be re-allocated inside Canada. How could this happen? Is it correct that Brother Jacob's first wife, Marion, if I remember correctly, has become an apostate and has encouraged her sister-wives to join her revolt?"

"Yes, I'm afraid that is so."

"Furthermore, she is refusing to sign over Brother Jacob's property to one of our Elders? She is refusing the new husband we have chosen for her?"

"Yes, that unfortunately is correct too. I was going to discuss the matter with you tomorrow."

"You knew about it since last week, right?" The silence on the other end confirmed his suspicion. "But you did not inform me right away because you were hoping to solve this mess before I heard about it?"

"Indeed. I did not want to trouble you with this upsetting development until I had checked all the facts. It seems that we made a blatant error when we signed half of the property over to Marion."

"We?" Brother Lucas interrupted.

"I did. I thought we could trust her implicitly. I take full responsibility for this. It looks like the Church has lost this compound, unless you order our men to go back and use more force to persuade Marion to return to the safety of our faith."

Brother Lucas startled to chuckle. This was just too good. He couldn't help but be amused. "It is not entirely the Church's loss, my dear Brother. I am pleased to hear that you accept responsibility for this fiasco. The Gatekeepers will have to be compensated, you understand."

Brother Mathew swallowed hard. "I don't know if I..."

"Oh, I wouldn't take all your possessions away from you. But you do own a large waterfront acreage along the Columbia River, don't you! I am sure the Brothers will agree to forgive you if you write it over to the Church. It will make a fine seminar compound for our young priesthood."

"But I might still be able to convince Marion. I will talk to her personally. I can fly to Vancouver immediately. Let me try..."

"You will do nothing of the kind!" Brother Lucas ordered sharply. Luckily, Brother Mathew could not see that he was still smiling. This was just too amusing. Marion an apostate! That bastard Jacob had stolen her from him and had enjoyed her for many years of his earthly life, but now he would be deprived of her company for all eternity – unless he followed her into the black abyss, where he actually belonged. What a delicious turn of fate and entirely without any interference from his side. Nobody could accuse him of vengeful manipulations. "Let her be. Marion is lost to us; and so is the compound. If we go back there for any kind of reprisal she may create trouble for the Church. Apostates tend to turn aggressive, actively seeking help from the authorities.

We don't need that kind of attention, not after the Zion Ranch raid. We have to let things cool down until the media has forgotten us. No, my dear Brother, you will not even attempt to contact the Canadian compound. Let them rot in hell. But we, the Brotherhood of Gate-keepers, thank you for your generous donation. You have willingly and without hesitation accepted your responsibility, which should be honoured. I will commend you for a position on the board of our Trust Fund Company. Such a selfless act of responsibility and generosity must be acknowledged so others within the Church will follow your example."

He could sense the tremendous relief in Brother Mathew. The Trust Fund position was lucrative and would compensate him for the loss of his valuable property in a few short years. It was never good to create enemies. With this appointment he had secured Brother Mathew's continued support.

"But now, let us talk about something more pleasant. While you have been busy trying to solve the Canadian crisis, I have made some arrangements myself. We must show our support in such situations and not just re-allocate the wives and children in Canada. I have therefore decided to take some of them into the holy covenant of plural marriage myself. Two of the girls rescued from the Canadian compound have been safely smuggled over the border and have just arrived at my home. I would like to invite you and Brothers John and Ernest to witness my marriage ceremony."

One hour later the limousines of the three Brothers arrived at his residence. Brother Lucas waited in his private office until they were brought to the formal living room and served some refreshments.

He waited a bit longer, savouring the moment. Soon he would see his new twins. Soon he would ask his first wife as the representative of all his other wives to accept them into his family. Soon he would retire with them to his private chambers. It had been too long.

He decided the time had come.

His brothers greeted him respectfully. Did he detect a touch of envy in their demeanour? Justifiably so. After all, they could only imagine what he would be enjoying tonight. He asked his wife to bring in the girls.

All heads turned to the door. When the first wife stepped aside to make space for the twins following her, it was for all to see what his eyes could not believe. This could not be! This was totally unacceptable! Totally wrong!

Brother Jacob had cheated him again!

The girls were incredibly ugly. Skinny. No, not just bone thin, they were shapeless. Narrow shoulders, no breasts, yet wide hips. Short. With unproportionally long arms and large hands. Their pasty, pimply faces featured squashed wide noses and protruding foreheads with a low hairline and eyebrows so bushy one could only guess where their deep set small eyes were hiding. The faces of simple minds, with annoyingly shy smiles. They did not completely look alike, but Brother Jacob had been right in his description that they were identical. Both were equally ugly.

They looked docile enough, standing there like mules. That bastard Jacob had cheated him again; haunting him even from his grave.

Brother Lucas turned away from the revolting sight and asked his first wife to remove the twins. He felt empty. Shallow. Drained of all energy. There was nothing left inside him, except a twinge of anger, directed at those disgusting girls. They had been sent by Brother Jacob straight from hell to make him suffer. How dare they become the instruments of his old rival and bitter enemy. He suddenly knew what to do. He addressed his Brothers.

"The wedding is cancelled. Forgive me for troubling you to come all this way. You could see for yourselves that I have been tricked. There can be no ceremony. I thank you all for coming."

They understood immediately and made their way to the door. There, Brother Mathew turned around and asked what should be done with the girls. He, Brother John and Brother Ernest were waiting for his instructions

Didn't they have any brains? Couldn't they think for themselves? Shouldn't the proper course of action be as obvious to them as it was to him?

Wherever Brother Jacob was, the twins would be sent his way!

"My dear Brothers", he sighed, "those creatures are here in this country without any documentation. They are no use to anybody. Do I really have to spell it out what should be done with them? Just get rid of them. But before you do, dedicate them to Brother Jacob for now and all eternity. They have done nothing wrong. They should not be punished by leaving this world without a husband. Marry them to him by the powers bestowed in us as Gatekeepers. They are his responsibility, make sure they join his eternal kingdom."

Epilogue

It was autumn again. The leaves had already turned yellow and red and would soon shrivel into a dry brown and be blown from the branches by the ever increasing northerly gusts that announced the approaching winter.

Lillian could not believe that only four years had passed since she had arrived here. It seemed a lifetime ago. She had come here to find solace with a husband who was supposed to share his future kingdom with her, but she had lost this husband, his kingdom – and the chance to share her eternity with him.

Lillian sighed involuntarily. Just thinking about this made the hair on the nape of her neck stand up. She shivered. An eternity with that man, who had raped her when she had been only thirteen, was her idea of eternal hell.

While a life time with her new husband would be bliss forever. Lillian sighed again. My God, how would she get through this day without constantly sighing? It was her wedding day, and it would be the happiest day of her life.

Marion had come into her room this morning to help her with her dress and her hair and had smiled wistfully when she had repeated those words to her. "This will be the happiest day of your life!"

Both women remembered. It was something that could not be forgotten.

"Yes," Lillian had replied to the older woman. "But this time, it is true!"

Acknowledgements

As a fiction novel writer I have always felt that it takes more than a vivid imagination to put a story together.

To build a solid foundation takes a lot of research. All references made in regards to the Fundamentalist Mormon Church, the FLDS, the Doctrine & Covenant and its Section 132, the polygamous cult in Bountiful, the raid of the Yearning for Zion Ranch in Texas, the child-bride trafficking, the Lost Boys, and much more, are facts. I have only altered minor details to accommodate the flow of the story.

The Gatekeepers, the compound north of Blue River and all characters in the story are pure fiction.

To let the imaginary scenes dancing around in my mind truly come to life, I have always drawn on my over the years wonderfully distorted memories – of places, of situations, of emotions, and above all, of people.

I thank all the people in my life for giving me the inspiration to write – and I apologize to those who believe they recognized themselves in one of my stories and feel unjustly treated. There is no one person who is portrayed specifically; it is always a mixture of human characteristics and behaviour that forms a novel persona.

But there are also those very real people who have contributed to my story in notable ways – be it through constructive criticism and corrections, or through continued encouragement. This novel needed to be written, and those dear and close friends are responsible for me not giving up in the two long years it took to research and write it.

I want to thank, in alphabetical order as it is impossible to rank my gratitude to them, Tom Baraniak, Cindy Berg, Sally de Boor, Erroll Brosnan, Shirley Dirkin, Waltraud Ewald, Dorothy Hartshorne, Linda Kenney, Cynthia Lauriente and Jackie Williamson. You were great! You were important!

But of course, as always, I thank the most important person in my life, the one who has given me the strength – and the free space – to withdraw into my own world, my husband Manfred Zeiner. He has never doubted my work, has always urged me on, and has given me a support base any writer can only dream of. I love him for it!

Made in the USA
Monee, IL
20 November 2024

70674511R00252